2011

D0728459

Jack Sheffield was born in 1945 and grew up in the tough environment of Gipton Estate, in north-east Leeds. After a job as a 'pitch boy', repairing roofs, he became a Corona Pop Man before going to St John's College, York, and training to be a teacher. In the late seventies and eighties, he was a headteacher of two schools in North Yorkshire before becoming Senior Lecturer in Primary Education at Bretton Hall College. It was at this time that he began to record his many amusing stories of village life as portrayed in *Teacher, Teacher!*, *Mister Teacher*, *Dear Teacher* and *Village Teacher*. *Please Sir!* is his fifth novel and continues the story of life in the fictional village of Ragley-on-the-Forest. He lives in York and Hampshire.

Visit his website at www.jacksheffield.com

PLEASE SIR!

The Alternative School Logbook 1981–1982

Jack Sheffield

CORGI BOOKS

TRANSWORLD PUBLISHERS
61–63 Uxbridge Road, London W5 5SA
A Random House Group Company
www.transworldbooks.co.uk

PLEASE SIR!
A CORGI BOOK: 9780552162203

First published in Great Britain
in 2011 by Bantam Press
an imprint of Transworld Publishers
Corgi edition published 2011

Addresses for Random House Group Ltd companies outside the UK
can be found at: www.randomhouse.co.uk
The Random House Group Ltd Reg. No. 954009

Typeset in Palatino by
Kestrel Data, Exeter, Devon.

2 4 6 8 10 9 7 5 3 1

The Random House Group Limited supports The Forest Stewardship
Council (FSC®), the leading international forest certification organisation.
Our books carrying the FSC label are printed on FSC® certified paper.
FSC is the only forest certification scheme endorsed by the leading
environmental organisations, including Greenpeace. Our
paper procurement policy can be found at
www.randomhouse.co.uk/environment

Printed and bound in Great Britain by Clays Ltd, St Ives PLC

For my sweet Elisabeth

Contents

Acknowledgements

I am indeed fortunate to have the support of my superb editor, the ever patient Linda Evans, and the wonderful team at Transworld, including Larry Finlay, Bill Scott-Kerr, Nick Robinson, Madeline Toy, Lynsey Dalladay, Sophie Holmes, Vivien Garrett, copy-editor Judy Collins, and the 'footsoldiers' – fellow 'Old Roundhegian' Martin Myers and the quiet, unassuming Mike 'Rock 'n' Roll' Edgerton.

Special thanks go to my industrious literary agent and Britain's most youthful forty-year-old, Philip Patterson of Marjacq Scripts, for his encouragement and good humour.

I am also grateful to all those who assisted in the research for this novel – in particular: Patrick Busby, Pricing Director, church organist and Harrogate Rugby Club supporter, Hampshire; Janina Bywater, nurse and lecturer in psychology, Cornwall; Rob Cragg, ex-European Director, Molex, and classic-car enthusiast, Hampshire; The Revd Ben Flenley, Rector of Bentworth,

Lasham, Medstead and Shalden, Hampshire; David Hayward, retired environmental scientist and radio-controlled model aircraft enthusiast, Hampshire; Steve Holford, postman and former potter from Stoke-on-Trent, Hampshire; John Kirby, ex-policeman, expert calligrapher and Sunderland supporter, County Durham; Jennifer Lines, retired headteacher and local artist, Hampshire; Roy Linley, Enterprise Architect, Unilever Global Expertise Team, and Leeds United supporter, Port Sunlight, Wirral; Sue Maddison, primary school teacher, Harrogate, Yorkshire; Kerry Magennis-Prior, ex-churchwarden, St Andrew's Church, Medstead, Hampshire; Sue Matthews, primary school teacher and John Denver enthusiast, Wigginton, Yorkshire; Phil Parker, ex-teacher and Manchester United supporter, Holme-upon-Spalding Moor, Yorkshire; The Revd Canon John Rendall, retired parish priest and Canon Emeritus of York Minster, Yorkshire; Charlie Shaylor, retired headteacher, lay reader and expert bread-maker, Hampshire; Pat Skinner, nurse and bread-pudding champion, Hampshire; Caroline Stockdale, librarian, York Central Library, Yorkshire, and all the wonderful staff at Waterstone's Alton, Hampshire, and Waterstone's York.

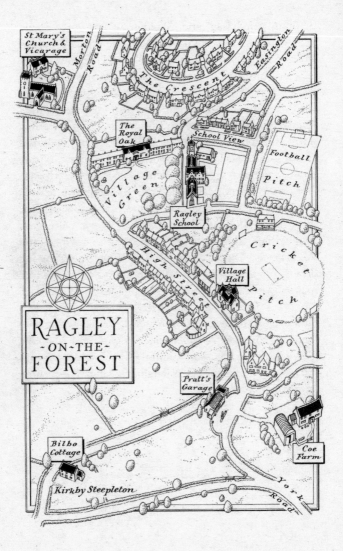

Prologue

Fate is a capricious companion . . . Just one look and I knew.

'So you didn't get the job?' Beth said quietly.

I shook my head. 'Not exactly.'

'Jack, what do you mean?' she said.

I took a deep breath and the words tumbled out. 'Well, Ragley School is staying open, so I chose *not* to go forward to the final interview.'

There was a hint of sadness in her green eyes. 'I see,' she said.

'But it's wonderful news, Beth, and . . . I love being a village teacher.'

She sighed deeply and shook her head. 'I know, Jack, I know.'

I put my arms around her slim waist and kissed her gently. 'This won't affect our wedding plans, will it?'

She looked at me as if she was seeing me for the first time and said nothing. The air was still and there were no clouds on this perfect day but the look in Beth's eyes made my heart sink. In the heaven that was once my heart, the sky was broken.

That was six weeks ago and the school summer holiday was now almost over. My interview at County Hall for a large primary school on the east coast of Yorkshire had ended abruptly. At the last moment I had withdrawn my application when Miss Barrington-Huntley, the Chair of the Education Committee for North Yorkshire, had informed me that Ragley Church of England Primary School was not on the list of schools to be closed. My fiancée, Beth Henderson – like me, a village school headteacher in her mid-thirties – found to her great relief that her school, Hartingdale, was also reprieved. It should have been a time for celebration. Instead it seemed to cause unease in our relationship. Falling in love had been easy; the next step was proving difficult.

It was Tuesday, 1 September 1981, and I was sitting alone in the school office. All was still and quiet. A watery sun streamed in through the high-arched Victorian windows and tiny motes of dust were suspended in the shaft of hazy sunlight waiting for a waft of air from the open doorway. Gentle rain was sweeping over from the Hambleton hills, but it was a quiet rain. Droplets caressed the bare branches of the avenue of horse-chestnut trees at the front of this lovely old school and I recalled the first time I had sat at my headteacher's desk. Later I had met Beth . . . and it was a perfect memory.

My fifth year as headmaster of Ragley-on-the-Forest Church of England Primary School in North Yorkshire was about to begin. It was a day of silent aspirations, a morning of new directions . . . and I wondered if I had made the right decision to return to Ragley School.

Then I unlocked the bottom drawer of my desk, took out the large, leather-bound school logbook and opened it to the next clean page. I filled my fountain pen with black Quink ink, wrote the date and stared at the empty page. The record of another school year was about to begin. Four years ago, the retiring headmaster, John Pruett, had told me how to fill in the official school logbook. 'Just keep it simple,' he said. 'Whatever you do, don't say what really happens, because no one will believe you!'

So the real stories were written in my 'Alternative School Logbook'. And this is it!

Chapter One

Enid Blyton and the Library Van

86 children were registered on roll on the first day of the school year. We were informed by County Hall that as part of the 'Reading for All' initiative, the North Yorkshire county library van will begin weekly visits to school. The newly appointed Computer Studies and Library Development Adviser will be visiting school to examine our reading policy and make recommendations.

Extract from the Ragley School Logbook:
Thursday, 3 September 1981

'Y'still 'ere, then!' shouted Mrs Winifred Brown through the open office door. 'Ah 'eard they were shutting y'down,' she added bluntly. As usual, our angriest parent had the demeanour of a snorting rhino and the finesse of a wrecking ball.

I looked up from my headteacher's desk. 'No, Mrs Brown, Ragley School is *definitely* open.'

'Pity,' she growled as she pushed little Damian

Brown back out of the entrance door towards the school playground. Her seven-year-old son, with his skinhead haircut and sticking-out ears, was simultaneously picking his nose and sucking a giant gobstopper. Multi-tasking came easily to Damian. 'Ah were jus' checkin',' retorted Mrs Brown. 'Y'don't know if y'comin' o' goin' in this school.' Then, with a parting withering look, she turned on her heel and stormed off.

I unwound my six-feet-one-inch frame from my chair and put on my old herringbone sports jacket with the frayed leather patches on the elbows. Then I gave my black-framed Buddy Holly spectacles a quick polish using the end of my outdated flower-power tie and walked out into the entrance hall.

'Tek no notice, Mr Sheffield. Y'can't please some folk.' It was Ruby the caretaker, her rosy cheeks flushed with the effort of sweeping the stone steps in the entrance porch. She leant on her yard broom and shook her head. 'Winifred's been proper vexed since 'er Eddie lost 'is job mekkin' them toilets.' Eddie Brown had been a fitter at Portaloo in York but was now resigned to sitting at home and listening to the regular tirades of his formidable wife. Only his pet ferret, Frankenstein, was a source of true companionship. It occurred to me that no matter how complicated my life seemed to be, there was always someone worse off.

I walked out to our tarmac playground surrounded by a waist-high wall of Yorkshire stone, amber in the sunlight and topped with black metal fleur-de-lis railings that cast long shadows. In the distance the church clock struck the half-hour. It was 8.30 a.m. on Thursday, 3 September, the first day of the autumn term, and my fifth year as headteacher of Ragley-on-the Forest Church of England Primary School in North Yorkshire had begun.

For this was 1981. The first computers had arrived in schools and Professor Ernö Rubik had announced that fifty million of his cubes had been sold. However, this went largely unnoticed by the ladies of the Ragley and Morton Women's Institute when they heard that Sue Barker, the darling of ladies tennis, had to retire from the American championships at Flushing Meadow with a swollen knee. In Liverpool the locals were trying to raise £12,000 for a bronze statue of the late John Lennon, while the new music scene had embraced the New Romantics. Adam and the Ants were riding high in the charts and young men in baggy shirts had begun to wear black eyeliner. Meanwhile, Prime Minister Margaret Thatcher knew her honeymoon period was over when Glaswegian factory workers welcomed her with a barrage of eggs and, on a distant horizon, there was trouble brewing in a group of islands in the South Atlantic. Closer to home, in the window of the Co-op in York, an incredible new electronic device from Grundig called a video recorder had gone on show and shoppers stopped to stare in wonder. The world was changing fast but, happily, in the quiet Yorkshire village of Ragley-on-the-Forest there was still time to pause a while and smell the flowers.

I walked down the cobbled driveway, through the school gates and breathed in the clean Yorkshire air. Then I stood back to admire our village school. It was a solid

Victorian building of reddish-brown bricks, a steeply sloping grey slate roof and a tall incongruous bell tower. On this perfect September day the sun reflected from the high arched window in the gable end. Recent fears of the closure of Ragley School, at least for the time being, were over.

Bordering the front of the school was a row of tall horse-chestnut trees, heavy in leaf and spiky fruit, and I stood under the welcome shade and watched the village coming alive. Off to my right in the centre of a row of pretty terraced cottages with pantile roofs and tall brick chimneys stood The Royal Oak with the autumn fire of Virginia creeper clinging to its whitewashed walls. Opposite me, on the village green, a group of mothers chatted nervously. Their four-year-olds were about to experience a first full day in Anne Grainger's reception class. The children looked relaxed and made daisy chains while their mothers stood anxiously with handkerchiefs at the ready. As usual, a few tears would be shed when the time came for them to say goodbye to their tiny offspring.

Down the High Street, Big Dave Robinson and his cousin, Little Malcolm Robinson, the council binmen, were collecting rubbish in their wagon from Prudence Golightly's General Stores & Newsagent, Piercy's Butcher's Shop, the Village Pharmacy and Pratt's Hardware Emporium. They paused outside Nora's Coffee Shop, where the assistant, Dorothy Humpleby, was leaning in the doorway, humming along to Soft Cell's recent number one record 'Tainted Love' and hoping for a glimpse of her boyfriend, Little Malcolm. Meanwhile, next door,

Diane Wigglesworth was putting a large poster of Farrah Fawcett in the window of her hair salon.

The tranquil scene was suddenly shattered by loud, excited voices as a posse of children appeared from the council estate and ran towards the school gates. Red-faced and panting, nine-year-old Jimmy Poole looked concerned.

'What's the problem, Jimmy?' I asked.

His sun-tanned, freckled face looked up at me with black-button eyes from under a fringe of ginger curls. 'Thorth, Mithter Theffield,' he lisped.

'Thoughts, Jimmy? You mean you're having unhappy thoughts?' I asked. Jimmy had always been a cheerful boy and it was strange to see him looking so downcast, particularly on the first day of term.

'No, Mithter Theffield,' replied Jimmy, shaking his head. 'Ah've forgotten me thorth for boyth gameth.'

'Ah, I see,' I said with a smile. 'Well, don't worry, we'll find you a spare pair.'

He looked relieved and ran into the schoolyard to talk to his friend Heathcliffe Earnshaw about the forth-coming conker season. Then he stopped and shouted over his shoulder, 'Mithter Theffield, don't worry . . . ah'm going thopping for thum after thcool with my mam and my thithter.'

I smiled as I watched the eager young faces of the children gathering in small groups on the playground, ready for another academic year. Like the changing seasons, there was a steady rhythm to the life of a village schoolteacher and, for me, it was the job I loved.

Suddenly a large cream and blue mobile library van

came into sight from Morton Road. It drove sedately past the village green and slowed up outside the Post Office, where the village postman, Ted Postlethwaite, had just finished his usual cup of Typhoo with the postmistress, Miss Amelia Duff. It pulled up outside the village hall and the driver, a short, portly woman in her mid-forties, got out and surveyed her vehicle with a critical eye. Then she leant in and picked up a Thermos flask in a mighty fist that had stamped countless thousands of library books. It was well known in the village that if you valued your knuckles you didn't shake hands with Rosie Backhouse.

Since leaving her home in Featherstone, Rosie had spent the past twenty years driving the county council library van round the cluster of villages to the north of York. One morning each week she parked in Ragley village and her regular customers would trundle out to select a new novel. Rosie ruled her empire with a rod of iron, to such a degree that Don Bradshaw, the barman in The Royal Oak, was convinced she had been trained by the Gestapo. Her husband was the timid Cyril, manager of the Cavendish furniture store in York, and he would probably have agreed. Rosie was a very fierce lady and woe betide anyone caught smudging the front cover of a book or, God forbid, turning down the corner of a page. She settled down on the bench outside the village hall, glanced up at the clock and unscrewed the top of her flask. A nice beaker of coffee before her nine o'clock start would be just the job.

On the school playground, Anne Grainger, the deputy headteacher, had come out to talk to the mothers of the new starters and, after a few reassuring words, they soon began to relax. Anne, a slim, attractive forty-nine-year-old, had been a loyal supporter of Ragley School for many years. Her hard work, patience and, not least, a mischievous sense of humour made her a priceless member of staff and it was always a joy to walk into her lively reception class of four- and five-year-olds.

'Jack, Vera needs a word with you in the office,' said Anne with a grin. 'You've had a telephone call from Miss High-and-Mighty.'

I hurried into school. A message from Miss Barrington-Huntley, the Chair of the North Yorkshire Education Committee, usually meant something important.

Vera Evans, our tall, slim, elegant fifty-nine-year-old school secretary, looked her usual immaculate self in a new charcoal-grey, pin-striped Marks & Spencer's business suit. She peered over her pince-nez spectacles at the shorthand message on her spiral-bound pad. 'Ah, Mr Sheffield,' said Vera in her usual formal manner, 'you need to ring Miss Barrington-Huntley at County Hall.' She saw my concern. 'Don't worry,' she added with a reassuring smile, 'it sounded routine.'

I relaxed and picked up the receiver. Although I was the headteacher, sometimes it felt as though it was Vera who ran the school. The calm manner with which she dealt with our regular crises and the occasional angry parent, as well as the increasing deluge of paperwork that arrived from the local authority, was a wonder to behold.

'Good morning, Jack,' said a confident and familiar voice.

'Ah . . . good morning, Miss Barrington-Huntley,' I

replied, a little nervously. The last time we had spoken was at my aborted interview for a large school headship at the end of last term.

'Just to let you know that our newly appointed adviser for computers and libraries, Mr, er . . .' there was the sound of ruffled papers, 'Mr, hmmn, Gilford Eccles, will be calling in to see you at lunchtime today. He's doing some research on reading policies in North Yorkshire schools prior to the national Reading For All conference next month.'

'Ah, I see. Thank you for letting me know,' I replied, with a slightly sinking feeling. Even though I was proud of our reading scheme, I guessed this new initiative was leading towards some form of common curriculum for schools. Also, I didn't know the first thing about computers.

'I'll call in when I can,' she added cheerily, 'but, in the meantime, very best wishes for the new academic year, Jack. Goodbye.' She rang off before I could reply.

I replaced the receiver. 'Vera, Miss B-H says we've got an official visitor at lunchtime today,' I said, '. . . by the name of Eccles.'

Vera wrote it on her pad. 'Did you say . . . Eccles?' she asked.

A diminutive figure appeared alongside. 'Oooh, I love Eccles cakes!' exclaimed Jo Hunter. Jo, an athletic twenty-six-year-old, taught the six- and seven-year-olds in Class 2 and was married to Dan Hunter, our friendly six-feet-four-inch local policeman. She was dressed in a body-hugging tracksuit and fashionable Chris Evert trainers with her long black hair tied back in a pony-tail.

'He's something to do with computers, Jo, so perhaps

you could look after him over the lunch break,' I said hopefully. 'And don't mention cakes.'

'Fine, Jack, no problem,' said Jo. She was clutching the instruction booklet for our new school computer which, for the rest of the staff, might as well have been written in Japanese. However, Jo was clearly a sign of things to come and she grasped the new technology with open arms. After collecting her new registers from Vera's desk, she hurried back to her classroom with the confidence of youth.

'Computers!' muttered Vera. 'My new electric typewriter was hard enough. Where will it all end?' She took the plastic cover off her wonder of the modern world: namely, an ergonomically designed, golf-ball head, IBM Selectric typewriter, and, not for the first time, she yearned for her old manual Royal Imperial and the familiar *ker-ching* of the carriage return.

Our first computer had arrived during the summer holiday, a large beige-coloured cube with software called Folio and a separate disk drive. Jo had called into school frequently and had begun to use it as a writing aid, whereas the rest of us simply looked on in wonder. We were all due to go on an evening course at the teacher-training college in York.

A smiling freckled face appeared in the doorway. 'Jack, please could *I* ring the bell this morning? It's sort of . . . *symbolic*.'

Sally Pringle, a tall, ginger-haired forty-year-old, had returned from maternity leave to teach the eight- and nine-year-olds in Class 3. Her mother was only too pleased to look after Grace, her seven-month-old baby, and Sally was excited to be back in Ragley School doing the job she loved.

'Of course, Sally,' I said.

'Thanks, Jack. It's good to be back . . . and I need the exercise.' Sally was wearing her usual loud colours, an outfit including an orange tie-dyed waistcoat and a voluminous bright yellow blouse that hung loosely over her green stretch cords. She patted her tummy. 'I wonder if I'll ever get my figure back,' she added with a grin and walked to the foot of the bell tower.

At the sound of the bell all the children hurried into school, while, down the High Street, Rosie Backhouse opened the doors of her library van. It was well known that Rosie's word was law. The sign SILENCE IS NEXT TO GODLINESS taped above the music section meant business. Anything more than a whisper, including coughing and sneezing, resulted in immediate expulsion. Rosie didn't suffer fools gladly.

As she waited for her first customer, she reflected on her life. Rosie had loved the late fifties and early sixties. She remembered listening to two-way family favourites on the Light Programme while drinking a tumbler of Kia-Ora Suncrush. She had played her latest Buddy Holly 45 on her Dansette record player, watched her television heart-throb Eamonn Andrews on her 14-inch Bush television set and shared a packet of Spangles with her boyfriend, Cyril, in the back row of the cinema. Finally, she had married the innocent and introverted Cyril in 1966, on the day England won the World Cup, and made quite sure it wasn't just Geoff Hurst who scored a hat-trick that day. Cyril soon became alarmed at Rosie's demanding nature once the lights went out and began to attend weekend management courses in order to provide much needed recovery time and a good night's rest. When he became manager of the Cavendish furniture store in York, Rosie bought the best kingsize bed in the shop and made sure their bedroom looked like the top prize from Nicholas Parsons' *Sale of the Century*. In Rosie's world, men were fine as long as they knew their place.

The ten- and eleven-year-olds in my class soon settled in and, although a few of them appeared to have forgotten how to write, they were soon busy filling in their new reading record cards, labelling mathematics books, putting their names in their *New Oxford Dictionary* and sticking a personalized label on the lid of their tin of Lakeland crayons.

Morning assembly was always a joyous occasion at the start of a new year, with the new starters waving cautiously to their elder brothers and sisters and all the staff weighing up the children they were about to teach. We sang 'Morning Has Broken' and 'Kumbaya', accompanied by Anne on the piano, and then we all recited our school prayer.

Dear Lord,
This is our school, let peace dwell here,
Let the room be full of contentment, let love abide
  here,
Love of one another, love of life itself,
And love of God.
Amen.

After the bell for morning playtime, I walked into the staff-room. Vera was frowning at the front-page article of her *Daily Telegraph* about Michael Heseltine, Secretary of State for the Environment, who had cut local authority grants by £300 million. Although Margaret Thatcher was Vera's political heroine, life in public service wasn't quite what she had imagined.

'Thanks, Vera,' said Anne as she collected her mug of hot milky coffee and walked out to do playground duty.

'A good start, Mr Sheffield,' said Vera, as she locked the metal box containing the school dinner money. 'It all added up.'

'It should do now school meals have gone up to fifty pence,' grumbled Sally as she hunted for a custard cream in the biscuit tin.

'They're still a bargain,' said Vera. 'Shirley makes wonderful meals.' Our school cook, Shirley Mapplebeck, was renowned for the excellence of her cooking.

'A few of the poorer families will struggle,' said Sally. It was well known that Sally's politics were a world away from those of Vera but somehow they always seemed to find a compromise for the sake of peace in the staff-room.

'Perhaps you're right, Sally,' said Vera, 'but I hope not.'

Jo looked up from her *Rules of Netball*. 'And how's Beth?' she asked.

The room suddenly fell silent as Sally buried herself in the new issue of *Child Education* and Vera sipped her coffee thoughtfully and stared out of the window.

'Fine,' I said with a strained smile.

Sally looked up. 'Well, *we're* all glad you're here, Jack,' she said bluntly, while Vera gave me a knowing look and said nothing.

'So I'm not buying my hat for the wedding yet, then?' continued Jo, not to be deflected.

'Not yet, Jo . . . but *soon*, I hope.'

The strained atmosphere was broken by Vera. 'Don't forget the library van will be in the car park over lunchtime, so I'll be out there and send word for you to bring your children a class at a time.'

'Thanks, Vera,' we all chorused. For me, the bell for the end of playtime came as a relief.

Meanwhile, in the High Street, a few villagers were selecting books in the mobile library van. Audrey Bustard was looking for the latest Jackie Collins; Betty Buttle was rummaging in the Mills & Boon section, while Petula Dudley-Palmer, the richest woman in the village, studied the back cover of a Jilly Cooper novel before making an informed and definitely more upmarket selection.

When Sheila Bradshaw, the barmaid from The Royal Oak, hitched up her tight black miniskirt to negotiate the steep steps into the van there was a strong smell of cheap perfume and a flutter of well-disguised interest from the other book-lovers. As always, she adopted the *direct* approach. ''Ello, Rosie,' she said cheerfully. 'Ah want *The Joy of Sex*, please.'

Don't we all? was the thought that flickered simultaneously through the minds of all the ladies in the van, but not a word was spoken.

'Top shelf, last bookcase on t'right, Sheila,' said Rosie in a matter-of-fact voice.

''E needs a bit of a shake-up, does my Don,' said Sheila.

Rosie nodded. 'Men,' she muttered, 'they're all alike.'

George Postlethwaite, the seventy-six-year-old champion fisherman who lost his right arm in the Second World War, entered and put his returned copy of *Coarse Fishing* on the small counter. 'Ah'm after that new book, Mrs Back'ouse,' he said, '*My Angling World*, an' ah wondered if you'd got a book, hmmn . . . on, well, y'know . . . *suicide*.'

Rosie looked up sharply. 'Second bookcase, bottom shelf for fishing,' she said.

George paused. 'An' what abart suicide?'

'*Definitely* no,' said Rosie fiercely.

'Why not?' asked George, who was a lover of the dark arts. Gutting fish on his kitchen table while watching a Vincent Price horror movie was George's idea of a good night in.

'Well,' said Rosie, 'it's not likely you'd bring it back, is it?'

The sharp logic escaped George as he shuffled away down the van.

At lunchtime I queued up with my plastic tray to enjoy one of Shirley's delicacies: namely, spam fritters, chips and peas, followed by jam roly-poly and vivid purple custard. I had just finished the last delicious mouthful when ten-year-old Theresa Ackroyd, who didn't miss anything going on outside the window, announced, 'Little sports car coming up t'drive, Mr Sheffield.'

A bright-red MG Midget roared into the car park

and drew up in the no-parking area outside the boiler-house doors. I walked into the entrance hall to meet the driver. He was a short, skinny man with long, curly, Bob Dylan-style hair, a fuzzy unkempt beard, John Lennon circular spectacles, a floral shirt, Mickey Mouse tie and a crumpled purple cord suit. 'Good morning, Mr Sheffield. I'm Gilford Eccles, the new Library and Computer Adviser for North Yorkshire.'

'Welcome to Ragley,' I said and shook his limp, delicate hand.

'I've brought this for you,' he said, holding up a smart spiral-bound, plastic-covered booklet entitled 'Reading in the Computer Age – a vision of the future by Gilford Eccles, Dip. Ed., Ed Psych, BA (Hons), MA'. Anne gave me a wide-eyed look that suggested we were in the company of a mad scientist with an over-inflated ego and what was I going to do about it.

'Thank you,' I said, handing the booklet quickly to Anne, who passed it even more quickly to Jo, who immediately began to flick through the pages.

'As you will see from my thesis, we shall *all* be affected by the silicon chip.'

We nodded and, as far as we could see, it sounded as though this tedious little man had just swallowed one.

'Thirty-six secondary schools in North Yorkshire now have a computer and one hundred and forty teachers have completed a training course,' he recited.

'Perhaps you could let us know the exact purpose of your visit, Mr Eccles,' I said.

He looked surprised. 'To advance the reading skills of your children of course,' he said with utter conviction.

31

'I'm here to check the content of your library and to ensure you're aware of the role of the computer in advanced reading techniques.'

'I see,' I said . . . but I didn't.

Sally came to the rescue. 'We've just built a new library,' she said firmly, 'and it's very well stocked.'

'Also, the mobile library van will be here over lunch-time to provide extra opportunities for children to take books home,' added Anne.

'And I've been on the computer course,' said Jo without a hint of modesty.

'Interesting,' said Mr Eccles with a superior smile. 'That sounds, hmmn . . . satisfactory.' He turned to survey our library area in the new extension to our entrance hall, which teemed with bright and attractive books. Most had been purchased thanks to the Parent–Teacher Association and there were others that had been donated by friends of the school. 'Oh no,' he said, picking up a copy of *Five Go Off in a Caravan* and *The Mountain of Adventure*, both by Enid Blyton. 'Dear me, these will have to go.'

'Why is that?' I asked.

Mr Eccles gave me a condescending look. 'How can we have an author who made a hero of a boy called Fatty and was turned down by the BBC's Director of Programmes in 1936 as a "second-rater"?'

'But Enid Blyton is still very popular and her books are in most homes,' I said, 'and there are lots of modern authors here, as you can see.'

'I'm sorry to say that Enid Blyton hasn't much literary value,' he scorned. 'Rather too much pink-winky, pixie stuff for me. So I'll remove these now,' he said and tucked them under his arm.

'But you can't take our books away,' I protested.

'I most certainly can,' bristled Mr Eccles. 'Remember the old adage, Mr Sheffield, *a place for everything and everything in its place* . . . and I know where these belong.'

I left the infuriating Mr Eccles to join Vera in the school car park, where Rosie had reversed her mobile library van up the cobbled school drive. By one o'clock all the children had finished their lunch and were excited about selecting a new library book.

Mr Eccles was ready to leave but, as he had parked in the wrong place, he was blocked in by the large van. 'Would you mind pulling your van forwards?' he shouted, clearly very annoyed.

'Shush . . . I'll move when I'm good and ready,' replied a fierce disembodied voice from inside the van.

Mr Eccles walked to the foot of the steps that led into the van and yelled through the open doorway: 'But you've blocked me in, so hurry up.'

A second later he took a quick step back as a fearsome sight appeared.

'How dare you shout in my library!' exclaimed Rosie as she stepped out of the van into the car park. 'This is a haven of peace and quiet.'

'Well, er, I'm in a h-hurry,' stuttered Mr Eccles.

Rosie folded her massive forearms and studied the unkempt figure before her. 'I know you,' she said, eyes widening in recognition. 'It's young Eccles, isn't it? From up near Linton. Always brought your books back late.'

Gilford Eccles looked at Rosie in horror. 'I think, er, you might be—'

'Ah, I remember now,' said Rosie with a fierce glint in her eyes. 'He used to love his Enid Blyton, did this one, Mr Sheffield.' She pointed at the books in Gilford's trembling hand. 'Your mother always said how much you enjoyed *Tales at Bedtime*. So how is she these days?'

'Er, very well, er, thank you,' muttered Mr Eccles. He thrust the books back in my hands. 'I'll, er, wait in the car until you've gone,' he said by way of apology.

'That's more like it,' said Rosie. 'A little patience and plenty of peace and quiet is what we need. No need to get uppity. Isn't that right, Mr Sheffield?'

'Definitely,' I said with a smile.

'I'll put these back on the shelves, shall I, Mr Sheffield?' said Vera triumphantly.

'Thank you,' I said.

'Under B in fiction?' said Vera pointedly.

'Yes, Vera . . . *a place for everything*,' I said.

Vera nodded towards the white-faced Gilford Eccles, sitting nervously in his sports car. '*And everything in its place*, Mr Sheffield.'

Chapter Two

Vera's Brief Encounter

*The Revd Joseph Evans recommenced his weekly RE lesson.
Miss Evans was absent for the first hour of morning school
for family reasons.*

Extract from the Ragley School Logbook:
Friday, 18 September 1981

Bright autumn sunshine lit up the platform as the early-morning train to London eased its way into York station.

Vera had enjoyed the annual two-day visit by her Aunt Priscilla. However, deep down she was looking forward to a return to the peace, quiet and general tidiness of her everyday life. Visitors were all very well but when, that morning, her aunt had stirred her tea and then returned the damp teaspoon to the sugar bowl, she knew with absolute conviction that their parting would not be one of sweet sorrow.

'Your train is here, Aunt Priscilla,' said Vera with a hint of relief. They were sitting in the station café and, while

Priscilla prattled on about the benefits of North Sea oil, Vera recalled her favourite film, the 1945 David Lean classic, *Brief Encounter*. There was, of course, a significant difference. While Celia Johnson had sat in the refreshment room at Milford Junction waiting for the handsome Trevor Howard, Vera was sitting with a cup of lukewarm tea, a tired scone and, sadly, her least favourite aunt.

Minutes later, with a final wave of a lace-edged handkerchief at the departing train, Vera turned on her heel and climbed the metal stairs of the bridge that spanned the platforms. It was Friday, 18 September, and once again all was well in Vera's orderly world. She glanced at her watch and was pleased she had allowed enough time to drive back to Ragley, collect her *Daily Telegraph* from Prudence Golightly in the General Stores, make a cup of Earl Grey tea and settle down at her desk to count the late dinner money. It was a routine she knew so well.

Commuters hurried past as she walked to the centre of the bridge and then paused to lean on the guardrail to admire the grandeur of this magnificent railway station. Huge metal arches spanned the great roof above her and Vera mused that these splendid buildings really *were* the cathedrals of Victorian Britain.

Vera lived with her younger brother, the Revd Joseph Evans, in the beautifully furnished and spacious vicarage on Morton Road. Her life was one of careful routine and order. Even her three well-behaved cats, Treacle, Jess and Maggie, were fastidious in their personal grooming – especially her favourite, Maggie, a black cat with white paws, named after Margaret Thatcher. Vera was content with her cross-stitch club, church flowers and Women's

Institute meetings. However, something was about to enter her peaceful world . . . something *unexpected*.

Below her, on the busy platforms, people waited anxiously for the next train, glancing frequently at the Roman numerals on the giant station clock. That is, all except for one man, who, to her surprise, appeared to be staring up at her. It was a look of sudden curiosity, of rapt intensity, a look she suddenly realized she knew so well. There could be no doubt. Twenty years had passed since their parting. The familiar long wavy hair was just as she remembered it, although now with the first wisps of grey, and his youthful angular frame had filled out a little with the approach of middle age. He waved and, to her surprise, she responded almost eagerly, raising a leather-gloved hand in swift acknowledgement.

Hedley Verity Bickerstaff set off with long strides along the platform. A handsome forty-seven-year-old with the confidence of the innately gifted, he launched himself up the steps. 'Vera, it really *is* you,' he called out and then paused with a look of admiration . . . and perhaps more.

'Hedley,' murmured Vera, almost to herself.

'After all these years,' he said, and bent forward to kiss her cheek lightly. His flaxen hair fell over his lean, sun-tanned face and his soft brown eyes crinkled into a smile. Over six feet tall, he cut an elegant figure, although his bright-yellow cravat and cream linen jacket gave him a rather foppish appearance among the thick tweeds and heavy brogues of this Yorkshire station.

Vera's mind was in a whirl. This was so unexpected. 'Hedley . . . how nice to see you again,' she said and her cheeks flushed with a distant memory of their last meeting.

Hedley glanced at the station clock and smiled. 'Just like *Brief Encounter*,' he said and Vera gave an imperceptible nod. They both knew it had always been her favourite film and the final evocative black-and-white scene, filmed in Lancashire's Carnforth station in 1945, still broke her heart. Celia Johnson, the apparently normal middle-class housewife, had found a true, if fleeting, love following a chance encounter with Trevor Howard. The brief affair that followed was never consummated and both returned to their humdrum lives. However, from that moment on, Vera was sure she knew how Celia Johnson felt and, on occasions, had pondered on the difference between infatuation and true love.

Hedley was proud of his distinctive name. He had been born in York on 25 June 1934, the historic day on which the England cricket team had defeated Australia at Lords, the home of cricket, for the first time since 1896. Hedley's father, Arthur Bickerstaff, a lifetime member of the Yorkshire Cricket Club, promptly insisted that his son be named after Hedley Verity, the legendary Yorkshire left-arm spin bowler, who, on that memorable day, had taken fifteen Australian wickets for a mere one hundred and four runs.

On 1 September 1939, when Hedley was five years old, Arthur had taken his son to Hove to watch Yorkshire beat Sussex and, much to Arthur's delight, Hedley Verity was the star performer, taking seven wickets for nine runs. Sadly, it was to prove his final day of cricket glory for, after becoming a captain in the Green Howards, he was killed in action in 1943 while leading an attack on a German-occupied farmhouse. All of Yorkshire mourned one of their favourite sons.

Finally, when Arthur Bickerstaff died on the beaches of Dunkirk, his wife, Iris, thanks to a useful sum of inheritance money, bought a large detached house in Ragley village for £515 and lived a comfortable life with her two sons, Hedley and his younger brother, Allan. Hedley had attended the Lawnswood Preparatory School for Young Gentlemen in Thirkby, passed his accountancy examinations and, in the late sixties, had begun work with Allan in the Easington accountancy firm of Bickerstaff, Bickerstaff, Crapper and Pugh.

Sadly, the artistic and musical Hedley never did follow in his namesake's footsteps as a cricketer. His mother gave him his father's old cricket flannels but, following the occasional game for the Ragley second XI when they were a man short, it was pointed out, rather cruelly, at the end of the season, that his cricket trousers had a higher batting average than he did. No one guessed why he suddenly fled to London to seek fame and fortune as a budding artist.

'So why are you here, Vera?' asked Hedley. 'I did wonder if I might see you . . . but not quite so soon.'

'I've just put my aunt on the London train after her visit,' said Vera quietly.

'Oh, I see,' said Hedley. 'Well, I'm here for my mother's seventy-fifth birthday tomorrow . . . and it's back to London on Sunday.' He glanced at his reserved first-class ticket. 'I'm on the fast train at two-thirty.'

There was a pause as they both looked into each other's

eyes and recalled a long-ago summer when Vera had so admired the dramatic oil paintings of a handsome young artist and Hedley had become infatuated with an elegant, attractive older woman. The memory of that single stolen kiss was distant now for the worldly owner of a London art gallery but was still seared in the mind of the village school secretary.

'I have to get to work,' said Vera quickly, looking up at the station clock once again. 'I'm the secretary at Ragley School and I have to drive back there now.'

'Perhaps you might consider giving me a lift, Vera, and then, well . . . perhaps we could talk.'

Vera's cheeks felt on fire. She couldn't very well refuse to give Hedley a lift, particularly as they were both going to Ragley. 'Very well,' she said, 'but I need to make a telephone call first,' and they walked out together into the sunshine.

At 8.45 a.m. a classic black Bentley purred up the school drive and parked in the space usually occupied by Vera's little Austin A40. Major Rupert Forbes-Kitchener, our sixty-three-year-old school governor and owner of the magnificent local country house, Morton Manor, stepped out. To my surprise he was accompanied by Vera's brother, the Revd Joseph Evans. The major's sharp eyes spotted me at the window and he waved his brass-topped walking cane in greeting.

We met in the entrance hall and I accompanied them into the school office. As always, the major, a tall, distinguished man with close-cropped steel-grey hair, looked immaculate. He was wearing his familiar thick tweed sports jacket, lovat-green waistcoat and regimental tie, his cavalry twill trousers with knife-edge creases and a pair of sturdy brown brogues with the toecaps polished to a military shine.

'Good morning, Jack. Jolly fine day, what?' he said and shook my hand in a powerful grip.

'It is, Major,' I said. 'Good to see you.'

'Rupert very kindly gave me a lift,' said Joseph. He was a tall, angular, slightly nervous fifty-seven-year-old with thinning grey hair. 'Vera telephoned from the station to say she's been delayed,' he said with a slightly concerned look. 'She was putting Aunt Priscilla on the train after her visit, so it must be something to do with that.'

'Oh, well,' I said, 'I'm sure she'll be here soon.'

'Absent without leave, old boy,' said the major with a deep chuckle. 'Pity, I had an invitation for her.' He held up an embossed envelope and placed it on Vera's desk. Since the death of his wife many years ago, the major had lived with his daughter, Virginia Anastasia, at Morton Manor, but it was well known that he had a deep affection for Vera. 'And there's one for you and that lovely young filly of yours,' he added. 'Nothing special, old chap,' he said: 'it's just tea and cakes at my place on Sunday . . . so hope to see you, what?'

'Certainly, Major, and thank you,' I said, putting the envelope in my pocket. 'I'll check with Beth and let you know.'

'Fine, Jack. Well, tally ho for now. Duty calls,' and he marched off back to the car park.

Joseph looked tense. 'Class 2 today, I believe,' he said, studying the timetable on the noticeboard.

'Yes, Joseph, and I'm sure it will be fine,' I said. 'So . . . what's the theme today?'

His lesson notes were inserted in his leather-bound, well-thumbed Bible. 'What is love?' he replied dolefully.

'Pardon?'

'No, that's it, Jack . . . *what is love?*'

'Ah, I see. Well, good luck, Joseph.'

'I'll probably need it,' he said. Joseph was always much more comfortable preaching sermons to his parishioners rather than a group of unpredictable six- and seven-year-olds. He stared out of the window as the major drove off. 'I wonder what's happened to Vera,' he murmured to himself.

In the spotless kitchen of St Mary's vicarage, Vera emptied her copper kettle, filled it with freshly drawn water from the cold tap and lit the gas ring. Then she selected a matching pair of bone-china teacups and saucers and placed them alongside a matching sugar bowl, a silver tea strainer and a small jug of milk on a dark mahogany tray. Atop a pure white doily on a plate she placed several home-made biscuits.

'You always were the most wonderful hostess, Vera,' said Hedley in obvious admiration.

Vera smiled modestly. 'I try,' she said and then stiffened as the grandfather clock in the hall struck nine o'clock. She would be late for school, a first in her regular life. It was just that there was something she needed to find out, something that had never been resolved . . . something important. She knew this might be her only chance and

Ragley School could survive without her for the time being. Meanwhile, there was the little matter of a *perfect* cup of tea.

Just before the water in the kettle came to the boil Vera poured a generous dash of hot water into a beautifully glazed china teapot. Her mother's wise words were always with her and she knew that warming the pot ensured the water stayed at boiling point when it hit the tea. Then, straight into the warmed teapot, she doled out a heaped teaspoonful for Hedley and another for herself, plus, of course, one for the pot. The kettle was now boiling frantically and Vera made sure it did not boil for too long as it could result in a bitter muddy brew. She poured in the water and stood back. It was time to let it stand for a few minutes before serving and she turned her attention back to Hedley.

'I hear you have a successful gallery in London,' said Vera.

'It's an inspiring place,' said Hedley. 'You would love it.'

'I'm pleased you found what you always wanted,' she said a little wistfully.

Hedley looked at Vera and sighed. 'Well, it took a long time, Vera, but eventually . . . I found happiness in my work.'

'You *still* paint, I hope.' Vera stirred the tea and re-placed the lid on the teapot. The memories that had been dormant for so long were now vivid in her mind. With measured restraint, she added the milk, cold and fresh, to each cup and then picked up the tea strainer to catch the leaves as she poured the tea.

Hedley smiled. 'So no tea bags, Vera,' he said softly. 'You don't change.'

Vera pursed her lips and made a small *moue* of displeasure. 'Oh dear, no!' she exclaimed and they both laughed. It broke the tension. 'Two sugars, Hedley?'

'You remembered.'

'Of course,' said Vera, stirring the cup with a silver teaspoon.

He raised the cup to his lips. 'Perfect, Vera. Then again . . . it always was.'

Vera touched her cheeks with her long, delicate fingers. She knew she was blushing again.

Back in school, Joseph was coping better than usual with the lively children in Jo Hunter's class. Remarkably, they had responded well to his 'What is love?' discussion. As he collected in the notebooks and glanced out of the window, he felt a little sad that his sister was not here to share in the fun. There had been no follow-up telephone call, which seemed unusual, and he hoped all was well with her.

Shortly before ten o'clock the children in my class were in the middle of a practical mathematics lesson and Theresa Ackroyd was pouring water into a litre jug and recording the results. 'Miss Evans coming up t'drive, Mr Sheffield,' she said without spilling a drop or appearing to look up.

Moments later, Vera popped her head round the classroom door. 'Sorry I'm late, Mr Sheffield. I'll get on with the late dinner money, shall I?' She collected the register from my desk and hurried out.

*   *   *

At morning break, Jo was on playground duty while the rest of us gathered in the staff-room. Sally picked up her September issue of *Cosmopolitan* and read out the title of an article by Quentin Crisp. 'Women will be free the moment they stop caring what men think about them,' she announced.

'I agree,' said Anne. 'What do you think, Vera?'

'Perhaps,' said Vera. She appeared to be in a world of her own as she stirred a pan of hot milk on the single electric ring.

Joseph walked in and immediately opened up the children's writing for us all to share. For once he was enthusiastic about their responses. 'No howlers today, Jack,' he said triumphantly. 'Have a look at these.'

Charlotte Ackroyd had written: 'Love is when my mummy puts on perfume and my daddy puts on aftershave and they go out to smell each other.' Mary Scrimshaw's careful neat printing was easy to recognize. 'Love is when my mummy kisses me to sleep at night.' Six-year-old Barry Ollerenshaw had other ideas: 'Love is when my great granddad ties my great grandma's shoelaces cos her fingers are all bent now'; and seven-year-old Benjamin Roberts had found a very practical example: 'Love is when Mummy gives Daddy the biggest pork chop.'

Joseph looked at his sister and wondered why she appeared so preoccupied. 'So you managed to pack Aunt Priscilla off back to London?'

'Oh, er, yes, Joseph,' she said as she rinsed the coffee mugs and peered out of the window.

'And the major left you an invitation on your desk,' he added.

'Thank you, Joseph,' said Vera in a distracted way. Although she was staring out on the playground and had a clear view of Heathcliffe Earnshaw hiding his new spud gun behind the school dustbins she appeared not to notice. Nor did she see his little brother Terry giving Jimmy Poole three marbles for one of his sherbet flying saucers. It was clear that Vera had a lot on her mind.

Fifteen minutes later, in the silent school office, Vera sat at her desk and reflected on her morning. She fingered the smooth edges of the elegant Victorian brooch pinned precisely on the neat lapel of her suit and wondered why her heart was still pounding. For a few brief moments she felt like a young woman again. Then she picked up her brass letter opener and reached for the thick, cream envelope with the Morton Manor crest. It was an invitation to afternoon tea at three o'clock on Sunday. She smiled when she saw the footnote in the major's firm, level handwriting. 'Hope you can make it, Vera – just a few special friends.' He had underlined the word *special*.

It was early evening and the school was quiet now. Out of the office window the distant Hambleton hills formed a hazy purple line beneath a darkening sky. The paperwork from County Hall was increasing year by year and I was working my way through a revised health and safety policy, which made me think twice about the adventurous activities that were fundamental to our outdoor education weekends, when the telephone rang.

'Jack, I thought you'd still be there.' It was Beth; she sounded tired. 'I've got a governor's report to complete. I thought if I did it tonight maybe I could come round tomorrow and make a meal.'

'That would be great, Beth,' I said.

'I was thinking about having a try at Delia's *bœuf bourguignonne* and maybe use some of your dry cider instead of wine to save a few pennies. It sounds scrummy in the book.'

'Can't wait,' I said.

'It takes a few hours so I'll come to the cottage around four, shall I?'

'Perfect,' I said, thinking it would give me time to do some housework.

'And I'll bring the report so maybe you could check it through for me.'

'Delighted,' I said.

There was a long silence. 'And we need to talk,' she added.

On Saturday evening darkness was falling and, in the evening breeze, the high elms were restless. On Morton Road bats swooped with blind confidence around the silent tower of St Mary's Church. Vera closed the lounge curtains in the vicarage and, shortly before seven o'clock, switched on BBC2 and settled down to watch the Leeds International Piano Competition. However, by the time the sixth finalist performed, her mind was elsewhere and she knew there was something she must do.

*　　*　　*

Meanwhile, at Bilbo Cottage, after a wonderful meal, Beth and I settled down with a bottle of wine to watch episode three of John Le Carré's spy thriller *Tinker, Tailor, Soldier, Spy*. The portrayal of the mole-catcher, George Smiley, by Alec Guinness had proved compulsive viewing for us and we relaxed together on the sofa in front of my first log fire of the season.

An hour later we stood together in the kitchen and I washed the casserole dish while Beth made some coffee. With her perfect complexion and honey-blonde hair and dressed in jeans and a baggy woollen sweater that merely enhanced her slim figure, I wondered how she could ever have wanted an awkward, bespectacled Yorkshireman like me. Nervously, I tried to flatten the palm-tree tuft of brown hair that refused to lie down on the crown of my head. From the empty lounge, I could hear a television interview with Ron Atkinson, manager of Manchester United. He wanted George Best to return to the club but it was *my* return to Ragley School that was uppermost in my mind. It was this decision that had caused tension between Beth and me.

Our recent conversations had become a collection of silences. I could see the ghosts of what we might become: silent partners in a comedy of manners, acting our parts in perfect harmony but never choosing our own pathway. There was distance between us. It was time to talk.

We took our coffee into the lounge and I switched off the television.

'Beth . . . I know you were disappointed in me when I pulled out of the chance to go for the bigger headship.'

'A little,' she said quietly and sipped her coffee.

'When I knew Ragley *wasn't* one of the small schools selected for closure, I was *so* relieved.'

'I know, Jack.'

'And I love my work. I'm really happy at Ragley.'

'As *I* am at Hartingdale, Jack, but I don't anticipate being there for ever.'

'I understand that, Beth.'

She replaced her coffee cup and went to stand by the fire. 'It's just that I thought we had similar ambitions,' she said as she stared into the flames.

I went to stand beside her in the flickering light. 'That's why we need to talk,' I said. Beth was silent. 'You see, I don't want to be a *disappointment* to you, Beth . . . not any more.'

She turned to face me. 'What *exactly* are you trying to say, Jack?'

I held her hands in mine and took a deep breath. 'Beth . . . I'll understand if you want to break off the engagement.'

There was a shocked expression on her face followed by confusion. 'Oh, Jack . . . Jack.' She put her arms round my waist and held me tightly. Her hair was soft against my cheek. '*You* are the man I want for my husband. How could you ever doubt that?'

'But we've been *drifting* for so long now, Beth, and I thought you might want to find someone, well, better than I am, someone who will *achieve* in the way *you* want them to succeed.'

She looked up at me with a firm intensity. 'Jack, even though I *was* disappointed when you decided not to go for the new headship, I could never be disappointed in you as a *person* . . . as a *man*.' Then she lifted her head and kissed me tenderly on the lips.

'It's just that we've not spoken about the wedding for ages,' I said. 'I thought you were avoiding it.'

'Jack,' she said, '*look* at me and believe it: *you* are the man I want to marry.'

I felt as though a weight had been lifted from my heart. 'Beth . . . I love you.' I put my arms around her as if I never, ever, wanted to let her go. Then we kissed again . . . and again.

'And I love you, Jack . . . so why don't we plan a wedding?'

'When?' I asked eagerly.

'How about now?' replied Beth.

'But it's late and I'm tired,' I said with a grin.

'Then let's have this conversation somewhere else,' she said with a wide-eyed stare. 'I've been thinking about hotels and wedding dresses and dates . . . and churches – for example, Yorkshire or Hampshire . . . In fact, your place or mine, Mr Sheffield?' She took my hand, turned out the light and led the way to the foot of the stairs.

On Sunday the weather was cooler and the first fires of autumn had been lit in the cottages of Ragley village. As Vera drove down the High Street, long streamers of woodsmoke were being tugged by a gentle breeze into a slate-blue sky. She glanced at her wristwatch. There was time for a final rendezvous and, as the miles raced by, she rehearsed her words carefully. Twenty minutes later, the sheer magnificence of York Minster came into sight, towering like a sleeping giant above the rooftops and snickleways of York. By the time she drove into the station car park she allowed herself a reflective, enigmatic smile.

Then she parked and looked at the clock. There was time to speak to Hedley but what was there to say? It was over and had been for a long time. In fact, it had barely begun. Now there was a wonderful man in her life. She put her hand in her coat pocket and read the invitation from Rupert once again.

And, as she waited, she smiled. There really was a difference between infatuation and true love . . . and she knew what it was.

Chapter Three

Ruby and the Butlin's Redcoat

Following a meeting with the school governors, permission has been granted by County Hall for Mrs Smith's caretaking duties to be extended by four hours per week.

Extract from the Ragley School Logbook:
Friday, 9 October 1981

'All the sixes, sixty-six,' announced the confident bingo caller as he flicked a comb through his Billy Fury quiff.

'You've got that one, Ruby,' whispered Betty Buttle, but Ruby looked preoccupied.

'Key of the door, twenty-one,' reverberated the voice from the giant speakers.

'An' that one, Ruby. C'mon, wekken up,' muttered Margery Ackroyd.

Ruby crossed off the numbers on her bingo card but her mind was elsewhere.

'Downing Street, number ten.'

The ladies of Ragley and Morton sat round their tables

in the Ragley village hall as the excitement increased. It was Thursday evening, 8 October, and the monthly bingo night was in full swing.

'Ah'd know that voice anywhere,' murmured Ruby almost to herself, a far-away look in her eyes.

'Two little ducks, twenty-two,' said the man with the faded red jacket and twinkling blue eyes.

'Ah'm sweatin' on eighty-eight,' said Julie Earnshaw.

'Yours and mine, sixty-nine,' boomed the voice again.

'Ah'm sweatin' an' all,' said Margery as she crossed off the penultimate number.

'Legs . . . eee-leven.'

'Ah knew it,' said Ruby, 'it's 'im . . . Well, ah never did, would y'believe it?'

'Seventy-seven, Sunset Strip. C'mon, ladies, somebody's got t'be close to a full 'ouse.'

Ruby didn't cross off number seventy-seven. She was staring at the only man in the hall.

'Two fat ladies, eighty-eight,' he cried.

"*Ouse!*' yelled Betty, waving her completed bingo card in the air.

'We 'ave a lucky lady on t'corner table,' said the tall, lean, chain-smoking fifty-year-old bingo caller. He stood up and waved at the group of ladies on Betty's table. 'Shout out y'numbers, luv, an' we'll check y'card.' Then he stared and went silent. 'Ruby,' he said quietly but forgetting his microphone was switched on.

'Does 'e know you?' asked Margery.

'Glory be,' muttered Ruby, 'it *is* 'im. Ah'd know that voice anywhere.'

'Who's '*im*?' whispered Julie Earnshaw, for whom

curiosity and correct grammar were not constant companions.

'After all these years,' said Ruby quietly.

'So . . . who is 'e?' asked all the ladies at once.

Ruby smiled and put down her pencil. 'It's Seaside Johnny.'

Outside the staff-room window Friday had dawned bright and clear. It was a perfect autumn morning. The season was changing and the leaves were tinged with gold. In the hedgerows busy spiders were making their intricate webs, robins and wrens were claiming their territory, while goldfinches pecked the ripe seeds from the teasels. It was 8.30 a.m. and, in the corridor outside the school office, the sound of Ruby singing 'Edelweiss' from her favourite musical, *The Sound of Music*, was distinctly louder than usual.

I smoothed some sticky-backed plastic over the fraying edges of a white card on which the one hundred words of the 'Schonell Word Recognition Test' were neatly printed. 'Ruby sounds cheerful,' I said.

Vera looked up from her pile of Yorkshire Purchasing Organization order forms and smiled. 'It's good to hear, Mr Sheffield. She's been a bit down lately.'

Suddenly there was the clatter of a galvanized bucket followed by a tap on the door and there stood Ruby. 'G'morning, Mr Sheffield, Miss Evans,' she said cheerfully. 'Ah'm trying t'finish a bit smartish this morning, if y'please.'

Ruby Smith weighed over twenty stones and her extra-large double X, bright-orange overall was tightly fastened over her plump frame as she pushed a few strands of damp, wavy, chestnut hair away from her eyes.

'That's fine, Ruby,' I said.

Vera always took a kindly interest in our good-hearted and hard-working school caretaker. 'Don't overdo it, Ruby,' she said, 'especially now the governors have granted those extra hours for you.'

'Ah'm fine, thank you, Miss Evans – reight as rain,' said Ruby as, absent-mindedly, she took out a soft cloth from her overall pocket and began to polish the door handle. 'It's jus' that sometimes ah want t'world t'slow down a bit,' she said, 'an' then ah can catch up, so t'speak.'

'So, Ruby . . . are you doing something special with Ronnie?' I asked, more in hope than expectation.

Ruby looked down at the door handle and the polishing slowed down to a standstill. 'Y'jokin', Mr Sheffield. Ah'm spittin' feathers wi' 'im. 'E won't get off 'is backside – sez 'e's gorra cold.'

'Oh, I see,' I said lamely.

'Anyway, Diane's doing me 'air at nine o'clock an' then ah said ah'd meet an old friend later in t'Coffee Shop.'

Vera looked up again with interest. 'Oh, who's that, Ruby?'

'Seaside Johnny, Miss Evans.'

'Seaside Johnny?' I said.

'Yes, Mr Sheffield,' said Ruby. ''E were t'new bingo caller las' night an' ah've not seen 'im f'years. 'E used t'work at Butlin's back in t'sixties.' She resumed polishing the door handle thoughtfully. 'An' 'e's jus' come back t'live in Easington an' opened a second-'and shop. Do y'remember 'im, Miss Evans?'

'I certainly do, Ruby,' said Vera. 'He used to have a stall on Thirkby market selling old paintings and bric-à-brac.'

'That's reight,' said Ruby with a smile. "E loved 'is art, did Johnny. 'E 'ad pictures all round 'is 'ouse – *Wrestler's Mother, Laughing Chandelier,* 'e'd gorrem all.' With that she picked up the wickerwork basket from under my desk, emptied the offcuts of sticky-backed plastic and torn manila envelopes into her black bag and dragged it out into the corridor.

When the door was closed, Vera resumed checking the carbon copy of an order form for large tins of powder paint and bristle brushes. Quietly, she murmured, 'Oh dear.'

'Problem, Vera?' I asked.

Vera didn't look up. 'No, Mr Sheffield . . . Well, I hope not.'

Morning school went well. In my class, ten-year-old Sarah Louise Tait wrote a wonderful poem, Debbie Clack's reading age caught up with her chronological age and Theresa Buttle finally cracked long multiplication. However, in Jo Hunter's class, life wasn't quite so smooth and a dispute had broken out.

'Oh, Terry!' exclaimed Jo.

'Ah never took 'er pen, Miss,' pleaded Terry Earnshaw.

Jo shook her head sadly at the absence of correct grammar. 'No, Terry: I *didn't* take her pen.'

'That meks two of us what never took it, Miss,' said Terry, quick as a flash.

'Oh dear,' said Jo. 'Come on, girls and boys, back to

our health education lesson . . . Now, who can remember, what are the bowels?'

Benjamin Roberts immediately raised his hand. 'A, E, I, O, U,' he shouted eagerly.

Jo sighed deeply. 'A good try, Benjamin,' she said, 'but . . . actually . . .'

In the High Street, Ruby had enjoyed a relaxing morning in Diane's Hair Salon. After deciding on a cut-price 'Farrah Fawcett', she had set off back to school wearing her favourite headscarf and feeling as though she had just got eight draws on Littlewood's pools. Although it crossed her mind that Farrah Fawcett didn't have to mop the hall floor and put the dining tables out, she was grateful that her caretaker's contract had been increased by an extra four hours per week and she knew the money would come in handy to feed her large family.

Finally, at half past twelve, Ruby hung up her overall in the caretaker's store, tightened the knot on her headscarf and tapped lightly on the open staff-room door. ''Scuse me, Miss Evans,' she said.

Vera looked up from her *Daily Telegraph* crossword. 'That's all right, Ruby,' said Vera. 'I was just studying this anagram.'

For a moment, Ruby was puzzled. She hadn't seen Ted the postman deliver any anagrams that morning.

'Ah'll be getting off, if it please, Miss Evans,' said Ruby. 'Ah need t'check on my Ronnie.'

'Why is that, Ruby?'

''E's got one o' them colds that men get.'

'I see,' said Vera. 'So . . . just a sniffle then.'

'That's reight, Miss Evans.'

'Any sign of a job on the horizon?'

'My Ronnie'll never knuckle down an' get a proper job, Miss Evans. It's not in 'is nature,' said Ruby. 'Ah know that now.'

'Oh dear, Ruby, I'm so sorry.'

Ruby shook her head. 'Sometimes ah wish 'e would sling 'is 'ook, but then ah took 'im f'better o' worse, so ah'm stuck wi' 'im.'

'But how do you,' Vera searched for the right word, '. . . *feel* about him, Ruby?'

'Well . . . ah do *luv* 'im, Miss Evans – allus 'ave, allus will. M'mother used t'say y'can't pick *who* y'love, it picks you.'

Vera smiled. 'She's a wise lady, Ruby.'

'She is that . . . Well, ah'll be off then, Miss Evans. See y'later.'

'OK, Ruby.' Vera shook her head sadly and wondered what would become of her downtrodden friend. She really did need something to cheer her up.

Ruby was deep in thought as she walked down the cobbled school drive. The distant forest at the foot of the Hambleton hills glowed with autumn gold but Ruby was too preoccupied to notice. She knew that her unemployed husband, Ronnie, would continue to drink the same considerable volume of beer regardless of the cost. To make matters worse, there was talk that Miss Golightly in the General Stores & Newsagent was about to raise the price of a loaf of bread to thirty-one pence. The outlook for Ruby and her family looked bleak. As she closed the school gates and turned towards home, Jo Hunter and Vera watched her from the staff-room window.

'I feel so sorry for Ruby,' said Jo sadly.

'So do I,' said Vera. 'She needs something to lift her spirits.'

Our forty-eight-year-old caretaker was married to un-employed Ronnie, whose life revolved around his racing pigeons, the bookmaker and Tetley's bitter. They had six children. 'The first 'n' last were accidents but ah love 'em all,' she had once said. Her elder son, thirty-year-old Andy, was in the army and her eldest daughter, twenty-eight-year-old Racquel, lived in York with her husband, a factory storeman. Racquel worked as a packer in the Joseph Rowntree chocolate factory and every Friday she delivered a free bag of Lion bars to her mother. ''Ere's y'little treat, Mam,' Racquel would say and Ruby would give her a hug and an expectant look. 'An' no, Mam, ah'm *not* pregnant.' Then Ruby would go into her cluttered kitchen to make a mug of tea and pray that one day she would be blessed with a grandchild.

Ruby and Ronnie shared their council house at number 7 School View with their other four children. Duggie, a twenty-six-year-old undertaker's assistant with the nickname 'Deadly', was content smoking his Castella cigars, playing with his Hornby Dublo train set and sleeping on his little wooden bunk in the attic; twenty-one-year-old Sharon had just got engaged to the local blond-haired adonis Rodney Morgetroyd, the Morton village milkman; nineteen-year-old Natasha was an assistant in Diane's Hair Salon, and eight-year-old Hazel, a happy, rosy-cheeked little girl, had just moved up into Sally Pringle's class.

As Ruby made her way home, she wondered if her life would always be one of toil in order to keep her family fed and healthy. There were too many days now when her bones ached and she simply wanted to sit down and shut out the world.

When she walked into her house, the sight that met her eyes was a long way from the elegant Christopher Plummer asking the demure Julie Andrews to dance.

'Ah'm proper poorly, Ruby,' complained frail, skinny Ronnie as he sat in the kitchen with a sweaty sock round his neck, a bread poultice on his chest and his feet in a bucket of hot mustard water. 'An' ah'm sweatin' cobs,' he gasped. 'Ah feel as though ah've gone three rounds wi' Giant 'Aystacks.'

Ruby ignored his plaintive cries and took a tin of sucking Victory V lozenges from the cupboard, rubbed off the dust from the lid on Ronnie's bobble hat and popped a sweet into his mouth. 'Suck that, y'soft ha'porth, an' shurrup!' said Ruby and went upstairs to find her best dress. 'Ah'm goin' out.'

'Where to?' croaked Ronnie.

'Never you mind,' said Ruby and she slammed the door.

On the High Street, Johnny Duckitt thought he ruled the road as he parked his 1975 four-door Vauxhall Viva. It was a recent purchase for £1,195 from Charlie Clack's garage and Charlie had thrown in a free car radio for good measure. In his knee-length leather jacket, tight stone-washed jeans and carefully coiffeured hair he imagined himself as a cross between sixties pop star Billy Fury and country and western singer Johnny Cash. After flicking a comb through his lacquered quiff, he lit up a Peter Stuyvesant luxury-length filter cigarette and waited in his car outside Nora's Coffee Shop. As he blew smoke rings through his open window he reflected on the conquests in his life. There had been so many . . . but Ruby had been different. For some reason she had resisted his charms and he had never forgotten her.

Johnny had worked at the Butlin's holiday camp in Filey on the east coast of Yorkshire in the sixties. He had strutted around with his red coat and baggy cream trousers and was always introduced as 'Seaside Johnny' to his adoring fans. His rendition of Frankie Vaughan's 'Green Door' regularly received a standing ovation. It was a carefree life and, for Johnny, every week meant an influx of holidaymakers and a new girlfriend.

In 1938 Billy Butlin had bought 120 acres of land at Hunmanby Gap near Filey for £12,000 and created one of the largest holiday camps in the country. At its peak there were eleven thousand holidaymakers and a railway station had been built near by to accommodate the huge weekly influx of visitors. It was on a balmy summer's evening over twenty years ago that Ruby had arrived at that station and two days later she danced with Johnny in the spectacular Viennese Ballroom. While Ronnie was propping up the bar and Ruby's mother, Agnes, was looking after young Andy, Racquel and Duggie, Johnny saw his chance. After a wild ride on the Big Dipper they held hands tightly on the 'Thrill of Thrills', followed by a lazy circuit of the boating pool in a little rowing boat with the number 48 painted on the side. Ruby had felt like a princess in the arms of this handsome Butlin's redcoat and when he had tried to steal a kiss she found she couldn't resist. It was a day she would never forget.

In Nora's Coffee Shop, Johnny bought two frothy coffees and Ruby sat opposite him at a corner table. There was a long silence until Johnny said, 'Yer 'air looks nice, Ruby.' It was an opening line he knew never failed.

'Ah've just 'ad it done. It's a *Farrah Fawcett*.'

Johnny carefully avoided a look of surprise. 'It's lovely, Ruby,' he said.

'Johnny . . . what 'appened t'you?' she asked. 'Y'said y'd write.'

'Ah'm sorry, Ruby,' he said. 'Truth is, ah never 'ad *confidence* like your Ronnie. Ah never *seized t'day*, so t'speak. Ronnie 'ad lasses 'anging on 'is every word. Ah were allus a quiet 'un, staying in t'background.' Telling lies was as easy as breathing for Seaside Johnny.

'But y'were a *Redcoat*, Johnny, y'were on t'stage,' said Ruby in surprise.

'That were jus' an act, Ruby,' said Johnny. 'It weren't real . . . it weren't *me*.'

'Ah kept that postcard y'sent me of t'Sunshine Chalets,' said Ruby. 'Then ah 'eard y'went an' married that erratic dancer from 'Alifax . . . an' ah never saw yer again.'

Johnny smiled. 'She were an *exotic* dancer, Ruby, but y'reight . . . she were *erratic* an' all. It didn't last long.'

'Ah'm sorry, Johnny,' said Ruby.

'No need, Ruby. Ah were eighth out o' ten kids . . . ah never knew what it were like t'sleep alone till ah got married,' he said with a grin. 'It were a relief when she'd gone.'

Ruby stared at her dumpy work-red hands. 'But did it mean owt . . . you an' me?'

''Course it did, Ruby. Ah could never forget you in that Tunnel o' Love,' said Johnny with the sincerity of a politician.

'But we never went on t'Tunnel o' Love: it were shut,' said Ruby, looking puzzled.

'Oh yes, ah remember now,' said Johnny quickly. 'It were that other one that y'liked.'

'Thrill o' thrills, it were, as ah recall,' said Ruby.

'Ah remember it well,' said Johnny.

'Ah'm glad y'do, Johnny. It were good t'feel, well, sort of *wanted*.'

Johnny looked sadly at Ruby. She had always been different from the others but now he knew why and, perhaps for the first time in his life, his selfish heart knew remorse.

At the end of school, Ruby came into the school office to collect the litter from the waste-paper baskets. She spotted the vase of roses on Vera's desk and sniffed appreciatively. 'Oooh, these are lovely, Miss Evans,' said Ruby. 'Teks me back.'

'You like roses, don't you, Ruby?' I said.

'Ah do that, Mr Sheffield,' she said. 'Ah 'ad roses on m'wedding day an' that time we 'ad that little party in t'school 'all.' She sighed and shook her head. 'Now me children are m'bed o' roses . . . an' ah luv 'em all.'

'I love roses as well, Ruby,' said Vera. 'They're so . . . *romantic*.'

Ruby picked up her galvanized bucket, leant on her mop and looked thoughtful. '*Romantic*, Miss Evans? Ah remember romance wi' my Ronnie but that were a long time ago – so long it's 'ard t'remember – an' after that . . . well . . . we jus' med babies.'

Vera gave a wistful smile as Ruby trotted off to mop the wood-block floor in the school entrance and I wondered about their different lives.

Meanwhile, Julie Earnshaw was in her kitchen dishing up fish fingers, chips and mushy peas to Heathcliffe, Terry and Dallas Sue-Ellen. She was thinking about the new bingo caller who had been keen to talk to Ruby Smith and she wondered why. However, with children like hers, the opportunity for private meditation was rare.

'Where are me other three dads, Mam?' asked Terry as he poured tomato sauce on his chips.

'Y'what? Y've only got *one* dad, y'soft ha'porth,' said his mother, looking offended but secretly recalling a few old boyfriends from her youth.

'But this morning t'vicar said we all 'ave *four* fathers!'

Mrs Earnshaw looked puzzled and wondered why they taught them all this stuff at school. Then she had a thought. 'Mebbe 'e means the 'Oly Trinity?'

Heathcliffe glanced up from his mushy peas sandwich. 'No, Mam, that's *Wakefield* Trinity. *They* play rugby league.' Heathcliffe was proud of his sporting knowledge.

Suddenly the baby of the family, Dallas Sue-Ellen Earnshaw, leant over the table and grabbed a squelchy handful of Terry's mushy peas. No one made a comment. After all, thought Mrs Earnshaw, her little pride and joy was still a month away from her second birthday and Mrs Grainger could teach her table manners when she got to school.

Margery Ackroyd was thinking about the handsome bingo caller who had definitely winked at *her*. He was what her mother would have called a 'ladies' man'. In the meantime, she served her husband, Wendell, with a pork chop, chips and peas. After all it was important to keep his strength up. As Wendell had told her on many occasions, packing Smarties into tubes was demanding work.

While Wendell daubed his meal with HP sauce, Margery picked up her *Woman* magazine and smiled. On the front cover there was a photograph of Prince Charles standing on a Scottish hillside, looking youthful and dashing in his kilt. Holding his hand was an adoring Lady Diana and this completed the perfect romantic picture. Sadly, emblazoned down the side were the highlighted articles, including 'Is there hope on the horizon for HERPES?' Margery thought to herself that for twenty pence you certainly got your money's worth from her favourite weekly magazine.

On Morton Road, Betty Buttle was preparing a giant shepherd's pie for her four children and wondering how the bingo caller, who clearly fancied himself, knew Ruby

Smith. It had not gone unnoticed that he had winked at someone on their table and Betty presumed it was her. Men had always fancied her fuller figure but not, of course, a figure as full as Ruby's. All in all, it had been a good night and, unknown to her husband, Harry, she had spent her winnings on a Breville sandwich toaster. She had seen one in the Dudley-Palmers' posh kitchen the last time Petula had hosted a Tupperware party and had wanted one ever since. Sadly, poor Harry had no idea what cremated offerings were about to appear in his pack-up. As she searched in the cupboard for a tin of Batchelors peas, she wondered if the sexy bingo caller would be there next time. If that was the case, perhaps she might wear the blue dress that showed off a little more of her substantial cleavage.

At six o'clock the school was quiet and I was writing a summary of our scheme of work for religious education that had been requested by County Hall.

The telephone rang. 'Have you by any chance done that scheme of work for RE?' asked Beth.

'I'm doing it now,' I said.

'Oh good, so . . . can I have a look at yours? I've not done mine yet.'

'It will cost you,' I said.

'That can be arranged,' she replied mischievously.

'Do you fancy a drink and a bite to eat in the Oak?'

'I'll be there soon after seven,' she said and rang off.

At seven o'clock I locked the school door and walked across the village green and into The Royal Oak. I carried a half of Chestnut Mild and a white wine over to the table in the bay window and sat down to wait for Beth.

The pub was filling up with regulars and Ronnie Smith, like Lazarus, had risen from his sick bed to join the Ragley Rovers football team in the taproom. After all, as manager of the team, it was important to show his loyalty to his players even though he didn't feel well. Ruby had seemed preoccupied but had agreed to join him and she was sitting on the bench seat by the dartboard, listening to Frankie Balls, the nine-fingered pianist, go through his Russ Conway repertoire.

'What's it t'be, Ronnie?' asked Don, wiping the bar counter.

'Pint, Don, an' . . . can y'put it on t'slate?'

Don Bradshaw, barman and retired wrestler, peered down at the little unemployed pigeon-racer and shook his head. 'Sorry, Ronnie, but ah 'ave an agreement wi' m'bank manager.'

'How come?' said Ronnie, scratching his bobble hat in confusion.

'Well '*e* doesn't sell beer an' *ah* don't lend money!'

'Oh, ah see,' said Ronnie and sloped off to find Ruby . . . and her purse.

Meanwhile, Clint Ramsbottom, Ragley Rovers' left-winger, local farm labourer and a 'New Romantic', had just put five pence in the juke-box and was singing along with Adam and the Ants to their recent number one hit, 'Prince Charming'.

'What y'dressed like that for, Clint?' asked Big Dave

Robinson. As team captain he was concerned when a team member began to show effeminate tendencies.

Clint pursed his lips and looked hurt. His big brother, Shane, full-back, farmhand and occasional psychopath, grabbed Clint by his embroidered shirt collar. His muscles bulged under his Sex Pistols T-shirt. 'Hey, Nancy, Big Dave asked yer a question!' he said.

Clint was always annoyed by his brother's insistence on calling him 'Nancy' ever since he had frequented Diane's Hair Salon. 'Ah'm a New Romantic,' he declared.

'What's romantic abart wearing frilly shirts?' asked Big Dave.

'An' fingerless gloves,' added Little Malcolm.

'An' black eye-liner,' shouted buxom Sheila Bradshaw from behind the bar.

Shane shook his head sadly. 'Nancy,' he said. 'Y'look a reight nancy.'

Sheila the barmaid was proud of her main asset. There was no doubt that her magnificent chest was something to behold and for the members of the Ragley Rovers football team it was an attraction that brightened up their day. This evening she had squeezed into a sparkly boob tube that left little to the imagination. A substantial sprinkling of Lentheric Musk in the vicinity of her cavernous cleavage had been the finishing touch.

''Ave y'got a bit o' loose change, Ruby, my love?' said Ronnie. 'Ah've come out wi'out m'dole money.'

'Ah've 'eard that one a few times,' said Ruby, rummaging in her purse for a pound note. 'It's a good job ah'm working extra 'ours.'

'Well, ah've worked 'ard this week, ah'll 'ave you know,' said Ronnie. 'Ah cleaned out m'pigeons.'

Sheila overheard the conversation and leant over the bar. 'Ah know,' she said, 'there's no rest for t'wicked.' She pulled on the hand pump and her magnificent bosom strained in the elasticated confines of the boob tube. 'Typical, Ruby,' she said, nodding towards Ronnie. 'A man's never too tired t'tell us 'ow 'ard 'e's worked.' As she handed the foaming pint to Ronnie she whispered, ''Bout time you got a job to 'elp your Ruby out a bit.'

Beth hurried in and, as usual, heads turned. Even at the end of a working day she looked stunning. She kissed me on the cheek, sat down and sipped her wine.

'Ah, that's better,' she said. Then she slipped off her jacket and relaxed into conversation. 'Jack, I've been thinking a lot since we last spoke. Your thought about breaking off the engagement made me realize that perhaps we haven't talked about the important things.'

'Such as?' I said, loosening my tie and leaning forward to look into her green eyes.

'Well, becoming a headteacher of a large school was an ambition I had for *myself* and I was imposing it on you . . . and that wasn't fair.'

'But there's nothing to stop you going for a large headship one day. You must know I would support you.'

'Really?' said Beth, sounding surprised.

'Why not, if that's what you want?'

'There aren't many women heads of large schools – in fact I can't think of any in North Yorkshire. It's dominated by men.'

'But you could break the mould, Beth; you're a good

headteacher and Miss Barrington-Huntley thinks the world of you.'

Beth went quiet as if searching for the right words. 'But don't you see, Jack? How would *you* feel if I was head of a large school and you remained a village headteacher – particularly as you're a better headteacher than I could ever be.'

I held her hand and squeezed it gently. 'Beth, that wouldn't trouble me because . . . I love you.'

'Oh, Jack,' she said softly.

'Look, I've an idea,' I said. 'Why not apply to do a Master's Degree in Primary School Management at Leeds University?'

'But how would I fit it all in?' asked Beth.

'You could do it part-time over a couple of years and then I think you have a year to do the final dissertation.'

'It sounds like a lot of work.'

'It is, but if that's what you want, then go for it and I'll be there to support you.'

'Jack, it's a wonderful idea.'

'So,' I said, standing up, 'before we organize this wedding . . . I'm starving – how about Sheila's famous battered cod and chips?'

Beth grinned. 'Perfect . . . and maybe a nightcap back at Bilbo Cottage.'

Ruby hurried past me as I was placing my order. 'G'night, Mr Sheffield,' she said.

'Good night, Ruby. Have a good weekend,' I said, but she had already gone.

Outside, Ruby walked to the old bench at the side of the

duck pond and sat down. She needed fresh air and time to think. Ronnie was propping up the bar and spending her hard-earned money. She knew it wouldn't change. The good thing was she had been blessed with children and she wouldn't swap them for all the tea in China. So maybe life wasn't so bad after all. If she had gone off with that Seaside Johnny, life would have got complicated and she didn't know what would become of her family. Little Hazel had given her a painting she had done at school and Ruby had taped it to the fridge door. It showed Ruby, Ronnie, Andy, Racquel, Duggie, Sharon, Natasha and Hazel all in a line and all holding hands.

Ruby sat back, stared up at the darkening night sky and dabbed her eyes with her frayed handkerchief. Then she thought to herself that some things in life are more important than others. Butlin's redcoats might come and go . . . but a family is for ever.

Chapter Four

Forgotten Harvest

Arrangements for tomorrow's Harvest Festival were confirmed at the staff meeting. We were informed that the new bishop would be accompanying Revd Evans at the service in the school hall.

Extract from the Ragley School Logbook:
Tuesday, 20 October 1981

'It's a Still Life drawing class,' said Vera, replacing the staff-room telephone and checking her neat shorthand on the spiral-bound notepad. 'At least, that's what it sounded like. Madame Laporte still has a distinctive French accent, even after all these years.' Then she stirred her Earl Grey tea thoughtfully. 'That should be perfect,' she added.

'You mean drawing fruit and veg,' said Sally, looking up from her last month's issue of *Cosmopolitan* magazine. The article 'Sexual jealousy is agony but you can use it to improve your love life' had definitely been worth reading again.

Vera frowned. 'Yes, Sally . . . but I'm sure the members will find it very stimulating.'

The ladies of the Ragley and Morton Women's Institute met in the village hall on the third Wednesday of each month and it was the highlight of Vera's busy life. Madame Jacqueline Laporte, the French teacher from Easington Comprehensive School, had stepped in at the last moment to organize an alternative event. This had followed the sad demise of Miss Edith Fawnswater, an eminent speaker from Bridlington, who had cancelled her talk entitled 'The Quickstep Made Easy' owing to painful blisters on her feet.

'Well, you won't be short of subject matter,' said Anne. 'After the Harvest Festival, all the produce is being taken to the village hall for distribution to the poor and needy.'

'Even better,' said Vera: 'a perfect end to a busy day.'

It was four o'clock on Tuesday, 20 October, and we had decided to meet in the staff-room to confirm arrangements for tomorrow's Harvest Festival. Letters had gone out to parents, Sally's choir had rehearsed the hymns, including an ambitious descant for 'We plough the fields and scatter the good seed on the land', trestle tables had been ordered from the village hall along with huge white tablecloths from the Women's Institute and the local champion gardener, George Hardisty, had just delivered one of his trademark giant carrots. All appeared to be ready for one of the highlights of the school calendar.

'OK, everybody, let's begin,' I said.

Suddenly there was a hurried tap on the door. It

was our local vicar . . . and he was out of breath.

'This is a surprise, Joseph,' said Vera, glancing up at the staff-room clock. 'I thought you were collecting me at *five o'clock*.'

Joseph tugged at his clerical collar. 'Please may I have a drink of water?' Jo jumped up, grabbed a heavy North Yorkshire County Council tumbler from the draining board, filled it with water and handed it to Joseph. He drank deeply and then looked around as if seeing us for the first time. 'Guess what,' he said.

'What?' we all said in unison.

'The bishop's coming!'

'Do you mean the *new* one?' asked Vera in surprise.

'Bishop thingummy,' said Anne.

'Yes, him,' said Joseph, wide-eyed. 'He telephoned to say he's coming *tomorrow*.'

'Oh,' said Vera, 'so what was the message?'

Joseph took a deep breath. 'Well . . . he was *really* pleasant.'

'Yes?' said Vera.

'And he said his name is Neil.'

'And?' said Vera.

Joseph wrinkled his brow. 'Well . . . he said, "Do call me Neil," which I thought was nice of him.'

'What did he *actually* say, Joseph?' said Vera firmly. 'Calm down and think.'

'Yes, er . . . let me see . . . He said he wants to visit us during afternoon school and stay for the Harvest Festival. Then he would like to have a look at St Mary's.' Joseph glanced nervously at Vera. 'So I invited him to come back to the vicarage for tea.'

There was an intake of breath from Vera. 'I see,' she said and gave Joseph her special *determined* look, one I knew so well. 'I need to get Joyce Davenport to help me with fresh flowers for the church and I'll get something nice for tea from Prudence at the General Stores.'

Anne had summed up the situation and looked at the clock. 'Jack, I think we know what we're doing tomorrow, so how about closing the meeting and I'll go with Vera to get the church ready?'

'And we'll help,' said Sally and Jo in unison.

'Good idea. Meeting closed,' I said.

'Thank you, everybody,' said Vera and hurried off to get her coat, 'and do come along, Joseph. There's lots to do: we have to make a good impression on the new bishop. Tomorrow needs to be *perfect*.'

We should have known life was never that simple.

The school was silent apart from the ticking of the school clock and the whisper of the wind in the bell tower. It was almost seven o'clock and I was at my desk completing the next day's order of service. Ruby had stayed late to give the hall floor an extra polish and had promised that she and Ronnie would put out the trestle tables for the Harvest Festival immediately after school lunch. Best of all, Beth had phoned and suggested we meet for a meal at The Royal Oak on her way home from Hartingdale.

Everything was ready, so I completed my daily entry in the school logbook, tidied my desk and locked the giant oak entrance door. As I walked out of the school gate I saw that Beth had already arrived. Her pale-blue Volkswagen Beetle was parked by the village green and she was sitting at our usual table in the bay window. Soon we were enjoying Sheila's special chicken and chips in a basket and a welcome drink.

Beth looked a little tired as she tucked a few strands of hair behind her ears. 'We need to arrange a date with Joseph – ' she said, 'that is, if we're agreed on getting married *here* and not Hampshire.'

'Only if you're happy about that, Beth,' I said.

'Well, it makes sense,' she said with a smile; 'all our friends are here.'

'What about your parents?' I asked anxiously.

'No problem, Jack. I had a chat with them on the phone last night and they were supportive.'

'That's a relief,' I said.

'And they want us to spend New Year with them down in Hampshire. What do you think?'

'Good idea,' I said. 'Then we can discuss all the details.'

She sipped her white wine and reached out to hold my hand. 'Exciting, isn't it?' she said.

'Vera and Joseph will be thrilled,' I said.

'They certainly will. Perhaps we should arrange to go to the vicarage one evening to discuss dates and arrangements.'

'I'll mention it after the Harvest Festival,' I said. She stretched and rubbed the tiredness from her neck. 'Another drink?' I asked.

Beth glanced at her watch. 'Just a tonic water, please, Jack. I've still got some marking to do tonight.'

*   *   *

At the bar, Jacqueline Laporte, the attractive French teacher from Easington, had just arrived with a Brigitte Bardot lookalike in a miniskirt.

'Hello, Jacqueline. Good to see you,' I said. We had both joined the Ragley tennis club during the summer holiday and had begun to get to know each other well.

'Hello, Jack. This is my little sister, Monique,' said Jacqueline in perfect English but with her familiar French accent.

'Pleased to meet you, Monique,' I said.

'Ah, *bonsoir*, Jacques,' said Monique with a mischievous grin as she stretched up to kiss me on both cheeks. 'I 'ave 'eard you play ze tennis wiz my sister.'

'That's right, Monique,' I said. 'We're in the Ragley mixed doubles team.'

'*C'est bon*,' said the effervescent Monique. 'Jacqueline is lucky playing with ze big strong 'andsome Yorksheer fellow.'

'Er, well . . . thank you,' I replied.

'Now behave, Monique,' said Jacqueline. 'Please ignore my sister, Jack – she is very high-spirited.' She gave her sister a stern look. 'And she is only staying with me for a *short* holiday before she returns to Paris.'

'And while I am 'ere,' said Monique, 'I weesh to learn ze Eengleesh and speak like ze Yorksheer native.'

'Can I get a drink for you and your sister, Jacqueline?' I said.

'Thank you, Jack. White wine, please,' said Jacqueline. 'French, of course,' she added with a smile.

'And for you, Monique?'

'I weel 'ave, as you say, ze swift 'alf, *s'il vous plaît*.'

Behind the bar, Sheila pulled on the hand pump. 'She's pickin' it up fast, Mr Sheffield,' said Sheila. 'My Don's been learning 'er.'

'Eee, Don, ecky ze thump,' said Monique. 'I am ze monkey's uncle, *n'est-ce pas*?'

Don the barman's stubbly face broke into a sheepish grin. Sheila leant over, pinned a York City tea towel to the bar with her prodigious bosom, and whispered in my direction, 'An' ah'm not s'prised wi' a figure like that.'

'*Merci*, Jacques,' said Monique. She sipped her half of Chestnut Mild. '*C'est delicieuse*.'

'So 'ave y'gorra 'usband back in France, then?' asked Sheila pointedly.

Monique gave me an enigmatic smile. '*Non*. I 'ave never been married . . . but I 'ave 'ad many 'uzbands.'

It was time to beat a hasty retreat.

On Wednesday morning I collected my copy of *The Times* from Prudence Golightly's General Stores & Newsagent on my way into Ragley. The headline declared 'I won't court popularity'. It looked as if Mrs Thatcher was having a tough time at the Blackpool Conference with the annual rate of price increases unlikely to be cut to ten per cent. However, that was far from my mind when I saw Sue Phillips, Chair of our Parent–Teacher Association, unloading a large wooden box from her Austin Metro.

'Morning, Jack. I've brought Resusci Annie in, as promised, for the staff First Aid training.' Sue, a tall, attractive blonde, was a staff nurse at the hospital in York and helped out as our school nurse. She had volunteered to lead a staff training session in mouth-to-mouth resuscitation on Thursday evening.

'Resusci-who?' I asked.

She glanced at her watch. 'Come on, Jack,' she said with a grin, 'I'll show you quickly.'

I carried the box into the staff-room and put it on the coffee table. Everyone gathered round as Sue removed the lid.

'Goodness me!' exclaimed Vera and stepped back in amazement.

'Wow!' said Jo.

'Impressive,' said Sally.

Revealed was the rubber head and torso of a vivacious blonde-haired naked woman. Her blue eyes stared back at us.

'What is it?' I asked.

'This is the model that my nurses use to practise their mouth-to-mouth resuscitation,' said Sue in a matter-of-fact voice. We all stared at Resusci Annie and couldn't help but notice that not only did she have breasts that would have done credit to a finalist in *Miss World* but her dark rubber nipples stood out like chapel hatpegs.

'She's a big girl,' said Sally cautiously.

Sue laughed. 'Yes. I think the designer based it on his girlfriend.'

'Oh dear,' was all Vera could say.

'Anyway, feel free to practise,' said Sue. 'The instructions are inside the lid. Well, must be off. See you later at the Harvest Festival,' and with that she hurried out.

Jo picked up the lid, took it to the corner of the staff-room and found the instruction booklet. 'I think my Dan did his police training on something like this,' she said thoughtfully, '. . . but it wasn't quite so glamorous.'

Sally chuckled and Anne gave me a knowing look. Meanwhile Vera, flushed with embarrassment, walked briskly back to the office to make copies of the Harvest Festival order of service from her carefully typed Gestetner master sheet. She smoothed it carefully on to the inky drum of the duplicating machine, peeled off the backing sheet and wound the handle to produce enough copies for parents and visitors, including, of course, the bishop. 'Today must be *perfect*,' she kept repeating to herself with every turn of the handle.

Shortly before morning break Theresa Ackroyd announced, 'Mr Ramsbottom's 'ere,' although she didn't appear to have raised her head from her School Mathematics Project workcard concerning the area of carpet needed to fit a large bedroom. A tractor and trailer pulled up in the car park and I walked out to meet one of Ragley's more colourful characters.

Derek 'Deke' Ramsbottom, local farmworker, part-time snowplough driver, singer of cowboy songs and father of Shane, Clint and Wayne, removed his Stetson hat. "Owdy, Mr Sheffield.'

'Morning, Deke. Thanks for coming.'

'Ah've brought all t'trestle tables on me trailer,' he said while absent-mindedly polishing the sheriff's badge on his leather waistcoat. 'Ah'll stack 'em in t'entrance, shall ah?' Deke's support for the school was legendary.

'Thanks, Deke,' I said. 'We're all grateful.'

'No problem, Mr Sheffield. Owt for t'school is fine by

me,' and he wandered back to his trailer, copying the distinctive walk of his hero, the late John Wayne. Once again, I was touched by the affection the villagers showed for their school.

After lunch, on the playground, life went on as normal. Heathcliffe Earnshaw, Ragley's undisputed conker champion, had been challenged to a conker match by a new girl who had just arrived in my class, ten-year-old Alice Baxter from Doncaster.

'Come on, then,' said the ever-confident Heathcliffe. Rarely, if ever, did he play with girls as he didn't see much point in them. However, there was something different about Alice: she wasn't like other girls who played with Tressy dolls and bought Donny Osmond records. She seemed to really understand the noble sport of conkers.

'Ah'm ready when you are,' said Alice.

Heathcliffe turned to his little brother Terry and whispered, 'Don't worry, ah've gorra coupla laggies.' These so-called 'laggies' were conkers from the previous year and left to harden in a tin in his father's garden shed. 'Ah've baked one in t'oven and t'other ah've soaked in vinegar.' His father had put the conkers in a vice and bored a small hole with his hand-drill. A length of orange unbreakable baling twine provided the final touch. Heathcliffe took his conkers very seriously.

However, Alice's father, Campbell Baxter – already nicknamed 'Two Soups' in the village – had also been a conker champion in his day. Every October he bought his unsuspecting wife a supply of a special brand of nail varnish and every year he used it to give his conker selection a rock hard, if shiny, finish.

To Heathcliffe's surprise, it was over in minutes. Alice made short work of his 'laggies' and their shattered remnants lay at his feet. However, she was gracious in victory and explained to Heathcliffe that she had been 'lucky'. Heathcliffe readily agreed and by the start of afternoon school he thought that perhaps for the first time in his young life it might be possible to be friends with a *girl*.

Meanwhile, Ruby and Ronnie were carrying the trestle tables from the entrance hall to the school hall and Vera was covering them with snowy-white table-cloths.

'We have to show *decorum* when the bishop arrives,' said Vera to Ruby and Ronnie.

'Dick who?' asked the bemused Ronnie.

'No, it means yer 'ave t'be polite, Ronnie,' explained Ruby. 'This bishop's *really* himportant.'

'Ah see,' said Ronnie. 'Well, 'ave no fear, Miss Evans, we'll watch us p's and q's an' ah'll do as ah'm told, even though me back is 'urting.'

Vera looked at Ruby and shook her head sadly. Then she returned to the hall to arrange the trestle tables while the nervous Joseph stood by the window, rehearsing his first prayer.

Back in my classroom the sharp-eyed Theresa said, 'Big flash car coming up t'drive, Mr Sheffield.'

A large white 1979 Volvo 245 Estate pulled up in the

car park and a short, cherubic, bespectacled man wearing a bishop's ankle-length purple cassock walked into the entrance hall. He was carrying his chimere, an outer, blood-red garment with snowy-white cuffs, his pectoral cross and a long thin case that looked as if he was going to a snooker tournament. We were later to discover it contained his solid silver pastoral staff in the shape of a shepherd's crook.

Joseph rushed to the entrance hall to meet him. 'Ah, Neil, Neil!' he exclaimed.

Ronnie immediately did as he was told. He knelt down on one knee, bowed his head and removed his bobble hat. After all, thought Ronnie, it *was* the bishop.

'Gerrup, y'soft ha'porth,' hissed Ruby in his ear. She gave a hesitant curtsy. 'Scuse us, your severance,' she said and exited quickly into the school hall, dragging Ronnie with one hand and a trestle table with the other.

'Good afternoon, Joseph,' said Bishop Neil, unperturbed by the unorthodox welcome. Joseph nodded nervously and gulped.

Vera suddenly appeared and smiled calmly. 'Welcome to Ragley, Bishop,' she said. 'I'm Vera Evans.'

'Hello, Miss Evans,' said Bishop Neil. 'I've heard so much about your good work in the parish.'

'Thank you, Bishop . . . I do what I can,' said Vera with, she hoped, sufficient modesty. 'Perhaps you would like some tea and then I'll let the headteacher, Mr Sheffield, know you have arrived?'

'That would be very welcome, Miss Evans,' said the bishop, with a charming smile. The thick lenses in his spectacles gave him the look of a friendly owl.

'I'll put the kettle on in the staff-room: it's more comfortable in there,' she said.

While Joseph and Bishop Neil talked in the entrance hall, Vera walked into the staff-room and, to her horror, saw Resusci Annie standing upright on the coffee table in all her naked glory.

'After you, Neil,' said Joseph, ushering him in.

With a burst of speed that would have impressed Seb Coe, Vera picked up the lidless box, turned it round and almost threw it on to the window ledge. Then she filled the kettle while composing herself. It had been a close thing.

After a cup of tea, the bishop donned his chimere, hung round his neck the pectoral cross, in which a precious ruby had been set, and screwed together his pastoral staff. Then he followed Vera into my classroom. 'What a lovely school you have here, Mr Sheffield,' he said.

'Thank you, Bishop,' I said and we shook hands. Joseph gave a strained smile and Vera appeared to relax for the first time.

The bishop stared at me myopically and asked, 'Perhaps I could take a brief look in one or two of the classrooms and talk to the children?'

'Of course,' I said.

Joseph decided to take the initiative and led the way into Jo Hunter's class. After introducing the bishop to Jo he turned to the class. 'Now, boys and girls,' he said, 'I hope you remember last week's Bible story.' A sea of blank looks and furrowed brows faced him. Undeterred he pressed on, 'Who knocked down the walls of Jericho?'

After what seemed an age, little Terry Earnshaw raised his hand. 'It weren't me, Vicar.'

Bishop Neil smiled kindly. 'Well, I'm pleased you tell the children Bible stories, Joseph.' Suddenly he was aware of a small boy tugging his robes.

'Our vicar's a bit like God,' said seven-year-old Benjamin Roberts.

'Really?' said the bishop, intrigued. 'And is that because he's kind to you?'

'No,' said little Ben, shaking his head.

'Or maybe because he helps all the boys and girls?' added the bishop.

'No,' said Ben.

The bishop was running out of helpful suggestions. 'Or is it because he tells you interesting Bible stories?'

'No,' said Ben defiantly. He was getting fed up with all these questions from this strange man in the *Star Wars* outfit and thick spectacles.

'So why is he like God?' asked the bishop, with a hint of desperation.

''Cause 'e's really *old*,' said Ben and he trotted off happily.

'Perhaps you would like to see the preparations in the hall,' said Joseph, eager to move on.

'Very well,' said Bishop Neil with a beatific smile.

Sally's children were in the school hall, helping to display all the produce that had arrived during the day. However, as always, and mindful of the eminent visitor, she was making every effort to generate teaching and learning opportunities from the activity.

'Here we have an orange, an apple and a pear, boys and girls,' she said, 'so what word do we use to describe all of these?'

Nine-year-old Elisabeth Amelia Dudley-Palmer raised her hand and Sally smiled in her direction. '*Fruit*, Miss,' said Elisabeth Amelia.

Sally was on a roll. The discovery of collective nouns was suddenly in everyone's grasp. 'And what about these?' she said, pointing to a potato, a cabbage and one of George Hardisty's carrots. 'What covers all of these?'

'*Gravy*, Miss,' shouted Heathcliffe quick as lightning.

Sally went bright red and the bishop retreated strategically to Anne's classroom.

Bishop Neil sat down next to five-year-old Jemima Poole. 'Now, what's this?' he said, pointing to a picture in her reading book of a farm with lots of animals.

Jemima looked up at him as if he had just landed from another planet. 'Farm,' she said bluntly.

The bishop nodded. 'Well done,' he said, quickly surmising this monosyllabic little girl was not very bright. 'And what's that?' he asked, pointing to a picture of a hen.

There was a lengthy silence and Jemima scratched her head. The bishop looked down sadly at the little girl. 'Don't you know what it is? Never mind, I'll tell you: it's a—'

'No, don't tell me,' said Jemima forcibly. 'I can't decide whether it's a Rhode Island Red or not. It's jus' that the picture isn't very clear.'

Bishop Neil chuckled and reminded himself not to jump to conclusions.

*   *   *

The Harvest Festival was memorable and Vera sighed in contentment. Parents and villagers had crowded into the school hall and no one could recall a finer display of produce, flanked by home-baked, plaited bread and sheaves of barley. The Revd Joseph Evans led the service of thanksgiving beautifully and he confirmed that God's bounty would be taken to the village hall after school and distributed tomorrow to those in greatest need.

Then the bishop, in a wonderfully clear voice, read from Deuteronomy, chapter twenty-four, verse nineteen: *'When you reap your harvest in your field and forget a sheaf in the field, you shall not go back to get it; it shall be left for the alien, the orphan, and the widow so that the Lord your God may bless you in all your undertakings.'*

After that, he led us in a final prayer and blessed the school and the congregation with the sign of the cross. The school bell rang out to announce the end of a success-ful day and we all breathed a sigh of relief.

In the school entrance hall, Bishop Neil was generous in his praise. 'Thank you, everyone, for a delightful visit. You have a wonderful school and very well-behaved pupils.'

Anne looked to the heavens and then caught my eye. I knew what she was thinking: we had survived.

Meanwhile, Vera, looking greatly relieved that every-thing had gone to plan and without mishap, was anxious to get back to the vicarage. 'Joseph, perhaps you could follow on with the bishop,' she said, 'and I'll go on ahead to prepare tea.'

'Certainly,' said Joseph and Vera hurried out to the car park, jumped in her Austin A40 and tore off up Morton Road.

It had felt like a royal visit and we all solemnly shook hands until, finally, Joseph and the bishop walked out to the smart white estate car. As they drove down the drive the bishop glanced back at the school and for the briefest heart-stopping moment he thought he saw a naked blonde woman pressing her ample bosom against the windowpane. He blinked quickly and readjusted his spectacles. 'I really must check my prescription,' he said to himself.

In the quiet nave of St Mary's Church, Bishop Neil was full of enthusiasm. 'Very well done, Joseph, on having such a thriving church community, and, Vera, what can I say? The flowers are exquisite – such style and understated artistry! Congratulations.' Vera smiled shyly; everything was going well.

Tea in the vicarage exceeded all of Vera's expectations. The Victoria sponge was, according to the bishop, the finest he had ever tasted and, at last, it was time to leave. Vera glanced at the clock. 'It's my Women's Institute meeting this evening, Bishop, so I need to go back to the village hall.'

'Perhaps I could give you a lift,' he said. 'It's on my way.'

It occurred to Vera that she would look very grand pulling up outside the village hall in this smart car with the bishop. Also, she could get a lift home with Joyce Davenport and relate the events of her *perfect* day. 'Thank you, Bishop. That would be so kind,' she said. Then she picked up her sketch pad from the hall table and put two sharpened pencils in her handbag. 'We're doing a little sketching this evening.'

'How delightful,' said Bishop Neil. 'Actually . . . I dabble as well.'

Vera was delighted with the impression she created when they arrived on Ragley High Street. Darkness had fallen and the lights shone brightly at the windows of the village hall.

'I'll walk you to the door,' said Bishop Neil.

'Thank you, Bishop,' said Vera.

As they arrived at the entrance they could see a group of ladies busy sketching in the hall and another group standing in the back corner, deep in animated conversation with Jacqueline Laporte. All did not appear to be as it should be and Vera wondered why sketching fruit and vegetables should create such fierce debate.

Vera and the bishop saw the reason at the same moment. There, at the front of the hall, was Miss Monique Laporte, reclining on a sofa in a languorous pose and naked as the day she was born apart from a strategically draped length of pink chiffon. Vera gasped and the bishop stepped back in alarm and dropped his spectacles.

His exit was a swift one. As Vera watched the rear lights of his white estate car disappear down the High Street, she reflected on misheard telephone conversations about *still*-life drawing. Meanwhile, Bishop Neil decided he would visit the opticians at the earliest opportunity.

*　　　*　　　*

The following afternoon I was in the school office, Vera was typing furiously and Resusci Annie was back in her box with the lid firmly closed. When the telephone rang I answered it. It was Bishop Neil ringing to say thank you for the visit. When I replaced the receiver, I looked across to Vera's desk.

'That's strange, Vera,' I said. 'The bishop sounded rather vague. It was almost as if he'd *forgotten* about the harvest.'

Vera's eyes never lifted from her typewriter. 'Er, yes, Mr Sheffield . . . He's probably got other things on his mind.'

Chapter Five

The World of Timothy Pratt

County Hall sent the document 'Rationalization – Small Schools in North Yorkshire' to all schools in the Easington area explaining why the high costs of maintaining small schools had resulted in the closure of four schools last academic year.

Extract from the Ragley School Logbook:
Wednesday, 11 November 1981

Timothy Pratt surveyed his Hardware Emporium and sighed. There was something missing, but he wasn't sure what it was.

He gazed with pride at his beautifully organized world of shelf brackets, boot scrapers and dome-headed screws. The floor had been swept, the shelves were dusted, the counter gleamed and the door bell had received its weekly burnishing with Brasso polish. Everything was as it should be and all the stock was, of course, in perfect alphabetical order. Timothy, or Tidy Tim as he was known in the village owing to his obsessively fastidious nature, liked *order*, particularly alphabetical order. Without it, life would be chaos.

Timothy reflected that he was now forty-one years old and had never had a special lady friend. He got on with women well enough and he was always happy to serve them when they came into his shop, especially Miss Evans, who was always very polite. However, when he showed them his Meccano set they tended to give him funny looks. He shook his head, sighed deeply and glanced up at the Roman numerals on the large clock behind the counter. Then he took out his shop door key from the pocket of his neatly ironed brown apron. It was shortly before nine o'clock on Wednesday, 11 November, and little did he know it but the world of Timothy Pratt was about to change.

Across the High Street, in the warmth of the Ragley School staff-room, Vera could hardly contain herself. 'I shall be missing tomorrow's cross-stitch class of course in order to get a good vantage point,' she said.

I looked up in surprise. It would normally take a momentous event like declaration of war with Russia for Vera to miss her twice-weekly class. She was holding up a *Yorkshire Post* and Jo, Anne and Sally were looking over her shoulder.

'Doesn't she look lovely,' said Anne.

'A perfect English rose,' said Vera.

'She's glowing,' said Jo.

'Probably because she's pregnant,' added Sally bluntly, 'and Charlie-boy looks a bit grumpy.'

'Yes, well, our future king has a lot on his mind,' said Vera authoritatively and with a hint of annoyance. As a staunch royalist, Vera believed Prince Charles and Princess Diana could do no wrong. Sally wisely kept her private thoughts about Prince Charles to herself.

The penny finally dropped. 'Ah, you're talking about tomorrow's royal visit,' I said.

The four women gave me a familiar *he's only a man* look and smiled condescendingly before returning to the small text under the headline 'Big Day for York Railway Museum.'

Three miles away in his brightly lit garage near Easington, Walter Clarence Crapper was polishing his propeller.

With a deep sigh, he glanced at his watch, returned his chamois leather to its precise place in his neat box of cleaning materials, said farewell to his model Sopwith Pup biplane with its magnificent sixty-inch wing span and turned off the light. Pausing only in the hallway to fill his two fountain pens with red and black Quink ink respectively and put his accountant's ledgers in his briefcase, he set off in his 1977 Toyota Corolla Estate, a tax-deductible bargain at £1,950, and headed at a sedate pace to Ragley village.

Walter, in his early forties, was the younger brother of Ernest Crapper, Ragley village's best and only encyclopaedia salesman. He had never married, mainly because he had yet to meet a woman who knew the difference between cyanoacrylate glue and wallpaper paste. In his neat, tidy garage he would spend his winter nights making model replicas of his favourite aircraft. This precise, exacting and uplifting hobby along with his detailed ledgers, columns of figures and slide-rule mathematics gave Walter an interesting and well-ordered life. While growing up with the name W. C. Crapper had been difficult, especially at school, he had found his niche and, apart from feeling a little lonely on those long, dark evenings when he lovingly recharged the nickel-cadmium battery on his model aircraft's transmitter, his life, if not *perfect*, was at least *satisfactory*.

'Well, almost,' he muttered to himself as he slowed up in Ragley High Street, parked outside Pratt's Hardware Emporium and picked up his briefcase.

The doorbell jingled as Walter, a balding, bespectacled man with a neatly clipped moustache and wearing a thick tweed suit, walked into the shop and paused for a moment on the coconut matting. He summed up the neat shelves, tidy counter and the sharp creases in Timothy's shirt sleeves. Then he nodded in approval. In the balance sheet of tidiness Timothy Pratt was already in credit. 'Good morning. I'm Walter Crapper, the accountant, here for our nine-thirty appointment,' he said in a clipped, precise voice. 'I presume you are Mr Pratt.'

'Oh, 'ello, Mr Crapper. Yes, I am and thanks for . . .' he glanced at the clock, 'being so *punctual*.'

Walter smiled modestly. 'We are here to serve, as they say.'

'Well, Mr Crapper, ah jus' need me books checking,' continued Timothy in his monotone voice, 'an' you came 'ighly recommended by y'sister-in-law, Elsie.'

'I'm pleased to hear it,' said Walter, with a reserved nod

of acceptance. Walter had never been a flamboyant man. He checked the neat Windsor knot in his aero club chairman's tie, walked up to the counter and looked around him. 'And may I say what a wonderful emporium you have.'

Timothy glowed with pride. 'Well, ah do m'best,' he said with slightly false modesty.

'And, of course, alphabetical order!' exclaimed Walter.

'I'd be lost without it,' said Timothy.

'So would I,' said Walter with feeling. '*Create order from chaos*,' he recited: 'that's my motto.'

'It's mine as well,' said Timothy, warming to his like-thinking accountant. However, when he saw the perfect columns of figures in Walter's leather-bound ledgers he could barely contain his excitement. Finally, at lunchtime, after he had invited Walter to join him next door for a quick sandwich in his sister's Coffee Shop, and he heard what Walter's plans were for the next day, he knew he was in the presence of greatness.

It was a quiet school day and at 3.45 p.m. the children in my class said their end-of-school prayer, put their chairs on their desks and walked into the cloakroom to collect their coats and scarves. Theresa Ackroyd and Debbie Clack had become friends and they smiled at me as they said goodnight. 'Thanks, Mr Sheffield. I enjoyed t'story,' said Theresa.

I had just read an extract from Frances Hodgson Burnett's *The Secret Garden*, and you could have heard a pin drop. 'Thanks, Theresa,' I said, 'and what are you doing tonight?'

'Debbie's coming back to my 'ouse f'tea,' said Theresa.

'An' we're gonna watch *Grange 'Ill*, Mr Sheffield,' said Debbie.

'An' then *Crossroads*,' added Theresa for good measure.

'*Grange 'Ill* should be good t'night,' said Debbie enthusiastically. 'Some 'ooligans are gonna cause some bother at t'school dance.'

They wandered off and I watched them skip happily across the playground. Their carefree world was something to be treasured and it seemed a shame that adolescence was just round the corner, waiting to spoil it.

On my way down the High Street the bright lights of Nora's Coffee Shop caught my eye and I pulled up outside. A relaxing cup of coffee was just what I needed. When I walked in, Dorothy Humpleby, the twenty-five-year-old, peroxide-blonde assistant and would-be model, was leaning on the counter and filing her nails while skimming through her latest *Smash Hits* magazine. She was dressed in a skin-tight pink polo-neck sweater, black leather hotpants and a pair of thigh-high white boots with four-inch heels. As Dorothy was five-feet-eleven-inches tall in her stockinged feet, conversations and neck strain were regular companions.

'Hello, Dorothy, how are you?' I asked politely but secretly hoped I would not be drawn into one of our usual *alternative universe* conversations.

'Fair t'middlin', Mr Sheffield,' said Dorothy. She stopped filing her nails and nodded towards a plateful of tired-looking pastries in the display case. 'What's it t'be? We got some cream 'orns fresh in yesterday.'

'Fine, Dorothy. I'll have a coffee and a cream horn, please,' I said quickly, seeking a speedy transaction.

'E's proper dreamy,' said Dorothy with a far-away look.

'Who's dweamy?' asked Nora Pratt, owner of the Coffee Shop and general know-all. Forty-four-year-old Nora was a short, stocky, self-opinionated lady who was very proud of her status in the village as president of the Ragley Amateur Dramatic Society. This helped her to secure the star part in the annual Ragley pantomime regardless of the fact that the pronunciation of the letter 'R' had always eluded her.

'Prince Albert of Meccano,' said Dorothy, selecting a slightly stale cream horn and putting it on a plate.

Nora looked up from the frothy coffee machine, caught my eye and shook her head. 'It's *Monaco*, Dowothy,' she said. 'He's the only son of Pwince Wainier and that film star Pwincess Gwace.'

Unmoved, Dorothy picked up my fifty-pence piece, gave me my change and wondered if her boyfriend, Malcolm Robinson, the local refuse collector, would ever surprise *her* with a trip to Monaco. As Malcolm had never been further than Bridlington, she guessed it was unlikely.

'Here y'are, Mr Sheffield,' said Nora: 'a fwothy coffee an' a cweam 'orn.'

I went to sit at a table and picked up a discarded copy of the *Easington Herald & Pioneer* and scanned the front page article headed 'Local Accountant to Meet the Royals'.

Meanwhile, Big Dave and Little Malcolm had called in for their end-of-work mug of tea. Dorothy's boyfriend, the five-feet-four-inch binman, Little Malcolm, was at the counter, staring at the love of his life, while his six-feet-four-inch cousin, Big Dave, went to sit with Deke Ramsbottom at the table next to the old chrome and red juke-box. Deke had just inserted five pence for one of his favourite records.

''E allus picks that Grindstone Cowboy,' said Dorothy to Little Malcolm.

'Y'reight there, Dorothy,' said Little Malcolm. ''E loves 'is cowboy songs, does Deke.'

'No, it's not Gwinestone, it's *Whinestone* Cowboy,' said Nora. She was a big fan of Glenn Campbell.

Dorothy ignored this correction and carried on regardless. 'Charles an' Di are coming t'York t'morrow, Malcolm. Ah wish ah could see 'er.'

'It'll be on t'telly,' said Little Malcolm.

'Ah know that, Malcolm,' insisted Dorothy, 'but ah think she uses that Max Factor eye-liner what ah like an' ah'd need t'be close up.'

'Oh, ah see,' said Little Malcolm . . . but he didn't.

'Ah know who will be *close up*,' said Nora triumphantly: 'that Mr Cwapper who's doing our Timothy's books. 'E 'elps out at t'Wailway Museum an' 'e'll be there tomowwow.'

'What does 'e do, then?' asked Dorothy.

''E looks after Stephenson's Wocket,' said Nora.

Dorothy looked blank.

'It's a twain, Dowothy.'

'Oy! 'Urry up wi' them teas, Casanova,' shouted Big Dave, giving Little Malcolm his big-girl's-blouse look.

Little Malcolm recoiled but composed himself

sufficiently to put three spoonfuls of sugar into both mugs and retreat to the table.

On my way home to Kirkby Steepleton, I noticed the lights were still on at Pratt's Garage and I pulled up by the single pump. Victor Pratt, elder brother of Nora and Timothy, lumbered out to serve me, wiping his oil-smeared hands on his filthy overalls. 'Now then, Mr Sheffield,' said Victor in a gruff voice.

'Hello, Victor. Could you fill her up, please?' He unscrewed my filler cap and, with some foreboding, I asked him the usual question, 'And how are you, Victor?' Victor's ailments usually defied all logic and were wonders of modern science.

'Ah've been stung by summat,' replied Victor with a pained expression.

'I'm sorry to hear that, Victor,' I said with feeling.

He pointed to a lump on his elbow as if it was a war wound. 'Ah've been t'Dr Davenport an' ah asked 'im for an anecdote.'

'An anecdote?' I said, trying to suppress a grin. 'And what did he say?'

'Nothing really,' said Victor looking puzzled. ''E jus' 'ad this sudden fit o' coughing. 'E does it reg'lar when ah go t'see 'im . . . ah don't know why.'

I gave Victor a ten-pound note and he wandered slowly back inside to resume battle with an ancient till that looked like something from a museum. When he returned to give me my change I noticed he was limping slightly. 'An' t'mek matters worse,' he grumbled, 'ah've got onions on m'feet.'

'Oh dear, Victor,' I said with feeling, 'I bet that brings tears to your eyes.'

'Y'reight there, Mr Sheffield,' said Victor. 'In fac', that's jus' what Dr Davenport said.'

In Kirkby Steepleton I bought a fish-and-chips supper and sat down at seven o'clock to watch *This is Your Life* on ITV. Eamonn Andrews had just surprised Cannon and Ball with his famous red book when the telephone rang.

'I've just finished at school,' said Beth. 'What are you doing?'

'Just about to start my fish-and-chips supper,' I said.

'Sounds lovely.'

'Why not join me?' I said.

'I think I will,' said Beth. 'Shall I pick some up on the way?'

'No. You come straight here and I'll nip into the village and buy some more.'

'Thanks,' said Beth. 'See you soon.'

Four hours later, after an evening of wedding-talk, Michael Parkinson was having a tête-à-tête with Joanna Lumley when we finally walked upstairs hand in hand.

On Thursday morning the first frost of winter had arrived and Vera put on her best suit, pinned on her grandmother's Victorian brooch and selected a warm scarf and a woollen royal-blue coat. Radio 3 was switched on in the kitchen and she hummed along to the music of Gershwin. Then, after scraping the ice off the windscreen of her Austin A40, she set off down Morton Road, through Ragley and on to the city of York, the jewel in Yorkshire's crown. She parked near Micklegate Bar, walked briskly to the railway station and selected a good vantage point in Tea-Room Square. Gradually the crowds began to grow around her and she leant against the metal barrier, waited patiently and smiled. She was about to see her future queen.

Timothy and Walter had already arrived. They were on first-name terms now and Timothy could barely contain his excitement. He had never met anyone as interesting as Walter in his whole life and the invitation to go with him to the Railway Museum simply couldn't be refused. After asking Deke Ramsbottom to look after his shop he had put on his best suit and Yorkshire county tie, featuring a single 'Tudor' white rose on a green background, and loaded his old camera with a roll of film.

'Good luck, Walter,' said Tidy Tim from behind the crowd barrier as Walter donned his spotlessly clean blue boiler suit.

'Thank you, Timothy,' said Walter and he took his place in the line of nervous museum volunteers.

At last the royal train arrived in bright sunshine and everyone cheered as the Prince and Princess of Wales stepped out of the carriage. They were due to become parents next June and there was much excited chatter among the ladies in the crowd. Princess Diana was radiant and looked stunning in her moss-green, woollen caped coat and a black Spanish-style hat. Vera was pleased to see she showed no sign of the illness that caused her to cancel engagements earlier in the week.

Immediately, Princess Diana mingled with the crowd and shook hands with as many people as she could, while Charles, Vera noticed, was more reserved and hung back. The princess received gifts of flowers with a smile and made sure she took time to speak with the old folk who had waited many hours. She appeared completely at ease, whereas Charles observed the formal protocol and walked stiffly alongside the Lord Lieutenant of North Yorkshire, the Marquis of Normandby, who was leading the prince towards the official welcoming party.

Suddenly Princess Diana was opposite Vera, who dropped an automatic curtsy. The princess smiled at the gesture and shook Vera's hand. It was a brief meeting of youth and experience. Both tall, elegant women, there was a moment when they looked levelly into each other's eyes.

'Do you want a boy or a girl, Your Highness?' Vera found herself whispering in their private cocoon of space.

Princess Diana looked thoughtful for a moment. 'I don't mind so long as it's healthy,' she said. Vera nodded in approval and, with her cool fingers, gave the princess's hand a gentle squeeze. 'God bless you, my dear,' said Vera as the princess was whisked away and presented to the director of the museum. Meanwhile, Vera took her tiny lace handkerchief from her handbag and dabbed away a few tears.

At last Walter's moment had arrived. As an official museum volunteer he had spent many hours polishing the miniature steam engine, a replica working model of Stephenson's Rocket. Princess Diana had been told by the museum director that many of the volunteer helpers had worked there for over twenty years.

'And how long have you been here?' she asked Walter, who was first in line.

'Since eight o'clock this morning, Your Highness,' replied Walter with a low bow.

The princess smiled, the shutter of Timothy Pratt's camera clicked and the moment that Walter Clarence Crapper met the princess was recorded for posterity.

Then, much to the delight of the crowd, this was followed by an unscheduled ride on the miniature train, and the princess, showing a good deal of her long, shapely legs as she crouched on the narrow seat, shouted, 'Perhaps I should have worn trousers, Charles!' The future king's sombre look suggested that he agreed.

It had been an exciting day and that evening I settled down with some marking and switched on the television for company. A new brand of superglue was being advertised. A man in overalls, looking unusually relaxed, had been stuck to a large board that was dangling from a helicopter. Whatever they were paying him wasn't enough.

At half past eight Judith Chalmers introduced the Miss World Competition from the Royal Albert Hall. It was won by an eighteen-year-old Venezuelan mathematics student who, in my opinion, didn't compare to Beth. Later I switched to BBC1 to watch *Tenko*, about a group of women prisoners in a camp in Singapore during the Second World War. I knew it was a series Beth enjoyed and I looked forward to the day we could relax together as a married couple.

* * *

Meanwhile, in the vicarage, Vera was listening to a concert on Radio 3 and was at peace with the music of Delius and Bizet. She was reading the front page of the *York Evening Press*. The headline read 'Isn't she lovely!' above a photograph of Princess Diana waving to the crowd. Vera smiled and reflected on her day and her brief meeting with the beautiful princess, a meeting she knew she would remember for the rest of her life.

On Easington Road, in Walter Crapper's garage, Timothy and Walter were looking at the same newspaper and remembering their very special day.

'Congratulations, Walter,' said Timothy.

'Thank you, Timothy,' said Walter. 'I'll never forget today.'

'And when ah've taken t'other thirty-five photos on this roll o' film, Walter, I'll take it t'Boots and we can see you being presented to t'princess.'

'That will be wonderful, Timothy,' said Walter. 'And now . . . would you like to see my undercarriage?'

'Yes, please,' said the eager Timothy, looking around at the wonderland that was Walter's workshop. Hanging from the ceiling was his Hi-Boy high-wing trainer and on his home-made wooden stand, supporting a half-finished model aircraft, was a fuel pump driven by a twelve-volt lead acetate battery.

'The fuel is made up of eighty per cent methanol, fifteen per cent castor oil and five per cent nitro methane which I can increase for competition flying,' said Walter.

'Competition flying?' said Timothy.

'Yes. In fact, there's a competition this Sunday,' said Walter. 'Would you like to come?'

'Ooh, yes, please,' said Timothy and he knew he had arrived in aero-modelling heaven when Walter let him cover the rib and spar wings in Solarfilm and then use an electric hot iron to allow the covering to shrink into place. Finally, he fitted the wheels with split pins and finished it off with a soldering iron. They both stood back in admiration. It was complete.

That evening as they each drank a cup of cocoa, Timothy felt that perhaps for the first time in his life he might have a real friend.

'Walter,' he said tentatively, 'one day, would you like t'see my Meccano set?'

On Sunday morning the weather was calm and the members of the Easington and District Aero Modellers' Club had gathered alongside their runway. It was one hundred and thirty yards long and twenty-five yards wide and the grass had been mown so it looked like a championship bowling green.

Walter had let Timothy help him attach the wings with six heavy-duty elastic bands to his pride and joy, a WOT 4 model aircraft. Then he picked up his transmitter and, attached to the aerial, his channel number fluttered on an orange and white pennant. 'I'm using a thirty-five megahertz waveband, Timothy,' said Walter, 'and the receiver in the aircraft has an identical crystal to the one in the transmitter,' he explained and Timothy looked on in fascination.

After a few final adjustments Walter looked at Timothy. 'Right, stand back,' he said. 'This is it.'

It was a moment that would live long in the memory of Timothy Pratt as the aircraft sped down the runway and lifted off into a cobalt-blue sky. He looked at Walter and smiled . . . and Walter smiled back. His heart soared like the tiny aircraft.

That evening Timothy Pratt surveyed the organized world of his Hardware Emporium. *'Create order from chaos,'* he recited quietly to himself. Then he turned out the lights and gave a contented sigh in the inky darkness. No longer was there something missing in his life . . . he had a friend.

Chapter Six

Separate Lives

Following a request from County Hall I updated our history and geography schemes of work.

Extract from the Ragley School Logbook:
Thursday, 19 November 1981

'Ah'll tell y'summat f'nowt, Mr Sheffield,' said Ruby, as she scattered salt on the frozen steps of the school entrance porch.

It was clearly an offer I couldn't refuse. 'And what's that, Ruby?'

'Y'look like death warmed up,' she said bluntly.

'I'll be fine,' I mumbled without conviction but with a hint of martyrdom. 'Just a bit of a cold.'

'Get some goose grease on y'chest, Mr Sheffield. My Auntie Gladys swears by it.'

'OK, Ruby,' I said and sneezed loudly.

'Huh, men!' she muttered under her breath as I walked into the welcome warmth of the school office.

It was 8.00 a.m. on Thursday, 19 November, and, as I sat down at my desk, I sighed. Then I reached for the telephone and dialled Beth's school number. I needed some sympathy.

Meanwhile, across the High Street, Big Dave and Little Malcolm had parked their dustcart outside Nora's Coffee Shop for their usual before-work large mug of tea and two rounds of toast. The juke-box was playing the new number one, 'Under Pressure' by Queen and David Bowie.

'Hey, laughin' boy, you're quiet,' said Big Dave, stirring his tea vigorously and biting savagely into a doorstep-sized slice of slightly burnt toast. Fortunately, Dorothy Humpleby knew exactly how Little Malcolm and Big Dave liked their toast and for the binmen of Ragley slightly burnt was perfection.

'Y'reight there, Dave,' said Little Malcolm, staring into his mug of tea and ignoring his toast. 'It's 'cause ah don't know 'ow t'say it.'

Big Dave looked puzzled. 'How d'y'mean?'

'It's *Match o' t'Day* on Sat'day neight, Dave, an' ah can't watch it.'

Big Dave nearly choked over his tea. He was thirty-nine years old, a year older than his diminutive cousin, and for all their adult life they had shared a council house in Ragley. He could barely believe what he was hearing. 'But we *allus* watch *Match o' t'Day*.'

'Ah know, Dave,' mumbled Little Malcolm, 'but this Sat'day ah can't.'

Big Dave shook his head. 'But it's *Sat'day* . . . We 'ave

telly warmed up, a couple o' cans an' a bag o' chips . . . It's our ritual.'

Dorothy Humpleby walked to their table with a huge teapot and topped up their mugs. ''Ave y'told 'im, then, Malcolm?'

Big Dave looked up sharply. 'Told me what?'

'We're off to t'pictures in York on Sat'day neight, Dave,' said a tense-looking Malcolm, 'an' we won't be back till late.'

'That's reight,' said Dorothy. 'We're off t'see them *Chariots o' Fire*.'

'What's that abart when it's at 'ome?' said Dave gruffly.

'Dunno, Dave,' said Little Malcolm, 'but Stevie sez there's a bloke in it called Abraham an' 'e can run reight fast.'

'Sounds like *Ben 'Ur* wi' Abraham an' chariots an' all,' grumbled Big Dave. 'It'll be one o' them Bible epics, not a patch on *Match o' t'Day*.'

'Mebbe so, Dave, but ah promised,' pleaded Little Malcolm. He knew he was breaking his big cousin's heart but it was too late to back out. Dorothy was the girl of his dreams. She only had to flutter her eyelashes and Jimmy Hill came a poor second.

Dorothy leant over the table and fixed Big Dave with a stare. 'Dave, mebbe *you* ought t'think abart gettin' a girl-friend.'

Big Dave was speechless. It wasn't until Little Malcolm picked up the empty mugs and took them back to the counter that a thought crossed his mind. Slowly a smile creased his stubbly face and it occurred to him that maybe Dorothy wasn't as daft as she looked. Perhaps there was more to life than beer, football and cricket.

He took his creased copy of the *York Evening Press* out of the pocket of his council donkey jacket, opened it and, for the first time in his life, he wasn't intending to read the sports page.

In Ragley School, just before morning assembly, Heathcliffe and Elisabeth Amelia were queuing in the corridor, waiting to walk into the hall in complete silence, while, on the record deck of our Contiboard music trolley, Vivaldi's *Four Seasons* was about to sprinkle over them like cultural confetti. This was their last chance to speak and they appeared to be concluding an argument about which was the best – cinder toffee, Pontefract cakes or liquorice bootlaces.

'Ah'm reight,' said Heathcliffe defiantly.

'Well,' responded Elisabeth Amelia, seeing an oppor-tunity to take the higher ground, 'my mummy says it's better to be *kind* than right.'

Heathcliffe was dumbstruck. It was on occasions like this it occurred to him that girls appeared to be higher in the intellectual pecking order and it wasn't a comfortable feeling.

On this freezing cold day, at morning break, Vera had prepared welcome hot milky coffees for all the staff. Anne wrapped up warm and went out on playground duty, while Jo and Sally sat near the gas fire. Sally had picked up Vera's *Daily Telegraph* and had begun to read an article about Princess Margaret, sixth in line to the throne. Life seemed turbulent for the Queen's younger sister. 'I wonder if she'll ever have peace in *her* life,' murmured Sally philosophically.

Jo looked across the staff-room at me. I was deep in my own thoughts. 'So have you and Beth picked a wedding date yet, Jack?'

It came out of the blue and I was unprepared. 'Er, not exactly, Jo, but we're getting there,' I said. 'We'll be discussing it with her mother and father over the Christmas holiday.'

Vera sensed my discomfort and went to stand by the window. The howling north wind battered the windows and they shook in their Victorian casements. 'The children are always a bit giddy when the wind blows so strongly,' she said. Then she smiled and said gently, 'More coffee, Mr Sheffield?'

'Thank you, Vera,' I said. It struck me that with her pince-nez spectacles perched on the end of her nose she looked like a wise owl.

During lunchbreak, ten miles away, Big Dave had travelled into York and was standing in the newspaper office of the *York Press*. In front of him in the queue was Mary Brakespeare, the matriarch of an Easington farming family.

"Ullo, Mrs Brakespeare,' said Big Dave a little sheepishly. He was hoping to make his visit short and sweet – and anonymous.

"Ullo, young David,' said Mary. 'Y've not 'eard, then?'

"Eard what?' he asked.

'My 'Arold . . . 'E's been tekken,' said Mary.

'Tekken?' said Big Dave in surprise.

'That's reight,' said Mary, looking out of the window and up to the heavens, 'to t'great shepherd in t'sky. Nivver went to a doctor in 'is life. If 'e ever 'ad owt wrong wi' 'im, 'e used to look in 'is book o' sheep ailments an' rub a bit o' stuff on 'is chest.'

'Oh 'eck,' said Big Dave, 'ah'm sorry to 'ear that, Mrs Brakespeare.'

'T'mek matters worse 'e jus' bought a new pig trailer an' ah'm stuck wi' it now.'

A short, attractive, pocket battleship of an assistant was sitting behind the desk. She was in her mid-thirties and didn't look as if she suffered fools gladly. The badge on her white blouse read: MISS FENELLA LOVELACE. She shook her magnificent mane of long, brown, wavy hair and removed her new large-lens, fashionable spectacles. 'Can ah 'elp?' she said to Mary.

'Yes, please, luv,' said Mary. 'Me 'usband's jus' died and ah want t'purrit in t'paper.'

'Ah'm sorry to 'ear that,' said Fenella and pushed a pencil and a slip of paper headed 'Obituary Column' across the desk. 'Here y'are, Mrs, er, Shakespeare. Y'write y'message on that an' it goes in Friday's paper.'

'It's *Brakespeare*, young lady, an' what do ah write?'

'Owt y'like,' said Fenella: 'usually who's dead an' a message.'

'An' 'ow much is it?' said Mary with a frown.

''Pends 'ow much y'write, but first six words are free,' explained Fenella.

'Ah see,' said Mary with a smile and proceeded to print

in large capitals: 'HAROLD DEAD – PIG TRAILER FOR SALE'.

Mary Brakespeare had never been one for sentiment.

At last it was Big Dave's turn. To his relief the office was empty of customers.

''Ello,' said Big Dave nervously.

'Good morning. What can ah do f'yer?' said Fenella, eyeing up this huge Yorkshireman appreciatively.

Dave took the crumpled newspaper from the pocket of his donkey jacket and pointed to the Personal column. 'Ah wanted t'put an ad in – er, for m'self.'

Fenella was curious but knew how to do her job. 'So yer lookin' for . . . a friend,' said Fenella quietly.

Dave took a deep breath. 'Yes, ah am.'

'Well, y'can 'ave a short 'eadline an' up t'thirty words an' y'can put abbreviations like G-S-O-H.'

'G-S-O-H?' said the perplexed Big Dave.

'That's reight. It stands f' "good sense o' 'umour".'

'Oh, ah see. Well, ah've got that all reight,' said Big Dave with a shy grin. 'An' 'ow much is it?'

'A pound,' said Fenella.

'A pound! That's more than three pints o' Tetley's!' exclaimed Big Dave.

Fenella, knowingly, nodded in agreement, and then gave Big Dave a form and a pencil.

'Ah 'aven't done owt like this before,' said Big Dave, feeling embarrassed.

'Don't worry,' said Fenella, ''ah've seen 'undreds. Ah'll check it when you've done.'

Dave took the paper to a counter near the window

and, slowly but surely, and with much crossing-out, composed a thirty-word masterpiece using bits of other advertisements. He took it back to Fenella, who read with interest: AVAILABLE NOW! *Tall, single, hardy outdoor-type, 39, brushes up well & likes driving large vehicles. WLTM good-looking 25–35 yr old with GSOH for friendship, pub visits & good times. York. Box 561066.*

'That's really good, Mr, er . . .' Fenella glanced at the top of the form, 'Robinson. An' then y'circle one o' these t'say which section it goes in,' she said. At the bottom of the form was printed 'M/M . . . M/F . . . F/M . . . F/F (*please circle*)' and Fenella looked thoughtful as he circled 'M/M'. Dave smiled: after all, he thought, there was no doubting he was a *man*.

Eager to escape he hurried out, jumped in his dustcart and tore off on the back road to Ragley village to meet up with his little cousin outside their house on School View. The previous week Little Malcolm had been to Dixon's in York and purchased a Merlin Pushbutton Car Radio, complete with long-wave and medium-wave bands, for £16.95. To Little Malcolm this was a fortune, but it had come with clear instructions and a fixing kit. He was installing it in his car when Big Dave pulled up. Little Malcolm grabbed his donkey jacket and jumped in.

He was aware that Big Dave was strangely silent as he crunched the dustcart into first gear. 'Ow did y'gerron?' he asked.

'All reight,' said Big Dave evasively. 'Jus' 'ad a bit of a wander round.' He sighed deeply. 'C'mon, Mal, let's shift some bins.'

* * *

At the end of school, as I said goodnight to the children in my class, ten-year-old Tricia Hensall came up to me to show me her new wristwatch. 'It's one o' them new Texas digital watches, Mr Sheffield,' said Tricia. 'There's a button t'light it up so y'can tell the time at night.'

'It's wonderful, Tricia,' I said and, as she ran off, I wondered where all this new technology would end.

Not all the children were in a hurry. Terry Earnshaw and Victoria Alice Dudley-Palmer were deep in discussion as they collected their coats and scarves from the line of pegs outside Class 2. Victoria Alice had always been attracted to little Terry Earnshaw. He wasn't like all the other boys her mother encouraged her to play with or invited to parties. He was a rough diamond, a daredevil: he was different.

She decided to plunge in with a question that had been on her mind. 'Terry, when we grow up will you marry me?'

Terry took a thick woollen balaclava from his coat pocket and pulled it over his head. Then he picked his nose expertly as he deliberated. 'Why?' he asked, stalling for time.

'Because you're my best *boy* friend,' said Victoria Alice.

They wandered out on to the dark playground. Mrs Dudley-Palmer was sitting in her Rolls-Royce, waiting just outside school and feeling relaxed. It was a cold night but the car's heating system was excellent.

A sudden thought gripped Terry so firmly that he forgot to continue picking his nose. 'Would you 'ave t'sleep in my bed? 'Cause it'd be right squashed,' he mumbled thoughtfully. He didn't mention the fact that Heathcliffe in the other bed continually flashed his three-colour torch at him, which could make life difficult for newly-weds.

Victoria Alice stopped to consider this unexpected development. Also, her knowledge of sex education was already two or three years ahead of little Terry's. 'Yes, of course,' she said indignantly, 'because I want to have lots of baby girls to play with.'

Terry shook his head in bewilderment. 'Ah don't fancy that,' he said forcefully, 'an' anyway what if we 'ave boys?'

Victoria Alice pondered for only a moment. 'I'd probably sell them,' she said defiantly, 'because boys are smelly.' It appeared that while her knowledge of sex education was superior, in terms of human rights the two of them were probably on a par.

'Ah see,' said Terry and, spotting a nearby and very inviting puddle, he veered off to take a running jump at it. At that moment it was a more attractive prospect than future nuptial agreements with the eloquent Victoria Alice. Also, talking to girls was bad for his super-hero image. Terry was glad of his balaclava as he walked through the bitter cold to his council house, while Victoria Alice joined Elisabeth Amelia on the back seat of their warm car.

They went their separate ways . . . as they were destined to do in their future lives.

I had stayed at school to update our history and geography schemes of work following yet another request from County Hall. Year by year, a new common curriculum appeared to get closer. As I turned the key in the lock of the huge oak entrance door of Ragley School, I sighed and breathed in the cold sharp air. My mind had been filled with the stuff of dreams and I reflected on the meaning of unconditional love. I knew what I really wanted and it was here spread out before me in this tiny Yorkshire village. Perhaps the headship of a large school would be mine some day in the far-distant future but not now . . . not now. I picked up my old brown briefcase and strode out to my Morris Minor Traveller. I was a village school teacher and another week was over.

That evening Big Dave Robinson had bought an early edition of the *York Evening Press* from the General Stores & Newsagent. Then he had sought privacy in the Gents' cubicle in The Royal Oak to read his advertisement in the Personal column. He stared at it in horror. 'Bloody 'ell!' he said out loud. While it had been printed exactly as he had written it, there was just one problem. Instead of being in the MEN SEEKING FEMALES section it was boldly displayed under the heading MEN SEEKING MEN. 'If t'lads find out ah'll never live it down,' he muttered.

Meanwhile, behind the closed doors of Ragley village there were others reflecting on their unusual lives.

Deadly Duggie Smith lay on his campbed in the attic of 7 School View and stared at the poster above his head of the woman he loved. He put a record on his record player and relaxed as Abba began to sing 'The Winner Takes It All'. The blonde and beautiful Agnetha Fältskog was the girl of his dreams. In a way it was a shame that they were never destined to meet. Duggie would have proved a faithful soulmate, but perhaps the Swedish superstar would not have been content as the wife of an undertaker's assistant.

Petula Dudley-Palmer was sitting in the new conservatory of their luxury home, reading a *Kaleidoscope* catalogue. Her daughters were playing with dolls in their bedroom and, in the home-office, her husband, Geoffrey, was playing 'Tennis' on his Atari 2600 video game with its woodgrain console, plastic paddles and stubby rubber joystick. In her catalogue there was a photograph of a white curly extension lead for a telephone. It meant you could actually walk around while using the phone, which seemed a novel idea. She knew she must have one to impress her friends. Then she wondered who her *real* friends were and couldn't immediately think of one. Petula looked around the conservatory, which was filled with the best in luxury cane furniture, and then at her reflection in the glass. She was alone and it occurred to her that *one* is a lonely number.

At nine o'clock on Saturday morning Big Dave was waiting outside the office of the *York Press* with Friday night's edition clutched in his giant goalkeeper fist. When Miss Fenella Lovelace opened the door she was surprised to see that the big gay Yorkshireman had returned.

'It's in t'wrong place,' said Big Dave.

'What is?' asked Fenella.

'T'advert. Y'went an' purrit in t'poofters section!' protested Big Dave indignantly.

Fenella rummaged through a pile of forms. 'It's 'ere,' she said, pointing to the circled 'M/M'. 'That's what y'wanted.'

'But ah wanted a *girl* friend, norra *boy* friend!'

Fenella's eyes crinkled into a smile. 'Oh, ah see. Well, we'd better change it, then.'

'Thanks, er . . .' Big Dave stared at the badge again, 'Miss, er, Lovelace.'

'Y'can call me Nellie, if y'like.'

'Nellie?'

'Yeah, well, Fenella's a bit of a daft name.'

'Oh, OK, er, Nellie. Pleased t'meet you. Ah'm Dave.'

They shook hands and Dave was impressed. Nellie had a grip like a car crusher. 'So what's a big lad like you doing looking furra girlfriend?'

He didn't quite know why but it all just flooded out: living with his cousin, Dorothy coming on the scene and, of course, the final straw – *Match of the Day*.

'Ah know 'ow y'feel,' said Nellie. 'Ah never miss *Match o' t'Day*. Ah luv football. In fac', ah played football at school i' Barnsley.'

Big Dave was impressed and was wise enough not to reveal his deep-seated beliefs concerning the ability of the fair sex to play a man's game. 'Ah play in goal. 'Ow abart you?'

'Ah were an overlapping midfielder what supplied square balls into t'box an' me 'lectric pace meant ah were never offside,' said Nellie without a hint of modesty.

Big Dave was stunned. He was in the presence of the impossible: a woman who understood football's offside law. Before he could stop himself he blurted out, 'Nellie, if

y'not already spoken for, ah don't s'ppose y'fancy comin'
to t'pictures tonight?'

'Ah might,' said Nellie coyly.

'There's two films on,' explained Dave. 'Fust 'un is
Gregory's Girl, abart this lass what plays football; second
'un is summat t'do wi' a bloke called Abraham what runs
fast in t'Bible.'

'Y'mean, go to t'fust 'ouse so we don't miss t'football?'

'O' course,' said Big Dave.

'OK, Dave,' said Nellie.

A thrill ran through Dave's body. It was a strange feeling, a bit like saving a penalty . . . only better.

On Sunday evening, the members of the Ragley Rovers
football team were exchanging stories about their weekend.

'Word 'as it y'gorra lass,' said Don, eyeing Big Dave
warily as he cleaned a pint tankard with his *England 4
West Germany 2* tea towel.

Dave went misty-eyed. 'She's a stunner,' he said.

'Gorra fancy name, ah 'eard tell,' said Don, fishing for
more news.

'Y'reight there, Don,' said Little Malcolm: 'Fenella
Lovelace.'

'By gum,' said Don, clearly impressed. 'Sounds like a
film star.'

'It does that,' agreed Big Dave.

Sheila looked up from behind the bar at the giant
binman and smiled. 'So where did y'tek this movie star?'

'Ah took 'er to t'pictures an' afterwards we 'ad a swift
pint an' a game o' darts in t'Bay 'Orse at Monk Bar i' York.

Then we watched *Match o' t'Day*,' said Big Dave. 'It were a good neight.'

The football team stared at him in amazement at this incredible news.

'Y'played darts wi' a woman?' spluttered Shane Ramsbottom, nearly dropping his pint tankard.

'An' did y'show 'er 'ow t'play?' asked Chris 'Kojak' Wojciechowski, the Bald-Headed Ball Wizard.

'Could she 'it t'board?' asked Clint Ramsbottom, suddenly interested in this dramatic news. ''Cause women aren't built f'darts,' he added, casting an admiring glance at Sheila in her straining boob tube, who was now at the far end of the bar and fortunately out of earshot.

'She sez she were in a women's darts team in Barnsley,' said Big Dave, 'an' she throws 'er darts real fast. She's only five-foot-two an' i' Barnsley she were called t' "Pocket Rocket".'

Little Malcolm was pleased to hear he was two inches taller than Big Dave's new girlfriend, but then a terrible thought struck him. 'Dave . . . y'did beat 'er?'

To their relief Dave nodded, but, unknown to them, their giant goalkeeper and male chauvinist secretly believed that Nellie had let him win after scraping the wire repeatedly on her finishing double. This was a secret Dave would never reveal. After all, there was a natural order to life and, in Big Dave's politically incorrect world, women were good at cooking and never beat men at darts or dominoes.

Chapter Seven

The Latchkey Boy

The Education Welfare Officer, Roy Davidson, is monitoring the new admission Nathan Penny following concerns raised by staff members.

Extract from the Ragley School Logbook:
Thursday, 3 December 1981

His name was Náthan. He was nine years old and he was alone.

It was the time of the fading of the light. A cold December mist swirled over Ragley village and its smoking chimneys and in the distance, over the purple bulk of the Hambleton hills, the setting sun glittered like beaten bronze. The days were short now. Winter had arrived.

At the back of the village hall the children's playground was surrounded by high chain-link fencing. A pair of swings swung to and fro in the cold north wind and a few flakes of snow settled on a wooden seesaw and a rusty tubular-metal climbing frame. On the top step of a tall ancient slide Nathan Penny, clad in an old green anorak, was staring into the growing darkness. Around his neck was a loop of string from which hung a brass Yale key. As he rocked back and forth it swung like a pendulum and reflected the glow of the amber street lights.

Nathan had arrived at Ragley just after the half-term holiday from a primary school in Chapeltown on the outskirts of Leeds. He was a pale, skinny, nervous-looking boy and in spite of all our efforts he had not appeared to make any friends. His mother had got a part-time job at the local chocolate factory and always looked as if she carried the worries of the world on her shoulders. I had yet to meet her husband, John Penny, who I gathered was a locksmith, travelling the length and breadth of Yorkshire in search of new work.

It was the first Wednesday in December, another school day had ended and the pupils had drifted home. Nathan was one of our 'latchkey' children who arrived home *before* his parents, unlocked the front door and walked into an empty house.

Jennifer Penny turned off the High Street, flashed her torch on the gravelled pathway and walked with light, crunching steps towards the playground. She had panicked when she had arrived home from her shift at Rowntree's and found that her son wasn't there. Spotting him on the slide, she sighed with relief. 'Nathan,' she called out, 'come 'ome. Y'll catch y'death o' cold.'

'Is 'e there, Mam?' said Nathan, his gaunt face pale in the shadows.

'No luv, 'e's not,' she replied and turned away to hide fresh tears.

In the playground there was silence apart from the creaking of the swings.

'Ah've got y'favourite f'tea,' said Jennifer, more in hope than expectation.

'So *'e's* not coming back tonight?'

Mrs Penny knew that scolding him would not work. This was one of his dark moods and she recognized the hunched shoulders, bowed head, and troubled eyes hidden behind his long black fringe. 'No, luv,' she said.

He stepped down. 'Sorry, Mam,' he said quietly.

She gave him a gentle hug. 'Let's go 'ome.'

They walked up the High Street, cold and huddled together like wraiths in the darkness, and turned the corner of the council estate. Jennifer looked down at her only son and, once again, she felt the pain of a mother.

On Thursday morning, a soft white quilt of snow had carpeted the back road from Kirkby Steepleton to Ragley village and my Morris Minor Traveller made slow progress. Ruby the caretaker, wearing a tightly knotted headscarf, was brushing the steps in the entrance porch when I arrived at school.

''Morning, Ruby,' I said. 'You're a saint.'

'No rest for t'wicked, Mr Sheffield,' said Ruby in a singsong voice. The freezing conditions clearly had no effect on this hardy Yorkshirewoman. She added a good sprinkling of salt to the stone steps as noisy conversation drifted out from the entrance hall. 'It's a bun fight in there,' she said as I hurried into school.

A group of parents under the supervision of Sally were making costumes for the forthcoming nativity play. Meanwhile, their children sat in a group round the old pine table, making paper chains from coloured paper. The loops were held together with a generous dab of white rubber glue, which had a strange but appealing smell, and high-pitched chatter reverberated around the walls.

It was just before morning playtime when Theresa Ackroyd made her first announcement of the day. 'PC 'Unter coming up t'drive, Mr Sheffield.'

Dan was Jo's husband, a loyal friend and our popular village bobby. A huge six-feet-four-inch rugby player, he looked smart in his navy-blue uniform with a small coat of arms on each collar.

I stepped out of my classroom door and across the corridor to tell Jo that Dan was here. As I walked into Class 2 the boys and girls were chanting their tables – all except for seven-year-old Benjamin Roberts. I stood behind him and listened. The rest of the class were singing 'Seven sevens are forty-nine', while little Ben was humming 'Dah, dah, dah, dee-dah'.

I leant over and whispered in his ear, 'What are you doing, Ben?'

He looked up and gave me a relaxed smile. 'Ah'm 'umming, Mr Sheffield.'

'Yes, I can tell that, Ben, but *why* are you humming?' I said, a little irritably.

Ben continued to be unperturbed. 'Well, ah know t'tune, Mr Sheffield. It's jus' that ah don't know t'words.'

I tried hard not to smile. It was clear Ben was not having the best of days. His 'Explorers of the World' topic folder was open in front of him. He had written, 'Christopher Columbus discovered a miracle.' To his credit he had looked up 'miracle' in his *New Oxford Dictionary* and the more I thought about it, the more it occurred to me that he was probably right.

I smiled at Jo as the bell rang. 'Dan's here,' I said.

'Oh, thanks,' she said. 'Wonder what *he* wants.'

Dan was waiting for me in the entrance hall, deep in thought and stroking his long, droopy moustache. He looked serious and was clearly on duty. 'Jack, there's been a burglary in Morton, next door to Beth's cottage. I've checked her doors and windows and all seems well.'

'Oh dear,' I said, 'that's bad news.'

'Thought you might want to let her know before she gets home,' he said.

'Thanks, Dan,' I said. 'I appreciate your letting us know.'

'Anyway, must get back to the station . . . See you Saturday. Beth told Jo to come around six.'

'OK, Dan, see you then.'

His little grey van bumped down the drive, turned right at the school gate and roared off up the Easington Road.

After I had telephoned Beth, the burglary was the main topic of discussion over lunch in the staff-room. Vera had just said, 'What's the world coming to?' when there was a tap on the door. It was Roy Davidson, our Education

Welfare Officer, calling in for his weekly visit. Roy, a tall, gaunt man in his mid-forties with a shock of prematurely grey hair, was a wonderful supporter of village schools and his knowledge of specialist educational support was second to none.

'You mentioned . . .' he checked his spiral notepad, 'Nathan Penny,' he said.

'He's in the library now if you want to have a word,' I said.

We were very proud of our wide range of books, accumulated thanks largely to the generosity of the Parent–Teacher Association and the local community. Our school capitation had been reduced once again and we were surviving on just a few pence per child per day. The extra funds made a huge difference to the experiences we could provide for the children of Ragley village.

Nathan clearly loved books. I had made him library monitor and he spent much of his spare time tidying and labelling, but mainly reading. When I walked into the carpeted library area he was engrossed in *The Voyage of the Dawn Treader* by C. S. Lewis.

'This is Nathan,' I said to Roy. 'He's a wonderful reader.'

'Hello, Nathan,' he said.

Nathan was thrilled to meet another grown-up who was interested in books. I left them to it, knowing that Roy's perceptive, gentle questioning would reveal how best to help this introverted little boy.

Ten minutes later, Roy came back into the staff-room. 'I could do with talking to his parents,' he said, glancing down at his copious notes. 'There's something I can't quite work out. His attendance is fine and there was no antisocial behaviour at his school in Leeds. Even so, the boy is clearly troubled.'

At the end of school I was in the office with Vera. She beckoned me over to the window. 'Mr Sheffield, watch the new boy Nathan Penny. See what he does,' she said. We peered out into the growing darkness. At the school gate Nathan took his *Ginn Reading 360* reading book and tucked it down the back of his shorts. When he was satisfied it was hidden from view he walked home.

Anne was collating her infant reading tests for end-of-term reports. 'Jack, there's something worrying about that little boy. I just can't put my finger on it,' she said.

Sally looked up from transcribing the sheet music of 'We Three Kings' into guitar chords for her beginners' group. She looked thoughtful. 'Perhaps we need to pull in a bit of additional support on this one, Jack. Better to be safe than sorry.'

'Sally's right, Jack,' said Anne.

'I agree,' I said, 'and in the meantime Roy Davidson wants to talk with his parents.'

'Jack, his mother is coming in tomorrow lunchtime to help with the nativity costumes,' said Sally. 'Maybe you could have a word then.'

It was Friday lunchtime and a large group of mothers were busy making costumes in the entrance hall. Jennifer Penny, in between shifts at the factory, was among them, eager to support.

'Excuse me, Mrs Penny. Any chance of a quick word?'
I said.

Soon we were in the school office discussing Nathan's
love of books. 'John won't allow no books in the 'ouse, Mr
Sheffield,' she said quietly. ''E says that 'e didn't need no
books when 'e were a lad.'

'And what do *you* think, Mrs Penny?' I asked.

She sighed deeply and picked at her bitten fingernails.
'Ah want t'give Nathan a chance in life, Mr Sheffield, an'
ah know 'e loves reading in your libr'y.'

'He's a good reader, Mrs Penny,' I said, 'and he seems
to have a natural gift for writing – in fact, his poetry is
exceptional.'

'Ah read to 'im when ah can, Mr Sheffield,' she said,
'but . . . not when 'is dad's 'ome.'

'I see,' I said.

'An' y'can't argue with him,' she added a little nervously,
rubbing her wrist. It was badly bruised.

'Perhaps if I have a word with Mr Penny he might let
Nathan take books home,' I said.

'Won't make no difference, Mr Sheffield, an' in any
case 'e says when Nathan's as tall as 'im 'e starts work. 'E
says 'e doesn't need books t'do manual work.'

The bell rang for afternoon school. 'Thanks, Mrs Penny,'
I said. 'I hope we can talk again.'

It was an impulse. At the end of school I gathered up the
complete series of Narnia stories and put them in a carrier
bag. Then I pulled on my duffel coat and old college scarf
and set off for the council estate. When I reached Nathan's
house a huge man was emptying the contents of his van

into a crowded garage. He stepped out quickly to meet me and blocked my way. 'Yes?' he said gruffly.

'I'm Jack Sheffield from the village school,' I said. 'Are you Mr Penny?'

'What d'you want? 'As Nathan been up t'no good?'

'No, just the opposite,' I said. 'He's a fine boy. You must be very proud.'

''E's no son o' mine,' he retorted. ''Is real dad ran off years ago. Ah met 'is mother when ah were working in Leeds.'

'I see,' I said and wished the system for the transfer of records from one school to another could be speeded up. 'Well, I hope you'll be very happy in Ragley and if you have any concerns please call in whenever you can. We want Nathan to be settled in his new school.'

'Is that it, then?' he said, still blocking my way.

I held up the bag of books. 'I've brought some books for Nathan to read at home.'

'Well, y'can tek 'em back again,' he said and turned away. Then, as an afterthought, he put his face close to mine. 'Y'know what teachers are,' he sneered: 'men amongst boys an' boys amongst men.'

'I've heard that before, Mr Penny,' I said, 'and it's a tired joke. I wouldn't go around repeating it if I were you.'

He watched me walk down the road before he turned back to his van and carried on unloading.

On Saturday evening, shortly after six o'clock, Beth and I were in the kitchen of Bilbo Cottage and my old pine table was covered in icing sugar. I had volunteered to ice Beth's Christmas cake. It was meant to be a joint effort but we both knew it wasn't really. The resulting masterpiece was due to be taken to Hampshire for our New Year's Eve visit to Beth's parents.

'If you dip the palette knife into the jug of hot water I gave you, Jack,' said Beth patiently, although through gritted teeth, 'then it's a lot easier and the icing will have a smoother finish.' It occurred to me she was beginning to sound like Delia Smith but I refrained from mentioning this.

In the meantime, the smell of Beth's cooking made my mouth water. She donned my Basil Brush oven gloves, a misguided and incongruous purchase at the recent PTA jumble sale, and removed the lid from a magnificent chicken casserole.

We had invited an unsuspecting Dan and Jo Hunter to join us for a meal before going into York for a wine-tasting evening at the Assembly Rooms. Soon the four of us were tucking in and it wasn't until Dan's third helping that he stretched out, patted his full tummy and sighed with satisfaction. 'Wonderful, Beth.'

I looked across at Beth and she took the hint. 'Jack's got something important to ask you, Dan,' she announced as she collected the plates.

Dan looked up. 'Is it anything to do with the washing-up?' he said with a broad grin.

'Actually, Dan, I was wondering if you would be my best man,' I said.

Jo gave a squeal of delight. 'Oh, say yes, Dan, before he changes his mind.'

'So, what's it to be, Dan?' said Beth. 'You could wear that lovely dress uniform of yours.'

'Well, what a surprise,' said Dan. He leant over the table and shook my hand. 'It would be a pleasure, Jack. I'm your man.'

'So have you picked a date?' asked Jo, barely able to contain her excitement.

'Yes. We went to see Joseph and it will be here at St Mary's on the last Saturday in May,' said Beth.

'In the Spring Bank holiday,' said Jo. 'A perfect time.'

'So not in Hampshire, then?' said Dan.

'No,' said Beth. 'My parents agreed it made sense to have it up here in Yorkshire. All our friends are here and this is where we're going to live.' She put her arm round my waist and looked at me. 'And Jack's finally persuaded me to move in here at Bilbo Cottage.'

Dan and I were ushered out of the kitchen, while Beth and Jo prepared coffee and talked about wedding dresses.

Over coffee we settled down to watch *Larry Grayson's Generation Game* with Isla St Clair and then, shortly after seven o'clock, when Stephanie Turner as Inspector Jean Darblay was about to solve another crime on *Juliet Bravo*, we switched off and prepared to set off for the wine-tasting.

'Jack, have you heard about the spate of burglaries in Easington?' said Dan.

'Yes. It was in the *Herald*,' I said, nodding towards the sofa. The headline in the *Easington Herald & Pioneer* read, 'Two more break-ins – police urge everyone to be vigilant'.

'People are getting nervous,' said Beth. 'My next-door neighbour is having new locks fitted and most of the villagers have started locking their doors for the first time.'

On Monday morning, Roy Davidson and Joseph Evans were waiting for me in the school office. 'I'm calling in to see Nathan Penny's parents today, Jack,' said Roy, 'and I'm taking Mary O'Neill from Social Services. We're getting reports that Mr Penny has a tendency towards violence.'

I recalled my meeting with Nathan's mother last week. 'I can understand that,' I said, 'and when I spoke with Mrs Penny there was bruising on her wrist. You might want to check that out.'

'He's certainly a busy man at present,' said Joseph reflectively, 'replacing all the broken locks following the burglaries.'

It was a hectic day with another group of parents putting the finishing touches to costumes and props for the nativity play. Only when I finally drove home to Kirkby Steepleton did I reflect once again on Nathan Penny and the difficulties in his life.

On Tuesday morning I was surprised to see Dan Hunter in the staff-room in animated conversation with Jo and Sally.

'More burglaries, Jack – all yesterday afternoon,' said Dan gravely.

'Six mothers worked in school yesterday, Jack, and three of them have been robbed,' said Jo. 'It's too much of a coincidence.'

Dan looked at his wife and nodded slowly. 'You've got a point there, Jo.'

'Well, that's my fault,' said Sally.

'How can it be your fault?' asked Jo.

'I advertised the rota for costume-making in the monthly newsletter,' said Sally, 'and listed the mothers who were coming along to help us and the dates and times they would be in school.'

There was silence while we all considered the implications. 'And does the newsletter just go to parents?' asked Dan.

'Parents and governors, that's all,' I said.

Dan stood up. 'I have to go,' he said abruptly. 'Something Joseph said last night.'

It was the end of the week when we all crowded round the *Easington Herald & Pioneer* in the staff-room and read the article. John Penny had been arrested on numerous counts of burglary.

'And then he had the cheek to return and repair their locks,' said Vera.

There was a knock on the door. It was Jennifer Penny with Nathan. She obviously wanted to talk. 'Perhaps you would like to sit in the library, Nathan,' I said, 'while I speak with your mother.' He smiled and trotted off at once.

'So how are you, Mrs Penny?' I asked when we were sitting in the office.

'Relieved,' she said simply.

'I'm really sorry,' I said. 'It must be difficult for you.'

She paused and looked sad. 'You never know 'ow life will turn out . . . 'ow a relationship will end.'

'What are you going to do? Nathan tells me you intend to move.'

'We are, Mr Sheffield, and ah've mixed feelings about that. Nathan was beginning t'settle here in Ragley and 'e was so proud when you made 'im library monitor. 'E loves his books.'

'So where are you going?'

'To my sister's just outside Skipton. It's a nice cottage with plenty o' room. We'll be 'appy there and there's a good school for Nathan.'

'That's encouraging news,' I said.

She looked out of the office window. 'Ragley's a lovely village, Mr Sheffield, but we can't stay 'ere after all that's 'appened. It would be too difficult for Nathan. He deserves a fresh start.'

'I understand,' I said, 'and . . . I was going to give him these,' I picked up the set of C. S. Lewis books, 'but Mr Penny refused them. Perhaps you would like to take them now.'

'You're very kind, Mr Sheffield. Nathan will be thrilled.'

It was a sad day when, the following Monday, Nathan and his mother came to say goodbye. 'Stick at your writing, Nathan,' I said and he gave me a relieved smile. Then they walked out of Ragley School for the last time. Vera and I watched them from the office window, mother and son setting out for an uncertain future. Vera had shown her usual efficiency and had forwarded Nathan's records to his next school along with a letter from Roy Davidson providing some of the family background.

When they reached the school gate, snow began to fall

135

again and I smiled as Jennifer Penny put a protective arm round her son's shoulders.

*   *   *

There is a postscript to this story. Twenty years later I received a Christmas card depicting a snowy picture of Grassington village in Wharfedale. The message inside said '*Do give me a call if you're in the area*', followed by a telephone number. It was signed . . . *Nathan Penny*.

So it was that on a bright, cold December day I found myself next to a roaring log fire in the Devonshire Arms in Grassington village, enjoying minced beef and Yorkshire pudding along with a pint of William Younger's Best Bitter. Opposite me was a wiry, athletic, weather-beaten young man, approaching his thirtieth birthday. He was a Yorkshire Dales Ranger, caring for the spectacular Yorkshire countryside with its limestone walls and wild moorland. Nathan Penny had flourished.

'Best thing you ever did was t'send that welfare officer round to our house, Mr Sheffield. It helped my mother see sense and it was the making of me.'

'It was a tough decision at the time,' I said. 'We had to tread carefully.'

'Well, all's well now. I've got a wonderful job, a lovely lass and my writing.'

'Ah, yes, your writing,' I said. 'Your stories were always beautifully written and your poetry was exceptional.' He smiled modestly. 'That reminds me, Nathan. I brought this for you.' I handed him an old paperback of mine that I had taken from my bookshelf that morning. It was a book of Roger McGough's poetry of the sixties.

'One of my favourite poets,' he said, flicking through the pages: 'a real man of the people . . . Humour and humility, a good combination.'

'I remembered you loved your poetry, Nathan,' I said.

'I still do,' he said, 'and it helped a lot.'

'How do you mean?'

He smiled. 'When my stepdad was around, Mr Sheffield, life was a series of frightening moments. It felt like a world of tall fences, no escape . . . But now I feel free.'

I nodded in acknowledgement. The nervous little boy I had known all those years ago had gone now and been replaced by the confident young man who sat before me.

'I learnt to open my box of secrets,' he said knowingly. Then he slipped out of his pocket an old leather wallet. Inside was a small photograph, which he took out and passed to me. It was Nathan with a young dark-haired woman and they were standing in front of a small cottage in the Dales. 'That's my Susan,' he said simply.

When we left the pub he shook my hand in farewell and, to my surprise, leant into his Land-Rover and drew out a package. 'For you, Mr Sheffield,' he said and thrust it into my hand. 'I did what you said: I stuck at it.'

Then he climbed into the driver's seat and, with a wave, drove off across the frozen cobbles of the market square. As he disappeared into the distance I recalled a long-ago December day when a troubled nine-year-old had walked down the driveway of Ragley School and disappeared into the darkness for the last time.

Finally, I opened the parcel and smiled. It was a book

of published poetry and the words on the front cover
read

THE LATCHKEY BOY

and other poems

by

Nathan Penny

Chapter Eight

A Doll Called Jesus

Three new admissions arrived today so our number on roll passed ninety for the first time in Ragley's history. The school Christmas party was enjoyed by a full attendance and was supported by the PTA.

Extract from the Ragley School Logbook:
Friday, 18 December 1981

'So remember, boys and girls, it's better to give than receive,' said the Revd Joseph Evans.

Most of the children in the school hall stared back at our friendly local vicar and looked bemused. It was Friday morning, 18 December, the last day of the autumn term, and our final assembly of 1981 was almost at an end. It had been a busy week with a successful nativity play on Wednesday, a carol service on Thursday and, finally, this afternoon, came the Christmas party. Excitement knew no bounds and the children fidgeted with anticipation of the forthcoming festivities.

Afterwards Joseph wondered if his message had fallen on deaf ears when his follow-up discussion about giving and receiving didn't go as he had anticipated.

'Ah don't reckon much t'Jesus's presents, Mr Evans,' said Terry Earnshaw defiantly. 'All this gold an' frankenstein an' t'other one. Ah reckon 'e would've rather 'ad a Darth Vader 'elmet an' a light sabre – or, if it 'ad been a girl, mebbe jus' the 'elmet.'

Joseph sighed but managed to smile at this forthright son of Barnsley with his spiky blond crewcut, runny nose and determined expression. However, he didn't notice that, next to Terry, little Victoria Alice Dudley-Palmer was looking distinctly thoughtful.

At morning break in the staff-room, Vera held up her copy of the *Easington Herald & Pioneer*. The headline read: 'York white Christmas on the cards'.

'I mustn't leave my Christmas food shopping too late,' said Vera, looking concerned. 'Morton Road soon gets blocked with snow.'

Jo glanced up from adding a seventh layer of newsprint to her Pass the Parcel prize. 'I just gave a list to my Dan and he said he would do it all.'

Sally and Anne looked at her as if she had just returned from the Galapagos Islands with a new species of man and decided to keep their thoughts to themselves. They returned to preparing their Pin the Tail on the Donkey game with an appropriate division of labour. Sally was drawing the donkey on an A2 piece of white card, as she had achieved a B grade in A-level Art. Anne was drawing the tail on a card offcut as she had failed Art but passed

A-level Geography, so at least she would know where to pin it.

I collected my hot drink, put on my duffel coat and old college scarf and walked outside. The playground was full of excited children who appeared to show no concern for the bitter cold as they ran red-faced and with bare knees. I sipped my mug of milky coffee and watched them sliding, throwing snowballs on the school field and playing 'What Time is it, Mr Wolf?' in the sheltered alcove by the boiler house.

I wandered over to the school gates and looked across to the village green. It resembled a picture from a Yorkshire calendar with the pantile roofs of the cottages covered in wavy snow patterns and woodsmoke drifting into the slate-grey sky. The boughs of the trees hung heavy with the weight of snow and the pond was frozen over. In the centre of the green had been erected the village Christmas tree, an annual gift from Major Forbes-Kitchener, and his gardeners had completed their task by setting a circle of hay bales around its base to prevent daring children from climbing it.

Down the High Street, outside Piercy's Butcher's Shop, Young Tommy was hanging up this year's batch of plump turkeys and Timothy Pratt was up a ladder checking the alignment of the perfectly horizontal chain of coloured lights that lit up his shop sign. Diane Wigglesworth had put a small Christmas tree in her window and was decorating it with small photographs of Farrah Fawcett, Kate Bush, Julie Christie, Twiggy and Wonder Woman. Ted Postlethwaite, the village postman, was shifting snow and had somehow found time to clear a path from the front door of the Post Office to the post-box, while in the doorway Amelia Duff, the postmistress, was watching, full of admiration.

Meanwhile Prudence Golightly's General Stores was doing a roaring trade with her newly acquired supply of mistletoe. Easington Comprehensive School had closed for Christmas a day before the local primary schools and teenagers Wayne Ramsbottom and Kenny Kershaw had risked life and limb to climb the tall lime trees on Easington Road, where huge round bunches of the parasitic plant populated the high branches. They were now returning their hard-earned money to Prudence by spending it on chocolate.

I was interrupted from my peaceful reverie by a shout from Terry Earnshaw. 'Ah'm froz', Mr Sheffield,' he said.

Victoria Alice was standing alongside Terry. 'So am I, Mr Sheffield. I'm froz' as well,' she said, with an admiring look at the Barnsley boy with the spiky blond hair and unconventional manners.

'Oh no,' I said, 'it's . . . I'm *frozen*.'

Terry gazed up at me sympathetically. 'Looks like we're all froz', Mr Sheffield.'

'Would you like to ring the bell for the end of play-time?' I said.

It was as if I had just offered them the crown jewels and they hurried off into the warmth of the school.

At the school gate a familiar face suddenly appeared. 'Good morning, Mr Sheffield.' It was Barbara Bryant clutching the hand of her six-year-old daughter. 'I've just brought

Stacey back from the dentist,' she said with a smile and crouched down next to her rosy-cheeked infant. 'She was desperate not to miss the Christmas party.'

'Hello, Mrs Bryant,' I said. 'How are things with you?' I recalled our first meeting a few Christmases ago. Her husband, Stephen, had been unemployed and it had been a difficult time for the family.

'Our Debbie's enjoying the big school and I'm still selling Avon cosmetics,' she said with a knowing smile, 'and my Stephen's doing really well now with his driving job, so everything's fine.'

This was good news. 'So you're OK, then?'

Barbara Bryant was a perceptive woman. She knew what I meant. 'We are now . . .' and she hugged her daughter. 'Anyway, must fly, Mr Sheffield – unless you're interested in some Avon cosmetics?' She laughed, kissed the little girl goodbye and walked back to her car.

Stacey waved after her mother and then looked up at me. 'Mr Sheffield, can I tell you something?'

'Yes, Stacey. What is it?'

'Every night I write a note to my mummy saying "I love you",' she said, 'and she keeps them in a tin in the side-board and she thinks I don't know.'

As she ran off to play with her friends, it occurred to me that Stacey had just described the best Christmas present of all.

After morning break the children in my class found it hard to concentrate on their final lessons of the term. They couldn't finish their English exercises quickly enough. In response to the instruction 'Name five Arctic animals', Theresa Ackroyd had scribbled: 'Four polar bears and a seal.' I hadn't the heart to mark it incorrect, particularly when, bursting with excitement, she asked breathlessly, 'Are we playing Musical Chairs this afternoon, Mr Sheffield?'

At twelve o'clock Vera popped her head round my door. 'There's a gentleman to see you, Mr Sheffield.'

In the entrance hall a huge, burly man wearing a boiler suit and a donkey jacket was waiting for me. He removed his thick scarf, gave me a shy smile and we shook hands. 'Pleased t'meet yer, Mr Sheffield, an' thanks f'seeing me at short notice,' he said.

'Good morning,' I said, 'and welcome to Ragley.'

'Ah wondered if y'could spare me a few minutes?' he said.

'Yes. Come in and sit down.' I opened the office door and gestured towards the visitor's chair.

'Well . . . ah'm John Hartley from Keighley, Mr Sheffield. Factory where ah worked closed down an' ah were made redundant.'

'I'm sorry to hear that,' I said.

'Ah've just moved into Ragley – into School View, number eleven,' he said, glancing out of the window and nodding towards the council estate. 'Ah've managed t'get a ware'ouse job at Rowntree's, mostly forklift-truck driving.'

'You've done well to find employment so quickly,' I said.

'Ah were first in t'queue, Mr Sheffield: early bird an' all that.'

I smiled and began to take a liking to this giant of a man. 'So, what can I do for you?'

'Well, ah've got five girls,' he said, taking out a sheet of notepaper from his rough donkey jacket and placing it on the table in front of me. It was a list of five girls' names with their dates of birth alongside. 'Ah wanted a rugby team an' ah finished up wi' a sewing class,' he added with a grin.

My eyes widened. Our number on roll was about to pass ninety for the first time.

'As y'can see, there's two teenagers, our Jean and Joanne, an' they're looking after t'three little 'uns – that's Tracy an' Louise, they're ten an' eight, an' then there's little Mo.'

I looked down at the list. The last name was Maureen and she was seven years old. 'Ah, I see,' I said: 'that would be Maureen.'

'She were named after 'er mother,' he said quietly.

'I understand,' I said.

'That's reight, Mr Sheffield, 'cept, like 'er mother,' he looked down at the carpet, 'she's allus gone by little Mo.'

'I see,' and I sensed something had been left unsaid.

'Well, y'see, my wife died three year back. It were cancer.' There was anguish in his voice and a long silence while he regained his composure.

'I'm very sorry to hear that, Mr Hartley,' I said, 'and we'll make your girls welcome in Ragley. We have a lovely school and I'm sure they'll be happy here.'

'So ah've 'eard, Mr Sheffield. Y'caretaker lives next door but one – a nice lady, med us reight welcome.'

'Ruby's a good neighbour,' I said, 'and our secretary,

Miss Evans, will take all the details and sort out which class they're in.'

Vera, ever perceptive, arrived and summed up the situation quickly. A few minutes later she had completed the admissions register and thanked Mr Hartley for being so efficient. She stood up and looked at me quizzically over her pince-nez spectacles. 'I was just thinking, Mr Sheffield, it's the school Christmas party this afternoon so perhaps Mr Hartley's daughters would like to come along.'

'Good idea,' I said.

Vera looked expectantly at Mr Hartley. 'It would break the ice, so to speak, and they could meet their new class-mates in a relaxed way.'

I glanced up at the faded Roman numerals of the office clock. 'The party starts at half past one, Mr Hartley.'

'Well, that's very kind of you,' he said; 'proper spirit o' Christmas. Ah'll be back then,' and he walked out and set off home with a spring in his step.

School lunch was a hurried affair even though Shirley had made one of my all-time favourite school dinners: mince and dumplings followed by gooseberry crumble and custard. Time was of the essence and all the staff, plus a few members of the Parent–Teacher Association, were already busy making preparations for the after-noon's party. Finally, at half past one, all the children were sitting on their chairs round the edge of the school hall and Jo was explaining the rules of the first game, Statues. Each class took its turn and was cheered on by friends in other classes and by brothers and sisters.

John Hartley's girls had soon settled in. Ten-year-old

Tracy had found a friend in Theresa Ackroyd, eight-year-old Louise was in animated conversation with Betsy Icklethwaite, while little Mo was sitting next to Victoria Alice Dudley-Palmer. Victoria Alice had brought her favourite doll to the party. It had been beautifully made and had a pretty porcelain face with ruby-red lips and long eyelashes. However, her long blue dress was slightly the worse for wear and needed stitching.

Little Mo Hartley was watching her. 'She's very pretty,' she said.

'Thank you,' said Victoria Alice.

'What's she called?' asked little Mo.

'Well, her real name is Annabelle Alexandra Dudley-Palmer and she's one of my favourite dolls, but last week she was Jesus.'

'Jesus?'

'Yes. In our nativity play.'

'Ah thought Jesus were a boy,' said Mo.

'Yes, he was, so Annabelle had to pretend,' said Victoria Alice.

'Did she get a clap when she was Jesus?' asked Mo. 'At my las' school, Jesus allus got a good clap.'

'Yes,' said Victoria Alice, 'and my mummy was crying and so was Mrs Earnshaw because Terry was a shepherd with a cough.'

'Ah 'ope Jesus didn't get a cough,' said Mo.

'No,' said Victoria Alice. 'I wrapped a tea towel round her face so she wouldn't get any germs.'

'What's germs?' asked Mo.

'Nasty things that give you a cold,' said Victoria Alice, proud of her medical knowledge.

'Please can ah 'old 'er?' asked Mo.

'Yes,' said Victoria Alice, 'because you're my friend.'

Little Mo beamed. 'Thank you . . . and *you're* my friend.'

The two tiny girls sat side by side. Mo rocked the doll gently and began to sing 'Rock-a-bye Jesus in a tree top'. Victoria Alice joined in and, totally oblivious to the noise of the party around them, they shared the peace of their private space and the sweetness of joint protectorship of a doll called Jesus.

After the games, while the children were enjoying afternoon break on the playground, we all helped Ruby to put out the dining tables. A few mothers had called in to help Shirley and Doreen in the kitchen to serve up jelly and ice cream following the crab-paste sandwiches, fairy cakes, jammy dodgers, mince pies and Penguin biscuits. The children considered this to be a feast and Doreen flexed her magnificent biceps as she walked around with a huge bowl of strawberry jelly, dolloping out second helpings as a reward to anyone who had actually eaten a crab-paste sandwich.

As usual, Ruby had been very generous and, with the help of daughter Racquel, she had bought a small gift for every child and these were hung on the Christmas tree. Early that morning, Jo had roped in Dan to blow up a hundred balloons and John Grainger had attached each one to a length of baling twine, ready to give out at the end of the day. At three o'clock when the last of the jelly had been devoured and the tables were put away, the children gathered round the

Christmas tree to sing carols accompanied by Sally on her guitar.

When parents drifted into the hall to collect their children and those belonging to friends and neighbours, Vera carefully checked off every pupil on her list to make sure each one went home safely and carrying a gift, a balloon, a miscellaneous collection of Christmas cards and any decorations they may have made. Slowly the hall emptied and Petula Dudley-Palmer collected Elisabeth Amelia and then sought out her younger daughter. She saw that Victoria Alice was sitting next to a little girl she did not recognize.

'Hello, Mummy. This is my new friend, she's going to be in my class and her name is Maureen but everyone calls her Mo,' said Victoria Alice breathlessly.

Petula crouched down. 'Hello, Mo,' she said and noticed that the little girl was hugging one of Victoria Alice's dolls. 'And do you like Annabelle?'

'Yes, thank you,' said Mo politely, 'but ah call 'er Jesus because it's Christmas time.'

'Ah yes, she was Jesus on Wednesday,' said Petula with a smile. She was also thinking that this little girl was very polite even if her clothing suggested she came from the council estate. Petula looked around at the throng of parents filling the hall. 'Where's your mummy?' she asked.

'She's in 'eaven,' said little Mo.

Petula looked at the little girl and cool fingers of sadness touched her heart.

'That means she must have been good, doesn't it, Mummy?' said Victoria Alice.

'Yes, darling, it does,' said Petula quietly.

Suddenly the giant figure of John Hartley arrived. He had collected Tracy and Louise and he smiled when he saw his youngest daughter. ''Ello, poppet,' he said softly. ''Ave you 'ad a good time?'

'Yes, Daddy,' said Mo, 'and this is m'new friend, Victoria, an' this is 'er doll, Jesus.'

'Jesus,' said John in surprise.

'It's a long story,' said Petula with a smile. 'I'm Petula, by the way – Victoria Alice's mother.'

'Pleased to meet you, Petula. I'm John Hartley.'

'Are these your daughters?' asked Petula.

'Yes,' said John. 'Well, three of 'em, an' there's two more starting at t'big school after Christmas.'

'You've got a busy time coming up with five daughters,' said Petula.

John grinned. 'I certainly 'ave,' he said.

'Mummy,' said Victoria Alice, 'please could Mo look after Jesus for Christmas because she likes her?'

'I thought she was one of your favourite dolls, dear,' said Petula.

'She is, Mummy,' said Victoria Alice.

'Then you mus' keep it, luv,' said John.

Victoria Alice gave her mother a searching look. 'But, Mummy, Mr Evans said it's more important to *give* than receive.'

Petula looked at her daughter and her heart melted. Then she glanced up at John. 'The vicar is right, of course, darling,' she said. 'So, if it's all right with Mr Hartley . . . ?'

John nodded and Mo picked up the doll and gave

it a kiss. 'C'mon, Jesus,' she said, 'y'coming 'ome wi' me.'

Petula took her girls to the cloakroom and made sure they were muffled up before they walked out to their Rolls-Royce. Snow was falling again.

'I think it's a tube of Smarties,' said Elisabeth Amelia to her little sister as they both felt the wrapping round Ruby's Christmas presents.

'It's very kind of Mrs Smith to give you all a gift,' said Petula and it occurred to her that such a gesture must have been difficult for our school caretaker with her small income.

'It's like Mr Evans said,' said Victoria Alice. It was clear that Joseph's words, each one like a perfect snowflake, had settled on the shoulders of this little girl. Her eyes were bright with understanding. 'Christmas is a time for *giving* as well, isn't it, Mummy?'

Petula Dudley-Palmer picked up her younger daughter and hugged her as only a mother can. 'Yes, darling, it is – and I am so proud of you.'

Elisabeth Amelia and Victoria Alice clambered into the back of the Rolls-Royce with their balloons and Petula started the engine. 'Oh dear,' she said as she tried to accelerate away. The wheels were spinning and sinking further into the fresh layer of snow.

There was a tap on the window. It was John Hartley. 'Would y'like a push?' he shouted.

'Oh, yes, please, if you would,' said Petula.

John was a man of great strength and he braced himself against the back of the car. Moments later the car moved forwards and spinning wheels began to grip.

'Thank you so much,' shouted Mrs Dudley-Palmer and her daughters waved out of the back window as they slowly accelerated away towards Morton Road.

John and his girls trudged off towards the council estate. Above their heads the full moon lit up Ragley village with cold white light and, beneath the skeletal branches of the horse-chestnut trees, shadows of black lace patterned the frozen snow beneath their feet.

'Well done, Daddy,' shouted Mo. 'Y'remembered . . . it's better t'*give* than t'receive.'

''Ow d'you mean, luv?' asked John.

She looked up with a big smile and wrapped her scarf round a doll called Jesus. 'Well, y'gave 'er a push.'

Chapter Nine

A Present for Christmas

Visited school to collect holiday mail.
Extract from the Ragley School Logbook:
Wednesday, 23 December 1981

I looked in Dixon's window and there it was, a wonder of modern technology, a VHS Home Video Recorder, and I knew I must have it. It was the perfect present for Christmas.

The centre of York looked and felt like Siberia and the pavements were crusted with ice. It was just before closing time on Wednesday, 23 December, and I walked into the brightly lit store and was soon in conversation with an assistant whose tufty hair and prominent front teeth gave him an uncanny resemblance to Bugs Bunny.

'Y'can record an' play back in colour or black an' white,' he said; 'in fac', y'can even record when y'telly is switched off!' This defied all logic but he clearly knew his stuff and was determined to milk every last drop out of his sales patter. Whoever had trained him had done a good job. 'An' best o' t'lot,' he said with his slightly scary Bugs Bunny grin, 'y'get a free 'older that'll tek *fourteen* cassettes.' The emphasis on the word fourteen was impressive and, in that moment, I realized my life would be incomplete without a VHS cassette holder.

'I'll take it,' I said.

For a moment he looked surprised, until he thought of his commission and then hopped triumphantly towards the till.

'You *will* show me how to use it, won't you?' I asked a little desperately. 'I'm not the most technologically-minded person.'

He looked at me with forced compassion. 'It's all in t'book o' rules,' he said, waving the instruction manual. 'A ten-year-old could do it.' It flickered across my mind that he was probably right. If I got stuck I could always ask the children in my class, particularly those who were already more competent than I was on the school computer.

With a heavy box under my arm, I negotiated the route back to my car and drove home to Kirkby Steepleton. I smiled as I neared Bilbo Cottage. A world of recording James Bond films every bank holiday for years to come stretched out before me.

Snow was falling again as I parked my Morris Minor Traveller on the driveway and staggered to the front door with the cumbersome box. I rattled the brass knocker and Beth opened the door. 'Hello, Santa,' she said with a grin. 'Whatever have you got there?'

'You'll love it,' I said. 'It's a present for *all* of us.'

I hung up my snow-covered duffel coat and old college scarf in the hallway and then took off my damp Kicker shoes.

'Your mother and Aunt May have been cooking,' said Beth with a wry smile. Every Christmas, my little Scottish mother, Margaret, and her sister, May, came to visit me for the Christmas holiday and then departed for Glasgow to spend Hogmanay with their friends. Cooking was not their forte. The Prestige pressure cooker I had bought for them four Christmases ago was still in pristine condition in its box. Meanwhile, the smell of burnt sprouts filled the air.

Beth and I walked into the kitchen, where a pan of something that resembled sheep droppings was steaming on the draining board.

'It's nae like the recipe in the book, May,' said Margaret doubtfully.

The two sisters were like two identical bookends with their grey curly hair and matching Glasgow Rangers aprons as they stared at the smoking cannonade of blackened sprouts.

'Well, I followed that wee girl, Dahlia Smith, to the letter, Margaret,' said Aunt May, who used a distinctive but entirely understandable version of the English language.

'I think it's *Delia*, Aunt May,' I said.

'Y'nae wrang there, Jackie-boy,' said Aunt May, who, like my mother, was also slightly deaf. 'That's what I said . . . She's the queen's knees at cookery, is Dahlia.'

Christmas was going to be a little different this year.

Beth had decided to stay at Bilbo Cottage over the holiday before our visit to Hampshire to spend New Year with her parents. My mother and Beth had hit it off immediately, particularly when she saw the transformation to my kitchen. Now everything had a place and there was a sense of order. 'It's nae like Fred Karno's any more in there, Jack. She's a cannie wee lassie,' she announced appreciatively.

I hurried back into the hallway to collect the large box. 'Well, I have a surprise present for all of us,' I said magnanimously. 'It's a video recorder, so we can record all our favourite programmes and then watch them whenever we like over the holiday.' It all sounded so simple. 'So, Mother, why don't you and Aunt May go in the lounge and make a selection?'

This seemed to go down well and Beth was relieved to have the kitchen to herself. While she prepared a hotpot supper, I unpacked the video recorder and Margaret and May flicked through the pages of the Christmas edition of the *Radio Times*.

'I'd like t'see that bonnie wee boy Cliff Richard in *Summer Holiday*,' said Margaret, 'and we nae canna miss the Queen's speech on Christmas Day, Jack.'

'OK, Mother,' I said with a frown. The instructions for the video recorder had been written by someone who no doubt had a doctorate in rocket science but, sadly, was unable to communicate in coherent sentences.

'And I dinna want t'blow my own crumpet, Jack,' said Aunt May, pointing to the Boxing Day film *Dr No*, 'but I once met that lovely Scottish boy Sean Connery in Glasgow.'

'Oh, that's good,' I said without conviction as I wondered why the diagram bore no relation to the back of the video box.

'There's too much tae see and not enough time tae fit it all in,' said Margaret.

I decided to leave them to it and walked into the kitchen. The smell of cooking was delicious. I walked up behind Beth and slipped my arms around her waist. 'Our first Christmas together,' I said and kissed her cheek.

'Jack, I'm concentrating,' said Beth with a smile.

'So am I,' I said and kissed her again.

She turned away from the bubbling pan and kissed me on the lips. 'There . . . Now go and play with your new toy while I get some hot food for everyone.' Her eyes were bright with light and love and, feeling content, I returned to do battle with my instruction booklet.

It was shortly before eight o'clock when we finally finished a hearty meal at the pine kitchen table. Then we wandered into the lounge and I added a few dry logs to the roaring fire. Beth put a bowl of satsumas and a box of sticky dates on the coffee table and helped me serve drinks. Soon, Margaret and May had kicked off their tartan slippers and were sipping port and lemon like contented kittens, while Beth curled up on the sofa with a glass of white wine. I filled my tankard from the huge can of Watney's Party Seven Draught Bitter in the kitchen and settled down next to her to watch the annual treat, *The Morecambe and Wise Christmas Show*, with Susannah York and Alvin Stardust.

'It's nae Christmas without Morecambe and Wise, Margaret,' shouted Aunt May.

'Och aye,' Margaret yelled back. Their deafness was clearly worse this year, so a noisy Christmas was in store.

My mother seemed to be shuffling about. 'Is everything all right, Margaret?' said Beth. They had quickly established first-name terms.

'Ah'm havin' trouble wi ma seet,' said Margaret.

'Oh dear,' said Beth.

'Would you like a cushion, Mother?' I asked.

'Nae, Jack. Use y'common sense: how's that gonna help me *see* better?' Margaret took off her spectacles and rubbed the lenses vigorously on the hem of her skirt, while Beth gave me a wide-eyed smile.

On Christmas Eve morning the back road from Kirkby Steepleton had been cleared by Deke Ramsbottom in his snow-plough and Beth and I negotiated the three-mile journey carefully. Beth had some presents to wrap, so I dropped her off at her rented cottage on Morton Road and agreed to pick her up before lunchtime.

A warm drink seemed a good idea so I pulled up on the High Street outside Nora's Coffee Shop. When I walked in, the Christmas number one record, 'Don't You Want Me?' by the Sheffield group The Human League was blasting out on the old red and chrome juke-box.

''Appy Chwistmas, Mr Sheffield,' shouted Nora from behind the coffee machine. 'Fwothy coffee?'

'Yes, please, Nora,' I replied.

'An' a cweam cake,' added Nora, always keen for extra business, 'fwesh in yesterday?'

'Thanks, Nora.' I glanced up at the large poster on the wall behind the counter advertising the Ragley Amateur Dramatic Society's annual New Year's Eve pantomime. This year it was *Goldilocks and the Three Bears*. Nora, as usual, had the star part and she was pictured in a bright-yellow dress and a tightly fastened alpine corset. At her feet sat the Buttle twins wearing a pair of moth-eaten bear costumes and, incongruously, eight-year-old Harold Bustard wearing a sheep costume as, at the time of the photograph, a third bear costume had not been obtained.

'Good luck with the pantomime, Nora,' I said, thinking that *Goldilocks and the Two Bears and a Sheep* had the makings of an interesting adaptation. A tired-looking cake and a cup of steaming froth appeared on the counter.

'Final dwess wehearsal nex' week, Mr Sheffield,' said Nora.

This year the producer, Felicity Miles-Humphreys, had decided to feature Abba songs and Nora had been given two solos. On reflection, the choices could have been made with a little more sensitivity as Nora could regularly be overheard singing 'I Have a Dweam' and 'Super Twooper' in the room above the Coffee Shop. You could not fault Nora for enthusiasm. She always sang with gusto but, sadly, without the letter 'R'.

I sat at the furthest table from the juke-box and picked up an *Easington Herald & Pioneer*. Over a photograph of the frozen River Ouse, the headline read, 'As bad as the mini-Ice Age of 1963'. I sipped my coffee and read the sports news. The England batsman, Geoffrey Boycott, had become the most prolific run scorer in test history when he overtook the 8,032 runs scored by Sir Garfield

Sobers. The forty-one-year-old Yorkshireman had passed the record after scoring eighty-two runs on the opening day of the Third Test Match against India in Delhi. With Yorkshire modesty, he had then presented the Indian prime minister, Indira Gandhi, with a copy of his book *In the Fast Lane*. I smiled: a knighthood couldn't be far away.

Meanwhile, Dorothy Humpleby was wiping the tables with a damp dishcloth and it was clear her mind was on other things. "Morning, Mr Sheffield,' she said. She was wearing a white polo-necked sweater, red hotpants, her favourite Wonder Woman boots and dangly Christmas-tree earrings.

'Good morning, Dorothy. Merry Christmas,' I said.

Dorothy launched into what was on her mind. 'My Malcolm's buying me summat special f'Christmas, Mr Sheffield,' she said. 'Ah took 'im into York and ah showed 'im.'

'And what's that, Dorothy?' I asked.

'It's a Toyah Willcox make-up set.'

'Toyah Willcox?'

'Yes, Mr Sheffield. She's a sexy rock singer an' real groovy wi' wild 'air.' She took a newspaper cutting from her hipster hotpants and put it on the counter. Under a photograph of Toyah Willcox the caption read: 'A palette of powders and lipsticks and power-packed angular make-up for the canvas that is your face'.

'Looks good, Dorothy,' I said dubiously.

'Ah love Toyah Willcox,' said Dorothy, 'an' she wears this black bodysuit when she's singing,' she added, a dreamy look in her eyes. 'It's reight good.'

Nora shuffled over and looked at the cutting. 'That'll be a weally nice Chwistmas pwesent, Dowothy,' she said. ''E's wight genewous, is Malcolm. What are y'getting 'im?'

'Dunno yet, Nora,' said Dorothy. 'Ah'm going to t'Christmas market this afternoon,' and she wandered off to wipe the grubby counter.

At a table on the other side of the Coffee Shop, Big Dave Robinson was deep in thought – and *not* about his new girlfriend, namely Fenella 'Nellie' Lovelace. An unexpected crisis had emerged in his life. He had just paid sixteen pence to Prudence Golightly for his weekly copy of *Roy of the Rovers* and he stared in horror at the cartoon-strip spread out before him on the Formica-top table. Roy Race, the Melchester Rovers player-manager, had been shot and rushed to hospital in a critical state. 'Bloody 'ell,' muttered Big Dave.

'What's up, Dave?' asked Little Malcolm as he arrived with two large mugs of sweet tea.

'Roy Race 'as been shot!' exclaimed Big Dave.

Little Malcolm recoiled in shock and spilled some tea down his donkey jacket. 'But Roy's t'greatest footballer that ever lived,' he said in a strained voice. Then he put down the tea, took off his bobble cap and bowed his head. 'They can't let 'im die.'

'It sez 'ere,' mumbled Big Dave, 'that Sam Barlow, t'club chairman, 'as appointed Blackie Gray as t'caretaker-player-manager, so ah s'ppose it meks sense.'

'Y'reight there, Dave,' said Little Malcolm. The two cousins took the fortunes of their favourite fictional football team very seriously. They were not the only ones. On the next page of the comic, 'get well' messages had poured in from the world of football, including Alf Ramsay, Trevor Francis, Malcolm Macdonald and Paul Mariner. There was even a message from Morecambe and Wise.

'Nellie'll be upset,' said Big Dave. 'She reads *Roy of t'Rovers* ev'ry week. She'll be 'eartbroken.'

Nora didn't miss any of the gossip in her Coffee Shop. 'What y'getting Nellie f'Chwistmas, Dave?' she shouted from behind the counter.

'Dunno yet, Nora,' replied Dave. 'Ah were thinking o' some shin pads f'when she plays football or a box t'put 'er darts in.'

Nora shook her head. 'No, Dave. It needs t'be summat womantic,' she said, ever the matchmaker.

Dorothy tottered over on her four-inch heels, gave the table a half-hearted wipe and put two huge bacon sand-wiches in front of Ragley's favourite binmen. 'Y'reight there, Nora,' said Dorothy. 'Women like a bit o' romance . . . don't they, Malcolm?'

Little Malcolm gave a nervous twitch and poured tomato sauce over his boiler-suit trousers instead of his sandwich. Dorothy immediately began to mop it off his lap with a damp cloth and Little Malcolm went a shade of puce. 'Y-yes, Dorothy,' he mumbled.

'Oh well,' said Dave, eager to get back to the crisis in his comic, 'ah'll prob'ly go to t'Christmas market.'

At a table next to the doorway, two fifteen-year-olds who had been in my class when I first arrived in Ragley, Claire Bradshaw and Anita Cuthbertson, were deep in conversation. The debate concerned whether Pixie boots were better than suede stilettos. They decided to get a pair of each from Easington market with the money they had been given for Christmas and share them, as they both took a size five.

''Appy Christmas, Mr Sheffield,' they chorused as I walked to the door.

'Happy Christmas, Claire . . . Anita,' I said, 'and I hope Santa pays you a visit tonight,' I added with a grin.

'We were 'oping f'Shakin' Stevens, Mr Sheffield,' said Claire. They both giggled and it occurred to me that teenagers grew up quickly these days.

On the High Street, outside Piercy's Butcher's Shop, assorted members of the church choir and a few passers-by were singing Christmas carols. Joseph Evans stood alongside, rattling a bucket of loose change as busy shoppers hurried past.

'Hark the herald angels sing,' they sang, 'glory to the new-born king.'

I walked in to collect my Christmas turkey and looked at the usual collection of pork pies, joints of gammon and pig trotters. It was clear that Old Tommy didn't exactly go overboard on Christmas decorations. There was nothing frivolous about the Ragley village butcher's. As a token gesture, on the counter was an empty bottle of India Pale Ale with a red candle stuck in the neck. Around the base were a few desultory sprigs of holly.

''Appy Christmas, Mr Sheffield,' said Old Tommy. 'Y'turkey's a reight big 'un this year.' He handed over the giant bird and I staggered out to my car, breathed on my key, unlocked the frozen double doors and put it in the boot.

Then I went back to join the choir and I stood beside Vera. It was good timing for, after a lively rendition of 'We Three Kings', Old Tommy came out with his grandson, Young Tommy, who was carrying a huge pan of steaming mulled wine made to Old Tommy's special recipe. 'There y'are,' he said. 'This'll mek y'toes curl.' He wasn't wrong. I sipped on a mug of the evil brew and gasped.

Vera's cheeks flushed as she drank the potent mixture. 'It gets stronger every year,' she said appreciatively.

Soon the cold was forgotten and I wandered off to complete my food shopping in Prudence Golightly's General Stores. When I walked in, Deirdre Coe was complaining bitterly. Deirdre was one of our least popular villagers for whom rudeness was a way of life.

'Thirty pence a pound f'sprouts!' she shouted. 'A fortnight ago they were only eighteen pence.'

'I'm sorry, Deirdre,' said Prudence gently, 'but it's because of the frozen ground. The farmers can't harvest the crops.'

'Well, ah'll tell y'summat f'nowt,' added Deirdre in disgust, 'ah'm not paying eighty pence for a small cauli'.'

'That's fine, Deirdre,' said Prudence politely, 'so is that all?'

Deirdre slammed a few coins on the counter and stormed out, almost knocking me over in the doorway. 'Move over, Mr 'eadteacher,' she grumbled as she left the doorbell ringing madly.

'Merry Christmas, Miss Golightly, and . . . merry

Christmas, Jeremy,' I said as I approached the counter. Jeremy, the teddy bear and Prudence's lifelong friend, was sitting on his usual shelf next to a tin of loose leaf Lyon's Tea and an old advertisement for Hudson's Soap and Carter's Little Liver Pills. Prudence made all his clothes and, on this festive day, he wore a bright-red ski suit, black boots and a white bobble hat.

'Merry Christmas, Mr Sheffield,' said the diminutive Miss Golightly, 'and how is Miss Henderson?'

'Fine, thank you,' I said. 'We're spending our first Christmas together.'

'Ah yes, that must be wonderful,' she said quietly with a faraway look in her eyes.

Five minutes later, with a large bag of fruit and vegetables, I walked back to my car. Jimmy Poole and his little sister, Jemima, were standing outside the village Pharmacy. Jimmy was gripping a straining dog lead on the end of which his Yorkshire terrier, Scargill, was eager to bite my ankles. Wisely, I kept my distance. 'Hello, Jimmy, hello, Jemima, happy Christmas,' I said, 'and a happy Christmas to you too, Scargill,' I added with a forced smile.

'Happy Chrithmath, Mr Theffield,' said Jimmy. He looked down knowingly at his little sister and gave me a wink. 'Thanta's coming tonight an' we're gonna leave 'im a glath of therry an' a minth pie.'

'That's right, Mr Sheffield,' said Jemima. 'I've asked him for a Sindy doll.'

'And I've athked for an Acthon Man Tholdier,' added Jimmy.

'Well, I'm sure he'll come to your house,' I said. Then I

loaded my shopping in my car and drove off up Morton Road to collect Beth.

After a late lunch at Bilbo Cottage we all set off to the Christmas market in Easington. Dusk was falling as we drove up Ragley High Street towards Easington Road and we slowed up outside Pratt's Hardware Emporium. Timothy's Christmas lights were the best I had ever seen. There was even an inflatable Santa tied to the chimney-pot.

'It's all lit up like Blackpool hallucinations,' said Aunt May, wide-eyed with appreciation.

When we arrived in Easington the Christmas market was brightly lit with stalls set up around the edge of the large cobbled square. A tall Christmas tree had been erected next to the war memorial and, on the stone steps, a choir was singing accompanied by the Ragley and Morton Brass Band. It was a festive scene and snow was falling again as I parked in one of the side streets.

Ragley villagers were out in force and many parents waved a greeting as they searched for a late bargain in the market or in the shops that bordered the square. Outside the toy shop, Heathcliffe and Terry were staring wide-eyed at a Hornby high-speed train set and Mrs Earnshaw was staring equally wide-eyed at the price tag, which read £29.95. She had fifteen pounds in her pocket and presents for three children to buy. While the boys were engrossed watching the train go round the track she bought a Connect 4 for £3.99, a Kerplunk game for £3.99 and, as an afterthought for little Dallas Sue-Ellen, a £1.85 Snowman soft toy based on the delightful 1979 book by Raymond Briggs. This left her with enough to buy some chocolate coins to put in their stockings.

'Come on,' she said hurriedly. 'Santa'll bring yer a train set when yer older.'

John Hartley was looking in the same shop window and with five daughters he had to make some careful choices. With little Mo in mind, he was looking at a Corgi Magic Roundabout Playground in a very large box. John knew that when you hadn't a lot of money it helped to go for *size*. A large box was always more exciting for children to open on Christmas morning. Then he wandered over to a stall where a man with a long pony-tail and a very loud voice was telling a gathering crowd that he had the perfect gift for teenagers. 'Gather round, ev'rybody. 'Ere's t'biggest bargain on t'market, all t'way from 'Ong Kong . . . state-of-the-art transistor radios shaped like a bottle o' Coca Cola an' a cheeseburger. Kids'll luv 'em! Six quid each or ten quid for the two.' John passed over a ten-pound note. 'Two down, three t'go,' he muttered to himself and walked back to the toy shop.

Meanwhile the two fifteen-year-olds, Claire Bradshaw and Anita Cuthbertson, were staring longingly at a small green plastic radio that hung from your neck on a strap. 'C'mon, girls,' shouted Pony-tail Man. 'This is the Strapper, t'latest in electronic innovation – an it's gonna be all t'rage f'Christmas 1981.'

Claire and Anita knew life wouldn't be worth living without one and started counting how much money they had got left altogether. 'We've only got four pound fifty between us,' said Claire.

"Ow much are they?' asked Anita.

Pony-tail Man quickly peeled off the sticky label with £4.00 written on it, leant over the trestle table and whispered, 'Your lucky day, girls: it's a bargain at four pound fifty.' After all, he thought, as his old granddad used to say, 'Christmas begins at 'ome.'

Across the road in the record shop, Ruby's son Duggie was staring lovingly at Abba's latest LP 'The Visitors', which was already riding high in the *Melody Maker* album charts. His favourite track, 'One of Us', had been released as a single and had shot into the top ten. 'It wouldn't be Christmas without an Abba album,' he said to the teenage girl behind the counter. She stared in admiration at his Boomtown Rats hairstyle that hid the half-smoked Castella cigar behind his ear and wondered if he had a girlfriend. Sadly, she was unaware that she would have to be Agnetha Fältskog's twin sister to stand a chance. Duggie placed the record lovingly in his off-licence carrier bag next to the four cans of Watneys Pale Ale he had just purchased for £1.09 and the new apron for his mother at 99 pence. With change out of a fiver and in less than twenty minutes, 'Deadly' Duggie Smith, the undertaker's assistant, had completed his Christmas shopping.

Geoffrey Dudley-Palmer was working late at the Rowntree's factory or, at least, he was sitting at his desk. Along with Easter, it was their busiest time of the year and, as a top executive, Geoffrey wanted to set an example. He was content in the knowledge that he had ordered his wife's Christmas present. A brand-new state-of-the-art

Jacussi whirlpool bath was being delivered from Leeds and installed next week. Geoffrey knew that Petula loved the latest in home gadgets and this was something very special. It also only took a single telephone call made by his secretary. Geoffrey was a firm believer in economy of effort.

Meanwhile, back in his luxury home, Victoria Alice and Elisabeth Amelia were sitting under their twelve-feet-tall artificial Christmas tree with silver-foil branches and looking curiously at a collection of beautifully wrapped presents that had just appeared. One of them had a torn edge and Elisabeth Amelia picked it up. 'You shouldn't look,' said Victoria Alice but Elisabeth Amelia's curiosity had to be satisfied. She peeled away a little more of the paper. 'It looks like dog food,' she said forlornly.

'Perhaps we're getting a dog,' said Victoria Alice. Their eyes shot wide with excitement. Elisabeth Amelia replaced the parcel carefully and they tiptoed away, crept back up the stairs and into their bedroom to hang up their stockings.

A mile away, in his bedroom in the vicarage, Joseph Evans was admiring his gift for Vera. He had bought a beautifully illustrated hardback book entitled *Advanced Cross-Stitch* by Emily Blenkinsop, one of Vera's heroines – in fact, probably a close third behind Margaret Thatcher and Mother Theresa. He had wrapped it in lavender tissue paper, Vera's favourite colour, and purchased a pink bow from the General Stores to complete the ensemble. He was sure she would consider it the perfect gift and he was right.

*   *   *

Vera, sitting at her dressing table in her bedroom, had also bought a book. She thought *Wine-making for Beginners* would be perfect for her younger brother. It didn't occur to her that Joseph considered himself to be at least in the *Advanced* class of this noble art. She only knew that he produced copious bottles of a brew that tasted like a subtle blend of Domestos and dandelion leaves and left a smell in her kitchen reminiscent of something the cat had dragged in. She would never know that on Christmas morning, when Joseph came to read the title of his gift, he would take a deep breath and pray for forgiveness for the unappreciative thoughts that flickered through his mind.

Back in Bilbo Cottage I was in my tiny study, wrapping my presents. I had bought a beautiful necklace for Beth and an assortment of gifts for my mother and Aunt May, including a large tin of Farrah's Original Harrogate Toffee, which, along with Kendal Mint Cake, was their favourite sweet.

It turned out to be a memorable Christmas, mainly because Beth and I were together. Late on Christmas Eve, I finally managed to set the new video recorder for a feast of festive viewing over the holiday period. Then, while Margaret and May switched on BBC1 and settled down to watch *The Good Old Days* from the Leeds City Varieties Theatre, Beth and I drove through the snow to attend the Midnight Mass service.

*   *   *

A Present for Christmas

Christmas Day flashed past in a whirl of presents and party hats. The giant turkey took longer than expected to cook so I had to record the Queen's speech. Beth loved her necklace and her present to me was an electric drill with lots of attachments and the step-by-step promise by a beautifully coiffeured man in a checked shirt that anything from a bookcase to a set of cupboards could be fitted in minutes. Unfortunately it seemed that the instructions had been written by the same mad scientist who had composed those for the video recorder. So, all in all, despite the bursts of laughter, it was largely a frustrating day of indigestion and drill bits.

It was Boxing Day when we all finally relaxed and settled down to watch my first attempts at recording. Anticipation was high as Margaret, May and Beth stared hopefully at the flickering screen. The good news was I had got the *times* of the transmissions correct; the bad news was I had clearly not mastered how to select the right *channels*.

So it was that on Christmas Eve, instead of *Summer Holiday* with Cliff Richard and the Shadows on BBC2, I had recorded *Playschool* on BBC1. It got worse. On Christmas Day, the Queen's speech was replaced by the end of a 1925 black-and-white Harold Lloyd film. Finally, instead of the big Christmas Day Bond film, *Dr No*, I had recorded *Charlie Brown's Christmas*.

This was an inauspicious start to my technological revolution. My present for Christmas had not quite worked out as I had hoped. However, it did mean we could play charades instead.

Chapter Ten

The Secrets of Sisters

Mrs Smith, caretaker, checked the school boiler to ensure frost protection over the rest of the holiday period.
Extract from the Ragley School Logbook:
Thursday, 31 December 1981

The tall forests of Hampshire were bare of leaves and stood like frozen sentinels guarding the icy road.

It was New Year's Eve and the journey from Yorkshire had been slow. Finally the orange street lamps of Little Chawton pierced the evening mist as my car crunched past the Cricketer public house next to the snow-covered village green and an ancient cast-iron, icicle-hung water pump. The year 1982 beckoned but some things didn't change. The flint-faced cottages of Hampshire were fixed in time, the heritage of a bygone age.

I turned left in front of a church with a square Norman tower and slowed up as we passed a row of neat half-timbered thatched cottages with crooked window frames. Finally, I coaxed my Morris Minor Traveller on to the gravelled driveway of Austen Cottage as another flurry of snow sprinkled the brightly lit porch.

'Here at last,' said Beth with relief, 'and Laura's arrived already.' Her sister's brand-new, crimson-red Audi Quattro was parked by the side of the garage.

Beth's father, John Henderson, a weather-beaten fifty-eight-year-old with steel-grey hair, appeared from the porch. He looked relaxed in a blue denim shirt, knitted cardigan and thick cord trousers and when he hugged Beth the bond between father and daughter was obvious. 'Welcome home,' he said softly.

'Hello, Dad. Good to be here,' said Beth.

I unlocked the rear doors and pulled out two overnight bags. John picked one up and shook my hand. His handshake was firm and, he being six feet tall, his eyes were on a level with mine. He gave me a warm smile. 'Well done, Jack,' he said. 'Glad you've made it safely.'

We walked into the spacious terracotta-tiled kitchen and it was just as I remembered it: neat, organized yet homely. A vase of holly with bright berries stood in the bay window and, on the old Welsh dresser, a collection of well-thumbed Jane Austen novels was stacked on the top shelf next to a set of *Wind in the Willows* decorative plates.

Diane Henderson was busy adding a few herbs to her famous watercress soup, a local speciality. Like both her daughters she had a slim figure, high cheek-bones and green eyes. She pushed a strand of soft blonde hair behind her ear, untied her blue-striped apron and threw it over the back of a chair. 'Beth,' she said, 'you must be tired. Come and sit down. You too, Jack.'

I gave her a hesitant peck on the cheek and sat at the old pine kitchen table. There was something about Diane that made me feel uneasy and I guessed I knew why. While Beth had always been the woman for me, in the past I had enjoyed a brief 'relationship' with her younger sister, Laura. I felt that Diane, unlike her husband, still had to make her mind up about me.

Laura was sitting at the kitchen table, blowing on the surface of a cup of coffee and sipping it gently. Even after all this time her beauty still surprised me. 'Hello, Laura,' I said, a little lamely, while pushing my Buddy Holly spectacles a bit further up the bridge of my nose.

She stood up quickly and looked me up and down. As always she was dressed to perfection, in a Daks country classic suit in herringbone tweed with patch pockets and knee-high brown leather boots. Her long brown hair tumbled over her shoulders as she reached up and kissed me on the cheek. The perfume was familiar. 'Hello, Jack,' she said lightly, 'and how's the village teacher?' I noticed that her cool fingertips gently stroked the back of my hand before she returned to her seat at the kitchen table.

'I'm fine, thanks,' I said. 'How about you?'

'Still at Liberty's in London,' she said. 'I'm the assistant manager in the fashion department, so can't complain.'

'Oh, are you still working with Desmond?' I said. Laura had been dating her wealthy manager, Desmond Dix, and I got the impression John Henderson didn't approve.

'No,' she said, shaking her head defiantly. 'He moved on . . . In fact we both did.'

'I'm sorry to hear that, Laura.'

'Don't be, Jack,' she said flippantly and tossed her hair

back from her shoulders. 'He's history now.' There was a hard edge to her voice but her green eyes were soft and vulnerable. 'He didn't come up to expectations.'

John Henderson glanced across the kitchen at his younger daughter but wisely kept his thoughts to himself, while Diane gave me a searching look and then returned to her cooking. I took a deep breath. The silence that followed felt like a raging storm.

Beth and I went upstairs to unpack. Significantly, we were in separate rooms and I found myself in the familiar small single bedroom that I had occupied the last time I visited. It was quiet and cosy with rough-plastered, whitewashed walls, ancient beams and framed pictures of steam engines and pretty watercolour views of Hampshire villages. I wondered where Beth and I might sleep in this house *after* we were married.

Soon we all gathered in the kitchen round a table covered with a snowy-white cloth and tucked into Diane's delicious watercress soup. This was followed by a wonderful supper of cold turkey, large slices of roast pork with apple sauce, new potatoes, pickled beetroot, ripe tomatoes, fresh bread and local butter, all washed down with a bottle of John's sharp, dry, home-made cherry wine. Diane's sherry trifle completed the feast and, finally, as we relaxed over coffee and mince pies dusted with icing sugar, Beth broke the growing silence. 'Come on, everybody, I'll tell you our wedding plans.'

Laura stared into her coffee, Diane gave her a searching look, while John smiled. 'We want to help as much as we can,' he said.

'Thanks, Dad,' said Beth.

'Beth . . . we thought we could pay for your dress,' said Diane, 'and the flowers.'

Beth stretched across the table and squeezed her mother's hand. 'That's very kind, Mother,' she said. She stood up and gave her parents a hug. 'And are you still happy about the wedding taking place in Yorkshire?' she asked.

'Yes. It makes sense,' said John.

'Most of your friends are up there,' said Diane, 'and, of course, the church is beautiful – and much bigger than our little church.'

'So roll on the twenty-ninth of May,' said John. He stood up and poured five glasses of his home-made wine. 'To the happy couple,' he said, raising his glass.

'To Beth and Jack,' said Diane.

'Beth . . . and Jack,' added Laura softly.

After the meal Beth and Diane did the washing-up and John went out to the woodshed to collect some logs for the fire. I walked out to the porch to get some fresh air. Around me the world was quiet under its mantle of snow. Now 1981 was almost over and I wondered what 1982 had in store. My life was about to change and I guessed the fields and forests of Hampshire and this thatched cottage would become a second home for me. I stepped outside and shivered in the cold night air.

'So, are you ready for married life, Jack?' It was Laura, a warm scarf thrown casually round her neck.

'Yes, I am.'

'And do you think you can live up to her expectations?'

Laura's gaze was steady and hard but her words were soft.

'I'll try,' I said, wondering where this was going.

'Jack, are you *really* happy?'

'Yes . . . Why?'

'I was just thinking that *we* had some good times together.'

'We did.'

'But not good enough.'

I thought it best to say nothing.

'She'll want to change you, Jack.'

'In what way?'

'You'll see.'

There was silence between us until John appeared with an armful of logs. 'Open the door, please, Laura,' he said and hurried inside.

I looked back at Laura. 'I don't understand,' I said.

She turned to walk back into the house. 'You will,' she said.

After she had gone her perfume lingered and I stood there until the cold began to seep into my bones. Above my head skeletal branches swayed in the breeze and whispered their ancient secrets beneath the eternal sky. Suddenly a falling star rent the heavens. It flickered briefly, a bright flame in the black velvet darkness, and burnt out, its life spent. It occurred to me that perhaps life really is an apocalypse: there is an end to everything.

Back in the low-beamed lounge, John was kneeling by the stone fireplace and putting logs on the fire. Beth and

Laura were chatting in the kitchen and Diane had gone upstairs to find a set of old but serviceable curtains that Beth thought would be perfect for our bedroom at Bilbo Cottage. John picked up the poker and levered some of the logs so that they crackled into life. 'Beth tells me she's given six months' notice on her cottage in Morton, Jack,' he said.

'That's right, John. She'll move in to Bilbo Cottage in early June after the honeymoon,' I said.

'I can give you a hand if you like, Jack. We'll be staying in her cottage for the wedding but I could stay on if you need me.'

'Thanks, John,' I said. 'I'll probably borrow a van to shift her belongings, so any help would be appreciated.'

'That reminds me,' he said, jumping up: 'there are some bits and pieces I promised Diane I would sort out for you,' and he walked out. I felt reassured that my future father-in-law was such a supportive man and, during the past year, we had become good friends. I guessed that Diane would take more time.

I wandered out into the hallway. The kitchen door was slightly ajar and Beth and Laura were whispering conspiratorially and sharing the secrets of sisters. Curious, I paused by the door.

Laura sounded insistent. 'Beth, are you *sure* about this wedding?'

'Why?' said Beth, sounding a little surprised.

'Well, it occurred to me that maybe Jack isn't the best person for you,' said Laura.

'Whatever do you mean?' asked Beth.

'Well, he's not exactly *ambitious*, is he?'

'Perhaps he's ambitious in a different way,' said Beth quietly; 'he has other goals in his life.'

'Beth, he'll never be more than a village schoolteacher,' said Laura. 'Is that what you really want?'

'Perhaps.'

'So . . . you're not sure,' said Laura.

'Yes, of course I'm sure. I didn't mean it that way,' insisted Beth.

There was a creak on the stairs above me and Diane appeared.

'Hello, Jack,' she said. 'Are you looking for John? I think he's in the garage.'

'Oh, thanks,' I said, feeling a little guilty. 'I'll go and find him.' Relieved to escape I put on my duffel coat and walked out to the garage, where John was searching through some old boxes in the rafters.

'Hi, Jack,' he said. 'Good timing. Can I pass this down to you?'

It was an old oak chest with a hinged lid. I put it down on the concrete floor and he descended the ladder and opened it. 'Diane's mother left all this stuff for her granddaughters. Doesn't look much but there's a lot of sentimental value here.' He lifted out a heavy brass candlestick and a few decorative plates. 'Diane wants the girls to have a look and share it out.' He smiled apologetically. 'Sorry if it looks as though we're trying to fill your cottage with junk.'

'Don't worry,' I said, 'we can take some back with us if you like.'

'Come on, then,' he said, 'let's get it in the hallway and then we'll have earned a pint.'

* * *

Back in the lounge, I sat down in an armchair next to an oak writing bureau and picked up a copy of *The Times*. The New Year's honours list included some familiar names, among them Sebastian Coe and Steve Ovett, gold-medal winners at the 1980 Moscow Olympics, who had been awarded, somewhat belatedly, the MBE. John returned with two bottles of local beer and two pint tankards. We settled down to share this unusual brew with its tooth-some malty aftertaste and a strange scent of lavender.

Beth and Laura arrived, each carrying a glass of wine, and sat on the sofa. Laura looked a little distracted and switched on the television set. Diane came in with a notebook and pencil, frowned at the television set and turned down the sound. Then she joined her daughters on the sofa and began chatting with them while *Elvis – the Movie,* with Kurt Russell, on BBC1 provided background entertainment.

'But, Laura, you *must* be chief bridesmaid,' said Diane, while scribbling in her notebook.

Laura was staring at the television set but her mind ap-peared to be on something else. 'I'm not sure,' she said.

'I was thinking of just *two* bridesmaids, Laura – you and Jo Hunter,' insisted Beth. 'So what do you think?'

Laura nodded and smiled but there was a hint of sad-ness in her eyes that had not gone unnoticed by Diane.

'Good, that's settled, then,' said Beth, but Diane was looking curiously at her younger daughter.

It was a relaxing evening and, as midnight approached, Diane turned up the volume on the television set. Barry

Took was looking back at 1981 with Judi Dench, Penelope Keith and Felicity Kendall. John retrieved a bottle of champagne from the fridge and poured five drinks. Then, as Big Ben chimed out twelve o'clock, we held hands in an awkward little circle and sang *Auld Lang Syne*. Beth was on my left and Laura on my right. 'Happy New Year, Beth,' I said and bent forward to kiss her. Then I turned to Laura. 'Happy New Year, Laura,' I said. 'I hope 1982 is all you wish for.' I leant forward to kiss her cheek.

She moved her face and our lips brushed lightly. 'So do I, Jack,' she whispered.

Half an hour later, we finished off the champagne and then settled down again to watch the *Hi-De-Hi!* team with Danny La Rue in their New Year programme from Pebble Mill. Laura still looked preoccupied and was the first to drift upstairs to bed. Finally, Beth and I kissed goodnight on the landing and it seemed strange sleeping alone on this special night. Outside, the wind sighed with the weight of memories while more snow pattered lightly against my bedroom window. I lay in my bed and reflected on the day. A new year stretched ahead and I prayed for happy times as sleep overtook me.

The next morning I opened my curtains and stared at the silent white world. There was no traffic as the villagers of Little Chawton enjoyed their bank holiday. Below me, weak winter sunshine reflected on the knapped flint walls. Suddenly there was a tap on the door and Beth came in with a cup of tea. She was wearing a short nightie and a warm dressing gown.

'Is this a vision I see before my eyes?' I said.

She sat down on the bed and put my hot drink on the bedside table. 'Don't get used to it, Jack. When we're at Bilbo Cottage I'll expect *you* to bring me tea each morning,' she said with a smile.

I pulled her towards me and kissed her. She responded and we lay in each other's arms. There was a creak of footsteps on the wooden floorboards outside the door. 'Now, why do I feel guilty about kissing my future husband?' she said, standing up quickly.

'Don't worry, I understand,' I said, 'and thanks for the tea.'

Beth squeezed my hand and hurried out again. Further down the corridor, Laura's door was open and, on impulse, Beth tapped on the door and walked in.

''Morning, big sister,' said Laura. She was sitting up in bed and yawning.

Beth sat on the chair by the window and stared thoughtfully at the frozen fields beyond.

'What's on your mind?' said Laura.

'Just thoughts,' said Beth.

'I know that look,' said Laura. 'We've shared too many secrets in this room, ever since we were children.'

Beth took a deep breath and gave her sister a level stare. 'Laura, you need to know that Jack and I are very happy together,' she said.

'I know.'

'So whatever happened in the past between you and Jack is *in* the past and that's where it needs to stay.'

'But—' said Laura.

'No, Laura, please don't,' said Beth quickly. 'In fact, don't say anything at all.'

Laura leant back against the pillow and hugged her knees.

'If Jack wants to remain as headteacher of his village school, then that's fine by me,' said Beth. 'I've come to realize that ambition matters nothing – especially if you haven't got the person you love to share it with.'

Laura sighed and pushed a few strands of hair behind her ears.

'Jack and I will be getting married on the twenty-ninth of May and we would both like you to be our bridesmaid. But if you can't cope with that, then that's fine.'

'I understand, Beth,' said Laura quietly. 'It's been difficult but I know I have to move on now . . . and I'll be happy to be your bridesmaid.'

Beth hugged her sister and, without another word, she walked back to her bedroom.

It was a lazy morning with tea and toast and conversations. Beth and Laura looked through the old chest and selected a few pieces of antique crockery and some miscellaneous brassware for themselves. They seemed at ease with each other and chatted about old times as each artefact brought back a special memory. Diane packed their treasures into two boxes and John and I loaded Beth's collection into the back of my car.

The grandfather clock in the entrance hall chimed midday. 'Come on, everybody,' shouted John. 'I've booked a table for half-twelve at the Cricketer.'

We all went to our rooms to change and Diane slipped into Beth's room.

'Beth,' she said, 'I have an important question for you.'

'Yes, Mother?'

'Are you *sure* he's the right man for you?'

'Yes, I am,' said Beth.

'I feel I have to ask,' said Diane: 'how can you be so sure?'

'Well, you see, Mother, I nearly lost him . . . and I never want to feel like that again.'

Diane nodded and hugged her daughter. 'That's how I felt with your father.' She smiled. 'Still do, in fact . . . And Laura, I worry about her.'

'I've spoken to her,' said Beth, 'and I don't think this will present any more problems.'

'Good,' said Diane, 'because if you hadn't spoken to her, I intended to.'

'I guessed you would, Mother,' said Beth with a smile. 'That's why I got in first.'

'Like mother, like daughter,' said Diane and her eyes were moist.

'I do love him, Mother.'

'I know . . . and, I have to admit, he's a good man.'

Downstairs I was standing with John and he was shaking his head. 'Why do women take so long to get ready, Jack?'

'No idea,' I said.

'And what can they find to talk about?'

I shrugged my shoulders. 'Don't know, John.'

'Women!' he muttered and went to find his car keys.

We all climbed in John's Land-Rover and drove out of the gateway of Austen Cottage. The three women were on the back seat, still in animated conversation about bouquets and bridesmaids, while I sat in the front with John and admired the scenery. Hampshire really was a beautiful county and I stared in awe at this land of water meadows and breath-taking forests. The snow-covered fields of rural England stretched out before us in the receding mist. Next to the ancient church the gnarled roots of a tall weeping willow gripped the edges of a frozen pond and the bell tower of the old schoolhouse, faced with undressed flint, reflected the low morning sun with refracted colours of broken light.

The Cricketer pub was as I remembered it, with a roaring log fire, an array of hand-pulled local beers and farmers playing dominoes. A large noticeboard next to the bar displayed posters for a New Year quiz, a meeting of the parish council and *Raiders of the Lost Ark* with Harrison Ford now showing at the tiny local cinema.

We found a table and John pointed towards the 'Specials' on the chalkboard. There were only two dishes: 'Breast of Locally Shot Pigeon – pan-fried on a bed of braised lentils' and 'Steak and Honeydew Pie with mushrooms and shortcrust pastry'. It made a change from a menu dominated by watercress and I selected the steak pie.

It was a wonderful meal and, for the first time, I relaxed and felt part of Beth's family. There were no more searching looks from Diane, while Laura was full of the new challenges in her professional life. I mentioned this to John when we returned to Austen Cottage. The women were in the lounge, looking through Beth's bridal magazines, and we were sitting in the kitchen. He grinned and opened a bottle of his courgette wine. 'This is liquid

dynamite, Jack, with an alcohol content of ten per cent.'
He poured two generous glasses. 'Now try that.'

It was when we were on our third glass that life's little
problems seemed to disappear. John raised his glass.
'Jack, a word of advice and make this your New Year's
resolution: don't try to understand my daughters. I gave
that up long ago.'

As resolutions go, it seemed better than most. After all,
understanding women is an elusive dream – always close
but for ever out of reach.

Chapter Eleven

The Knock on the Door

At the end of the first week of the Spring Term there were 91 children registered on roll.

Extract from the Ragley School Logbook:
Friday, 8 January 1982

Winter, bound in iron, cloaked in frost, had tightened its grip on Kirkby Steepleton.

Out of the bedroom window of Bilbo Cottage, I saw that fresh snow lay heavy on the silent land and freezing fog shrouded the back road to Ragley village. It was Friday, 8 January, the end of the first week of the spring term, and the outside temperature was minus ten degrees centigrade. We were experiencing the worst winter since 1963. I switched on my Bush radio and shivered as I walked into the bathroom.

Three miles away in Ragley village, Ruby was making a bacon sandwich for Deadly Duggie, who had tuned in as usual to Radio 1. Mike Read had introduced Blondie singing 'Atomic' and Duggie, Natasha, Sharon and Hazel were all singing along. The walls were shaking.

Further up Easington Road, in the Graingers' tidy house on the Crescent, Anne was adding chopped banana to her bowl of Weetabix. Terry Wogan on Radio 2 had just introduced David Soul singing 'Silver Lady' and Anne was humming along and gyrating her hips in time to the music. Sadly, her husband John had long since forgotten the art of hip-gyration and he missed what could have been interpreted as an early-morning mating ritual. Instead, his head was buried in his *Do-It-Yourself* magazine. After all, the promise of a free grouting tool with the next monthly issue was compelling news.

A mile away on Morton Road, in the calm oasis of the vicarage kitchen, Vera was feeding her three cats, Maggie, Treacle and Jess, while listening to the *Morning Concert* on Radio 3. It occurred to her that Prokofiev and Shostakovich were ideal companions for their morning bowl of meaty chunks.

The new year of 1982 stretched out before me. With my lesson plans in my battered leather briefcase, I wrapped my college scarf a little tighter, fastened the toggles on my duffel coat and walked out to scrape the ice from the frozen windscreen of my Morris Minor Traveller. It was a slow journey to Ragley village and I drove through a white world, devoid of life, with frozen trees etched against a forbidding sky. Heavy clouds hung over the Hambleton hills with the promise of more snow.

As I peered at the desolate beauty of this countryside

I reflected why I loved this spectacular part of North Yorkshire. The wind in the tall elms was the song of winter and, while it froze my bones, it served to nourish my soul. My thoughts were somewhat less lyrical when finally I arrived in the school car park and a sharp wind stung my cheeks as I hurried towards the school entrance. Beneath my feet, tiny frost crystals edged the cobblestones like scattered stardust.

Ruby, in a tightly knotted headscarf, was sweeping the path clear and seemed oblivious of the bitter cold. She was singing the recent number one, 'Begin the Beguine', by the Spanish singer Julio Inglesias.

'G'morning, Ruby,' I said. 'I like the singing.'

'Oh, 'ello, Mr Sheffield. Y'can't beat 'im, 'e's a proper 'eart-throb,' said Ruby, leaning on her broom.

'Who's that?' I asked.

'That Hoolio Doubleglazias,' said Ruby.

'Yes, er, well . . . thanks for all your hard work, Ruby,' I said. 'We've done well to stay open this week.'

'Well, at least all t'children are enjoying t'snow,' she said with a smile.

On the playground, Alice Baxter and Theresa Ackroyd, like Arctic explorers, were making first footprints in the fresh snowfall.

'And how's Ronnie?' I asked.

Ruby banged her broom against the school wall in annoyance. ''E's stayed in bed, Mr Sheffield,' grumbled Ruby. ''Is chest is playing 'im up again.'

'I'm sorry to hear that, Ruby,' I replied, thinking privately it was probably because he smoked thirty a day and took no exercise. 'Have you called the doctor?'

"E dunt need no doctor, Mr Sheffield,' said Ruby dismissively. 'Ah jus' rubbed some Vic on t'soles of 'is feet an' told 'im 'e'll be reight as rain.' She wandered off to pour salt on the entrance steps and I wondered if Dr Davenport was aware of Ruby's encyclopaedia of rural remedies.

I hurried to the entrance porch, where coal tits were perched on the crate of milk. They were pecking holes in the foil tops of each third-of-a-pint bottle to reach the precious head of cream.

As I walked into the school office and sat at my desk, I felt that little thrill that comes with uncertainty. For a village schoolteacher, no two days were alike and I wondered what was in store. Also, you never knew who would call in and ask for advice, or seek to complain, or merely to pass the time of day. Today was such a day and, as usual, it began with a knock on the door.

'Come in,' I said.

The office door was flung open and it banged loudly against the metal filing cabinet. Our least favourite villager, Stan Coe, local landowner, pig farmer and habitual bully, had wedged his sixteen-stone frame in the doorway. Stanley always seemed to be up to no good and there was a history of conflict between us. Ever since he had been removed from the Governing Body at the end of my first year at Ragley he had held me in contempt.

'Sheffield, ah need a word,' he shouted. He pointed a stubby nicotine-stained finger at me and his oilskin coat crackled. 'Ah've said it afore about t'kids in this school o' yours: y'don't teach 'em any bloody manners.'

'You'd better come in and tell me about it, Mr Coe,' I

said with a sinking heart. This was not the start to the school day I was hoping for.

He remained stubbornly where he was. 'Nay, ah'm a busy man. Ah don't sit on me arse all day an' then 'ave long 'olidays.'

'So what's the problem, Mr Coe, because I'm a busy man as well – and I'd be grateful if you would watch your language.'

'Ah want your kids well away from my livestock. They lean over t'fence an' shout at me pigs. They'll be leaving t'gate open next. Y'can't trust 'em.'

'I'll have a word in school assembly about it, Mr Coe,' I said. 'So, is that all?'

'It is f'now,' he said and slammed the door behind him. I heard him shout as he stormed out into the entrance hall. 'An' gerrowt o' m'way, y'stupid woman.' Through the window I saw him stride out to his Land-Rover, which was splattered with frozen mud and parked in the STRICTLY NO PARKING area outside the boiler-house doors.

This was followed by a timid knock on the door.

'Come in,' I said.

It was Mrs Daphne Cathcart, mother of eight-year-old Michelle in Sally's class. With her pink candy-floss hair, and teeth that resembled a rickety fence, Daphne was an interesting lady.

'Sorry about that, Mr Sheffield,' she said, blushing furiously and with a Darth Vader wheeze, 'but ah wondered if y'could spare me a minute.'

'Certainly, Mrs Cathcart. Come in and sit down,' I said.

'Thank you,' she said and closed the door. 'That man

allus picks on me. Ah bet 'e wouldn't if ah 'ad a 'usband.' She
sat down and fiddled with her huge purple earrings.

'Now, what can I do to help, Mrs Cathcart?'

'Ah 'ave t'go t'York this afternoon, Mr Sheffield,' she
said, 'so ah'll be late picking up our Michelle. Ah wondered
if she could 'elp mebbe tidying libr'y for 'alf an 'our after
school? But if it's not convenient ah can get m'sister to
come from Easington.'

'That's fine, Mrs Cathcart,' I said, eager to help. Sadly,
Daphne often had problems in her life. 'Michelle's coming on well with her reading. She'll enjoy looking at the
books in the library and I'll make sure she's supervised.'

Mrs Cathcart blushed again, this time with pride, and I
recalled that blushing was one of her personal problems.
'She's tekking after 'er big sister,' she said proudly, 'who's
doing real well up at t'big school.'

I had taught twelve-year-old Cathy last year. 'That's
good to hear,' I said. 'So, is it something special in York,
Mrs Cathcart?' I asked.

'Ah'm off t'this,' she said, thrusting a leaflet under my
nose. It read 'Move towards Success and Happiness with
Positive Programming – let American Hypnotist Werner
Finkletoes change the direction of your life.'

'Oh, er, I see,' I said. 'Well, I hope it goes well for you,
Mrs Cathcart.'

'Thanks, Mr Sheffield. Ah knew you'd understand
. . . 'Cause ah'd like t'be 'appy again an' mebbe stop all
m'blushing.' She blushed visibly and I felt a great sadness
for this lady who needed a boost of self-confidence more
than any parent I had ever met.

She paused at the door before she left and was silent

for a heartbeat. It was as if she was reluctant to open a window on her inner struggle. 'Ah've come t'learn in life, Mr Sheffield,' she said, 'that if you 'ave problems as a parent, then your children will 'ave 'em too, an' ah don't want that to 'appen to our Cathy an' our Michelle.' Then she quietly shut the door and set off to the bus stop and her date with 'success and happiness'.

Almost immediately, there was another knock on the door.

'Come in,' I said.

It was Vera. 'Our visitor, Miss Makepiece, is here, Mr Sheffield,' she said, 'to support Mrs Pringle's History of Ragley Village project.'

Vera opened the door wide and a tiny lady in her seventies walked in. She was wearing a smart, royal-blue Marks & Spencer's overcoat, matching woollen hat, scarf and gloves and fur-lined boots. 'Perhaps you would like a hot drink, Miss Makepiece,' said Vera with a gentle smile, 'and then I'll let Mrs Pringle know you're here.'

'Thank you, Miss Evans,' she said, 'you're very kind.' Her bright-blue eyes twinkled with mild amusement behind her spectacles as she looked around the office as if it was a long-lost friend. Then she removed a glove to shake hands. 'Good morning, Mr Sheffield. Pleased to meet you. I'm Miss Makepiece – Lily Makepiece,' she said.

'Oh yes. I heard you were coming in. Please . . . do sit down, Miss Makepiece, and thank you for your support,' I said.

'Well, I'm here for the weekend, Mr Sheffield,' said Lily. 'I'm visiting my sister at the Hartford Home for Retired

Gentlefolk. It was she who told your secretary and then Miss Evans told Mrs Pringle,' she said, holding up a letter on school headed paper and written in Sally's expansive handwriting. 'Fifty years ago I was an infant teacher here in Ragley School,' she said, 'and I've brought some photographs with me of those times.'

'That's wonderful,' I said. 'Sally's our historian and she'll be thrilled you can help her bring the project to life.'

'Well, if I say it myself, I've had an interesting life and it's a pity my eyesight is failing so that I can't write it all down.'

Sally appeared at the door. 'Oh, thank you for coming, Miss Makepiece,' she said. 'I'm Sally Pringle and I know from your sister that your mind is still sharp as a razor.'

'We shall see, Mrs Pringle,' she said and, after she had drunk her coffee, she set off with sprightly steps to Sally's classroom.

It was morning assembly when I saw Miss Makepiece again and I introduced her to the rest of the children. Anne played the first bars of our morning hymn and I noticed that Miss Makepiece didn't need a hymn book to refer to the words. She sang 'When a Knight won his spurs in the stories of old' from memory.

I gave out a few notices, including a warning not to go near Mr Coe's pig farm, at which point Miss Makepiece looked up with keen eyes. Then, after our prayers, the children trooped out to get their coats and scarves for morning playtime. I was on duty so I grabbed a hot coffee and walked out on to the playground.

Around me, the sharp cries of children were muffled

in the icy blanket of snow. Still as stone, the fresh layer deadened sound. Even the raucous cawing of the rooks in the high elms was muted. In the nearby woods, a startled woodcock skittered through the branches, eager to resume its solitude. On the village green, small animals had stripped bare of bark the fallen branches.

On the school field, children were enjoying games in the snow. Heathcliffe Earnshaw and his brother Terry were throwing snowballs at a snowman. Their Auntie Hilda in Cleckheaton had knitted matching grey balaclavas for the two boys, which made them look like evacuees from the Second World War.

'Great shot, 'Eath,' shouted Terry excitedly: 'reight on 'is nose.'

When I walked closer I was amused to note that their snowman, with his twig spectacles, had an uncanny resemblance to me.

The bell rang for the end of playtime and the children walked back into school. Anne and Jo, with the experience of countless wet and snowy playtimes, helped their infants to return their wet clothes and boots to the right places in the cloakroom.

'This takes me back,' said Miss Makepiece as she was met with the familiar smell of damp gloves, scarves and socks and the regiment of wellingtons.

She was soon into her stride in Sally's class. 'Well, boys and girls,' she said, clapping her hands for attention, 'fifty years ago school was very different. We taught the three Rs – words and sums – and these were written on slate boards and cleaned with spit.'

Heathcliffe looked at her with admiration and wished he could have lived in those days. He was particularly impressed with the practical use of spit.

'We taught the children folk dances in their hobnailed boots,' continued Miss Makepiece, 'and it made such a racket on this wooden floor.' The children stared at the floor in amazement.

'Please, Miss, what did you do in the war?' asked eight-year-old Betsy Icklethwaite.

'Well, during the Second World War, I worked in the Sheffield steelworks. We were known as the Women of Steel and we worked a seventy-two-hour week for £3 13s and £5 18s if we worked nights. So I spent the war making bullets.'

The children were perfectly silent. After years of making bullets this was clearly not a woman you would want to cross.

'Our postman was George Postlethwaite,' added Miss Makepiece, glancing up at the clock. It was almost lunch-time. 'After the war he continued even though he had only one arm. He used to call into school with the post and a brace of rabbits for the pot.'

'And did you eat 'em, Miss?' asked Rowena Buttle.

'Oh yes, it all went in the stew for school dinner,' she said with a smile.

The twelve o'clock bell suddenly rang. 'Miss . . . Ah wonder if Mrs Mapplebeck does that to our school dinners?' questioned Heathcliffe on his way out.

After a lunch of shepherd's pie, which the children in Class 3 insisted was in fact rabbit pie, the staff all gathered in the staff-room to chat with Miss Makepiece. She proved a fund of stories and gave me an insight into what life at Ragley School was like all those years ago.

'Best of all,' she said, 'I earned ninety-two pounds a year, and guess what I spent my savings on – a two-and-a-quarter horsepower Raleigh motorcycle.'

'Impressive,' said Sally.

'I bet that caused a stir in the village,' said Jo.

'Well, I certainly turned heads,' said Miss Makepiece. 'I wasn't what you might call a *conventional* schoolteacher.'

Vera was in awe of this very special lady. 'It must have been exciting coming to school in those days on a motor-powered bike,' she said.

'It certainly was. I recall the pond was full of geese and when I roared past the village green they used to chase me. I can see them now: running, with their necks stretched out, and hissing at me.'

We all laughed and continued to swap stories until the bell rang for afternoon school.

At the end of the school day I had just finished reading the next chapter of our new class story, 'Tom's Midnight Garden', and the children had hung on to every word. Few of them ever had the opportunity to enjoy a good story in homes where the television set blared out constantly and adults were too busy to take time to read to their children.

After putting their chairs up on their desks and saying our end-of-school prayer, the children in my class hurried out into the darkness. They set off to their homes to watch *Animal Magic* with Johnny Morris, featuring a seal sanctuary in Cornwall, followed by a new eighteen-episode series of *Grange Hill*. Life was never dull for ten-year-olds in 1982.

For my part I had a pile of paperwork to complete and I walked back to the school office. Jo was classifying some of the books in our non-fiction library and Michelle Cathcart was helping her. I could hear the clink of teacups in the staff-room, where Anne and Sally were reminiscing with Miss Makepiece on a successful day, while, back in the school office, Vera had prepared Form 8, the annual report for County Hall, for me to complete with our numbers on roll and staffing hours.

'Sorry, it's that time of the year again,' said Vera. 'I've done most of it but you need to check my figures.'

'Thanks, Vera,' I said and sat down with a sigh. I had just removed the top of my fountain pen when there was a hurried knock on the door.

'Come in,' I said.

It was Ruby and she was out of breath.

'Oh 'eck, ah'm all beside m'self, Miss Evans,' said Ruby, panting.

'Are you all right, Ruby?' I asked.

'Yes, Mr Sheffield, beggin' y'pardon.' It wasn't like Ruby to sit down in the school office but she flopped down on the visitor's chair.

'What is it, Ruby?' asked Vera.

'Ah've 'ad some news – wonderful news.'

Vera sat back in her chair and gave Ruby her full attention.

'It's our Racquel: it's 'appened at last,' she said, the words tumbling out.

'Oh, I'm so pleased for you,' said Vera.

'What's happened?' I asked.

Vera gave me her sympathetic *he's only a man* look and Ruby appeared puzzled. 'Ruby's come to tell us that Racquel is pregnant, Mr Sheffield. So she's going to be a grandmother for the first time.' She stood up and gave Ruby a hug. 'Congratulations, Ruby,' she said.

'Great news,' I joined in.

'And when is it due?' asked Vera.

'July, Miss Evans,' said Ruby, dabbing her eyes. 'Ah'm thrilled t'bits,' and she rushed off to the staff-room to tell Anne, Sally and Miss Makepiece.

Vera closed the door. 'I'm so pleased for Ruby,' she said and went to collect her coat.

I sat down at my desk and a few minutes later there was a loud knock on the door and it burst open. Stan Coe had returned and he was breathing fire.

'Ah've 'ad enough o' this,' he shouted: 'kids everywhere y'look an' strollin' bold as brass past my pigs.'

'Probably because they're walking home, Mr Coe, and the lights in your pig sties attract them. It's only natural to look and I can't see what harm they're doing.'

'So that's it, is it, Sheffield?' he yelled. 'Ah might 'ave known ah'd get no 'elp from a bloody down-at-'eel school teacher.'

The noise had attracted Ruby, Anne, Sally and Miss Makepiece from the staff-room and they stood in a line in the entrance hall, witnessing Stan Coe's tirade. Suddenly a firm, commanding voice was heard. 'It's young Stanley Coe, isn't it?'

Stan turned in surprise. 'Who's asking?' he said gruffly.

Lily Makepiece bristled and walked to face him. 'You don't remember me, do you, Stanley?'

'No, ah don't.'

'I'm Miss Makepiece.'

'Bloody 'ell!' exclaimed Stan, taking a step back. He looked as if he'd just come face to face with the Ghost of Christmas Past.

'Yes, Stanley, I was your teacher when you bullied all those girls. As I recall, you were excluded for three days in November 1932.' Stan took a step back towards the entrance door in alarm. 'I rarely forget a face and I could never forget yours, Stanley Coe,' said Miss Makepiece firmly. 'So you had better go home and stop all this nonsense before I alert the local police that you're bullying again.'

Stan Coe ran out and we heard the skid of tyres as he raced down the drive.

Spontaneous applause broke out. Miss Makepiece turned to me, eyes bright with mischief. 'Thank you for a lovely day, Mr Sheffield,' she said. 'I'm pleased to see that Ragley School is still in good hands,' and, with that, she walked out with Sally into the darkness.

An hour later I was alone in school. Anne, Vera and Jo had set off home with Ruby, while Mrs Cathcart, after a successful trip to York, had collected Michelle. It had been a day of long hours and the ticking of the school clock echoed mournfully around Ragley's Victorian rafters as the casements shook in the bitter wind.

I was surprised by another knock on the door. It was

Beth. She looked tired. 'Wondered if you'd like a drink and a meal in the Oak,' she said.

'Great idea,' I said, clearing my desk.

'What sort of day have you had?'

I thought for a moment as I grabbed my coat and scarf. 'Well . . . you know . . . the usual.'

Chapter Twelve

The Leeds Pals

Two First World War veterans visited school as part of Class 4's Food project. Miss Evans sent a revised copy of our history syllabus to County Hall for the attention of their 'common curriculum' working party.

Extract from the Ragley School Logbook:
Friday, 29 January 1982

There are times in the life of a village headteacher that live long in the memory. The day I met Billy and Harry Gaskin was such a time. It was during the bitter winter of 1981/82 and it began with a loaf of bread.

The last Friday morning in January was one of the coldest I had known during my time in Ragley village. Outside my classroom was a frozen bird table constructed from an old tree branch and the oak seat of a broken chair. It was primitive but effective and each morning three 'bird-table monitors' from various classes took turns to load it with scraps from Shirley's kitchen and the bacon rind left-overs from Ruby's regular breakfast fry-ups. This morning it was the turn of children in my class and three ten-year-olds, Sarah Tait, Amanda Pickles and Theresa Ackroyd, wrapped in scarves, gloves and bobble hats walked out on to the playground and waved back at the school windows as if they were intrepid Antarctic explorers. A large thermometer, a recent purchase from the Yorkshire Purchasing Organization catalogue, hung from the bird table, swaying in the bitter wind. Sarah, by far the most able of the three, noted the line of mercury, and remembered the reading.

'It's minus fourteen degrees Celsius, Mr Sheffield,' said Sarah excitedly when she came back into class.

'Could you record it please, Sarah?' I asked and she trotted off to our temperature chart on the display board above the bookcase in our Reading Corner and put a small cross close to the bottom edge of the squared paper.

'Any colder an' we'll 'ave t'move t'bookcase,' remarked eleven-year-old Jonathan Greening, the ever-practical farmer's son.

It was a busy morning during which I managed to complete the mid-year reading tests using the Schonell Word Recognition Test. The children applied themselves to their School Mathematics Project workcards followed by written work in their English exercise books. This often produced some imaginative responses, not least from Amanda Pickles, who, in answer to the question 'What was Sir Walter Raleigh famous for?' had written, 'He invented bicycles,' and I put a tiny red question mark in the margin.

When the bell went for morning playtime, Joseph, who

had just completed his weekly Bible stories lesson with Class 3, was in the corridor in animated discussion with Heathcliffe Earnshaw.

'If we can't see God, 'ow do we know what 'E looks like?' asked an indignant Heathcliffe.

'God *is* all around us,' said the Revd Joseph Evans in a knowing voice.

'Well, ah can't see 'Im,' said Heathcliffe with conviction, 'an' anyway, my dad said if God were from Barnsley, 'E'd 'ave knocked Satan into t'middle o' nex' week an' 'ad Sat'day off as well as Sunday.'

Joseph smiled uncertainly, pleased that his lessons were having some impact on young minds, but too nonplussed to reply.

In the school office, Vera had completed her late dinner-money register.

'Any messages, Vera?' I asked when I walked in.

'Yes, Mr Sheffield,' said Vera, checking the shorthand notes on her pad. 'County Hall want yet another updated history syllabus, Shirley's got everything organized for the bread-making demonstration and the major is bringing the Gaskin brothers into school after lunch to support your Food topic.'

'Thank you,' I said. 'I'm looking forward to meeting them.'

'They're both sidesmen at church, Mr Sheffield,' said Vera; 'lovely men, both in their eighties, and inseparable friends. Both of them lost their wives a few years ago and they moved from Leeds into one of the little cottages on Morton Road.'

I noticed that Vera was especially elegant today with yesterday afternoon's perm at Diane's Hair Salon looking especially striking. It crossed my mind that perhaps it wasn't a coincidence as the major was visiting school today.

It was just before twelve o'clock when the ever-watchful Theresa Ackroyd made her latest announcement. 'Major's posh car comin' up t'drive, Mr Sheffield.' Theresa never missed a trick. It was just a shame that her observational skills outweighed the written work in her Health Education project folder. The questions had been set by Staff Nurse Sue Phillips after a recent talk to the class. In answer to the question 'What is a fibula?' Theresa had written 'a small lie'. However, next to her, the new girl Tracy Hartley was displaying an interesting view of human development. She had written: 'My big sisters say when we grow up, the next stage is puberty and the one after that is adultery.'

Major Rupert Forbes-Kitchener smiled when he walked into the school office and his steel-blue eyes twinkled when he saw Vera. 'Good afternoon, Vera,' he said, 'and how are you?'

'I'm fine, thank you, Rupert, in spite of this dreadfully cold weather.'

'Too true my dear,' he said and his gaze softened but he didn't reveal what had passed through his mind. Behind him were two elderly men who looked remarkably similar: both short, balding and wiry and more like twins than brothers a year apart. They wore thick tweed three-piece suits, huge old-fashioned greatcoats and each carried an old leather bag. When they smiled there was laughter in their eyes.

'And I've brought two jolly brave men with me, Vera, who I believe you know . . . Mr Billy Gaskin and Mr Harry Gaskin,' he said.

The two men bowed. 'Good afternoon, Miss Evans,' said Harry, 'and thank you for t'invitation. Billy's been practisin' 'is speech all mornin' for t'bread-making. 'E's more of a do-er than a talker, is our Billy.'

'An', er, this is f'you, Miss Evans,' said Billy Gaskin, reaching into his leather bag, and he held out a freshly baked loaf wrapped in tissue paper. 'Oh, what a treat, Mr Gaskin,' said Vera, looking as if she'd just been presented with the crown jewels.

'An' one for t''eadmaster,' said Harry, and Billy produced another loaf from his bag.

'That's very kind, Mr Gaskin,' I said. 'It looks . . . and smells wonderful.' I weighed it in my hands. The loaf was dark and surprisingly heavy. It lacked the symmetry of mass-produced loaves and the smell was scrumptious. 'Perfect,' I said appreciatively.

'Mr Gaskin is known as "Billy the Bread" in church, Mr Sheffield, and he and his brother are great supporters,' said Vera. 'Every week, Billy gives Elsie, the organist, a loaf of home-made bread.'

'That's very generous of you, Billy,' I said.

'Well, my way o' thinkin' is that we pass this way but once,' said Billy, 'so we might as well do a bit o' good on t'journey.'

''E's reight there,' said Harry.

'Well said, that man,' said the major, 'and what's the recipe? I'll give it to my cook.'

'Well, Rupert,' said Vera, 'Mr Sheffield is going to write Mr Gaskin's recipe on the blackboard so that the children can copy it into their "Food" folders . . . I'll make a copy for you.'

'Jolly good show, Vera. Well, duty calls, what?' said the major, lifting his brass timepiece from his waistcoat pocket. 'See you chaps later at the end of school.'

Billy and Harry stiffened automatically to attention. 'Yes, Major,' they said in unison.

'At ease, men,' said Rupert with a smile. 'Old habits die hard, what?' He walked out to his classic Bentley while Vera and I led the two men through the little corridor from the office to the staff-room for a cup of tea. Anne, Sally and Jo were there. Anne was helping Sally refill the Roneo Spirit Duplicator and Jo was immersed in a new North Yorkshire booklet, *Computers in Primary Schools*, by our adviser Gilford Eccles.

'These are our visitors,' I announced, 'Billy and Harry Gaskin – and look what they've brought.' I put the loaf on the coffee table and everyone gathered round.

'What a lovely gift!' said Anne.

Billy and Harry smiled shyly.

'You can't beat the smell of fresh bread,' said Sally.

'We'll share it out later today,' I said.

'Oooh, thanks,' said Jo. 'I love newly baked bread. There's something, you know, special about it.'

'The colour's interesting,' said Anne, intrigued.

'That'll be t'treacle,' said Billy with a modest smile.

*   *   *

After a cup of tea, Shirley the cook came in and took Billy and Harry to the kitchen to collect the mixing bowls and set up the demonstration table in the school hall. It was Vera, of course, who knew the story of their lives and we all gathered round to hear about the two brothers.

Billy had been born in a terraced house in a soot-blackened street in Leeds in January 1895 and Harry arrived a year later. They were best friends as well as brothers, sharing a tough working-class experience. However, though they were often hungry, they were regularly reminded by their grandmother that they were the luckiest boys in the world because they were children of the Empire and Queen Victoria was on the throne. It was a simple, frugal life of bread-and-dripping sandwiches, cobbled streets and the expectation of work in one of the local mills.

However, the brief pleasures of childhood soon passed and in 1914 they stood side by side at the foot of the statue of the Black Prince in Leeds City Square and stared up at Kitchener's poster appeal 'Your Country Needs You'. Above their heads an armada of high cirrus clouds sped across a cornflower-blue sky towards the distant Pennines. It was a day of hope and expectation, a day of daring and defiance, but, for Harry and Billy, it was the day they signed up for a date with destiny. They were about to enter a conflict that would shape the rest of their lives and, with tens of other volunteers, they queued to serve their country.

Billy and Harry joined the 15th West Yorkshire Battalion following Earl Kitchener's idea that units of men should be drawn from one town or city. So it was they became part of a band of brothers, a regiment known as the 'Leeds Pals'.

In the school hall at a quarter past one, the children were wide-eyed with excitement as they watched Billy and Harry, assisted by Shirley the cook, begin their demonstration. 'Well, ah weigh out one and a 'alf pounds of wholemeal flour,' said Billy, 'and ah add yeast and salt . . .'

'Let me write this down,' I said and I noted the first part of the process on the blackboard.

'After that,' continued Billy, 'ah add a 'alf pound of malted brown flour, then ah dissolve a tablespoon of treacle in 'alf a pint of hot water and add it and another 'alf a pint of cold water. Then ah mix in a tablespoon of olive oil.' I scribbled furiously as the children took turns to weigh and measure the ingredients. 'I knead the dough and then ah put it, covered with a tea towel, in a warm place to rise for an 'our,' said Billy.

While this was going on, the children prepared a collection of much smaller individual loaves that were destined to be taken home. Vera had already sent a letter explaining this to parents. Aprons were passed from boy to girl and hands were scrubbed. Jonathan Greening stared in amazement at his hands. 'Ah've never seen 'em look so clean, Mr Sheffield,' he said. 'Me mam'll be thrilled.'

'After oiling a few bread tins,' continued Billy, 'ah knead t'dough again, put it in t'tins and allow it to rise for a second time for 'alf an 'our in a warm oven. Then ah bake 'em for 'alf an 'our at 190 degrees Celsius. Last of all ah cool t'loaves on a tray.'

'And that's 'ow t'make a perfect loaf, Mr Sheffield,' said Harry, with an admiring glance at his elder brother.

When the bell rang for afternoon playtime, the children went out to play in the snow and Shirley began baking the bread in her ovens. Vera had prepared a large pot of tea and some dainty slices of Billy's bread, spread with fresh butter from Prudence Golightly's General Stores. Jo was on duty and we could see her helping to build an igloo with some of the older children. Meanwhile, we all settled down to our feast of fresh bread and butter and soon Billy and Harry were regaling us with their stories.

'So what was it really like in the war?' I asked. 'My grandfather never came back to tell me.'

'Well, it were s'pposed t'be t'war to end all wars, but it wasn't t'be,' said Harry thoughtfully.

'Y'reight there, 'Arry,' said Billy.

'Ah recall t'16th and 18th Battalions of t'Prince of Wales Own West Yorkshire Regiment – all brave lads.'

'Then some general got it wrong,' said Billy.

'It were first of July, 1916,' said Harry, 'a day we'll never forget.'

There was silence in the staff-room as both men struggled to find the words.

'You mean the Battle of the Somme?' said Sally.

'That's reight, luv,' said Billy. 'It were a massacre.'

There was silence as they reflected on their world of ghosts and shadows.

'T'Leeds Pals were cut down by t'German machine guns,' continued Harry, 'an' then t'Bradford Pals were shot to pieces.'

'T'Leeds Pals lost twenty-four officers an' five 'undred an' four men,' said Billy. 'T'nex' day there were only forty-seven of us f'roll call.'

'How terribly sad,' said Anne.

'It robbed our community of a generation of young men,' said Vera.

'Over fifty-seven thousand men lay dead and wounded on the uplands of Picardy,' said Sally softly.

'Anyway, we're still 'ere,' said Billy, 'an' it's a real treat t'come t'your school, Miss Evans.'

I smiled. Ragley really was *Vera's* school.

'Mind you, we're gettin' on a bit now,' said Harry with a grin. 'There's seven ages t'man: "spills, drills, thrills, hills, ills, pills and wills". Ah'm up to t'last one, Mr Sheffield.'

'Y'know what they say,' said Billy with a smile: 'where there's a will, there's a relative.'

We all laughed. The spell was broken, the bell rang out and we all hurried back to our work.

It was a different end to the school week. Parents came in to collect their children and finished up talking to Billy and Harry. Many of them looked with interest at the collection of tiny loaves as, one by one, they were wrapped in tissue and taken home.

'Thank you, Mr Gaskin,' said Theresa Buttle. 'That were a great afternoon.'

'Y'welcome, luv,' said Billy.

'Can I give you a lift, Vera?' asked Rupert.

'That's very kind of you,' said Vera and she hurried off to get her coat and scarf.

*　　*　　*

The Bentley drove smoothly over the crusted snow through the gateway to the vicarage and pulled up outside the entrance porch. The north wind whipped up a fresh flurry of snow and Rupert and Vera stared out at the bleak but beautiful landscape. 'Another year, Vera,' he murmured.

'Yes, Rupert,' said Vera: '1982 . . . I wonder what it will bring.'

'A wedding in the village,' he said.

Vera glanced at the major and thought how handsome he looked. 'You mean Mr Sheffield and Miss Henderson?'

'Yes, my dear. They will make a good couple.'

'I'm glad they've both found happiness,' said Vera.

The major turned back to look at her. 'Vera . . . it makes you think, doesn't it?'

'What's that, Rupert?'

'About what those two old soldiers said about growing old,' said Rupert quietly. 'Maybe it would be good to have a companion to share happy times.'

'It might,' said Vera, unwilling to commit herself further.

'Vera, you are a wonderful lady,' said Rupert with sudden intensity, 'and you must know that I hold you in great esteem.'

'That's kind of you to say,' said Vera, wondering where the conversation was leading.

'It's just that life is so precious.'

'I agree,' said Vera.

'Perhaps one day we could be together,' he said.

There was a long silence. Finally Vera looked up at Rupert. 'Perhaps,' she whispered, '. . . perhaps.'

*   *   *

In the years that followed I visited Billy and Harry from time to time. More often than not they were in their delightful cottage garden and the memories are sharp in my mind. In late spring, aquilegias, wallflowers and forget-me-nots filled the crowded borders and throughout the year it was a haven for what they called 'proper old-fashioned plants': honeysuckle and lavender, pinks and sweet peas, foxgloves and hollyhocks. A dusky pink clematis wound its way through the branches of an old apple tree and espalier-trained pears hugged the south wall during the bounty of autumn. Best of all were the roses, a profusion of colour, filling the pergola and scenting the air.

Occasionally the brothers would call into school unannounced and leave a familiar gift for the staff to enjoy. It was always wrapped in white tissue paper and the smell was heavenly. I recall there was a great sadness in the village when, ten years later, they both passed away, first Billy and then, two months later, Harry – friends in life and partners in death. Old soldiers may pass away but friendship never dies.

Chapter Thirteen

Routine and Romance

Final preparations were made for the PTA Valentine Dance to take place in the school hall on Saturday, 13 February, 7.30–11.00 p.m.

Extract from the Ragley School Logbook:
Friday, 12 February 1982

True romance takes many forms and in the tiny village of Ragley-on-the-Forest it occasionally appeared in disguise.

Heathcliffe Earnshaw took the half-sucked gobstopper from his mouth and looked at it thoughtfully. He was impressed to see it had changed colour from red to the next layer of lurid purple.

This was a big moment in his young life. He had never thought of girls as friends – with the possible exception of Alice Baxter, who had defeated him at conkers – but there was something different about Elisabeth Amelia Dudley-Palmer. She was aloof and distant and she certainly knew more words than he did, which puzzled him because they were the same age. He guessed it was because she read different books from the gory tales of pirates, robbers and superheroes that he enjoyed. 'Lizzie,' he said and he stretched out his hand, 'would y'like my gobstopper?'

Elisabeth Amelia had always admired Heathcliffe. He was a rough adventurer in her predictable world of dolls, dresses and dinner parties. 'Oh, thank you, Heathcliffe, you're very kind.' She took the sticky sweet and grimaced for a moment as it stuck to her spotlessly clean fingers. 'I'll wrap it in my handkerchief and eat it at playtime.' From beneath the cuff of her royal-blue cardigan she took a tiny embroidered monogrammed handkerchief and wrapped up the huge spherical sweet.

It was 8.30 a.m. on Friday morning, 12 February, and Heathcliffe wandered off to scuff his new shoes on the school wall. Shiny shoes were not for tough superheroes, even those who were beginning to have romantic inclinations.

In the school office Sue Phillips, the tall, blonde, blue-eyed Chair of the Parent–Teacher Association, gave that familiar mischievous smile and put a poster on my desk. It read 'Ragley School PTA Valentine Dance, tickets £2.50 including disco, light refreshments and wine'. Sue was on her way to the District Hospital and looked immaculate in her light-blue staff nurse uniform, which included a starched white apron, black lace-up shoes, a navy-blue belt, on which the buckle depicted the God of Wind, plus her silver General Nursing Council badge.

'Good morning, Sue,' I said.

"Morning, Jack. We're all set,' she said: 'the tickets are selling like hot cakes.'

'That's good news,' I said. 'Beth and I are looking forward to it.'

'Yes,' said Sue. 'I guess she must be really busy these days at Hartingdale.'

'She'll certainly enjoy a break from paperwork,' I said.

Sue grinned and pointed to the bright-red love heart on the poster. 'And perhaps a bit of romance.'

I smiled and pinned up the poster on the noticeboard. 'It sounds a bargain at that price.'

'Yes, I suppose it does,' said Sue, with a hint of a frown. 'To be honest, Jack, our finger buffet should be fine but I'm slightly dubious about Clint Ramsbottom's disco. Having said that, at least it's free – and what can you expect these days for two pounds fifty?'

'*And* a glass of wine,' I added.

Sue shook her head. 'Yes, Jack, but I wouldn't get too excited about that either: it's the vicar's home-made variety.'

'Oh dear,' I said.

'Exactly,' said Sue. 'Anyway, must rush, and I'll see you tomorrow evening. We'll be setting up shortly after six if you could make sure the school is open.'

A few minutes later Joseph Evans appeared in the doorway followed by his sister. Vera sounded animated. 'But your elderflower has a distinctly *stewed* taste, Joseph,' she said. 'It's because you use too many flower petals.'

'It's an *acquired* taste,' said Joseph defensively and then looked relieved to see me. 'Hello, Jack. I believe I'm doing some Bible stories with Class 2 this morning,' he said, 'and then the Ten Commandments with Class 3.' With a furrowed brow he hurried away. Another demanding morning was in store for our timid vicar.

Predictably, the lesson in Class 3 didn't quite go to plan.

'Why are there *ten* Commandments, Mr Evans?' asked nine-year-old Joey Wilkinson. 'It's too many to remember and it makes my head hurt.'

While Joseph was pondering how to respond, Heathcliffe Earnshaw had an inspiration and raised his hand. 'Mr Evans,' he said, 'we only need *one* Commandment: "Thou shalt share thy last gobstopper".'

'Oh really, Heathcliffe,' said Joseph in exasperation.

'But that's a good answer, Mr Evans,' insisted Elisabeth Amelia Dudley-Palmer defiantly. Elisabeth Amelia still had a soft spot for the unconventional Heathcliffe. He was so unlike the other boys that her mother invited to her birthday parties. Also, her vocabulary was developing at a remarkable rate, as Joseph was about to discover.

'And why is that?' asked a bemused Joseph.

'Because it's a *symbolic* gobstopper, Mr Evans,' said Elisabeth Amelia with gravitas.

Joseph blinked. In the years to come he recalled it was the day he learnt never to underestimate children.

At morning break in the staff-room Sally Pringle looked up from her milky coffee and her second custard cream. 'By the way, Vera, that cardigan you knitted for Grace was a lovely gift. Colin and I were both thrilled.'

Baby Grace was now a year old and had been for her

check-up with the nurse at Dr Davenport's surgery. Sally's pride and joy weighed 20lb 4oz and was declared the healthiest baby in all creation by the smiling nurse. As Sally walked out she decided she would never again complain about a smelly nappy.

'It was a pleasure for such a beautiful baby,' said Vera.

Meanwhile, Anne and I looked up from our collection of Yorkshire Purchasing Organization order forms. With the cuts in public spending every penny had to be accounted for.

'Are you going to the Valentine dance, Sally?' asked Anne.

'Yes,' she said cheerfully. 'My mother's looking after Grace, so I'm hoping it will cheer Colin up. Stopping smoking has been difficult for him. He spends half his life sucking sherbet lemons.'

'I wouldn't recommend the wine,' warned Vera. 'It's Joseph's.'

Everyone nodded but felt it would have been disloyal to Joseph to agree out loud. After all, even though it tasted like floor polish, he meant well . . . and it was free.

By lunchtime Joseph was looking distinctly gloomy as he flicked through the children's exercise books and wondered why the six- and seven-year-olds in Jo Hunter's class just didn't seem to get the message. Charlotte Ackroyd insisted that 'David was a Hebrew king who was very skilled at playing the liar' and Harold Bustard had written: 'Samson killed the Philistines with the axe of the apostles.' Not for the first time he wondered about his role as a teacher of young children. He never had this trouble with the older ones in his confirmation classes.

At the end of school I worked late. Beth rang to say she was going out with her staff into Thirkby to see *Raiders of the Lost Ark*, starring Harrison Ford, and we could meet up on Saturday.

By seven o'clock, after I had locked up the school, the bright lights of The Royal Oak looked particularly inviting for a hungry headteacher. The frozen grass crunched beneath my feet as I walked across the village green.

At the bar Old Tommy Piercy was sitting with one of his farming friends.

'Good evening, Mr Piercy,' I said.

'Nah then, young Mr Sheffield,' he replied between puffs on his pipe of Old Holborn tobacco.

'This snow's getting worse,' I said.

'Snow,' muttered Old Tommy, shaking his head. 'Call that snow? That's nowt but fairy-dust, tha knows. Ah'll tell y'abart snow. Nineteen forty-seven were proper snow, waist 'igh an' enough t'freeze y'nadgers.'

All the football team nodded in agreement and I politely joined in. After all, what Old Tommy didn't know about snow wasn't worth bothering about.

Big Dave and Little Malcolm were ordering their usual round of thirteen pints of Tetley's for the football team, Stevie the substitute, and, of course, Ronnie Smith, the manager.

'She's fit as a butcher's dog, Don,' said Big Dave proudly.

Don the barman pulled the hand pump with his

mighty fist and nodded in absolute understanding and deep appreciation. In the pecking order of praise, this was a Yorkshireman's ultimate accolade. 'So are y'keen, then, on this lass wi' t'fancy name?' asked Don.

'It's fancy all reight, Don,' chipped in Little Malcolm. 'It's Fenella Lovelace.'

'Sounds like summat from James Bond,' added Sheila the barmaid as she adjusted the shoulder pads under her sparkly pink blouse.

'Well, ah call 'er Nellie . . . an' ah'm tekkin 'er out f'Valentine's Day,' said Big Dave proudly.

'We're all goin' to t'school dance,' said Little Malcolm.

'Did you 'ear that, Don: *romance* is not dead f'some people,' said Sheila.

Don shuffled off to the far end of the bar. I was waiting my turn to be served and Sheila fluttered her false eyelashes at me and pressed her substantial cleavage across the counter.

''E's like that Olympic flame, Mr Sheffield,' said Sheila.

'Olympic flame?'

'Yes, 'e never goes out.' As usual I focused on the shelf of bottled shandy as I placed my order. This wasn't to hide my embarrassment, more a case of self-preservation. Her husband Don, an ex-wrestler and built like a fork-lift truck, was standing at the other end of the bar and he thought the world of his gregarious wife. Then she looked up at me and smoothed the creases in her black leather miniskirt. 'What's it t'be, Mr Sheffield?'

'A pint of Chestnut, please, Sheila, and a pie and mushy peas.'

'Comin' up, Mr Sheffield,' said Sheila. 'So no Miss 'Enderson, then?'

'No, Sheila. She's gone out with her staff to see *Raiders of the Lost Ark*.'

'Oooh, 'Arrison Ford!' swooned Sheila. 'Now, that's one ah wouldn't kick out o' bed.'

A short while later I was sitting at a table, supping my pint and scalding my tongue on Sheila's famous meat pie. I took out my notebook and added a few more reminders to my wedding list, including buying a wedding ring and a London theatre visit for our honeymoon. Then I returned to the bar for a refill. Old Tommy was still there, sitting on his usual stool next to the signed photograph of Geoffrey Boycott.

'Ah see tha's cack-'anded, Mr Sheffield,' he remarked. 'Ah saw y'writing.'

'I'm making a wedding list,' I said.

'Ooooh, 'ow romantic,' said Sheila. 'My Don never makes no lists. In fac' there's no *excitement* any more, if y'know what ah mean. It's jus' routine . . . nowt else, jus' routine.'

I gave her thirty pence for my pint of Chestnut. 'So, have you mentioned it to him, Sheila?' I asked tentatively.

'Nowt said needs no mending, Mr Sheffield,' said Sheila with a wink. She looked at Old Tommy. 'I bet you were *romantic* in y'day, Mr Piercy.'

Old Tommy puffed on his pipe and contemplated. He was a gruff, stubborn, opinionated Yorkshireman, proud of his county of stone cities and grassy dales, wet moorlands and dry humour. 'Aye, lass,' he said. He held up his hands and wiggled his fingers. 'But these won't be un-doing any more whalebone corsets,' he said. He turned to his lifelong friend Alf Wight, whose sheepdog, Floss, was crouched at his feet. 'Gi' me a dog any day,' said Old Tommy.

''E's best sort, is my Floss,' said Alf, who was a proud member of the Yorkshire Sheepdog Society: 'allus pals at t'end o' day. 'E's at 'is peak tha knaws, five year old now.' Sadly, the mystical union between Alf and Floss was something that he had never quite established with his wife. 'So y'can keep y'romance,' said Alf, which probably explained why he spent Friday nights drinking with his dog while his wife stayed at home with a crate of bottled stout.

There were raised voices further down the bar. 'Salt 'n' Shake crisps?' said Big Dave, 'Salt in a bag . . . in yer *crisps*?'

'That's reight,' said Don.

'We used to 'ave proper flavours like vinegar or cheese an' onion,' said Big Dave. 'Who wants t'shake salt on their crisps?'

Stevie 'Supersub' Coleclough, eager to defuse the great crisp debate, changed the subject. 'No entertainment t'neight, then, Don?' he asked.

'Nay, Stevie,' said Don. 'Las' week's were a poor do.' Apparently the 'turn' was a pensioner singing 'Mule Train' while repeatedly bashing his head with a tin tray.

'Y'not kidding,' said Shane Ramsbottom. 'It went down like t'*Titanic*.'

Old Tommy Piercy looked up. 'Y'reight there, young Shane,' he said: 'it were rubbish. In fac' if ah were comin' again, ah wouldn't come.'

'Sorry, Tommy, but *proper turns* are expensive,' said Don and he hurried off to collect some empty glasses.

''E's an ol' skinflint, is that one,' said Old Tommy. ''E'd nip a currant in two.'

In the annals of Yorkshire put-downs, this was up among the best of them.

Saturday morning dawned bright and bitterly cold with fresh snow covering the distant hills. Sparrows and chaffinches were busy in the hedgerow and a solitary robin perched on my garden seat, looking hopefully for a few crumbs.

I decided to do some shopping in Ragley and Beth said she would meet me in the village. By the time I pulled up on Ragley High Street I was ready for a hot drink on this freezing morning. Rod Stewart was singing 'Da Ya Think I'm Sexy?' as I walked into Nora's Coffee Shop. In my case, in my old duffel coat, steamed-up Buddy Holly spectacles and wavy brown hair sticking up in frozen spikes, the answer was definitely no.

Dorothy Humpleby was sporting her new image. Her Super-Straight-Leg jeans from Levi's womenswear range involved rolling up the legs to create a different look. She was deep in conversation with Nora.

'Ah luv Valentine's Day,' said Dorothy. 'It's proper romantic.'

'Y'never know, Dowothy,' said Nora conspiratorially, Malcolm might s'pwise you with a wing.'

Dorothy wandered off to the coffee machine and Nora looked up at me and shook her head. 'She weally is a sandwich short of a picnic, is our Dowothy.'

*   *   *

Unknown to Dorothy, the love of her life had just entered the Village Pharmacy, where the owner, Eugene Scrimshaw, wearing his white coat over the top of his Star Trek uniform, was dreaming as he waited for his wife Peggy to take over. Eugene had converted his attic into the flight deck of the Starship *Enterprise* and he had got a bit carried away on his latest voyage to discover lost worlds. Peggy Scrimshaw was now in the General Stores with Margery Ackroyd, the local gossip, and there was no such thing as a short conversation with Margery.

Eugene came back to earth. 'What is it t'be, Malcolm?' he said.

Malcolm looked furtively around him. 'It's personal,' he whispered.

''Ave no fear, my lips are sealed,' said Eugene.

'It's summat f'Dorothy,' said Malcolm; 'ah've seen 'em advertised.'

Eugene looked at the doorway. There was no sign of any other customer or Peggy outside. ''Ow about these?' he said, holding up a packet of Durex. 'All different colours. They're all t'rage these days.'

Malcolm flushed furiously. 'No, not them!' he exclaimed. 'Any road, it's Dorothy what buys stuff like that.'

'Oh, ah see,' said Eugene. 'So what is it?'

Malcolm looked over his shoulder again and took out a cutting from the *News of the World*. 'It's a Buf-Puf cleansing sponge,' said Malcolm, pointing to a photograph of Michelle Hobson, otherwise known as Miss Great Britain 1981. 'It sez it'll give yer a beauty queen complexion . . . an' if this lass were taller, an' mebbe wi' blonde 'air an' a bigger nose, she'd be t'dead spit o' my Dorothy,' said Little Malcolm earnestly.

The doorbell jingled and Peggy walked in. Little Malcolm quickly bought a tube of toothpaste. 'Er, ah'll see y'later, Eugene,' he said and hurried out.

Peggy frowned at Eugene and walked past the counter. As she hung up her scarf and took her white coat from the coat stand in the back room she mimed a Mr Spock Vulcan nerve pinch in Eugene's direction. Something was going on with Captain Kirk and Little Malcolm and she knew it.

I called into Prudence Golightly's General Stores & Newsagent, picked up my copy of *The Times*, along with a sliced loaf for 29p, 80 PG Tips tea bags for 51p and a packet of McVities milk-chocolate biscuits for 31p. As usual, the shop was bustling with customers. It appeared that all the needs of the village community could be found here. Every shelf was full to bursting with flour, butter, fresh-baked bread, sugar and salt. Stock hung from hooks on the beams and tins of shoe polish sat alongside heavy-duty scouring pads. On the noticeboard by the counter were postcards advertising shoe repairs, dog walking and Kelvin Froggat the chimney sweep. There were children clutching small coins and making agonizing decisions about the colourful range of sweets, including love hearts, gobstoppers, sherbet dabs, hazelnut creams, homemade locust beans, aniseed balls, pear drops, marzipan tea-cakes, liquorice torpedoes and, my personal favourite, Sharpe's chocolate butter dainties. It was also the home for local gossip and Margery Ackroyd was telling Betty

Buttle why the wire supports in Sheila Bradshaw's bra gave her the best cleavage in the village.

'Oh, one more thing, Miss Golightly: I need a Valentine card for Miss Henderson,' I said.

'I've got just the one,' she said. For Prudence, her customers' affairs of the heart were all part of a normal day. She rummaged in a wooden drawer under the counter. 'This one should be perfect, Mr Sheffield.' The picture on the front showed a man and a woman sitting on a bench, under a cherry tree full of blossom, and looking out to sea.

'Er, thank you, Miss Golightly,' I said. 'I'm sure Beth will love it.'

'Don't forget, Mr Sheffield, it's supposed to be anonymous, so put a question mark on it,' said Miss Golightly.

'Good idea,' I said and scribbled on the card.

The doorbell jingled. It was Beth. 'Hello, Miss Golightly,' she said. 'Hello, Jack. Are you ready?'

I snatched up my card and shopping list, shoved it in the envelope and thrust it in the pocket of my duffel coat.

As we walked back to my car, Mrs Dudley-Palmer's Rolls-Royce drove smoothly up the High Street. It occurred to her that perhaps romance wasn't dead after all. Her husband, Geoffrey, had arranged a visit for her to the Céramique Internationale showrooms in Bradford. So, following a trip to the Debenham's department store in Leeds where she ordered a top-of-the-range 'Style Fine Line' fitted kitchen in Snowdon Oak, she visited the Bradford showrooms and selected the 'Monsoon' range of French ceramic tiles. The salesman told her the French provincial range suited her obvious taste and, although she was initially flattered, she recalled that 'provincial' meant something to do with 'proletariat' and she didn't want her new kitchen to look as though it had been designed by a French peasant. However, she felt sure that Geoffrey would be delighted with her purchase from the men's shirt section of Debenham's. The blue-and-white-striped shirt, made from the finest Macclesfield silk, was a bargain at £45. At least, this is what the young salesman had told her and she always believed anyone who resembled a youthful Nicholas Parsons.

The Parent–Teacher Association dance went surprisingly well and those with a strong stomach thought Joseph's wine was a psychedelic journey into the unknown.

Clint Ramsbottom weighed up his audience, put his Sex Pistols collection to one side, and began with 'The Land of Make-Believe' by Bucks Fizz and Abba's 'Waterloo'. Parents, staff and villagers danced, relaxed together and chatted with Joseph about his unique blend of wine.

At the end of the evening, in the darkness of the school hall, Beth and I were sipping a surprisingly palatable parsnip wine. Her head was on my shoulder and her hair had the fragrance of summer.

'Looking forward to the wedding?' I whispered in her ear.

'Yes, Jack, I am.'

'Joseph suggested we should go to church tomorrow morning to arrange when our banns should be read out.'

'That should be fun,' she said.

'Not if someone objects,' I replied with a smile. Beth

looked up at me, concerned. 'I was only joking,' I said.

'I know. I was just thinking of Laura.'

'Oh, I see,' I said, 'but, Beth, there was never anything between me and your sister.'

'I know, Jack, but Laura didn't see it like that. You were special to her and so different from the high-flyers she mixes with in her career.'

'I never wanted to be part of her world, Beth, you must know that.'

She smiled. 'That was part of your charm, Jack.'

I shook my head in confusion. 'I'll never understand women.'

'You don't need to. You only need to understand me.' She stretched up and kissed me on the lips.

'This doesn't feel right,' I said. 'I'm in *school*.'

'Then perhaps I should take you home,' said Beth with an unblinking gaze.

'You mean Bilbo Cottage?'

'Yes, Jack, *our* home.'

On Sunday morning Beth and I were sitting in St Mary's Church and Joseph, looking slightly worse for wear, was in full flow.

As we rose for the first hymn, Beth whispered, 'By the way, thanks for the card . . . Good to see romance isn't dead.'

'How on earth did you know it was from me?' I asked in mock disbelief.

Beth pretended to consider the matter before replying. 'Well, Jack, it could have been because you left your shopping list in the envelope.'

Chapter Fourteen

Ted Postlethwaite and the Missing Cat

County Hall requested a copy of our revised scheme of work for science in support of their proposal for a 'common curriculum' for schools in North Yorkshire. Our local policeman, Acting Sergeant Dan Hunter, was in school to lead morning assembly on the theme 'Don't Talk to Strangers'.

Extract from the Ragley School Logbook:
Thursday, 4 March 1982

It was a cold Thursday morning in early March and a fitful sun was trying to pierce the iron-grey clouds. As I ate my breakfast cereal in the snug kitchen of Bilbo Cottage, I scanned the headline in the *Easington Herald and Pioneer*, 'Scargill and Maggie – problems ahead', and frowned. Trouble was looming.

It had been a murky dawn and the fields were cloaked in a heavy mist as I drove on the back road from Kirkby Steepleton to Ragley village. In the distance the

Hambleton hills looked bleak beneath the wind-driven sky. As I drove up the High Street, Deke Ramsbottom, perched on his noisy tractor, gave me a cheery wave, while Ernie Morgetroyd and his son, the handsome Rodney, trundled by on their electric milk float on their way home to Morton. On the far side of the village green, Ted 'Postie' Postlethwaite had finished his morning round and was looking forward to his cup of tea at the Post Office. Ted was a renowned 'early bird' and made sure all his customers received their mail before they left for work. He had been the local Ragley and Morton postman for over twenty-five years and, at fifty-six years old, he was wondering about his future. Ted had never married and was beginning to realize there was more to life than going fishing with his father.

On this chilly morning he smiled as he reflected that the gentle, talented and graceful Miss Amelia Duff was the apple of his eye. No one played the flugelhorn or made a cup of Typhoo tea like Miss Duff. So it was that, in this happy introspective state, he was slow to take evasive action when Jimmy Poole's Yorkshire terrier, the aptly named Scargill, ran from behind the weeping willow tree at the side of the duck pond, attacked his ankles and shredded his woollen socks.

Up Morton Road, in the vicarage kitchen Vera Evans was equally distressed.

'Maggie, Maggie, where are you?' she said in a soft coaxing voice. 'Come to mummy, my little darling.' Her other two cats, Treacle and Jess, were tucking into their breakfast with joyous intensity. Each had a personal feeding bowl but the ceramic dish with the word 'Maggie' painted decoratively on the side remained untouched. 'Oh dear,' said Vera, 'where on earth can she be?'

She put on her coat and scarf and went to search the outbuildings. Vera rarely ever missed her twice-weekly cross-stitch class in the village hall but today it would have to wait. Her beautiful black cat, with distinctive white paws and named after Vera's favourite politician, was nowhere to be seen.

'Ah'm thorry, Mithter Pothlethwaite,' said Jimmy Poole as he attached a dog lead to the frenzied Yorkshire terrier. 'Thcargill liketh to 'ave a run when we go thoppin' for m'dad'th *Daily Expreth* an' Mithter Ramthbottom'th tractor gave 'im a thock.'

'It's a menace, is that dog,' retorted Ted, rubbing his ankle. 'Allus chasing ducks an' cats. It needs keeping under control.'

'Thit, thit,' urged Jimmy, but the lively Scargill didn't want to sit.

'Y'need t'feed 'im once in a while,' said Ted.

'' 'E 'ad 'ith breakfatht at theven o'clock,' said Jimmy plaintively.

'An 'e's just 'ad another,' said Ted, pointing at the hole in his sock.

'Thorry, Mithter Pothlethwaite,' said Jimmy and he ran off to collect his father's newspaper from the General Stores.

'It's on the kitchen table, Ted,' said Amelia as she unlocked the door of the Post Office.

'Thank you, Amelia,' said Ted. 'Ah'm ready for a 'ot drink.'

Amelia took the post from Ted into the back room, removed the rubber band and laid out the letters on the counter behind the sturdy wire grill.

'Busy morning, Ted?' asked Amelia as she poured a second cup of tea for herself from an ancient china teapot.

'Ah'll swing f'that dog one day,' said Ted, showing Amelia his torn sock.

'Oh, you mean Scargill. Yes, he can be a bit of a pest sometimes,' said Amelia with a calm smile.

Ted decided to drop the subject because Amelia never thought ill of anyone and he didn't want to appear grumpy. After all, this was the highlight of his day. As they sat there drinking tea, Amelia reflected on the life of the Ragley village postman. He had become a good friend and she welcomed their morning tête-à-tête and, on occasions, wondered if there could ever be something more between them.

Ted was a good postman and a true village character. 'It's a *public service*, not a business,' he used to tell his customers when he relaxed in The Royal Oak. Each day he started work at the depot at 4.45 a.m., tipped the letters and small packages out from the bags and began 'internal sorting'. He delivered letters, bills, postcards, packages, magazines, Christmas cards, birthday cards and small presents. His mail always fitted into *one* bag because, happily for the Ragley village postman, there was no junk mail. At 6.15 a.m., after packing it into his tarpaulin waterproof bag, which kept all the letters and packages snuff dry, he put it on his bicycle – a formidable construction, built like a Centurion tank, and, with a full bag of mail in the wire basket, it felt as though it weighed as much.

For Ted, early morning was the best time of the day. He had the village to himself, with only birdsong and the weather for company, except for the clinking of milk bottles as Ernie Morgetroyd and his son Rodney whirred past on their electric milk float. All the villagers of Ragley could read their mail over breakfast and knew they could set their watches by Ted's regular routine. His last delivery was always at precisely 8.15 a.m. to Miss Duff in the Post Office.

'It's Miss Golightly's birthday on Saturday,' said Ted. 'She got her first card this morning with a Kent postmark – probably 'er cousin.' Ted knew *everybody's* birthday, as well as whether they were late with their gas payments.

'Thanks for letting me know, Ted,' said Amelia.

'Ah know m'customers, Amelia,' said Ted with false modesty.

'I must give her a card. She's a lovely lady,' said Amelia.

Ted wanted to say, 'And so are you,' but didn't have the courage. Instead he just stared at the woman of his dreams.

Amelia was a slight and diminutive fifty-nine-year-old spinster and had been postmistress for the past seventeen years. Her late father, Athol Duff, had been a mill worker and he had played the flugelhorn in the famous Black Dyke Mills Band. Helped by Athol's prowess, they had won the prestigious *Daily Herald* National Championship

Trophy three times in the 1940s. Amelia had continued the tradition in the Ragley and Morton Brass Band and the tone of her flugelhorn was both mellow and haunting. She glanced up at the old sepia photograph of Queensbury Mills, a Victorian colossus set against the smoky chimneys of Bradford, and sighed. Time was a great healer but the pain of loss was always there.

'Amelia . . . what are y'thinkin'?' asked Ted.

'Just about life and what might have been,' said Amelia.

There was a long silence. Ted finished his tea, put down his 1935 King George V Silver Jubilee mug and looked across the well-scrubbed pine table.

'Even postmen 'ave dreams, Amelia,' he said.

'And what's yours, Ted?'

'The trumpet, Amelia,' he said quietly. 'Ah allus wanted t'play the trumpet, ever since ah were a boy. It's a marvellous instrument.'

Amelia looked at Ted as if for the first time and wished her father could have been here, sat beside her.

Then she smiled. Perhaps he was.

When I drove into the school car park, Dan and Jo's two-tone-green 'F'-registered Wolseley Hornet was already there.

Dan had come into school to deliver a safety talk to the children on being careful about speaking to strangers and, as headteacher, I was growing increasingly aware that health and safety issues were becoming more pressing as each year went by. Dan was rightly very proud of himself, having just passed all three parts of his promotion exams, including the traffic and crime papers as well as general police duties. It meant that he was qualified to act as sergeant while the regular sergeant was on holiday.

Jo was clearly delighted for her husband. 'He's *Acting* Sergeant this week, Jack,' she said, 'so he gets *two* stripes on his uniform instead of three. Apparently, Sergeant Grayson at the Easington police station is on holiday. He's gone back to Hull to support his favourite football team.'

'Well, somebody has to,' I said, slightly uncharitably. Hull City, as usual, was languishing in one of the lower divisions of the football league.

Jo grinned. 'Don't forget to mention the stripes, Jack. He's so chuffed. In fact I nearly sewed some on his pyjamas!' She laughed and set off to her classroom, ready for the morning bell.

The huge figure of Dan Hunter was in the school hall, pinning up a few posters of people in assorted uniforms, including nurses and firemen. 'Good morning, Dan,' I said, 'and congratulations on passing your exams.' I shook his giant fist and he smiled a little shyly.

'Thanks, Jack,' he said, looking down self-consciously at his gleaming white chevron stripes. 'Takes some getting used to, and the other lads at the station are pulling my leg something rotten.'

'I can imagine,' I said. 'Anyway, thanks for coming in. It must be a busy week for you with all the extra responsibility.'

The morning assembly went well and Dan was truly a gentle giant with all the children, guiding them carefully through the difficult concept that strangers might not be all they seemed.

When the bell rang for morning break I was on duty and I pulled on my old duffel coat and college scarf while Anne made me a welcome hot coffee. The children seemed oblivious to the cold weather. Tracy Hartley was teaching a group of infants to play hopscotch while Amanda Pickles was bouncing a tennis ball and chanting, 'Red, white and blue, the Queen's got the flu, the King's got the tummy ache, and I don't know what to do.' Meanwhile, against the school wall, a type of leapfrog game was in progress and Dean Kershaw and a group of younger boys were chanting, 'Jimmy, Jimmy, knicker knacker, one-two-three.'

In the shelter of the school porch, eight-year-old Betsy Icklethwaite had looped a length of thick string around Louise Hartley's hands. 'Hold it still,' said Betsy, 'and I'll show you 'ow to make a cat's cradle and afterwards you can 'ave a go.' Then she used a series of careful moves with her index finger, little finger and thumb to create patterns just as her mother had taught her. Louise's eyes were wide with interest. 'Now,' said Betsy, 'what's it t'be nex', a soldier's bed or a fish in a dish?'

A hammering noise on the other side of the village green caught my attention. Sixty-six-year-old Oscar Woodcock was pinning a poster that read RAGLEY ANNUAL SHED WEEK on one of the telegraph poles outside his terraced cottage next to The Royal Oak.

Oscar was proud of being the president of the Ragley Shed Society and especially so during the first week in March. Posters all round the village announced it was Shed Week, the time when the men of Ragley opened up their sheds to reveal their private world to other like-minded and equally eccentric shed-owners.

The favourite was undoubtedly Oscar's shed as he used it for brewing cider. Oscar would pick apples from the trees in his garden, let them mature for a week and then tip them into his 'scratcher', a home-made cider press. He knew that a sack of apples would make a gallon of apple juice. Then he would pour the liquid into a one-gallon glass demijohn and add wine yeast to start the fermentation. Growing up in Somerset and making scrumpy as a boy had provided him with a special expertise. For Oscar, one glass of his potent mixture tended to solve all his problems; two glasses, and he couldn't remember what they were in the first place.

It was lunchtime when a worried-looking Vera pulled up in her Austin A40 in the school car park. In the staff-room, Sally was turning the handle of our spirit duplicator to produce multiple copies of guitar-chord shapes for her beginners' group and Jo was preparing a teacher's guide for our new computer. I was putting the final touches to our revised scheme of work for science as County Hall had requested yet another document for the proposed 'common curriculum'.

Anne was making a fresh pot of tea while chuckling over an article in the *Yorkshire Post* under the headline 'Women firefighters'. Apparently, the Deputy Chief fire officer had said, 'Women of suitable physique can be trained as firefighters and, under the Sex Discrimination Act, we are obliged to recruit women. They will undergo the same physical tests as men. There should be no problem

apart from the slight difference in chest measurements.'
Too true, thought Anne.

It was at that moment that Vera hurried into the staff-room, looking distraught.

'Is everything all right, Vera?' said Sally.

'Come and sit down,' said Jo.

Anne was concerned. 'You look a little pale,' she said.
'Would you like a cup of this tea?'

'What is it, Vera?' I asked.

Vera put her head in her hands and burst into tears.

While this drama was being played out, Oscar Woodcock, the recently retired manager of the local refuse tip, had finished putting up the poster and was tidying his shed ready for the influx of visitors on Saturday morning. Like a modern-day 'Stig of the Dump' he recycled everything he could and over the years had collected the cast-offs of the villagers of Ragley and Morton.

His huge wooden shed resembled an incongruous home, with a three-piece leather suite, a discarded but very fine Axminster carpet, a nest of G-Plan tables, an ornately carved antique pine bookcase stacked with old hardbacks and a complete set of *Encyclopaedia Britannica* and a paraffin heater. Also, thanks to Mrs Dudley-Palmer he wasn't short of the latest electrical appliances, including a soda stream and a Breville sandwich toaster. He wiped the surface of an out-of-stock Habitat kitchen unit and arranged a set of 1953 Coronation mugs next to his electric kettle. Then he sighed with satisfaction. There was something about his shed that made him feel secure, safe and wonderfully sanguine . . . probably linked to the ever-present smell of potent cider. Sadly, it was a feeling that quickly dissipated when his wife's piercing voice called him to come in and help with the housework.

In Ragley School, it was a difficult afternoon and Vera insisted on staying at her desk until afternoon break, when everyone in the staff-room ganged up on her and sent her home to look for Maggie. At the end of school Anne completed reading *The Tale of Squirrel Nutkin* to her class and then encouraged a discussion, but it wasn't *squirrels* that the children had in mind.

'Has Miss Evans found her cat?' asked a concerned Jemima Poole.

'I don't think so, Jemima,' said Anne, 'but I'm sure she will turn up.'

At four o'clock we gathered in the staff-room as the telephone rang and Sally took the call. It was Vera. Maggie was still missing.

'Don't worry,' said Sally, 'she'll turn up and, in the meantime, I'll prepare some posters and we'll distribute them around the village tonight.'

Anne, Sally and Jo took the High Street shops and I was given a poster for Pratt's garage. As I pinned the poster to the scruffy noticeboard next to the counter, Victor had other problems on his mind.

'Ah've gorra touch o' t'pneumonics,' said Victor, rubbing his chest, 'an' ah'm short o'wind.'

'I'm sorry to hear that, Victor,' I said.

'An ah've gorra sceptic throat. Ah told Dr Davenport

ah'd allus 'ad a sceptical throat and 'e said 'e weren't s'prised.'

'I see,' I said.

'So, all in all, ah'm not feeling m'self, so t'speak,' said the mournful Victor. 'Ah'm proper poorly, but like all men ah don't complain, ah just battle on,' he added with a touch of martyrdom. 'An' ah 'ope Miss Evans finds 'er cat,' he shouted after me as I walked out into the gloom.

On Friday morning Vera was up early, searching the grounds for her beloved Maggie. Around her, in the vicarage garden, birds were pairing up and claiming their territory and chattering with new vigour. Snowdrops, aconites and crocuses should have cheered the spirit but, for Vera, her senses were blunted. When she returned to her spotless kitchen, the fragrant scent of hyacinths on the window ledge went unnoticed. Maggie had not been found.

Meanwhile, the villagers had been mobilized and, in the grey early-morning light, parents and children were looking in outbuildings and gardens. Even Ronnie Smith had been pressed into service. Ruby had mixed an old-fashioned remedy of butter, honey and lemon juice into a mugful of boiling water and forced him to climb out of his sick bed.

At eight o'clock, when Dan Hunter dropped off Jo in the school car park, there was the sound of a dog barking. Jimmy Poole was being pulled by Scargill on his lead across the village green towards Oscar Woodcock's gate, where Ted Postlethwaite was about to deliver a letter. 'Oh no,' shouted Ted, 'not again!'

The little terrier seemed more excited than usual and, to Ted's surprise and great relief, he scampered down Oscar's path and resumed his barking outside the shed. Dan, in his smart uniform, walked across the green to see what all the fuss was about.

'Ah think there's summat in Oscar's shed,' said Ted.

Oscar came out to investigate and then went back indoors for his shed key. When he unlocked it, both Oscar and Ted looked up at Dan, unwilling to set foot inside.

'Well, I never,' said Dan as he emerged with a sleepy cat in his arms. Maggie had enjoyed her rest, fortified by the occasional mouse washed down with the spillage from Oscar's cider.

'Well done, Scargill,' said Ted with a smile and Jimmy beamed from ear to ear.

'Miss Evans will be thrilled,' said Dan.

Vera never heard the true story. Each morning for several weeks Maggie had enjoyed taunting Scargill, the bossy little Yorkshire terrier, from the safety of the high wall that surrounded Oscar's garden, before returning home for breakfast at the vicarage. However, yesterday morning was different. A sudden backfire from Deke Ramsbottom's tractor had caused her attention to be diverted at the very moment Jimmy Poole had let loose his beloved Scargill. With bared teeth and pent-up vengeance, Scargill had chased Maggie through an open gateway and down an overgrown path towards a garden shed, where Maggie took refuge at the very moment Oscar emerged and locked the door behind him. Then Scargill ran back to the village green, spotted an old adversary, and promptly satisfied his vengeance on Ted Postlethwaite's ankle. Maggie was forgotten and honour had been satisfied.

By Saturday morning, life had returned to normal in Ragley village.

For Ted Postlethwaite it was his 'job and knock' day; there was no second post and he could go home after his morning delivery. However, when he called in at the Post Office, Amelia had begun to prepare a magnificent meat and potato pie with an upturned egg cup to support the golden crust. 'I thought you might like a celebration meal, Ted,' said Amelia.

'Celebration?' said Ted.

'Well, all the village is talking about how you and Scargill found Miss Evans's cat.'

Ted smiled and reflected that perhaps Scargill wasn't so bad after all. His bark was definitely better than his bite.

Meanwhile, in Prudence Golightly's General Stores, Ruby stood in the queue, holding her shopping bag and clutching a 3p-off coupon for Bird's Instant Whip from the *Daily Mirror*. In front of her Vera had just presented Prudence with a birthday card.

'Thank you, Vera,' said Prudence: 'you *remembered*.'

'Of course, Prudence,' said Vera.

'And what can I get you?' asked Prudence.

'A large tin of your best Whiskas cat food, please, Prudence,' said Vera.

Prudence peeled off the 31p label and handed the tin over the counter. 'On the house, Vera,' she said with a smile.

'That's kind, Prudence,' said Vera. 'Maggie will enjoy this.'

'It was terrific news, Vera,' said Prudence.

'Yes, such a relief.' She held up a Piercy's Butcher's bag that contained a juicy bone. 'And I'm about to deliver a present to Mrs Poole for her clever dog. You never know, my Maggie and little Scargill may be friends one day.'

Chapter Fifteen

Oliver Cromwell's Underwear

A group of parents assisted in the making of seventeenth-century costumes for the children in Classes 3 and 4 in preparation for tomorrow's visit to Clarke Hall, Wakefield.
Extract from the Ragley School Logbook:
Thursday, 25 March 1982

It was early on Thursday, 25 March, and Beth and I had spent the previous night together. It had been a wonderful night followed by a slightly tense morning.

She looked around the kitchen in dismay. 'Jack, we really do need to bring Bilbo Cottage into the twentieth century – starting with a decent washing machine.'

'Sorry, Beth,' I said, 'I'd never really thought about it.' We had been using Beth's old washing machine in her rented cottage in Morton but a permanent remedy was required.

'I've done some research on it,' she said, 'and this should be perfect.' She gave me a cutting from the *York Evening*

Press. It read 'Caravell DL500 fully automatic washing machine with a 9lb load capacity, £149.00'.

'It looks really . . . er, modern,' I said hesitantly. Washing machines were not in my comfort zone.

'And they'll deliver it immediately.' Beth sounded determined. She looked at her watch. 'Well, must rush, Jack. I'm due at High Sutton in an hour.'

Beth had been invited by Miss Barrington-Huntley to join a North Yorkshire curriculum working group for an intensive four-day course. It was clear the concept of a 'common curriculum' for all schools was gathering momentum and Beth was keen to be involved. I carried her suitcase out to her slightly rusty, pale-blue Volkswagen Beetle and kissed her goodbye.

'Drive safely, Beth,' I said, 'and I'll see you on Sunday evening.'

As she roared off, the scent of Rive Gauche perfume lingered.

Then I took the washing machine ad from my pocket and smiled. I would give her a surprise.

My journey to school was uplifting. The harsh days of winter were over. Rooks cawed in the elm-tops and the first cuckoo announced the arrival of spring. In the bare hedgerows the sharp buds of hawthorn guarded the arrowheads of daffodils and on Ragley High Street the first primroses splashed the grassy banks with fresh colour. As I pulled into the school car park it was good to be alive as the early-morning sunshine washed over me.

In the entrance hall, it was a hive of activity. A group of mothers were deep in conversation with Sally and Jo about seventeenth-century costume. Sally, our history enthusiast, had organized an educational visit tomorrow to Clarke Hall, near Wakefield, for the children in the top two classes. It was part of our joint history project and costume-making had dominated the past week. As usual, of course, there were a few who had left it to the last minute.

'Our 'Eathcliffe sez 'e wants t'be a *buccaneer* – at least ah think it were a buccaneer,' said Mrs Earnshaw.

'A buccaneer?' said Sally in surprise.

'An' our Terry wants t'be a pheasant or summat,' she added for good measure.

'He probably meant a *musketeer*,' said Sally politely.

'And a *peasant*,' added Jo, who wasn't going on the visit but was always willing to show solidarity.

Mrs Earnshaw, unmoved, pressed on and pulled two pairs of her husband's cut-down trousers and two of his old shirts from a carrier bag.

'These will be perfect, Mrs Earnshaw,' said the ever-supportive Sally. Meanwhile, the lively toddler Dallas Sue-Ellen Earnshaw had pulled a garment out of the 'finished costumes' bag and was tugging the waistband out of a pair of breeches.

Sue Phillips and Petula Dudley-Palmer had brought their sewing machines into school; Petula's, naturally, was the latest in modern technology. Betty Buttle, Margery Ackroyd, Marion Greening and Cynthia Clack were cutting, sewing and stitching as if their lives depended on it. Sally was the self-appointed shop steward, while Vera appeared to be in charge of quality control. It resembled the backroom of Burton's, the Leeds-based tailor's shop.

'First of all, you have to decide your station in life,' said Sally: 'maybe a lord or a lady.'

'Or a soldier or a peasant, Mr Sheffield,' added Vera.

'Well, we've used wool or cotton for authenticity,' said Sue Phillips and all the mothers nodded knowingly.

'And I've read skirts and breeches were particularly baggy,' added Petula Dudley-Palmer, not to be outdone.

I nodded politely and hurried into the office to escape their clutches. Sadly I was the product of a boys' grammar school education and, for me, sewing was an elusive art. A few minutes later I was busy ordering a set of brass metric weights and a box of wooden thirty-centimetre rulers when there was a tap on the door. Sue Phillips and Sally came in, each clutching a bundle. Sue held up a large bright-red, embroidered shirt and Sally draped a pair of brown breeches on my desk. 'You'll look good in these, Jack,' said a whimsical Sue Phillips.

I stared in disbelief. The outfit looked perfect for Adam and the Ants but not for a Yorkshire headteacher.

'Oh, thanks, Sue,' I said hesitantly. '. . . As long as I don't look, well, er, you know.'

'Don't worry, Jack,' said Sally with a broad grin, 'you'll blend in nicely. I've even decorated your breeches with rows of shiny buttons down the outside seams.'

'Very fetching,' I said dubiously.

'Actually, Jack,' said Sally, 'they had a practical purpose. Musketeers used them as ammunition when they ran out of musket balls or shot.'

Not for the first time I wondered how Sally knew all this.

*   *   *

Our morning lessons went well and it was encouraging to see that the children had already done a lot of background reading on our 'England in the Seventeenth Century' project.

'So what do we know about Oliver Cromwell, boys and girls?' I asked.

'He won the Battle of Naseby, Mr Sheffield,' said Jonathan Greening.

'And he overthrew King Charles I,' said Alice Baxter.

'Well done,' I said.

The children had obviously enjoyed researching the battles and politics of this tempestuous time. Best of all, everyone was looking forward to Friday morning when we would dress up in costume and visit Clarke Hall, near Wakefield. There we would go back three hundred years and experience life as it was then. It would bring history to life and the children were full of excitement. I recalled doing a turgid history course at A level in the 1960s and wished it could have been like this.

In the staff-room at morning break, Vera was glancing through the headlines of her *Daily Telegraph*. The number of unemployed had dipped below three million and the harsh winter had resulted in a £200 million insurance payout, the largest ever recorded for a natural disaster. Also, in Parliament, the former Prime Minister, Jim Callaghan, stated he was concerned to hear that a party of Argentinians had landed in the Falkland Islands and hoisted the Argentinian flag, and something ought to be done about it.

Meanwhile, Sally was concerned about her weight

again. She was munching on a chocolate digestive biscuit and reading her March issue of *Cosmopolitan*. The article 'Are You Twice the Woman Your Husband Married?' had got her thinking. She read, 'Are you finding extra inches in all the wrong places?' and nodded. Fortunately, *Cosmopolitan* had all the answers, with a recommendation to purchase a Black and Decker Home Exerciser, including a Rower at £45 and a Pacer at £40. 'You can then suggest a second honeymoon', it went on to say, and Sally selected a custard cream from the biscuit tin and nibbled on it thoughtfully.

'I've just ordered a surprise for Beth,' I said, eager to share my news.

'For the wedding?' asked Anne.

'Well, not exactly. It's a washing machine and they're delivering it on Saturday morning.'

Sally looked up. 'Was that Beth's idea?'

'Yes,' I said, slightly puzzled.

'Oh, that's all right, then,' said Sally and went back to her article.

'Who's fitting it?' asked Anne. 'John made a real mess of ours – water all over my kitchen floor.'

'I don't know,' I said, 'but I'm keen to have it up and running for when Beth gets back on Sunday evening from her course.'

'Mrs Ackroyd's husband, Wendell, fits washing machines in his spare time, Mr Sheffield,' said Vera. 'You could trust him with the key: he's perfectly reliable and, unlike his wife, he's very discreet.'

*   *   *

After school an idea occurred to me. I parked on the High Street and called into Pratt's Hardware Emporium. The frayed clothes line in my back garden had seen better days and, as Beth had reminded me, I needed to y'move with the times.

'It's a brand-new, state-of-the-art rotary drier, Mr Sheffield,' said Timothy Pratt in his monotone voice.

'It looks perfect, Timothy,' I said, 'and I know just where to put it.'

'It's a proper space-saver, Mr Sheffield, an' perfect for the modern 'ousewife.'

'Well, actually, Timothy, it's for me.'

'An' then f'Miss 'Enderson when y'get married, so t'speak,' added Timothy quickly and anxious not to offend.

'Is it difficult to put up?' I asked.

Timothy pondered this for a moment. 'Well, if y'like, ah could mention it to John Paxton. Ah bet 'e'd fix it f'you.'

John Paxton was the village odd-job man. 'Thanks, Timothy,' I said. 'I'll put a whitewash cross on the lawn where I want it erecting and then he can do it when he's got time.'

'Fine, Mr Sheffield. Ah'll keep it 'ere f'now an' 'e can collect it and do t'job.'

'Thanks again,' I said and hurried back to Kirkby Steepleton to try on my seventeenth-century costume.

On Friday morning the pupils in Sally's class and my class lined up on the cobbled driveway. Sally and all the children, plus half a dozen mothers, looked authentic in their costumes, whereas I got a few strange glances from the parents by the school gate.

'Who's Mr Sheffield s'pposed to be?' whispered Margery Ackroyd to her daughter.

'Oliver Cromwell,' said Theresa confidently. 'We've been doing 'im in 'istory.'

Margery looked at my bright-red New Wave baggy shirt, punk-rock breeches studded with steel buttons and Status Quo waistcoat. Then she shook her head sadly. 'Oliver Cromwell must 'ave been a funny feller,' she mumbled to herself.

With a farewell wave to Anne, Jo, Vera and the crowd of parents, I boarded William Featherstone's familiar ancient cream and green Reliance bus, clutching the usual shoe box full of sick-bags. 'You Can Rely on Reliance' had been painted in bright-red letters under the rear window. William, in his neatly ironed, brown bus driver's jacket, white shirt and ex-regimental tie, doffed his peaked cap with old-fashioned charm as we boarded. Then, with parents waving as though they would never see their offspring again, we set off down the High Street.

It was a bright chilly morning as we drove along the A642 on the outskirts of Wakefield and, finally, approached Clarke Hall. It stood frozen in time, a magnificent late-seventeenth-century brick-built gentleman's farmhouse set in West Yorkshire countryside. With its contemporary and replica furnishings it had become a living-history museum and perfect for a school visit.

Our guides for the day came out in full costume to meet

us. 'I'm Master Benjamin,' said the bearded man with a cheerful smile, 'and this is Mistress Bella.' He looked at me. 'And this is obviously Oliver Cromwell,' he said and some of the children giggled. We all walked inside and waited for our instructions. 'Now, boys and girls,' said Benjamin, 'when we talk to each other, we must be polite and we begin by saying, "Prithee, Master Benjamin" or "Prithee, Mistress Bella",' he glanced up at me, 'or "Prithee, Master Oliver".' There was another chuckle from the children. I was beginning to tire of my seventeenth-century alter ego.

After we had all practised addressing one another with a bow or a curtsy, Benjamin explained the programme for the day. We were in groups that rotated so that we all had an opportunity to do the various activities. These included preparing vegetables and making soup in the kitchen; going outside to do charcoal drawings of the building and leaded windows; playing a variety of seventeenth-century musical instruments; learning how to use a spinning wheel and being taught a seventeenth-century dance. A parent or teacher was with each group and I began with Bella, who gave us a brief curtsy and beckoned us into the huge kitchen. It was a marvellous experience and I soon forgot that I looked like an extra in *Mutiny on the Bounty*. We prepared our own lunch in huge cooking pots and, while stirring too vigorously, I splashed my shirt with copious amounts of the thick soup. During lunch, little Terry Earnshaw looked up hesitantly and muttered the memorable words, 'Prithee, Master Benjamin, can ah leave m'carrots?' and everyone laughed. After that, the day progressed well and, while I was hopeless at the dancing, I enjoyed using the authentic spinning wheel and practising with quill pens.

So it was a tired but happy party that finally arrived back in Ragley as darkness began to fall and I drove home to change. With Beth away there was no incentive to cook for myself, so I drove back to The Royal Oak for a drink and a meal.

When I walked in, the television, on its high shelf above the bar, was droning on unnoticed. It was a programme about Sunday trading and Lady Trumpington in the House of Lords was in full flow. 'On a Sunday, a mother may buy gin for herself but not powdered milk for her baby, a newspaper from a newsagent but not a Bible from a bookseller; chemists can make up a doctor's prescription but will not sell you a lipstick!' Meanwhile, a Woolworth's store in Slough was about to be prosecuted for announcing its intention to open on a Sunday.

'Sunday should be a day o' rest,' said Old Tommy Piercy at the bar.

'Not when y'work in a pub, Tommy,' said Don as he served me with a pint of Chestnut and shouted to Sheila for another portion of dumplings and minced beef.

I sipped on my pint and looked around. The bars were filling up with the usual crowd. By good fortune I noticed that, in the corner of the lounge bar, Margery Ackroyd was sitting with her husband, Wendell. They were deep in conversation.

Margery considered herself to be at the cutting edge of fashion and had taken special care to position her double-flapped Velcro shoulderpads under her bra straps. She modelled herself on the television star Linda Gray, who, as the downtrodden Sue-Ellen in *Dallas*, always looked the image of early-eighties elegance. Margery, a part-time assistant manager at a travel agent's in York, was determined 'to be the boss but stay sexy'.

Wendell, however, thought the effect was very strange and wondered why Margery's salmon-pink frilly blouse looked as though she had forgotten to remove the coat hanger. When I approached him, he said he would be happy to help me out with the installation of the washing machine, while Margery listened intently, eager not to miss any opportunity for gossip. 'No problem, Mr Sheffield,' he said. 'Ah'm a dab 'and at fittin' washin' machines. Ah can do it in m'sleep.'

'So when can you come round?' I asked.

''Ow about early Saturday morning?' said Wendell.

'Perfect,' I said, 'and how much?'

'Call it a fiver, Mr Sheffield,' he said.

I shook his hand in relief. 'It's a deal; see you then.'

On Saturday morning the washing machine arrived at nine o'clock and Wendell Ackroyd was as good as his word and began fitting it. Then he yawned and stretched.

'Are you tired, Mr Ackroyd?' I asked.

'Ah am that, Mr Sheffield,' he shouted from under the draining board. 'Ah 'ave trouble sleeping. Margery says ah talk in m'sleep.'

It was soon fixed and I gave him a five-pound note. 'Is it easy to operate? I want to try it out tomorrow morning, you see,' I said.

He gave me a quick demonstration and it seemed simple enough. 'Ah'll call by on Sunday, if y'like, t'check it's OK,' he said.

'Thanks,' I said, 'and if I'm out I'll leave the key under the mat.'

On Saturday afternoon Dan Hunter pulled up outside in his Wolseley Hornet. I needed to order a new suit for the wedding and Dan knew the perfect place. 'Good stuff, Jack – and cheap,' he said with appropriate Yorkshire logic.

We parked in Duncombe Place in the shadow of York Minster. 'I'll meet you in half an hour in Parliament Street, Jack,' he said. 'I've got to get something for Jo's birthday.' Jo had dropped a big hint to Dan that she would like a bottle of Babe cologne, a new fragrance product by Fabergé, and Dan, as a new-age eighties man, was both willing and confident enough to oblige.

I set off to walk down Petergate, when a man and a woman wearing Stars and Stripes baseball caps approached me. The portly American had a large name badge pinned to his checked shirt. It read: 'Dwight Clearwater III'.

'Excuse me, mah friend,' he said, 'but is this,' he glanced down at a typed list, 'er, Stonehenge?'

'No, this is York Minster,' I explained politely. 'Stonehenge is down south in Wiltshire.'

His partner's badge read 'Emmylou Clearwater' and she nodded knowingly. 'That's raaaht, mah lil' honeybunch, Stonehenge is that lil' bitty pile o' stones near London, England.'

'Ah, you mean where that good ol' boy Billy Shakes-peare was bawn,' said Dwight.

'That's so raaht, mah lil' chickpea,' said Emmylou.

Dwight looked at me, expecting praise for his knowledge of our greatest playwright. It wasn't forthcoming.

'We were kinda wond'rin' if you maaht know Chuck an' Betty, our dear friends, in Ker-narras-bruff,' he said, pointing to a map of Great Britain.

'Ker-narras-bruff?' I was losing the will to live. 'Oh, you mean, Knaresborough.'

'Knaresborough?' said Emmylou. 'Ah do declare you have the strangest way of saying things here in your pretty lil' state of York-sheer.'

'Well, if you'll excuse me, I have to get on,' I said hurriedly. Anglo-American relations could be damaged if I continued this conversation.

'One las' thing, mah good friend,' said Dwight: 'can you kindly tell us where we can try your York-sheer puddin'?'

'Yes. Try the Guy Fawkes pub across the road. They do a lovely lunch,' I said.

'Guy Fawkes?' said Emmylou.

'Yes, mah lil' sweetie-pie,' said Dwight, with the appropriate modesty of a man with an American degree. 'He was the limey that invented fireworks.'

'You are sooooo heestorical, mah sweetness,' said Emmylou, and they wandered off to the birthplace of Guy Fawkes, where, after a traditional roast-beef dinner, Emmylou asked the puzzled waiter, 'For the sweet course, mah friend, can we have your good ol' York-sheer puddin'.'

The waiter scratched his head. 'Y've 'ad it, luv. It were that round thing wi' gravy in that came wi' y'main course.' He didn't get a tip.

Early on Sunday morning, after hanging my new suit in the wardrobe, I put my Oliver Cromwell shirt in the washing machine and added my week's supply of underwear. Following Wendell's instructions, I pressed a few buttons and watched in complete admiration as everything seemed to work perfectly. Then I went out to the garden to inspect my new rotary drier. John Paxton had erected it in exactly the right spot. The sun came out, all was going to plan and I knew Beth would be impressed.

I had decided to go to the eleven o'clock Communion Service at St Mary's, partly because our banns were being read out but mainly because it was the most peaceful time of the week. In a busy life it was good to relax in the serene quiet of the church and enjoy Joseph's sermon and the organ music, as well, of course, as the good companionship of the church community.

So, at ten o'clock, it was with a feeling of inner peace that I emptied the washing machine into my wicker basket in order to hang the clothes on the rotary drier. Then I looked in horror at the collection of damp garments piled before me. The red shirt was clean again, if a slightly paler shade of red. However, all my white underwear had turned a violent shade of bright pink. The answer soon became clear: the colour from the shirt had run. With suitable self-restraint, I avoided kicking the washing machine and pegged the washing on the rotary drier, secretly pleased it was hidden away in my back garden. Before I left for church, as an afterthought I left the key under the mat for Wendell Ackroyd.

Later that evening, Beth was thrilled to see our modern, twentieth-century washing machine and rotary drier. I didn't mention the fact that my underwear was now a startling shade of rose-pink and an early visit to the men's department in Marks & Spencer beckoned.

On Monday morning it was the turn of my class to lead assembly. I began with a round of questions about our visit and, at first, all went well.

'So what do we know about Oliver Cromwell, boys and girls?' I asked.

Dean Kershaw's hand shot up. ''E were a Round'ead, Mr Sheffield.'

'An' 'e defeated t'Royalists,' added Tracy Hartley for good measure.

'My mother said 'e were a big girl,' announced Theresa Ackroyd.

'A big girl!' I exclaimed.

'That's reight, Mr Sheffield, a big girl.'

'And why is that, Theresa?'

''Cause 'e used t'wear pink underwear.'

'Pardon?'

'Well, that's what me mum said, Mr Sheffield.'

Everyone giggled, Sally and Jo suppressed a smile and Anne simply gave me a knowing look.

It would appear that Wendell Ackroyd really *did* talk in his sleep.

Chapter Sixteen

The Busby Girl

*A temporary kitchen assistant commenced work today.
Mrs Mary Attersthwaite will support our school cook,
Mrs Mapplebeck, for three days during the absence of
Mrs Critchley. A selection of artwork from all classes was
prepared for display by Mrs Pringle. This will be exhibited
at the Children's Art Exhibition in York Art Gallery on
Saturday, 24 April.*

Extract from the Ragley School Logbook:
Tuesday, 20 April 1982

There is a water-colour painting on the wall above
the headteacher's desk in the school office. It is a view
of Ragley School with its distinctive bell tower and set
among horse-chestnut trees that are bursting into life.
Many years have passed now since that April morning
when the artist set up her easel on the village green and
watched the bright sunshine light up the school walls like
amber honey. If you look closely at the bottom corner of

the painting you will see a small neat signature. It reads, 'Mary Attersthwaite 1982', but I shall always remember her as the Busby Girl.

Tuesday, 20 April 1982, was a morning that lifted the spirits. My drive from Kirkby Steepleton was filled with the sights and sounds of new life. Bright-yellow forsythia glowed in the hedgerows and, in the distant fields, the ewes baa-aad protectively over their new-born lambs. As I approached Ragley, a pheasant's flapping wings shattered the tranquillity, followed immediately by its harsh, shrieking cry to protect its space. On the grassy borders of the High Street clumps of daffodils and tulips waved in the gentle breeze as I pulled up outside Prudence Golightly's General Stores to buy my morning newspaper.

The front page of *The Times* was full of gloomy news. Britain and Argentina appeared to be on the brink of war and the headline 'Every man willing to die in Battle for South Georgia' suggested troubled times ahead. Meanwhile, Sir Keith Joseph, Education Secretary, had informed the House of Commons that seventy-nine village schools had closed in the past twelve months. Fortunately, Ragley wasn't one of them.

In the entrance hall, Shirley Mapplebeck, the school cook, was waiting for me. Next to her was a delicate lady with greying hair tied in a bun and the brightest blue eyes I had ever seen. She looked to be in her mid fifties and had the fresh complexion of someone who enjoys the out-doors.

'This is Mary Attersthwaite, Mr Sheffield, m'cousin from near Thirkby,' said Shirley. 'She's taking over t'day as assistant in t'kitchen until Doreen comes back on Friday.'

Doreen Critchley, our fiercesome dinner lady and kitchen assistant, had taken three days compassionate leave to attend her Uncle Willie's funeral in Wales, so a replacement had been required and Vera had completed the necessary paperwork.

'Good morning, Mr Sheffield. I'm pleased to meet you,' said Mary. Her accent was definitely Yorkshire but what Vera would describe as 'refined Yorkshire': in other words, Mary didn't drop her 'aitches.

'Pleased to meet you, Mary,' I said, 'and good luck in the kitchen. Shirley's a wonderful cook.'

Shirley smiled shyly. 'And so's our Mary, Mr Sheffield. She were Bradford Bread Pudding Champion,' said Shirley with pride.

Anne and Sally walked into the entrance hall carrying a large pile of children's artwork. 'Ooooh, I love bread pudding,' said Anne.

'And so do I,' said Sally. 'I know I shouldn't, but it's my favourite.'

'We'll 'ave t'see what we can do, won't we, Mary?' said Shirley and they hurried off to the kitchen.

For the next two days life was busy and Sally worked hard to collect and mount our artwork for the Children's Art Exhibition at the gallery in York. It was Thursday lunchtime when Vera came to tell us all that a surprise awaited us in the staff-room. When I walked in, Shirley was giving out plates and spoons and Mary was serving large helpings of bread pudding.

'This is the best bread pudding I've ever tasted,' said Sally.

'I agree,' said Jo.

'Please would you give us the recipe, Mary?' asked Vera, notebook in hand.

'Certainly,' said Mary. 'I use twelve ounces of bread, twelve ounces of mixed dried fruit, three ounces of brown sugar, three ounces of suet, a teaspoonful of mixed spice and one egg.'

Vera made her shorthand notes with swift strokes. 'And what's the process?'

'That's easy,' said Mary. 'I just break the bread into small pieces in a large mixing bowl, cover it with cold water and soak for ten hours.'

You could have heard a pin drop. One of the great secrets of the universe was being revealed and the ladies of Ragley School hung on to every word.

'Then I drain the bread in a colander and remove as much water as possible,' continued Mary: 'using the back of a large spoon helps. After that I return the bread to a bowl, add the rest of the ingredients and mix it well.'

Vera's pencil continued scratching for a moment and then stopped, poised in mid-air. The denouement had arrived.

'Finally, I line a baking dish with greaseproof paper and pour in the mixture,' said Mary. 'It should be soft and drop into the dish; if not, just add a little water. Then I bake it at 180 degrees Celsius for about one hour and, last of all, I sprinkle it with sugar when it's still hot from the oven.'

As we ate our scrumptious bread pudding, Shirley

looked with affection at her favourite cousin. 'She's 'ad an interesting life, 'as our Mary. She were a Busby girl.'

'A Busby girl?' I said.

'Oh, you mean that wonderful department store in Bradford,' said Vera. 'I used to go there with my mother, especially at Christmas.'

'That was the best time, Miss Evans,' said Mary, 'and the *happiest* time of my life.'

'Busby's?' said Jo. 'What was it like?'

A faraway look came into Mary's eyes. 'Well, I started there in 1941 on my sixteenth birthday. I was in the hairdressing department and I earned fifteen shillings per week, plus a five shillings war bonus. Shopping was different then, Mrs Hunter,' she said and Jo nodded. 'The staff thought of themselves as one big family and we all took pride in customer service. The Busby family were wonderful. They really cared for all their staff and knew all our names. It was a proper *family* store. Then, after the war, my pay went up to seventeen and sixpence per week. I remember working late on a Thursday night and all my friends came in so I could practise on their hair.'

Mary had a captive audience and we all settled back to enjoy her reminiscences. Having been brought up in Leeds, I was familiar with Busby's department store. Founded in 1908, it was a grand Victorian building that became a Bradford shopping emporium and was famous for quality merchandise at bargain prices. Opposite the old Theatre Royal Picture House, it commanded an ideal location for the shoppers of West Yorkshire and was rightly known as 'the store with the friendly welcome'.

The founder of the store was Eric Busby and, in later years, his three sons had carried on the tradition of excellent service and value for money. Mary was one of many with happy memories of this famous store.

'I remember it well,' said Vera. 'It was particularly exciting at Christmas when Santa arrived in the Busby Grotto.'

'That's right, Miss Evans,' said Mary. 'My boss heard I was good at art so at Christmas I went to help out in the Display Department . . . which is where I met my Gerald. I had to make up buckets of glue size and whitening and then paste grey-coloured paper over wire-mesh "mountains" to make Santa's magical kingdom.'

'Gerald is Mary's 'usband,' explained Shirley. ''E's a picture-framer now in a shop in Thirkby.'

'Yes,' said Mary with a smile. 'Gerald and I used to see each other in the canteen. You could get lobster patties for five old pence and green figs and cream for six old pence, a real treat. Gerald bought me a transistor radio. He paid for it with 'saved-up' threepenny bits . . . I've still got it now. We did our courting behind lift number six. It wasn't the most romantic spot but, in those days, beggars couldn't be choosers.'

Everyone laughed. It was good to hear this animated lady relive her working life. We sipped our tea and finished off the bread pudding.

'I remember going with my mother to the sales,' said Vera. 'They were something to behold – queues as far as you could see, chairs outside for the elderly and the first seventy-five got a cup of tea.'

'So were you always a hairdresser?' asked Anne.

'No. After that, I worked in the Lamson Room, collecting the tubes,' said Mary.

'Lamson?' queried Jo.

'Yes. When you bought something in the store, the assistant put your money into a small numbered tube and then inserted it into a pipe that ran right through the store. It was incredible how it worked and we would send it on its way back to the right department, carrying your change, with a terrific whooshing sound. It was like a miniature spaceship.'

'I remember those,' said Vera.

'Altogether there was ten miles of tubing to take each transaction to the right place,' said Mary. 'Each department had a number – for example, Haberdashery was number six – so nothing went astray. The whole process only took two minutes to get to us and back, so, while the customer was waiting for her purchase to be neatly wrapped, there was no delay.'

'And you always got the correct change and a receipt,' said Vera.

'What a good idea,' said Sally. 'It's certainly got more style than all these new electronic systems.'

Jo looked puzzled but nodded anyway.

'I agree,' said Mary, 'and all the Busby family made sure it worked well. They used to *walk the floors* and there was always a lovely atmosphere. Our motto was 'Do unto others as you would have them do unto you' and that's what we did. Mr Arthur and Mr Eric were always polite and friendly. Best of all was Mr Paul, who always stopped for a chat . . . He was a very handsome man . . . and then there was Mr Ernest, who gave me a lovely cosmetic tray when Gerald and I got married. You don't get bosses like that any more.' She looked up at me and blushed. 'Present company excepted of course.'

Everyone smiled and gazed in admiration at this eloquent lady. However, it was obvious to us all that Mary still missed the *ker-ching* of the cash registers, the whoosh of the overhead Lamson cash carriers and the chatter of shop girls.

'So what happened to Busby's?' asked Jo.

'Sadly, it changed,' said Mary. 'It merged with Debenham's in the late fifties and the name Busby disappeared. Then three years ago the whole store burnt down.'

'Oh dear,' said Anne.

'It was the end of an era,' said Vera.

'I still miss it, but I'm trying to do something worthwhile with my life, so now, in my spare time, I paint with my water-colours,' said Mary.

'You'll have to have a look at the children's artwork for the exhibition on Saturday,' said Sally.

'Of course,' said Mary.

'And perhaps show the boys and girls how you paint in water-colours,' I added.

'It would be a pleasure,' said Mary.

The bell rang for afternoon school and we all hurried off full of bread pudding and happy thoughts of shopping in the world before supermarkets.

It was before school on Friday morning when, from my office window, I saw Mary Attersthwaite walk into the middle of the village green and stare up at the school.

She was carrying her artist's materials. A large leather bag was over her shoulder and an easel was under her arm. Curious, I went out to see her.

As I approached, Mary opened up her folding canvas seat, picked up her notebook and opened it to the next clean page. With swift confident strokes of a soft B pencil she sketched the broad outline of the school and the tall horse-chestnut trees. Then she shielded her eyes from the sharp April sunshine and shaded in the patches of shadow as they would appear in morning sunlight. It was a brilliant instant drawing.

'Good morning, Mary,' I said: 'a beautiful morning.'

'Perfect for a painting, Mr Sheffield,' she replied with a smile. 'No wind and good light.'

I watched her as she erected her wooden easel, spending time getting the legs level on the tufted grass. On a board of thick plywood she had attached a sheet of water-colour paper, held fast with masking tape, and then she fixed it at a slight angle on the easel, tilting towards her. With a soft pencil, so as not to leave any grooves on the smooth paper, she sketched the school once again with its bell tower and sloping slate roof. I said nothing, her concentration being intense.

Finally, satisfied, she sat down, filled her water pot from her bottle of fresh water and hung it from its loop of string on a hook at the side of the easel. 'Time to begin,' she said.

'Mary,' I said, 'perhaps, later this morning, you might allow some of the children to see how it progresses.'

'Of course, Mr Sheffield. It would be a pleasure,' she said.

Then, with the confidence of experience, she picked up a large soft brush, opened her tin box of paints and began with broad sweeps to create a damp wash of pale-blue sky.

'Well, I'll leave you to it, Mary,' I said. 'What a wonderful way to spend the morning,' I added a little wistfully.

Mary paused and looked up at me reflectively. 'I've walked a long road, Mr Sheffield . . . and it's been a life full of light and shade.' As she resumed her painting, a mantle of peace surrounded her.

Back in my classroom, while the majority of answers to some of the questions in our Countryside Project were well informed, Theresa Ackroyd once again provided alternative, if perfectly logical, solutions. In answer to the question 'Why are electricity pylons dangerous?' Theresa wrote, 'You might walk into one.' Likewise, to 'What problems might hedgerow removal cause?' her response was: 'All the cows will escape.' I smiled and wrote in the margin, 'We need to discuss this, Theresa.' It also occurred to me that, on occasions, children provide better answers than the 'right' ones.

Ten minutes before morning break the children in my class were surprised when I asked them to stop work. They looked up at the clock, thinking I had made a mistake, but, significantly, no one complained. I led them out of school on to the village green, where Mary glanced up from her painting and waved in acknowledgement.

By the time we gathered round her easel, I noticed the water-colour had progressed dramatically. She was clearly a quick worker. Her keen eye had identified the lightest parts of the subject and she had painted these first, gradually moving on to the detail. The children were fascinated by the techniques described by Mary. 'Then, boys and girls,' she said, 'I use this square-ended brush for the gable end of the school and for the windows.' She dabbed on a little more paint and the roof tiles and windows sprang into new form.

'Cor, can we 'ave a go, Mr Sheffield?' asked Dean Kershaw.

'Good idea, Dean,' I said. 'We can do some painting this afternoon.'

While the children walked back into school I stayed with Mary. Soon a group were playing 'Kiss-Catch' on the playground while the younger ones were enjoying a game of 'What Time is it, Mr Wolf?'

Alice Baxter and Theresa Ackroyd were turning the ends of a large skipping rope and children were jumping in and out, singing their skipping rhyme.

Mary chuckled. 'Some things don't change, do they, Mr Sheffield?' and she murmured the familiar rhyme along with the chanting children.

'Each, peach, pear, plum,
I spy Tom Thumb,
Tom Thumb in the wood,
I spy Robin Hood,
Robin Hood in the cellar,
I spy Cinderella . . .'

'The happiest time of their life, Mr Sheffield,' said Mary. I smiled and walked back into school.

*   *   *

On Saturday morning I set off to do some shopping in Ragley on my way to Beth's cottage in Morton. We had decided to go into York to see the Children's Art Exhibition and, in the meantime, Beth was doing some packing, which made me realize how close the wedding was.

I pulled up alongside the single pump on the courtyard in front of Pratt's Garage. Victor lumbered out to meet me while rubbing his grease-blackened hands on the bib of his filthy overalls. 'Could you fill her up, please, Victor?' I asked. He didn't look happy. On the other hand he never did. Through gritted teeth I asked the inevitable question, 'And how are you, Victor?'

He sucked air through his teeth and I knew it must be bad news. 'Well, Mr Sheffield,' he said mournfully, 'ah get pains in m'back when ah put mi jim-jam bottoms on at bedtime.' He winced painfully. It was a tough life being a martyr.

'So have you been to Dr Davenport?'

'Yes, ah 'ave, but that were no good.'

'Why not, Victor?' I asked.

'Well, 'e sed ah've got t'go to an Austria-path, but ah told 'im ah've no wish t'go abroad an' Yorkshire's jus' fine f'me.'

'And what did Dr Davenport say to that, Victor?' I asked.

''E jus' gave me one of 'is septic looks,' said Victor; 'y'know the sort.'

'I certainly do,' I said as he ambled off to get my change.

*　　　*　　　*

Ragley High Street was busy with shoppers and I pulled up outside Piercy's the Butcher's. When I walked in Old Tommy Piercy was serving a young man in a smart suit, who said curtly, 'I'd like some steak.'

The ladies behind me winced visibly. He hadn't said 'please' and it hadn't gone unnoticed.

'Rump or sirloin?' asked Old Tommy, equally unimpressed.

'Sirloin,' said the young man. 'Four slices, each one a half inch wide.'

Again there was a muttered reaction from the ladies in the queue. Old Tommy glanced up at the man, weighed up his pinstripe suit and his aloof manner and began to carve.

'I said a *half* inch,' repeated the man.

'That's what y'gettin',' said Old Tommy brusquely.

'I'll have you know that in *my* profession I work to ten thousandth of an inch,' he said.

Old Tommy leant over the counter and waved the sharpest knife in Yorkshire under the visitor's nose. 'Well, young man,' he said firmly, 'watch 'n' y'll learn summat . . . 'cause ah'm *exact*.'

Following his departure, the ladies in the queue gave Old Tommy a round of applause and he bowed modestly. 'Off-comers,' he muttered: 'ah've no time for 'em.' Then he turned to serve me with a smile. 'Now then, young Mr Sheffield, what can ah do for our village 'eadmaster?'

'Please may I have two steaks, Mr Piercy, and perhaps you could select them for me.'

He sliced two large sirloin steaks. "Alf inch each,' he said with a chuckle.

'Exactly, Mr Piercy,' I said.

The door of Nora's Coffee Shop was open and the gentle sound of Simon and Garfunkel's 'April Come She Will' drifted outside from the juke-box. I walked in to find Nora, Dorothy, Big Dave, Little Malcolm and Timothy Pratt staring in wonderment at a large British Telecom poster on the wall. It read, 'It doesn't cost much to stay in touch.' Apparently, direct dialling to Australia was now available for only £1.38 per minute and there was no longer any need to go through the operator.

'Our Kingsley's been t'Australia,' said Timothy.

'Is that 'im what keeps fewwets?' asked Nora.

'That's 'im, Nora,' said Timothy.

'Y'can wing diwect to Austwalia now,' said Nora.

Dorothy shook her head forlornly as she rearranged a pile of two-day-old hot-cross buns. 'Ah don't know *nobody* in Australia, Nora,' said Dorothy, 'but ah wish ah did.'

'Well, ah've got Auntie Wuth in Canbewwa,' said Nora, 'but she's ex-diwectowy.'

'Mus' be a long cable under t'sea,' said Big Dave philosophically.

'Y'reight there, Dave,' agreed Little Malcolm: 'mus' be a long 'un under that Specific Ocean.'

'No, ah don't think so, Malcolm,' said Dorothy. 'It's summat t'do wi' stalactites that fly up in space.'

'No, not stalactites, Dowothy,' said Nora, 'it's them *satellites* they send up in wockets. Isn't that wight, Mr Sheffield?'

'Er, yes, Nora . . . So it's just a coffee and a hot-cross bun, please.'

'Comin' up, Mr Sheffield,' said Nora. 'C'mon, Dowothy, f'get Austwalia; you choose a nice hot-cwoss bun f'Mr Sheffield an' ah'll get 'is fwothy coffee.'

Half an hour later, with a bootful of shopping, I pulled up outside Beth's cottage on Morton Road. The hallway was full of cardboard boxes with labels on them that read, BEDROOM, KITCHEN, LOUNGE and, of slight concern to me, GARAGE, as I had always considered the garage to be *my* domain.

'I hope Bilbo Cottage has elastic walls, Jack,' said Beth with a grin. She looked relaxed in a checked blouse, a fashionable 'Sherpa' woollen quilted waistcoat, tight stonewashed jeans and calf-high leather boots. Reaching up to kiss me, 'Missed you last night,' she said mischievously.

We set off for York and, twenty minutes later, parked on Lord Mayor's Walk alongside the city walls. The grassy banks were swathed in daffodils that lifted the spirits on this sunlit morning. We held hands and I felt content knowing that, in a little over a month, this beautiful woman would become my wife. Under the magnificent archway of Monk Bar we scampered up the narrow stone stairway on to the Roman walls, one of the great sights of England. We paused to enjoy the glorious views of the Minster and peer over the lovely gardens of Gray's Court, behind the Treasurer's House, where as a student I used to sit on the spacious lawn and read the poems of T. S. Eliot. Then, at Bootham Bar, we descended into

York's medieval streets and there before us was York Art Gallery.

We joined a queue and waited behind two harassed women. It appeared their view of children's art was slightly jaundiced to say the least. One was leaning on a push-chair filled with groceries and the other was clutching a holiday brochure. A heated debate had ensued. 'Ah 'ate art,' said Push-chair Woman. 'Ah prefer photos.'

'So do I,' said Holiday Brochure Woman, 'but ah 'ad t'come cos of our Clifford's penguins. God knows why 'e painted penguins.'

'Tell me abart it!' replied Push-chair Woman. 'Our Darrell painted a picture of 'is tortoise. 'E were gonna paint 'is ferret but t'little bugger wunt keep still.'

'Ah know what y'mean. Anyway ah'm jus' showin' me face an' then ah'm goin' t'travel agents. We're off t'Benidorm.'

'Benidorm? What's it like, then?'

'Like Skegness wi' sun.'

'Oh well, we're goin' back t'Butlin's. We love Butlin's: everything's free f'kids an' y'get proper food – no foreign rubbish.'

'It says 'ere in t'brochure y'get good food where we're stayin',' persisted Holiday Brochure Woman.

Push-chair Woman shook her head knowingly. 'Yeah, but y'don't get spam fritters in Benidorm.'

There was a long pause. This was clearly the knockout punch. 'So where's these bleedin' penguins, then?' said Holiday Brochure Woman and, as the queue moved forward, they disappeared into the crowd.

It was an excellent exhibition and while we were admiring Jimmy Poole's painting of Scargill, his Yorkshire terrier, chasing Maggie, Vera's black-and-white cat, a familiar voice said, 'Aren't children's paintings tremendous, Mr Sheffield?' It was Mary Attersthwaite.

'Hello, Mary,' I said. 'Good to see you . . . This is my fiancée, Beth Henderson.'

Mary smiled and, after introductions, she had an in-depth conversation with Beth about children's art. To Beth's surprise she discovered that Mary lived near her school, just outside Hartingdale, and, before long, they had both agreed to begin a water-colour painting club in the school for children and adults.

So it was that a long and happy relationship began and Mary found her new niche in life.

A week later, Shirley brought into the office a large package, neatly wrapped in brown paper, and placed it on Vera's desk. 'A gift for the school from Mary,' she said.

Vera unwrapped it and, to our delight, we saw it was a beautifully framed, water-colour painting of Ragley School signed by Mary Attersthwaite. 'I know just the place,' said Vera and, by the end of the day, she had hung it on the wall above my desk.

On the small card that came with the painting was the message *'To all at Ragley School, with happy memories, from the Busby Girl'*.

Chapter Seventeen

The Enemy Within

The PTA authorized the purchase of a new football and netball strip prior to the Annual Small Schools Football & Netball Tournament at Easington on Saturday, 8 May.
Extract from the Ragley School Logbook:
Wednesday, 5 May 1982

It was Wednesday morning, 5 May, and Ruby the caretaker was leaning against the pine table in the entrance hall. A mop and bucket lay discarded at her feet. It wasn't like Ruby to just sit around and I wondered what could be the problem. Then I realized as she held up her newspaper. The headline on the front page of the *Sun* simply read: 'GOTCHA!'

'Ah'm worried about our Andy,' said Ruby. Her eyes were red with recent tears.

I looked at her newspaper. In its inimitable style the *Sun* had reported the sinking of the *Belgrano*. Under the headline 'The navy had the Argies on their knees last night after a devastating double punch . . . Wallop' it read: 'Our lads sink gunboat and hole cruiser'.

'I'm sure he'll come home safe and sound, Ruby,' I said with as much conviction as I could muster.

'Not like them poor Argies, Mr Sheffield. There'll be a lot o' mothers who won't 'ave their sons coming 'ome.'

I had to agree, but others would say it was unpatriotic to do so. I recalled my grandfather, killed at the age of twenty-one on the first terrible day of the Battle of the Somme, and my father, floundering in the South China Sea while being strafed by Japanese fighter pilots. War was a bloody business and I had been one of the fortunate generation who had lived during a time of peace.

Vera suddenly appeared from the school office and quickly summed up the situation. She put her arm round Ruby's shoulders. 'Come into the staff-room and have a cup of tea, Ruby,' she said gently.

There had been a surprise escalation of political events. In early April, Argentina had occupied the Falklands with ten thousand troops and, in response, Margaret Thatcher had sent a large British task force on a 7,500 mile journey to liberate this tiny group of windswept islands in the South Atlantic. It was the biggest naval action since the Second World War and included the 5th Infantry Brigade and the British 3rd Commando Brigade. Sergeant Andy Smith was among them.

We didn't know it then but the war was destined to last seventy-four days and account for the lives of two hundred and fifty-five British and six hundred and forty-nine Argentine soldiers, sailors and airmen and three civilian Falklanders. But in Ragley-on-the-Forest Church of England Primary School in a quiet corner of England, life simply went on as normal and the milk continued to be delivered on time.

As I sat at my desk, it seemed trivial to be thinking about a new football strip.

On Saturday it was the Annual Small Schools Football and Netball Tournament in the spacious grounds of Easington Primary School. Our Parent–Teacher Association had recently purchased a new netball strip with blue skirts, white polo shirts and smart bibs with large letters on them such as GK and GA, denoting their positions. The girls looked really smart and were thrilled with their new outfits. However, our football team regularly turned out in blue shirts of widely different shades, scruffy shorts and multicoloured socks. As Eric Earnshaw, father of Heathcliffe and Terry, commented in his broad Barnsley accent at our last football match, 'They look a reight ragtag 'n' bobtail, Mr Sheffield.'

The telephone rang as I sat at my desk. It was Sue Phillips, the Chair of our Parent–Teacher Association. 'It's about a new football strip, Jack,' she said. 'My husband plays golf with the man who owns that new sports shop in Goodramgate in York and they've got an offer on at present. I could call in after my shift at the hospital and check it out if you like.'

'Thanks, Sue, that's really helpful,' I said. 'I appreciate your support.'

'Oh, and by the way, Jack,' added Sue before she rang off, 'I've just bought the most wonderful hat for the wedding.'

I glanced at the calendar on the wall. Sally had circled

29 May in red felt pen. In a little over three weeks I would be marrying Beth Henderson.

It was morning break when Vera raised the Falklands problem. Anne was on playground duty while the rest of us met in the staff-room. 'Ruby was very upset this morning,' said Vera as she handed out the milky drinks. 'It's sad that all this has suddenly flared up again.'

'We've been in dispute over these islands for centuries,' said Sally. 'Apparently they were named after Lord Falkland, Treasurer to the Navy, by Captain Strong, who landed there almost three hundred years ago to replenish his water supplies.'

'So when did the Argentinians get involved?' I asked.

'Well, I seem to recall it was in the early nineteenth century that Argentina claimed the islands,' said Sally, 'but then they were quickly repossessed by Britain in 1833.'

'And presumably this General Galtieri has stirred it all up again,' said Jo, scanning Vera's *Daily Telegraph*. 'It says here that after taking over the presidency of Argentina in a coup in 1981 he immediately set about planning to retake what he calls *Las Malvinas*.'

'Yes . . . That's their name for the Falklands,' said Sally.

'And Margaret definitely won't back down,' said Vera, shaking her head in dismay. 'She's not the type.' It was a dilemma for Vera: she hated war but always supported the venerable Margaret.

During the afternoon in my class we looked at a selection of newspapers as part of our Communication project. The children had brought in a copy of the newspaper their parents bought each day and we examined how the same story was reported by the different journalists. It threw up some interesting discussion, particularly relating to the promise of extra television channels. The BBC had announced that direct broadcasting by satellite channels would be introduced in 1986 and all the children were most enthusiastic. For my part, as I only ever watched BBC1, BBC2 and ITV, I couldn't imagine the need for more choice.

However, it appeared that Dean Kershaw hadn't completely grasped some of the arguments. In answer to the question 'What is the meaning of "free press"?' he wrote, 'When your mother irons your shirts', and I put a red exclamation mark in the margin.

On the way home that evening I bought a fish-and-chips supper and ate it on my lap while watching Frank Bough and Sue Lawley in *Nationwide*. They reported that the Tottenham Hotspur team manager, Keith Burtenshaw, had announced that the Argentinian Ricky Villa was to be left out of the FA Cup Final team due to play Queen's Park Rangers at Wembley later this month. Fed up with Argentina, I decided to change channels. It was a choice between snooker from the Crucible on BBC2 or a programme on post-natal depression on ITV. It wasn't difficult: I went for David Vine and the snooker.

On Thursday morning as I drove out of Kirkby Steepleton, the first rays of sunshine were gilding the high cirrus clouds. Wisps of mist caressed the distant fields with ghostly fingertips and the vast sky over the plain of York was washed clean. It was a pink dawn, a new day and, on my car radio, I hummed along to Paul McCartney and Stevie Wonder's 'Ebony and Ivory'.

Even Ruby looked a little more cheerful when I arrived at school. 'Our Duggie's painting t'kitchen t'brighten t'place up f'when our Andy comes 'ome, Mr Sheffield,' said Ruby. She looked really excited.

'That's great news, Ruby,' I said, 'and what colour will it be?'

'Well, 'e gorrit cheap off Tidy Tim – some old stock,' said Ruby. 'It's gonna be Mongolian and white.'

I couldn't wait to see it.

Our History lesson went well apart from a few of the usual howlers. In answer to the question 'What was the Romans' greatest achievement?' Tracy Hartley had written, 'Learning Latin', and Dean Kershaw thought that 'Round his garden' was the perfect answer to 'Where was Hadrian's wall built?' Neither did Amanda Pickles hesitate in her response to the question 'Where was the Magna Carta signed?' She wrote, 'At the bottom of the page', and, once again, I couldn't fault her logic.

It was lunchtime when Sue Phillips popped her smiling face round the staff-room door. 'I've got the shirts, Jack,' she said, 'and they look great.'

She put a cardboard box on the coffee table and held up a football shirt with pale-blue and white vertical stripes.

'Terrific,' I said. 'We'll be the smartest team at the tournament.'

'Well done, Sue,' said Anne. 'What about shorts and socks?'

'Marion Greening is going into the Co-op this afternoon for the shorts and Freddie Kershaw knows a market trader in Thirkby and he's picking up a set of socks. I've asked them to bring all the kit to the tournament and the boys can change there.'

'Good idea, Sue, and thanks again,' I said.

'So we're all set,' she said, 'and with everything at rock-bottom price.'

She settled down for a well-earned coffee and struck up a conversation with Vera, Anne, Sally and Jo about wedding hats, at which point I made a hasty exit.

That evening, in fine weather, I decided to get some fresh air and began work on my vegetable plot in the back garden of Bilbo Cottage. After an hour of digging I took a breather on the old bench and thought about my new life with Beth in this lovely old cottage. Around me were the sights and sounds of this picturesque part of North Yorkshire. The swallows had returned with their familiar acrobatics, a sign of the summer months that stretched ahead. They had migrated from southern Africa after spending winter there and had survived the five-thousand mile journey to return to the eaves of Bilbo Cottage and I welcomed them like long-lost friends. They swooped down to their familiar nesting site in order to produce the first of their broods. I had learnt not to mistake them for house martins any more and reflected that my knowledge of country life was increasing with each passing year.

'So this is what you get up to,' said a familiar voice.

It was Beth. She looked casual and relaxed in a crew-necked raglan jumper, stone-washed jeans and Chris Evert trainers.

'This is a surprise,' I said.

'Well, I've got another car-load,' she said. 'It's more books and a few knick-knacks.'

'Perhaps we need a new bookcase,' I said, trying to be positive but realizing with some concern that my home was changing before my eyes.

'There's no *perhaps* about it, Jack,' said Beth with a grin. 'I thought we could nip into York on Saturday after the netball tournament.'

I glanced at my watch. 'Do you fancy a drink?'

'*After* we've unloaded,' said Beth. 'Don't try to put me off.'

Somehow we found a place for all the boxes, including Beth's complete set of Jane Austen novels and a surprisingly large collection of sports trophies from her school-days in Hampshire. 'Looks like you were quite athletic in your day,' I said.

'I still am, Jack,' said Beth with a knowing look.

Married life promised to be fun.

The Royal Oak was busy as usual and 'Town Called Malice' by The Jam was playing on the juke-box.

'Hey, Mr Sheffield,' said Don from the other end of the bar, "ave a dekko at this.' He held up today's edition of the *Sun* with the slightly more sensitive headline 'Did 1,200 Argies Drown?' which was a distinct improvement on 'GOTCHA!' 'Looks like we're giving them Argies a reight pasting,' he said triumphantly.

I nodded in acknowledgement as we walked to a quiet corner. 'Difficult times, Jack,' said Beth thoughtfully as we sipped our drinks.

'So, how about the wedding . . . Are you looking forward to it?' I asked, eager to change the subject.

She smiled. 'Very much. How about you?'

I raised my glass of Chestnut Mild. 'To us,' I said.

'To us,' she replied and she sipped her white wine.

'Your parents have been very generous,' I said.

'It's dominated my mother's life,' said Beth. 'She rings me every night with updates on flowers and what everyone is wearing.'

'How's your father bearing up?'

'He's his usual laid-back self – apart from concern about giving a speech at the reception. That's not really his forte.'

'Are you still happy with the village hall for the evening party? I thought you wanted something a bit, well, more *grand*.'

'No, it's worked out fine, Jack, now that we've booked the Dean Court for a formal Wedding Breakfast for family and the main guests. So the hall will be perfect for all our friends from Ragley, Morton and Hartingdale.'

'And have you heard about the major's offer?' I asked.

'What's that?'

'He's offered us his chauffeur-driven Bentley to take you to the church and for the Sunday morning to the railway station.'

'Well done Rupert,' said Beth. 'I wonder if Vera twisted his arm.'

For our honeymoon, Beth and I had decided on a

London theatre holiday and we had spent an enjoyable evening planning which shows to see. It was all coming together.

'And the dress?' I asked.

'It's all sorted, Jack. Laura gave me some great advice during our trip to the Harrogate Fashion Fair. So the dress is lovely . . . but you won't see it of course until the day.'

'I'm pleased Laura's OK,' I said.

'That's just my sister, Jack – always blowing hot and cold, never anything in between. She and Jo will make super bridesmaids and they've both been really support-ive.'

I finished my drink, put down the glass and looked into her green eyes. 'I love you,' I whispered quietly.

'Yes, but will you still love me when I bring another collection of boxes to the cottage tomorrow?' She squeezed my hand and we walked out into the darkness.

On Friday morning, as I drove on the back road to Ragley village, it was good to be alive on this fine Yorkshire day. The hedgerows were coming alive, the air was warm and the sweet scent of wallflowers drifted on a gentle breeze. Early purple orchids lit up the woodland floor along-side the swathes of bluebells, and the lambs in the fields were still drowsy with sleep. Around me, the peace of the countryside and the soft sound of wood pigeons soothed the soul and healed the scars of winter.

However, harsh reality was an unwelcome companion as I gave Prudence Golightly twenty pence for my copy of *The Times* and read the front page. It said that the

Queen was 'deeply concerned' following the sinking of HMS *Sheffield* in the South Atlantic. It also included a graphic account of the moment when Captain Sam Salt, Commander of the *Sheffield*, gave the order to abandon ship as the paint peeled off the hull following a direct hit by an Argentine missile.

With a heavy heart I walked into the entrance hall, where Sally and Vera were doing their best to cheer up Ruby.

'You smell lovely, Ruby – what's the perfume?' asked Sally.

'It's summat Frenchified, Mrs Pringle,' said Ruby. 'Our Andy bought it for me las' Christmas.'

'He made a good choice, Ruby,' said Vera quietly.

'Ah sed ah'd only wear it on special occasions, but then ah thought that might never come. So ah'm wearing it ev'ry day for 'im . . . till 'e comes 'ome safe.'

'That's a lovely thought, Ruby,' said Vera.

'I pray he does come 'ome safe 'n' sound,' said Ruby, '. . . and all t'other young men an' women. War's a terrible thing.'

We stood there quietly, all with our own thoughts.

Ruby put down her box of paper towels. 'Life's tough, Miss Evans.'

'Yes, Ruby,' said Vera firmly, 'but *you're* tougher,' and she handed her a lace-edged handkerchief. Ruby rubbed the tears from her eyes, blew her nose vigorously and offered the handkerchief back to Vera. 'You keep it, Ruby,' said Vera.

Then Ruby picked up the box and set off for the staff toilets and Vera walked into the office, removed the cover from her electric typewriter and began to write a thank-you letter to parents following the purchase of our new football strip.

Love is impatient. It doesn't respect the hands of time. So it was with my feelings for Beth. Occasionally, a carefree, reckless urgency scattered my senses. Logic was cast aside, which is why I set off to Morton very early on Saturday morning. Beth and I had arranged to travel to Easington together for the tournament. When I knocked on her door, above my head a parliament of rooks shattered the silence of the sycamores as they wheeled in a balmy blue sky and fed their young.

Beth was in her dressing gown. 'You're early,' she said, glancing at her watch. 'I haven't put my tracksuit on yet.'

'I noticed,' I said. 'I just couldn't wait to see you.'

'You'd better come in,' she said with a smile.

An hour later in the General Stores Ruby was waiting to be served behind Vera, who was collecting her *Daily Telegraph*. Prudence had been upset by her previous customer, the aggressively rude Deirdre Coe, Stan Coe's bossy sister.

'She's *always* complaining, Vera,' said Prudence. 'I don't know what to make of her.'

Ruby was the only other person in the shop, waiting to buy a bag of sugar, and she was listening in.

'At times she can be a most dreadful woman,' said Vera, 'an absolute virago.'

Ruby was puzzled. She knew for a fact that Deirdre was a Gemini. However, she would never dream of contradicting Miss Evans and kept her thoughts to herself.

'And how are you, Ruby?' asked Prudence.

'Only middlin', Prudence,' said Ruby. 'Ah'm all at sea t'day wi' all t'worry.'

'I hope your Andrew will be safe,' she said.

Ruby gave a big sigh. 'Ah'd like t'pray for 'im, y'know, proper-like, but ah don't really know 'ow.'

Vera stood for a moment, looking thoughtful. 'Ruby,' she said quietly, 'I think I can help.'

The netball and football tournament was destined to live long in the memory for two special reasons.

'Come on, Ragley,' shouted Jo Hunter. Our girls were about to win the netball final, a terrific achievement and a tribute to the many hours of coaching by Jo. The leggy Theresa Ackroyd had just scored another goal.

'Well done,' shouted Dan Hunter. During the last hour he had gradually picked up enough of the rules of netball to appreciate what was going on. 'It's sort of a lady-like basketball, I suppose,' he said to me, still slightly bewildered at Beth's judgements as referee. A crowd of Ragley mothers shouted encouragement from the side of the court and everyone was in good spirits.

It was after the girls had been presented with the trophy that Sue Phillips whispered in my ear, 'Jack, you'd better have a look at this.' The football tournament was about to start and Eric Earnshaw and Freddie Kershaw, our self-appointed coaches, had gathered the Ragley School football team round them and they were issuing final instructions. The boys looked really smart in their new kit. Marion Greening had bought a set of black shorts and Freddie had bought pairs of white socks with pale-blue hoops.

It was Freddie who broke the news. 'Mr Sheffield, we've gorra bit of a problem wi' this new strip.'

'But it looks great,' I said. 'It's the best we've ever looked.'

Eric Earnshaw walked over. 'Trouble is, Mr Sheffield, we're likely as not gonna get booed.'

'What do you mean?' I said. 'There's never any booing at this event; it's always been good-natured and played in a good spirit.'

As our boys walked on to the field there was a rumble of cheerful disapproval from the large crowd on the touchline, including a few half-hearted boos.

'What's going on?' I said.

Sue looked at Eric and Freddie. 'Shall I tell him?' They both gritted their teeth and nodded. 'Jack, don't you recognize the kit?'

I stared at the team as they kicked off and realization dawned. 'Oh no!'

'Oh yes,' said Sue. 'We've kitted the poor boys out in the *Argentinian* football strip.'

It was a good afternoon with lots of friendly banter, particularly by the headteacher of Easington School, who, at the end of the first game, announced on the loudspeaker system, 'Morton Primary School, nil . . . Argentina 2.'

It was later that day when Vera drove her Austin A40 on to the vicarage forecourt and came to a stop.

'Here we are, Ruby,' said Vera gently.

'Thank you, Miss Evans,' said Ruby. 'You're very kind.'

The two women got out of the car and stood side by side. Next to them, in the last of the afternoon sunlight, the light-pink petals of magnolia brightened the red brick wall and espalier pears were swelling with new growth. As they walked towards the church entrance, branches of yellow forsythia bordering the grassy banks brushed their legs.

In the quiet of the church, only the ticking of the old clock could be heard. Installed in 1912 to commemorate the coronation of George V, it had marked the passing of two world wars, the coronation of Queen Elizabeth II and, through the years, the seasons of village life. Now it was Ruby's turn to listen to the clock and count the heartbeats.

'Ah've never been all that religious, Miss Evans, but ah'd like t'pray for our Andy. Ah want 'im t'come back safe.'

Vera held her hand and they walked together to the first pew and sat down side by side. 'Would you like to be alone, Ruby?' whispered Vera.

'Ah'd 'ppreciate y'company . . . please,' said Ruby. She was dabbing her red eyes with a damp cleaning cloth.

Vera passed her yet another of her precious lace-edged handkerchiefs. 'Take mine, Ruby.'

And so it was that, as the sky slowly darkened over the vast plain of York, two women, separated by circumstances but united in compassion, whispered private prayers for a son of Ragley village.

Chapter Eighteen

Perfect Day

The Parent–Teacher Association presented Mr Sheffield with a dinner service prior to his wedding at St Mary's Church tomorrow.

Extract from the Ragley School Logbook:
Friday, 28 May 1982

It was a slow dawn and, as I looked out of the window of Bilbo Cottage, the scent of wallflowers drifted on the air and bright cherry blossom gladdened the eye.

For this was May, a time of renewal. It was good to be alive on this special morning. In the distance the flower candles on the horse-chestnut trees foretold of the season to come. A perky robin, its beady eyes bright with anticipation, was perched on the handle of my garden spade. It was a day of new promise and expectation.

It was also Saturday, 29 May . . . our wedding day.

*   *   *

There was the sound of a car outside and a loud rat-a-tat of the door knocker. I hurried downstairs in my dressing gown. It was Dan looking magnificent in his dress uniform, shiny black boots and a pair of spotless white gloves trapped neatly under his leather belt. He had taken Jo to Beth's cottage in Morton and then driven on to Kirkby Steepleton.

'I'm getting married in the morning,' he sang tunelessly as he strode into the hallway, 'ding, dong, the bells are gonna chime . . .'

''Morning, Dan,' I said. 'You're an early bird.'

He looked me up and down. 'How are you feeling?' he asked.

'I'm fine. Have you got the ring?' I asked nervously.

He tapped his uniform pocket and smiled. 'Fancy a cuppa?' he said as he walked into the kitchen. It was a good feeling to have him around: he appeared relaxed and confident.

I looked at myself in the hall mirror. 'I need a good shave,' I said.

'That's not all,' said Dan, taking a crumpled piece of paper from his inside pocket. 'You also need to help me improve this best man's speech.'

'Beth had better go first,' said Diane Wigglesworth, quickly unpacking her hairdressing kit on the kitchen table. Diane was used to busy mornings such as this and she had a routine: first the bride, followed by the bride's mother and then the bridesmaids. Not for the first time, Diane reflected that ladies' hairdressing was fifty per cent skill and fifty per cent psychology.

It was eight o'clock in Beth's cottage and it was already a hive of activity. Jo Hunter had arrived and begun helping Laura with the tray of bouquets, headdresses and the carnations for buttonholes. John Henderson was giving his car a final polish, but actually keeping out of the way, and Beth's mother, Diane, was laying out the wedding dress, her own mother's necklace and a blue garter from Laura. 'Something borrowed,' said Diane. 'And something blue,' added Laura with a smile. Finally, Diane put a silver sixpence in Beth's shoe and prayed it would bring her good luck.

At eleven o'clock I locked the front door and we climbed into Dan's Wolseley Hornet and drove out of the driveway. It occurred to me that the next time I walked into Bilbo Cottage I would be a married man and I cherished the thought.

It was rare for me to be a passenger on this familiar journey and I took in the sights. When we reached Ragley, the High Street seemed quiet for a Saturday. I later discovered that many of the shops had employed temporary staff. Prudence Golightly and Old Tommy Piercy, Eugene and Peggy Scrimshaw, Timothy Pratt and his sister Nora, along with Amelia Duff and Ted Postlethwaite, had already left their premises and set off up Morton Road. Many parents and children, dressed in their Sunday best, waved at me as we drove past. The wedding was clearly a big attraction and all roads led to St Mary's Church.

As we drove past the village green, I glanced up at Ragley School and thought about the first time I had arrived in the village and walked through the gates. So much had happened, highs and lows, good times and bad, but always there had been Beth and the hope that one day we could share a life together. That day had arrived.

Meanwhile, by the duck pond, untouched by wedding plans, a group of pre-school children were making daisy chains and feeding the ducks. It was the springtime of their lives and I recalled that innocence is no passing fancy but something to be treasured.

St Mary's Church shimmered in the morning heat haze but inside it was cool and calm. Vera and Joseph were going through their usual ritual and making sure everything was ready for the big occasion.

In the vestry, Vera looked the picture of elegance in a lavender two-piece suit. Her matching wide-brimmed hat had been placed on the pew nearest the north transept, reserving her place and ensuring an excellent view without encroaching on immediate family. It also meant she could keep an eye on the unpredictable Elsie Crapper, the Valium-sedated organist.

Now she stood before Joseph, scrutinizing his garments and checking there were no creases in his white surplice and his full-length cope. Then, with delicate care, she placed round his neck a white stole that she had stitched with intricate gold crosses and stood back to admire him. Vera was immensely proud of her younger brother and she gave him a nod of approval.

'Perfect, Joseph,' she said, 'and, don't worry, I'll keep an eye on Elsie and I'll point the ushers in the right direction.' She indicated her reserved pew. 'I'll be sitting there, Joseph, near at hand . . . next to Rupert.'

Joseph smiled. 'I'd be lost without you,' he said, and he meant it. It had become clear that her attraction to the devoted Major Rupert Forbes-Kitchener had grown during the past year and he wondered if the day might not be far away when it would be Vera's turn to be a bride in this beautiful church.

Vera was preoccupied and didn't notice the moment of uncertainty in Joseph's eyes and she hurried off to put her beautifully embroidered wedding kneeler in place on the steps in front of the altar. Then, as she always did, she stood back to check that everything was perfect – from the candles to the flowers to the altar cloth.

Dan parked round the back of the church, in the shade of the vicarage wall. 'We're early, Jack,' he said, looking up at the clock in the bell tower. 'Let's go into the church-yard where it's quiet.'

We sat on a bench and Dan pulled out his speech and began mumbling to himself. 'I'd better not tell the one about the Welsh shepherd,' he said doubtfully, 'although it went down well at the rugby club.' I decided to leave him to it and walked slowly up the gravel path and paused next to a tall, weathered gravestone covered in lichen. It read:

In loving memory of
JOHN HAWKSWORTH
Born 18th August 1882
Father in thy gracious keeping
Leave we now thy servant sleeping
Killed at Passchendale 17th October 1917.

I sighed at the symmetry of the dates. He was born almost one hundred years ago and we shared the same birthday, but we led very different lives.

A few minutes later, Dan tugged my sleeve. 'It's time to go, Jack.'

I took a deep breath, checked the knot in my silver-grey tie, buffed the black toecaps of my shoes with my handkerchief and we walked round to the front of the church, where excited Scottish voices could be heard. My mother, Margaret, and her sister, May, were waiting in the entrance porch. They had stayed overnight at the vicarage and looked resplendent in matching dark-blue two-piece suits and dainty little hats with tartan bows. They were each clutching a huge carton of confetti.

My mother rushed to greet me. 'My son . . . my dear wee boy,' she said and gave me a big hug. 'Y'nae canna looked smarter if y'tried,' she said, casting an appreciative eye up and down. 'Your father would have been proud tae see you like this.' A tear ran down her cheek and she quickly dabbed it away.

'Oh, the poor wee dear is weeping again,' said Aunt May, 'and all her cascara is running.'

'Well, you look lovely, both of you,' I said, 'and were you comfortable last night?'

'Och aye,' said my mother. 'Vera and Joseph made us welcome.'

'And the wee vicar kept serving up his home-made wine, Jack,' added Aunt May, 'so it's good we've got strong constipations.'

Dan stifled a laugh. He wasn't used to Aunt May's malapropisms.

'So, are you going in?' I said.

'Och aye,' said Aunt May. 'We're nae gonna wait for y'toffee-nosed wee cousin frae Kilmarnock.'

I couldn't even remember which distant member of the family that could be and I didn't ask.

Inside in the quiet sanctuary of the church, the ushers, a surprisingly smart John Grainger and the strapping, flaxen-haired Simon Graveson, Beth's deputy headteacher from Hartingdale, were sorting out hymn-books and the Order of Service sheets. Simon looked at me curiously, while John just grinned and said, 'Good luck, Jack. Hope all goes well,' before guiding Margaret and May to one of the front pews.

In the stillness of the nave, Joseph was waiting to greet us. 'How are you, Jack?' he said softly.

'I'm fine, thank you, Joseph,' I said a little nervously.

A week ago, Joseph had joked, 'Don't worry, Jack, it's the revised 1928 service, not the 1662 one with lines such as "carnal lust and appetite".' Today his demeanour was different: serious and quiet, yet reassuring and supportive.

He put his hand on my shoulder. 'Jack, it's a wonderful day and you are to be married in the eyes of God. I'm so pleased for you and Beth.' He glanced up at the imposing figure of Dan. 'And I must say, Daniel, you look very grand today.'

'Thank you, Vicar,' said Dan a little self-consciously, 'and fear not, I've got the ring.' He held it up proudly.

'I never doubted it,' said Joseph with a smile. 'Now, if

we go into the vestry we can complete the formalities of payment for the legal fees and bell ringers and so on.' It was clear that, unlike at school, Joseph was in his comfort zone; he had done this many times.

As we walked into the vestry, Vera suddenly appeared at my side. She squeezed my hand and stretched up to kiss me on my cheek. 'Good luck, Jack,' she said softly, '. . . and God bless you.'

'Thank you, Vera,' I said. It took a few moments to recall what it was that was different about her greeting and then I smiled. Vera had called me by my first name. Minutes later, after a reminder of the order of service, Joseph gave Dan his final instructions, checked that he had replaced the ring in his uniform pocket and ushered us to the front pew.

Outside, on the vicarage lawn beside the church, the wedding guests were gathering. The men looked smart and sober in their three-piece suits, whereas the ladies created a spectacular riot of colour in their summer dresses and striking hats as they chatted in relaxed groups. Miss Barrington-Huntley had caused a stir with the sheer magnificence of her new hat. Even though it resembled an electrocuted flamingo, no one dared offer anything other than expressions of praise.

Meanwhile, Dan's police colleagues, in their smart, ceremonial uniforms and pristine-white gloves, talked about last week's FA Cup Final and the barrel of beer they had seen being rolled into the village hall by Don Bradshaw.

Sally Pringle arrived in a bright-yellow outfit she

had made herself and a startling, brave hat. Baby Grace had suddenly grown into a happy toddler and was wearing a similar outfit to Sally, created from the left-over material. Sadly, Colin Pringle, looking hot in a creased suit, was sucking sherbet lemons, desperate for a cigarette.

Don and Sheila Bradshaw wandered over to talk to the Pringles. 'Bar's all set up in t'village 'all, Mrs Pringle,' said Don. Colin's eyes lit up, but not at Sheila's dress revealing Ragley's most magnificent cleavage. He had forgotten about the free beer.

'Thanks,' said Sally. 'Jack and Beth will be so grateful for your support.'

Sheila looked up at her great bear of a husband. 'Well, 'e can show a lot o' gumption when 'e shapes 'imself, can my Don,' she said proudly.

Don stood there awkwardly in his ill-fitting suit and went bright red. For someone who had once wrestled under the name 'The Silent Strangler', he definitely had a gentle side to his nature.

Parents and children of Ragley School were now lining the pathway from the gate to the church entrance.

'Aren't they lucky to 'ave such a perfec' day?' said Margery Ackroyd to Betty Buttle. 'It rained on my weddin' day.'

'Y'reight there, Margery,' said Betty. 'Ah remember it well.'

'Come on, Wendell,' said Margery, grabbing her husband's hand. 'Let's get in for an end-pew, then we'll 'ave a good view – ah don't want t'miss owt,' and they joined the procession that was moving slowly into the church.

Outside the vicarage gates, Stan Coe pulled up in his filthy Land-Rover and glowered at the gathering. Mrs Pauline Paxton, mother of eight-year-old Molly, bristled. 'An' you can sling yer 'ook,' she said. Pauline was a former Yorkshire girls' discus champion, the current captain of the Ragley tug-of-war team and renowned for her ability to geld pigs. She was not someone you would want to cross. Stan nodded nervously and roared off to the Pig and Ferret to calm his nerves.

Gradually, the church filled and I glanced across at Diane Henderson, immaculate in a two-piece cream silk suit. She was sitting with a few members of her extended family and she gave me a gentle wave and a reassuring smile.

A few pews behind me, the modest and undemonstrative Anne Grainger was undoubtedly the real surprise. Her dramatic royal-blue and white, wide-brimmed hat would have graced Ladies' Day at Ascot and she blew me a kiss. Behind her sat Ruby, who had treated herself to a perm at Diane's Hair Salon and was wearing a straw hat covered in primroses. She was already dabbing away a few tears. 'Good luck, Mr Sheffield,' she said, waving her handkerchief. Next to her was daughter Racquel, now seven months pregnant and looking happy and flushed. On the end of the pew, Ronnie sat stiffly in his best suit, feeling out of sorts. He was missing the reassuring comfort of his bobble hat.

*   *   *

It was the moment the ladies of Ragley and Morton had been waiting for. The major's chauffeur opened the door of the gleaming Bentley and John Henderson stepped out and turned to take his daughter's hand. When Beth appeared there was a spontaneous cheer from the children and a ripple of applause from the ladies gathered at the church gate.

'What a beautiful dress,' said Shirley the cook to Doreen Critchley. 'Ah knew she'd pick a good 'un.'

'Must 'ave cost a fortune,' retorted the practical Doreen.

Beth looked beautiful. The dress had a white fitted bodice with a scooped neckline and was covered in delicate lace. The long narrow sleeves reached to her wrists and the full skirt, of a lighter material, extended at the back to a small train that fluttered behind her. The bouquet of delicate spring flowers was perfect.

It was typical Beth: no flamboyance . . . simply under-stated beauty.

Laura and Jo had pinned a beautiful circlet of flowers to her ringlets of honey-blonde hair and the full-length veil lifted in the slight breeze as she walked on the gravel path to the church. Behind Beth came Laura and Jo, both slim and stunning in matching long lilac dresses, bare shoulders and each capped with a headband of tiny flowers.

'She's marrying our teacher,' shouted five-year-old Jemima Poole from the crowd.

Four-year-old Katie Icklethwaite looked puzzled. 'Will she teach me when I start school, Jemima?'

'Who?' replied Jemima.

'That lady – *Mrs* Teacher,' said Katie.

'No,' said Jemima. 'She teaches somewhere else. You'll 'ave my teacher, Mrs Grainger. She's old but she's nice.'

'She's got a pretty dress,' said Katie thoughtfully, 'jus' like my Barbie.'

A hushed whisper amongst the congregation and a turning of heads indicated the arrival of the bride. The bridal party had gathered in the porch and Laura and Jo were making final adjustments to Beth's dress.

Dan gave me a nudge and we stepped out from our pew and took our places in front of Joseph. Vera gave a signal to Elsie at the organ and the first bars of the 'Bridal March' echoed round the ancient walls. As I looked around I saw Diane Henderson wiping away a tear as she glanced back at John leading her elder daughter down the aisle. It was an image I shall never forget: John looking so straight and proud with Beth on his arm and, in a halo of sunlight from the open church door, she looking more beautiful than I could imagine.

Suddenly Beth was beside me and she looked up and smiled. All sound around me seemed hushed, and in that moment we were in our private cocoon, just the two of us. In a spinning world we had found a moment of stillness and there was a special intimacy in our sheltered space.

I had come to realize that love was no easy journey; rather, a pathway of ice and fire. My relationship with Beth had been steadfast but never safe. In the past few years my emotions had been heated and hammered in the forge of life but now the first journey had ended and a new one was beginning. As I stood beside her there was only a gentle peace in my heart and time for cool reflection.

The service seemed to pass by in a dream. We sang two of our favourite hymns, 'Love divine, all loves excelling' and 'Lord of all hopefulness'.

Joseph led us calmly through each stage of the service with practised ease and we gave our responses with confidence. 'Wilt thou have this woman to thy wedded wife?' he asked, '. . . and, forsaking all others, keep thee only unto her, so long as ye both shall live?'

'I will,' I said.

I had chosen my destiny and I was bound to its promise.

When we emerged once again into the sunshine the world around us exploded with cheers and confetti.

Beth squeezed my hand as we gathered on the lawn for the official photographs. 'Wasn't that wonderful, Jack?' she said.

'I love you, Beth,' I whispered in her ear.

The harassed photographer was going through his ritual of interchanging parents for the family photographs. John Henderson stood next to my mother and she held his arm as if she never wanted the moment to end. Predictably Aunt May insisted on clutching his other arm and there he was, sandwiched between two smiling ladies of Scotland. Diane had Dan, the Adonis of the police force, beside her and didn't complain when the giant policeman slipped his arm round her waist. It was a time of joy and tears in equal measure and it seemed as if the whole village had turned out to share our day.

'Jolly fine wedding, what?' said a familiar voice. The major was at my elbow and he was pointing towards a gleaming Bentley and a smartly dressed chauffeur. 'Your carriage awaits . . . Mr and Mrs Sheffield.'

When we pulled up outside the Dean Court Hotel in the shadow of York Minster we were welcomed by the maître d'hôtel. As always, the service was impeccable, the table settings were perfect and the champagne flowed.

It was a happy and relaxed occasion for family and close friends and everyone applauded the speeches and the cutting of the cake. Again, it seemed to pass by in a blur, for I had eyes only for Beth and longed to be alone with her.

At last the opportunity came when our chauffeur-driven Bentley returned us to Bilbo Cottage and I carried Beth over the threshold. Above our heads, a rook cawed in the high elms and a mouse scuttled in the moss-covered eaves. In the cool of the hallway I kissed my bride and then we walked into the lounge and collapsed on the sofa in each other's arms.

It was an hour later when Beth said, 'Jack, I haven't packed yet.'

'Do it tomorrow morning,' I said, reluctant to move.

'Have *you* packed?' she asked a little sleepily.

'No, but I've got all the rail and theatre tickets.'

As we only had a one-week spring bank holiday we had decided to go to London the following morning for a short theatre break. Beth had planned it to begin on

Monday with *The Pirates of Penzance* featuring Tim Curry, George Cole and Pamela Stephenson. Then on Tuesday it was Agatha Christie's *The Mousetrap*, now in its thirtieth year, followed by a real treat on Wednesday: namely, Glenda Jackson in a new comedy, *Summit Conference*.

We were due to return to Bilbo Cottage on Thursday and miss the historic occasion on the bank holiday Monday when one hundred thousand pilgrims were due to gather on the Knavesmire to welcome the visit of the Pope. However, thoughts of papal helicopters and popemobiles were far from my mind. I had just married the woman I loved.

When we arrived in the village hall, Clint Ramsbottom was playing the new hit record 'House of Fun' by Madness, and Old Tommy Piercy was complaining that we ought to have some *proper* music.

It was a night to remember. It seemed as though everyone we knew had turned up and Don and Big Dave returned to The Royal Oak for a second barrel. As dusk finally arrived and coloured lights flickered around the hall, Beth went off to dance with her father. Suddenly, Laura was in front of me. She stood close and gently stroked out the creases in my jacket. I could smell her perfume, Opium by Yves Saint Laurent.

'Congratulations, Jack,' she said, smoothing the wide lapels. 'Great suit, by the way.' Then she looked at me with questioning green eyes. 'Make my sister happy, Jack,' she said.

'I shall, Laura,' I said.

Clint Ramsbottom put on Abba's 'The Winner Takes

It All' and Laura smiled wistfully. Her long hair was hanging free over her bare, suntanned shoulders and, as always, she looked lovely. 'One last dance?' she said quietly and took my hand.

After the dance, Beth arrived and gave her sister a hug. 'Thanks, Laura,' she said, '. . . for everything.'

'Have a good life, big sister,' said Laura. 'You have the love of a man who will never break your heart.' Then she reached up, kissed my cheek and walked away into the crowd.

It was midnight when we made our escape and our chauffeur delivered us back to a silent Bilbo Cottage.

The road to love has many pathways and I had reached my destination. No more the ache of distance and the silence of spaces. We were together at last and her hair was on my pillow. It was the beginning of a new life and the end of a perfect day.

Chapter Nineteen

The Summer Ball

The children completed paintings for the children's art display at the Annual Morton and Ragley Agricultural Show in the grounds of Morton Manor on Saturday, 26th June. The 4th-year juniors in Class 4 visited Easington Comprehensive School prior to transfer in September.

Extract from the Ragley School Logbook:
Friday, 25 June 1982

Vera held up her *Daily Telegraph* in delight. 'Isn't it wonderful,' she said, 'a son for Charles and Diana, and it says here that he weighed just over seven pounds and that he "cried lustily".'

It was the last Friday in June, a new school day was about to begin and Vera was flushed with excitement.

'So is he second in line to the throne?' asked Jo.

'Yes,' said Vera, who had become our unofficial royal correspondent ever since Princess Diana had given birth earlier in the week.

'Personally, I'd get rid of the lot of them,' said Sally rather grumpily, 'and let them survive on a teacher's salary.'

'Actually, I think Di is a breath of fresh air for the royal family,' said Anne.

'And it says here that Prince Andrew is still flying "round the clock" during operations, based on HMS *Invincible* – so *he's* doing his bit for Queen and country,' said Vera.

Sally picked up her register from Vera's desk. 'Yes, you're probably right, Anne, and . . . I do like Diana,' she said with a tired smile. 'Sorry, Vera,' she added as she paused in the doorway. 'I'm not quite feeling myself today. My new diet is making me grumpy.'

'Sally,' Vera said, trying to change the subject, 'I hope that you and Colin will be coming to the Manor House on Saturday evening.'

Sally smiled. 'I wouldn't miss it for the world, Vera. The Summer Ball will be just the thing to cheer me up.'

The social gathering of the year was only one day away and the major had invited all the staff to attend a grand ball at his manor house on the evening of the Annual Morton and Ragley Agricultural Show. As Anne Grainger had insisted to her husband, John, when he complained he couldn't dance and asked did he really have to go, 'These tickets are like gold dust!'

At nine o'clock the bell rang for morning school but the fifteen children in their final year at Ragley lined up by the school gate to board William Featherstone's Reliance bus. It was a special day for them and they were all full of anticipation at the prospect of visiting Easington Comprehensive School prior to their transfer to secondary education in September.

'Mr Sheffield, ah've 'eard they 'ave science labs an' woodwork an' a big canteen an' a trampoline like on t'Olympics,' said Jonathan Greening as he boarded the bus. The words tumbled out. He was about to discover a new world of uniforms, examinations and adolescence and his eyes were bright with excitement.

It was morning playtime when Ruby made a surprise entrance. I hadn't seen much of her recently as Racquel's baby was due in a few weeks and she had been spending all her spare time sewing furiously and making a decorative christening shawl. Her twice-weekly cross-stitch class had provided the opportunity to apply the finishing touches.

'Ah've finished m'shawl, Miss Evans,' said Ruby, holding it up for all to see, 'an' ah've got some good news.'

'Oh, well done, Ruby,' said Vera.

'What beautiful stitching!' said Anne.

'And what's the news?' asked Sally.

Ruby looked around the staff-room at our expectant faces. 'Our Andy's comin' 'ome,' she said triumphantly.

It was true. The war with Argentina was over. After Argentine planes had killed forty-three British troops at Bluff Cove, over eleven thousand Argentinian soldiers had surrendered in a final battle at Port Stanley. 'White flags are flying,' Mrs Thatcher had announced to a cheering House of Commons.

Everyone jumped up and there was a burst of

spontaneous applause. 'Oh, Ruby,' said Anne, 'that's wonderful news.'

'And do you know when he's coming home?' I asked.

'Some time next month, so ah've 'eard,' said Ruby.

Vera got up from her chair, put her arms round our tearful caretaker and gave her a hug. 'I'm so pleased for you,' she said.

'An' thanks t'you, Miss Evans,' said Ruby quietly. 'A bit o' prayin' didn't do no 'arm, did it?'

Vera smiled. 'It never does, Ruby . . . It never does.'

Meanwhile, outside on the school field, the concept of life and death was being accommodated at a different level. Terry Earnshaw's understanding of *life* and *girls*, but not necessarily in that order, continued to be a little fragile.

'Oh!' shouted Victoria Alice, 'a wasp!' She jumped back as the fierce little insect landed on the grass in front of her. Terry saw his moment had come to demonstrate he was a true super-hero and he promptly stamped on it.

Victoria Alice stared in horror. 'Oh, Terry, you've killed it!' she exclaimed.

'Ah know,' said Terry puffing out his chest, 'an' ah weren't frit either.' Past tenses had always eluded young Terry.

'Mummy says when you die you go to heaven,' said Victoria Alice.

They both stared at the dead wasp for what seemed like an eternity, until Terry, becoming restless, broke the silence. 'Well, it's tekkin' its time abart it,' he said testily.

*   *   *

At lunchtime, in the corner of the staff-room, Sally had taken out a bag of muesli and was munching away as if her life depended on it. She clearly wasn't her usual cheery self. Her daughter, Grace, was now over sixteen months old and was toddling around, opening cupboard doors and giving Sally a few sleepless nights because of teething problems. Also, it appeared that Sally had begun yet another diet.

'I'm starving,' she said mournfully while eyeing up the box of biscuits on the coffee table. She took out of her shoulder bag a small Penguin paperback with the words *Audrey Eyton's Extraordinary F-PLAN Diet* emblazoned on the front cover. The sub-text read: 'At last! Look great and feel fabulous with this effective and healthy new diet'.

'This is my new slimming book,' she said, 'and the idea is you have a high-fibre diet, so you should feel satisfied on fewer calories.'

Anne and Jo suddenly looked interested. 'What do you do?' asked Anne.

'Well, every day I drink half a pint of skimmed milk and never go beyond fifteen hundred calories,' said Sally, holding up another little paperback, this one entitled *F-PLAN: Calorie and Fibre Chart*, 'and I check the calorie count in this book.'

'So, is it working?' asked Jo and then immediately wished she hadn't as Vera and Anne gave her a stern look.

Sally grinned. 'Hope so . . . but I could murder a custard cream.'

*   *   *

On Friday evening Beth and I went into York to the Odeon cinema and settled down to share a bag of Liquorice Allsorts and enjoy *On Golden Pond*, with Jane Fonda, Henry Fonda and Katharine Hepburn. Beth explained that, apparently, the father–daughter rift in the film was echoed in real life and, as I carefully selected all the coconut whirls in the pitch darkness, I wondered if that made acting the part easier.

It was Saturday morning and a dawn of pearl grey crested the distant hills as the first fingers of sharp shadows spread across the land. A new day had begun.

The rattle of the letter-box woke Beth. Since getting married, I had begun to have a newspaper delivered at the weekend. 'The paper's here,' she said sleepily, 'and I'd love a cup of tea if you're going downstairs to collect it,' she added coyly. Married life had seemed to suit us both and, with the exception of my having no wardrobe space any more, life was bliss.

When Beth emerged, in her dressing gown and with tousled hair, I was eating my Weetabix and reading the paper. There was the usual mixed bag of news. Arthur Scargill and forty thousand miners had brought forty-four Yorkshire pits to a halt and the American President, ex-film star Ronald Reagan, had told the House of Commons that Britain's young men had fought in the Falklands 'not for mere real estate'. Meanwhile, on the back page, Bobby Robson said he would consider replacing Ron Greenwood as the England manager . . . if he was offered the job. Also, the price of four-star petrol had gone up again by 7p to 169p per gallon. It was tough keeping pace with inflation.

Beth looked up at the kitchen clock. 'I'm having my hair done at nine,' she said, 'so shall we go into Ragley together?' Diane's Hair Salon was fully booked this day of the Summer Ball.

'Yes, fine,' I said through a mouthful of cereal. 'I'll drop you off on my way to the barber's.' My hairdressing experience was due to be in complete contrast to Beth's two hours of pampering. Trev the barber, known locally as 'Chainsaw Trev', was an old-fashioned, no-frills barber who provided a standard 'short back and sides' and a shave that involved an executioner's chair, copious lathering, stropping a cut-throat razor, followed by a styptic pencil to stop the inevitable bleeding and a boiling-hot towel held up with tongs and dropped on the patient's face – in other words, ten minutes of hell.

Shortly before nine o'clock, I dropped Beth off in Ragley High Street. 'See you in the Coffee Shop around eleven,' she said and I drove off to Easington for my appointment with Chainsaw Trev.

In the meantime, Ragley village went on as normal. In her back garden, Amelia Duff, the Ragley postmistress, was feeding her chickens with an interesting mix of chickweed, dandelions and stale bread. Tidy Tim had just finished cutting his lawn in regimented rows of perfect, weed-free parallel stripes. 'Nature's all right, Mr Sheffield,' Timothy had once explained to me, 'so long as she's kept in 'er place, if y'get m'meaning.' In Pepperpot Cottage on Morton Road, Joyce Davenport, the doctor's wife and Vera's dearest friend, was assembling a bowl of nettle tops, vegetable stock, peas and coriander to make her famous chilled pea and nettle soup, and, incongruously, she was humming along to the latest Bucks Fizz record.

Outside The Royal Oak, mothers and children were sitting by the pond and feeding the ducks. The ducks, in turn, were showing their appreciation by preening themselves and splashing happily in the warm sunshine. On the village green, Katrina Buttle was holding a buttercup under her twin sister's chin and studying the reflected glow of the bright petals in the early-morning sunshine.

Meanwhile, Heathcliffe Earnshaw and his brother Terry were sitting on the roof of their garden shed and eating huge sticks of rhubarb. Next to their grubby knees they had a large brown paper bag full of sugar. In turn they dipped the end of their rhubarb into the bag and then they chewed the sweetened stalk. It was their idea of Saturday morning heaven.

At eleven o'clock I ordered a coffee and a Wagon Wheel in Nora's Coffee Shop. Dorothy Humpleby was studying her horoscope in the *Easington & District Pioneer*.

'Yurra Leo, aren't you, Mr Sheffield?' asked Dorothy.

'Yes, Dorothy.'

'Well, in y'Starscope it says 'ere, "The feeling of anticlimax could be giving you the blues: you could well have made a mistake in your past with a romantic involvement."'

'That's not vewy bwight, Dowothy,' shouted Nora. 'Mr Sheffield only wecently got mawwied.'

*   *   *

It was over lunch at Bilbo Cottage that I suddenly remembered to compliment Beth on her new hair-do, although to my undiscerning eye it didn't look any different. To be perfectly honest, if I hadn't seen her walk into the salon, I wouldn't have guessed. Her hair looked just the same to me. Fortunately, it was the early stage of our married life and, at that time, I had no idea of the cost.

Conversely, Beth suggested I go to a 'proper hair-dresser' in future as I now looked like an escaped convict, whereas I was pleased I had got my money's worth. Beth glanced at her watch. 'I said I'd help Sally with the art display at the show, Jack, so we'd better get going.' It was the day of the Annual Morton and Ragley Agricultural Show and one of the main events in the local calendar.

We walked out to my emerald-green Morris Minor Traveller with its ash-wood frame and brightly polished chromium grill and I gave my chrome and yellow AA badge an involuntary polish.

'Jack . . . have you ever thought about changing this car?' asked Beth.

I looked at her in horror. 'Change my car . . . my lovely car?'

She grinned. 'I'll take that as a "no", shall I?'

It took me the full four miles to the grounds of Morton Manor to recover from the shock.

The show comprised all the classic English village attractions including the Ragley and Morton brass band, a coconut shy, bowling for a pig, cream teas, home-made cakes and a fancy-dress parade.

315

Sarah Louise Tait's magnificent black-and-white rabbit, Nibbles, won the Pets' Competition with Tony Ackroyd's tortoise, Yul Brynner, a close second. Dominic and Damian Brown had brought their father's psychopathic ferret, Frankenstein, but it was unplaced as the judges couldn't get close enough to make a decision, such was the ferocity of its attack on the wire mesh of its cage. In the meantime, Jimmy Poole's Yorkshire terrier, Scargill, was disqualified for nipping the ankles of the chief judge, along with Cleopatra, Jodie Cuthbertson's talking parrot, who told the whole of the Women's Institute committee who were walking by at the time to 'f*** off!'

In the Women's Institute refreshment tent, a bottle of Joseph's courgette wine with no label had got mixed in with Vera's fresh mint lemonade and traditional ginger beer. So it was that Walter Sparrow, the president of the Ragley and Morton Temperance Society, was unwittingly enjoying a glass of Joseph's home brew with an alcohol content of ten per cent and announcing to the world that his arthritic hip was no longer painful and didn't the two octogenarian ladies serving the drinks look 'en-shanting'.

On the showground, Virginia Anastasia Forbes-Kitchener, in her skin-tight jodhpurs, won the show jumping with a clear round on her spirited horse, Banjo, much to the delight of her father. 'Good show, old girl,' shouted the major. His words of encouragement could be heard in the Women's Institute tent, where Vera was judging the Six Butterfly Buns competition although her mind was elsewhere. The Summer Ball was only a few hours away and she knew it was decision time.

*　　*　　*

As we approached Morton Manor the scent of honey-suckle was in the evening air.

Having driven past a narrow, cobbled yard and a row of sleepy cottages with leaded windows, I parked in a small grassy field. Then we slipped through a gap in the tall yew hedge and walked along an avenue of espaliered pears, joining other couples heading towards the turreted, Yorkshire-stone manor house. The gravel pathway meandered under a pergola of metal arches supporting fragrant sweet peas, bright climbing clematis and Victorian roses. Beth's fingers lightly caressed a row of lavender plants and she paused to enjoy the scent of the mauve flower spikes. Thomas, the gardener, had worked hard and, next to the stone pillars of the entrance porch, tubs of pink aubretia, fiery red pelargoniums, green-and-cream variegated ivy and trailing magenta lobelia vividly enhanced the summer scene. The light breeze stirred Beth's summer dress and I sensed the whisper of silk against her skin.

The major, immaculate in dinner suit and sporting regimental medals, was there waiting to greet us and, by his side, stood Vera. She was holding a rose in her hand, a pale-pink Blush Noissette, and, in her beautiful evening gown, looked the perfect English lady.

'Welcome to the newly-weds, what?' said the major, shaking my hand and kissing Beth lightly on the cheek.

Vera and Beth were soon engaged in conversation and the major leant over and whispered in my ear, 'A fine filly, don't you think, my boy?'

'I agree, Major,' I replied, though I wasn't entirely sure whether he was referring to Beth or Vera.

*   *   *

It was a relaxing evening, a time for the meeting of friends and of happy reunion in the balmy air. During the champagne reception, conversation ebbed and flowed among the 'country set'.

'Our cars used to be made by *British* manufacturers,' said the major. 'And Morris and Austin dominated the roads,' added the son of the local MP, keen to join in but secretly hoping for time alone with the shapely Virginia. The conversation then turned to the problems at Yorkshire County Cricket Club, where no one seemed to want Geoffrey Boycott as club captain. There was great unrest among the men of Ragley and Morton, who longed for Yorkshire supremacy on the cricket fields of England.

The nine-piece band struck up a slow waltz and the wine flowed. Waiters with silver trays kept appearing with mouth-watering canapés and Beth and I danced under the glittering chandeliers. We saw Anne trying, with limited success, to teach John how to quickstep, while Dan and Jo glided around the polished ballroom floor like professionals. Eventually, the six of us collected our drinks and walked out to join Colin and Sally in the octagonal bandstand overlooking the croquet lawn. Together we swapped stories of learning to dance as we sipped our wine and gazed at the charming scene.

'Ah, now that looks intriguing,' said the observant Sally. She gave Anne, Beth and Jo a knowing wink. 'Girls, are you thinking what I'm thinking?'

Near by, under the graceful branches of a weeping willow, Vera and the major sat on wickerwork chairs at a wrought-iron table, deep in conversation. The major was holding her hand and Vera was looking into his steel-blue eyes and hanging on every word. In her diaphanous evening gown and with a silk shawl over her shoulders she looked relaxed in his company. A smile played on her lips as if she had found a lost chord in the symphony of her life. They were content in each other's company and the major's gaze never left the woman he had grown to love.

Then, to our surprise, he stood up suddenly and set off purposefully back towards the house. Vera walked over to join us.

'Good evening, Vera,' I said, standing up from the bench. 'Do come and join us.'

Vera took a deep breath. 'Hello, everybody,' she said, 'but I do believe I'm too excited to sit down.'

'Is everything all right, Vera?' I asked.

Vera glanced back at the major as he entered the open French windows. 'We are all driven by destiny, Mr Sheffield,' she said softly, 'and I believe I have found mine.'

'Oh, Vera!' exclaimed all the women, while the men stared nonplussed.

'I should like you all to be the first to know that Rupert is asking my *younger* brother for permission to marry me,' said Vera with a smile and a distinct emphasis on *younger*.

'Oh, how romantic!' said Jo.

'That's wonderful news,' said Anne.

'I want to be the first to give you a hug, Vera,' said Sally.

The men, including myself, were struck speechless

but eventually we came to our senses and joined in the celebrations. Another wedding . . . and this time it was Vera.

Joseph shook hands with the major and congratulated him. He felt the request for his sister's hand in marriage was a token of politeness from a very correct man but went along with it anyway. 'My sister is very precious to me, Rupert,' he said with feeling. 'I know you will look after her.'

'With my life,' said Rupert.

It was after midnight when Joseph left the party alone. He was finding it hard to come to terms with the thought of living on his own in the vicarage. Wrapped in a cold cloak of uncertainty, he trudged into the night.

However, unknown to all of us, under the bright stars on that special night, in the far distance heavy cumulus clouds were filling the sapphire sky with ominous intent. A storm was coming.

Chapter Twenty

Please Sir!

Fifteen 4th-year juniors left today and will commence full-time education at Easington Comprehensive School in September. At the Leavers' Assembly, book prizes were presented by Major Forbes-Kitchener and Sergeant Andrew Smith.

School closed today and will reopen for the new academic year 1982/83 on Monday, 6 September 1982.

Extract from the Ragley School Logbook:
Friday, 23 July 1982

It was the time of the quiet dawn when the earth awakes from its slumber. In the far distance the purple line of the Hambleton hills shimmered in the morning heat haze. The final day of the school year had arrived and the breathless promise of gathering storm clouds hung heavy on the silent land.

On the driveway of Bilbo Cottage, Beth was looking cool and elegant in a green linen suit that exactly matched her eyes. She smiled up at me. 'So, I'll see you tonight, Jack,' she said. 'I'll drive home and change first and then come on to your after-school party.'

'That's great,' I said. 'It starts just after five o'clock.'

'Yes, but don't forget I'm picking up my mother from the station at six-thirty, so I can only stay for an hour at most.'

'Ah, er, yes . . . I remember now,' I said. Diane Henderson was coming up from Hampshire for a short visit.

Beth grinned. 'OK, 'bye,' and she unlocked her car.

'Fine, see you then and . . . I love you.' My mother had once told me never to part with a loved one on a sad note because, in life, you never know what might happen. It was good advice.

'And *I* love you,' she said. We kissed goodbye and she climbed into her pale-blue Volkswagen Beetle and roared out of Kirkby Steepleton on her journey to Hartingdale.

As I watched her car disappear in the distance I reflected on the changes in our lives during the past year. The wedding and honeymoon were still fresh in our minds and now I had replaced tired routines for the bold taking of one shared life, borne upon the memories of hopeful youth and shaped for the joy of giving. In the cool fire of creation our new life had begun.

With a contented sigh, I locked the front door and threw my battered briefcase and my old herringbone jacket on the passenger seat. Then I polished the lenses of my Buddy Holly spectacles using the end of my new slimline eighties tie, a present from Beth, and drove off on the back road to Ragley.

On this warm summer day the journey was calm

and peaceful midst the abundance of nature. In the hedgerows, wild flowering raspberry canes competed with the waving ferns of bracken and purple thistle heads. The cow parsley sparkled with cuckoo spit and the scent of wild garlic drifted through my open window from the shady woodland floor. As I approached Ragley I heard the distant warning cry of a pheasant. I didn't heed the warning . . . Perhaps I should have done. It was Friday, 23 July, a day I was destined never to forget.

Ragley High Street looked a picture. Honeysuckle clambered over the porch of the village hall, Young Tommy Piercy was pulling out the blue-and-white-striped awning over the Butcher's Shop window, Dorothy Humpleby was on the Coffee Shop forecourt putting pots of bright-red geraniums on the picnic tables and Timothy Pratt was watering his display of perfectly horizontal hanging baskets outside his emporium. As I pulled into the school car park next to Vera's Austin A40, I admired the magenta bells of foxgloves, tall and elegant, that graced the border at the side of Sally's classroom. All seemed well on this beautiful Yorkshire morning.

When I walked into the school office, Vera was absent-mindedly fingering her beautiful sapphire engagement ring. 'Oh, good morning, Mr Sheffield,' she said. 'Forgive me, I was miles away.'

'Good morning, Vera,' I said with a smile. 'I'm not surprised; life has been an adventure for both of us this year.'

'Too true,' she said and then gave a deep sigh and looked out of the window at the dark clouds on the distant horizon. 'But what is life but a million memories and a few precious moments.' Vera was clearly in a reflective mood and she sighed with the weight of recollections.

'Well, this is *your* time, Vera, and we're all so happy for you. The major is a good man.'

'Thank you for saying so,' she said; 'and I do believe that Joseph is gradually coming round to the idea, particularly as, next summer, I shall be living almost next door to the vicarage.'

'So, is that the plan . . . for you and the major to marry next summer?'

'Yes,' said Vera with a calm smile. 'Probably after the end of term, at the beginning of the summer holiday. We didn't want to rush things and we thought a one-year engagement was right and proper, if only for the sake of my dear brother.'

'That sounds perfect, Vera,' I said, 'and how is Joseph?'

'As he always is, Mr Sheffield,' said Vera with an enigmatic smile. 'He's a lovely, caring and supportive brother, but an *innocent* in an experienced world. In fact,' she looked up at me and chuckled, 'his telephone call with Bishop Neil last night summed it up.'

'In what way?'

'Well, in the middle of a conversation about the ecclesiastical conference, he suddenly mentioned that *next year he would be marrying his sister.*' She chuckled again at the memory. 'Then he had to explain what he *actually* meant.'

'I see what you mean,' I said, 'but perhaps he's worried about living alone in the vicarage.'

'He is, Mr Sheffield, that's the problem, and I have to help him as much as I can.'

'Just as you support *me*, Vera,' I said. 'You know I'd be lost without you.'

'Well . . .' she looked around the office at the old metal filing cabinet and the lines of school photographs on the wall, 'I love my work here in Ragley School.' She sighed and removed the cover from her electric typewriter. 'And I'm sure I always shall.' Then she began typing a note to parents confirming that school would reopen for the autumn term on Monday, 6 September. My brief insight into Vera's personal world was over and it was back to business as usual.

During morning break the children in my class set out the chairs for our annual Leavers' Assembly. This was a popular event when the fourth-year juniors in my class were each presented with a book prize provided by the Parent–Teacher Association. The assembly was led by Joseph and supported by parents, grandparents and friends of the school. This year we had two principal guests to present the prizes, our school governor, Major Rupert Forbes-Kitchener, and Ruby's son, Sergeant Andrew Smith.

Ruby had worked late to make sure the hall floor had received an extra polish before the assembly. When I walked into the entrance hall, Ruby had hung up her overall and locked her caretaker's store.

'Thanks, Ruby,' I said: 'the hall floor looks lovely.'

'Thank you, Mr Sheffield,' said Ruby. 'Ah'm so excited an' our Andy's proper thrilled t'be invited.' She was clearly full of pride for her son.

'I trust Ronnie will be here, Ruby.'

'Ah 'ope so, Mr Sheffield. Ah've jus' read t'riot act to

'im,' said Ruby, 'an' ah've told 'im t'shape 'imself an' get 'ere sharpish t'see our Andy gettin' 'onoured.'

'Well, Ruby,' I said with a smile, 'I'll see you later.'

'Y'will that . . . an' ah'll be in m'best frock,' and she hurried off down the school drive and back to 7 School View, where Andy was cleaning his army boots to a mirror-like shine with good old-fashioned spit and polish.

When I walked into the staff-room, Vera was holding up the front page of her *Daily Telegraph*. 'Doesn't she look radiant?' said Vera.

'I bet she was relieved it was a boy,' said Anne.

Sally nodded but kept her thoughts to herself.

Under the headline 'A beautiful baby boy' was a photograph of Princess Diana with her son, now a month old. The royal baby had been named William Arthur Philip Louis, with the royal command that *'the name William will not be shortened in any way'*.

'And so it shouldn't,' insisted Vera: 'it wouldn't be right and proper.'

'I suppose "Prince Willy" doesn't have the same ring to it,' mumbled Sally through a mouthful of biscuit crumbs.

By eleven o'clock the hall was full and the major, in a charcoal-grey three-piece suit, regimental tie and a row of medals on his chest, introduced Ruby's son. Andy, with his white sergeant's stripes, looked immaculate in his army uniform with its knife-edge creases.

Rupert was a brilliant public speaker and Vera looked on in admiration. However, he was also wise in his choice of words and took care not to glorify war – something that was appreciated by all the adults present, including Old Tommy Piercy, who nodded sagely. Rupert merely expressed how pleased we all were that Sergeant Smith had served his country with honour in the Falklands and, thankfully, returned home safe and sound. Ruby was dabbing away the tears, with yet another of Vera's handkerchiefs, long before the book-presentation ceremony began.

With something of a lump in my throat, I read out the names of the school leavers in my class. I had watched them grow from tiny infants into confident eleven-year-olds and it was sad to see them go. They came out, one by one, to shake hands with the major and receive their book from Andy Smith, who had a kind, encouraging word for each of them. The books had been chosen by the Parent–Teacher Association to suit the interests of each individual pupil, so the selection included the Narnia stories, model aircraft, modern farm machinery and how to look after a horse.

The assembly was conducted by Joseph in a calm and sensitive manner and it proved the perfect way to say goodbye to a group of children who were about to take their next step in life. It was also a poignant moment when the group of school leavers bowed their heads and joined in our school prayer for the very last time.

'*Dear Lord,*
This is our school, let peace dwell here,
Let the room be full of contentment, let love abide here,
Love of one another, love of life itself,
And love of God.
Amen.'

Finally, Joseph gave thanks to everyone who supported the school, including the governing body and the Parent–Teacher Association, but, particularly, the teachers and the ancillary staff. Vera, in her usual trim business suit, and Ruby, Shirley and Doreen, dressed in bright summer dresses, looked suitably modest when the audience broke into spontaneous applause. I looked across the hall to Anne, who gave me that familiar gentle smile, and I guessed what she was thinking. Somehow, we had survived the round of village school closures and another year had been completed without mishap. I was lucky to have such a loyal and talented deputy headteacher and Anne had made it clear she wanted to remain at Ragley and not seek a headship for herself.

It was almost lunchtime when the hall emptied and Ruby, Ronnie and Andy walked down the drive together and stopped at the school gate for a word with Old Tommy Piercy.

'Nah then, young Andrew, y'back, then,' said Old Tommy bluntly.

'Yes, Mr Piercy,' said Andy, 'an' ah'm reight glad.'

'There's been a lot o' changes since y'went gallavantin' off t'fight them Argies,' said Old Tommy, lighting up his pipe and sucking contentedly.

'So ah've 'eard, Mr Piercy,' said Andy, 'what wi' t' 'eadteacher gettin' married.'

'An' Miss Evans gettin' a man at last,' added Ronnie for good measure, though Ruby gave him a stern look.

'Mark my words,' said Old Tommy with a twinkle in his eye, 'she'll be a good bit o' pensioner-crumpet.'

'Oh, Tommy,' said Ruby, 'y'can't say that about Miss Evans. She's a proper lady . . . an' she deserves 'er bit o' 'appiness.'

However, Old Tommy was a quintessential Yorkshireman. 'Well, ah say what ah like an' ah like what ah say,' he replied defiantly through a haze of Old Holborn tobacco and walked off down the High Street.

'Mam,' said Andy, 'ah wonder 'ow our Racquel's gettin' on.'

'She's fine, luv . . . Not long now,' said Ruby, and she linked arms proudly with her elder son as they walked home.

At lunchtime I went into the kitchen to thank Shirley and Doreen for all their hard work during the year and to confirm arrangements for our after-school party.

'Don't worry, Mr Sheffield,' said Shirley, 'I'll get t'Baby Burco fired up an' sort out all t'best crockery.' She looked at the formidable Doreen Critchley. 'An' Doreen's made a lovely apple an' cinnamon lattice tart, special, like. Ah'm sure y'll like it.' I looked at the bulging muscles in Doreen's forearms and agreed that I definitely would.

Then Shirley made me a large mug of tea just the way I like it, black with a slice of lemon, and together we sat chatting while watching the children on the school field. The ten-year-olds in my class were sitting in a group and discussing who might be tuck-shop monitor next term, while, near by, the fourth-year junior girls were acting out Irene Cara's 'Fame' dance routine. On a much less aesthetic level, the boys who were about to leave Ragley were leaning against the school wall and musing about the craft lessons that were coming their way next term with *real* woodwork benches. Secondary-school life was suddenly full of new possibilities and Ragley School had begun to appear very small.

I recalled that my own childhood seemed to be made up of play, food, sleep and books – but mainly play. I was a cowboy in the morning, a super-hero in the afternoon and, in bed at night, I would read my *Eagle* comic and join Dan Dare on his latest interplanetary mission. It was a time of long summer days and imagination knew no bounds.

As I walked back to my classroom for afternoon school, I reflected that I was about to complete my fifth year as headteacher of Ragley School and the five-year-olds who had arrived with me back in 1977 were now ten-year-olds in my class. In another year's time it would be *their* turn to leave for Easington Comprehensive School and I would have been in charge of a complete generation of primary children for a full cycle of six years. They would have known only me as their headteacher and I wondered about my impact on their lives. I knew I had helped to teach them to read and write, to count and paint, to solve problems and to talk with confidence, to share and speak the truth, but more than anything I hoped I had instilled a love of learning.

At the end of school, Ruby was collecting the waste paper from my office when Petula Dudley-Palmer called by. 'We're going to Venice for our holiday, Mr Sheffield,' she said.

'That should be a wonderful experience for the girls,' I said.

'Yes,' said Petula; 'I can see us now drifting under the Bridge of Sighs with a gondolier.'

Ruby was puzzled. She had heard of 'glue-ear' but not 'gondol-ear'. She said nothing, though, and wandered off with her black bag.

An hour later, the hall was filling up with staff, governors and a few members of the Parent–Teacher Association. The major arrived in his chauffeur-driven Bentley with Joseph as a passenger and they walked in together. The major was still in his three-piece suit but now without the medals, while Joseph was in his summer attire with a cream linen jacket, the obligatory dog-collar and a straw panama hat.

Sue Phillips got chatting with the major about her family's forthcoming caravan holiday in Cornwall and Devon.

'It's a topping place, Susan,' said the major, pointing vaguely south with his brass-topped cane, 'and there's some jolly drives around there.'

Then there was a cheer as Shirley and Doreen wheeled in the trolley from the kitchen on which the cups and saucers rattled and a Baby Burco boiler steamed merrily. Vera, Sally and Jo had laid out on some of the dining tables a simple buffet, including a large plateful of Vera's perfect scones and a huge jar of home-made raspberry and strawberry jam. Shirley had prepared a plateful of sandwiches and Doreen, of course, made sure her magnificent apple and cinnamon lattice tart had pride of place.

*　　　*　　　*

Under the welcome shade of the horse-chestnut trees by the school gate, eight-year-old Betsy Icklethwaite was telling her sister, four-year-old Katie, about what it would be like when she started school next term.

'You'll 'ave t'be able t'write y'name,' said Betsy.

'I can do that,' said Katie.

'Y'can't,' said Betsy.

'Ah can . . . 'cept f'catti-pull letters,' said Katie defiantly.

'Y'mean *capital* letters,' corrected Betsy.

'That's what ah said,' retorted Katie.

'And you need t'know which is your coat peg,' said Betsy.

This was unexpected. 'Oh,' said Katie, 'an' will you 'elp me?'

'Yes,' said Betsy magnanimously and feeling quite grown-up.

Suddenly Beth arrived in her Volkswagen Beetle, turned carefully into the school entrance and waved at the two little girls.

'She's a nice lady,' said Katie.

'That's 'er who married Mr Sheffield,' said Betsy with the voice of experience.

'Ah know,' said Katie, 'it's *Mrs Teacher.*'

Beth walked into the hall and, as always, a few heads turned. She looked so attractive in her new Debenham's outfit, a Hawaiian-print dress with a linen straight-style jacket.

'Good to be here, Jack,' she said and turned to Vera. 'Can I do anything to help?'

'Well, if you're brave enough, you could cut Doreen's lattice tart and serve it out,' said Vera cheerfully.

It was a happy occasion and a relaxing end to the school year and, although the sky darkened as we chatted, everyone was in good spirits until gradually, in small groups, people took their leave.

'Don't wait for me, Rupert,' said Vera. 'I've got some tidying up to do in the office before I go home.'

'Very well, old girl,' said Rupert, 'but perhaps I could offer Joseph a lift.'

'Thank you, Rupert, that would be helpful – and less of the *old girl*, if you don't mind,' she said with mock admonishment.

'Of course, my dear. Message heard and understood,' and he gave her a kiss on the cheek.

'I'll see you later,' said Vera.

'Tally ho. Come on, Joseph,' said Rupert. 'We've got our marching orders.' He put his hand on Joseph's shoulder. 'Just a couple of errands before going home, old chap, and then I'll drop you off at the vicarage.'

'Thank you, Rupert,' said Joseph. He turned to Vera and gave her a gentle smile. 'See you soon,' he said and the two men walked out together to the waiting Bentley.

'Please Sir!' It was Beth tugging my sleeve and looking up anxiously at the hall clock. It was 5.55 p.m. 'My mother's train gets into York at half six.' She picked up her handbag, gave Vera a quick hug and, with a wave, hurried out to the car park and drove into the High Street behind the major's car.

Finally, only Anne, Sally and Jo were left in the staff-room, winding down with a cup of tea, and Vera and I were in the school office. It was quiet as we completed our end-of-year tasks. However, Vera was comfortable with silence: for her it spoke volumes.

I unlocked the bottom drawer of my desk and took out the ancient leather-bound school logbook. Then I filled my fountain pen with black Quink ink and stared at the next clean page. The academic year 1981/82 was almost over and I was about to pen the last entry of the school year.

I had just decided what to write when Ruby burst into the office. 'Miss Evans, Miss Evans!' she exclaimed. 'It's our Racquel! T'baby's comin' an' she's been rushed into 'ospital.'

Vera remained calm and quickly summed up the situation. 'Where are Ronnie and Andrew?' she asked.

'Dunno, Miss Evans,' gasped Ruby frantically. 'They're not at 'ome. Ah think they went t'York wi' Andy's mates.'

'Can I help?' I said.

Vera looked out of the window and stared up at the gathering storm. 'No, you stay here, Mr Sheffield. It will be better if *I* take Ruby,' and she picked up her coat and handbag and the two women dashed out to the car park. It was 6.05 p.m.

The sultry calm lay heavily on the land and, amid the heat of pressure, a stifling electric tension was waiting for the moment of release. It came with ragged fingers of fiery lightning and the boom of heaven's marching army. The storm had arrived and, as Vera and Ruby drove down the High Street towards York, the first heavy splashes of rain bounced off the top of the car. Moments later the rain fell harder and there was a flash of lightning followed a few seconds later by a crash of thunder. The storm was over-head now and the York road became slick with running water.

Up ahead the major's Bentley slowed. Cars were putting on their headlights and pulling off the road to seek safety. Beth was anxiously peering through her wind-screen as her wipers failed to clear the deluge of water. She glanced down at her wristwatch. It was 6.10 p.m.

'Are we goin' t'get there in time, Miss Evans?' asked a desperate Ruby.

Vera was trying to remain calm but she could barely see the road ahead. 'Don't worry Ruby,' she said: 'not far now.'

Back in the school office, I wrote, 'School closed today and will reopen for the new academic year 1982/83 on Monday, 6 September 1982.' Then I blotted the page carefully, closed the logbook and locked it in the bottom drawer of my desk.

I sighed. Another year was over and I had now completed five years as headteacher of Ragley-on-the-Forest Church of England Primary School. There was a rattle of crockery from the staff-room and I went to join the others.

The approaching lorry braked suddenly to avoid getting too close to the car in front and then its back end began to aquaplane across the rain-soaked carriageway.

Seconds felt like slow-motion minutes but the driver

saw what was coming and tried desperately to veer to the left and on to the grassy verge, where the near-side tyres spun helplessly.

The words tumbled out: 'Oh, please God . . .'

The crash of the rear offside of the lorry hitting the car's bonnet was like a bomb blast. Then there was flying glass, the crunch of metal, a final scream and . . . darkness.

I was in the staff-room with Anne and Sally, while Jo was collecting her coat, when the telephone rang. It was 6.45 p.m.

'I'll get it,' called Jo from the cloakroom area.

We heard a hurried mumble of words from Jo and then, 'Oh, no . . . oh, no!'

'Something's wrong,' said Anne.

Sally was first to react. She walked through the little corridor to the school office and Anne and I hurried behind her. 'What is it?' asked Sally.

Jo, her face ashen, was staring at the receiver.

'What's wrong?' asked Anne.

Jo replaced the receiver as if in a dream. 'It was Dan,' she said quietly. She looked up at us as if seeing us for the first time. 'There's been an accident . . . water on the road . . . a lorry skidded . . . two cars are involved.'

'Is anyone hurt?' asked Sally.

Jo took a deep breath, as if searching for the words, and stared at us for what seemed like an eternity. 'Yes,' she said simply.

Her eyes were soft with sorrow.

And in a heartbeat our lives had changed for ever.